COMING S

Apocalypse U...

Praise for the books of the New Praetorians series:

"…an intriguing world of futuristic technology, made more familiar by contemporary references."

"Radiant descriptions also enhance the story."

—Kirkus Reviews

From the ashes of Notre Dame Cathedral to the cosmic mysteries lurking inside the CERN supercollider to bone-strewn labyrinths of the Paris Catacombs to the gilded halls of all-corrupting wealth and power in Davos comes an unprecedented technothriller adventure.

*"The intrigue of **The Da Vinci Code** combined with the big-scale action of **James Bond**."*

A heinous genocidal attack threatens Europe, a monstrous bioweapon is unleashed on Moscow, and Ellie Sato, a young British reporter, finds herself caught in the middle of *Apocalypse Europe!*

> Reader Suitability:
> Scenes of violence, moderate profanity,
> sexuality, and torture.
> Recommended for 18+

APOCALYPSE: EUROPE

THE PANGEA PROTOCOL

RK SYRUS

Cover: James "Tiberius" Egan of Bookfly Design

Formatting: Pikko's House

Paper book
ISBN10: 1-910890-14-6
(ISBN13: 978-1-910890-14-1)

Ebook
eISBN10: 1-910890-13-8
(eISBN13: 978-1-910890-13-4)

"The world order of tomorrow is not a world order based on nation-states, on countries, it's a world order that is based on empires."

—Guy Verhofstadt, the most influential Global Imperialist Member of the European Parliament (MEP) and former Prime Minister of Belgium

"These people have an agenda and they are penetrating a continent that has no agenda… we all know from history what that leads to."

—Ayaan Hirsi Ali, women's rights activist, author, former member of the Dutch Parliament

"…politicians fired by moral ideas do not respect the electorate. Their plan is to exchange the electorate for a better one."

—Sir Roger Scruton, writer and philosopher

POPULATION DENSITY EUROPE

**TOTAL:
779.3
MILLION**

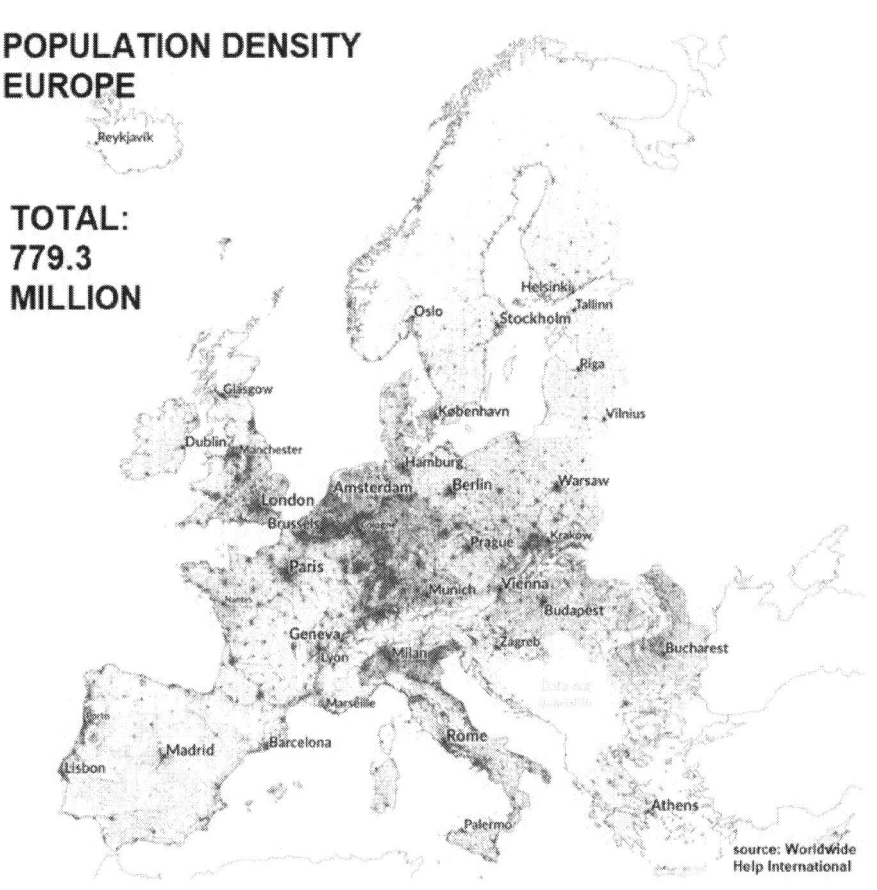

source: Worldwide
Help International

1

A MAN

A man walked past Notre Dame; the night air was cool on his lips and tongue. He looked up at the rebuilt cathedral and icy tendrils of pain and the mortification of shameful failure seized him. The obscene structure was illuminated from the front by a row of small floodlights along its stone walls and backlit against the night sky by a halo of Parisian city lights. From four kilometers away, the Eiffel Tower sent out rhythmic lances of illumination from its rotating searchlights. Low-hanging clouds reflected this spectral pulse of the city. The man paused and, resting his clean hand on the grimy railing of the bridge over the Seine, forced himself to look up.

This old bitch looked better when she was on fire, he thought.

The man had set fire to Notre Dame Cathedral twelve years ago. Much had changed since then, he knew, but there it was. The decrepit monument was still standing on the Île de la Cité, a disgusting leper's sore persistently oozing foul-smelling pus onto the face of Paris. That thought, and others, made him shudder.

Memories, only memories.

It was after midnight, someone would wonder where he was. Still, he continued slowly along the river, his head angled a few degrees to one side as though he were listening for a melody which was just about to begin. The halogen light made the walls and the rebuilt spire both appear to be made out of stone. A latticework of restoration scaffolding crisscrossed above the foremost towers. Easter Vigil had concluded hours ago. The cathedral and the park surrounding it on the Île de la Cité were as silent and gloomy as a graveyard.

The man, intending at last to go home, turned towards the car and the shadowy figures following him at a distance. Something slid under his foot. The ground was wet and had soaked through the paper of a small, homemade handbill. All he could read was:

"Joyeuses Pâques! Christ est ressuscité!"

Oh fuck, thought the man. *"Happy Easter, Christ is risen." Couldn't the bastard stay dead?*

Not wanting to touch the despicable paper with his hand, he pushed at it with a tasseled loafer, scraped it under a railing and over the edge of the bridge. A balled-up dirty mess, the flyer fell into the dark waters.

The man felt the cool wind from the river at his back. It made him realize how hot and flushed his face had become as he stared up at the cathedral. In his mind, the cathedral was burning again. In his vision, Notre Dame was gloriously aflame, utterly collapsing into ruin, the ashes sinking into a pit. The pit then widened, taking in not only the terrible medieval monument but Square Jean XXIII as well, finally engulfing the entire Île de la Cité. The river waters would rush down through the gaping sinkhole and spew into rat-infested sewers and into the catacombs, bringing up the stored bones of six million disinterred corpses.

A boat horn sounded. The man realized it was not the cathedral that was burning. It was him burning with utter hate. For a moment, he raged silently at the church, its new spire, and most violently of all at the obscenity of all obscenities: the Christian Cross.

By now, this was supposed to be the Mosque of Notre Dame, or the brothel of Notre Putain.

During the French Revolution, Notre Dame had been turned into a seedy warehouse for turnips and cabbages. To him, it was not important what they used it as: a garbage dump, or a whorehouse, or a mosque. What mattered was that this blight must be gone from Paris. This leprosy of the mind called Christianity had to be scraped away from humankind.

That was why he had set the fire and tried to burn down the damned place. That was why the shame of his failure smoldered in him like an ember that had fallen on fireplace tiles just short of a fluffy wool rug, yearning to set the house aflame but in the end merely sitting there sizzling impotently.

In 2019, setting the fire had by no means been a certain thing. For days he had worked caught up in a frenzy, completely alone, coming up with one fanciful plan after another: crashing a light plane or helicopter full of fuel into the roof, tampering with natural gas lines. And rejecting each idea in turn.

It had been April 15, just before Easter. He had not touched water or food for two days, maybe three. He had not been able to stop moving since the moment the desire for destruction had seized him.

His specialty was engineering, not demolition; he only knew basic formulas of materials science. He could not risk making a detailed online search for the information he needed to bring down the grand old slut of the Catholic Church in Paris. His old textbooks from university were inadequate. He needed a better source. Finding it led indirectly to his epiphany and the genesis of his fire.

During the early months of 2019, Notre Dame had been in the middle of extensive repairs. Scaffolding had been erected across the transept and around the base of the wooden rooftop spire. The public was still being admitted to view the relics inside the cavernous monstrosity. Access to the ground floor was not a problem, but it might also be a trap.

Early on he was inclined to favor inspiration over deliberation. If he spied the layout first and formulated his plan based on rotating guard schedules or where workers were assigned on a given day, his scheme could be obsolete the very next day. Worse, his frequent visits could be noted and might lead to his capture.

Emerging from his apartment that morning eager for knowledge, he found his way to a used book shop. There he found a fat tattered binder entitled *Criminal Fires: Chemistry and Physics of Fire Behavior*. When the clerk was busy, he had quickly shoved it into his briefcase and left. As he walked along the alley behind the book shop, he was still in the throes of anxiety. Could he do it? Could he do it without being caught? Perhaps he should delay and create a defense strategy if he should be apprehended. Could he find a lazy psychiatrist who would unwittingly help him document a fake mental illness?

Fate provided a final push. In the alley behind the book shop a homeless man was selling junk, it was all laid out on the filthy cobblestones. Among these items was a can of oil-based wood stain. He grabbed it and paid the grizzled old beggar with a hateful stare and a closed fist.

Kerosene or some unusual accelerant would cause suspicion during the detailed investigation that was sure to follow. Notre Dame was rife with woodwork; from his knowledge of chemistry, linseed oil was just what he wanted. The other components necessary he already had in his flat: painter's overalls and a mask retained from a part-time job he had years ago.

He found himself back in his modest apartment and looked at the time. Still early. He could do it that very day. He became drunk on his own audacity. Killing one person was only a murder—this act, so sudden and unexpected, would strike at the heart of France and the soul of Europe. He sat at his small kitchen table and greedily studied the fire prevention manual. In an hour he felt fully prepared.

Walking to the cathedral, he took the most logical route for someone not in a hurry on a spring day in Paris. Mindful of being watched by the street surveillance cameras, he behaved precisely as an engineering consultant working for a large international investment firm would on his day off. His wallet was in the pocket of his suede jacket; everything else was tucked in a medium-sized leather shoulder bag.

He walked toward the Île de la Cité like an automaton. He was risking everything—his career, his money, his life, his family's good name—and for what? The answer was too big for his brain. All he knew was he could not stop. It was as though he were in a dreamlike state, acting out events that had already happened.

What if they questioned him? Why was he going to the cathedral? He knew Catholic liturgy but was not a regular at Notre Dame. Attacks against Christian and Jewish places of worship had recently escalated; there was always security. As he approached the entrance, he considered cover stories.

The firm at which he worked was a large multinational conglomerate involved in construction and finance globally. The connections his position provided him would, over the next twelve years after the fire, provide him links to money and secret avenues of power in Brussels and Davos. Those covert economic and political partnerships would lay the foundation of his future success and entrée into a very special society.

But on April 15, 2019, he was just a junior consulting engineer. If questioned as to why he was visiting Notre Dame, he decided to say his firm was considering reinsuring an Armenian state restoration project, which was actually true. He wanted to see how work on the cathedral was progressing in order to write a memo to his firm's risk assessment department.

Boring, credible, perfect.

His overalls and mask, which were rolled up into a very tight bundle, were for his work—also true. His department was bidding on a contract to remediate the hundreds of kilometers of limestone quarry catacombs which lay under Paris, mostly on the Left Bank. At some point he would have to climb down into the musty caverns which honeycombed through the foundations of Paris.

Nothing about him would appear out of place, as long as no one looked into his small leather grooming bag and analyzed the contents of his bottle of hair oil. He had emptied out the original product to make a receptacle for the wood oil. As a finishing touch, he'd added an extra sheen of organic argan hair oil to his thick dark hair. Obviously he was a man who liked to take care of his appearance.

What he did not carry was a lighter or even so much as a single match. One did not need those to start a fire.

He reached Notre Dame. At the sight of a long line of white-and-blue police vans stretching along the street leading to the entrance, his hands started to shake. He quickly thrust them into his pockets.

As it was, the officers were more interested in their lunch than providing security. People wandered around the sunlit square in front of the cathedral. Despite a sign cautioning baggage was not allowed, people entered and left with large shopping bags and backpacks. His small satchel was not noticed. He paused directly in front of a security camera, checking his watch and making sure the lens got a good look at him.

Then, with the vigor of a man with a full bladder, he strode down the side street that flanked the cathedral on the river side, and entered a tented area which contained a line of portable toilets. He entered the last one.

He waited for a knock; waited to be challenged and told these latrines were for registered renovation workers only. No one came. No one knocked. He changed into is overalls and stuffed his satchel up through an air hole to rest on the plastic roof of the latrine.

After putting on his paint mask, he took a deep breath. He smelled chlorine and urine. He began.

That Monday afternoon, noon Mass was in full swing. The sounds of liturgy filtered through to the side of the cathedral. Hearing it nearly made him sick to his stomach, but he forced himself to swallow the acidic bile which his empty stomach had tried to rid itself of. It would not do to vomit into his mask.

He walked out, mixing in with the contractors and tradesmen leaving for their lunch break. Passing the lower rung of a scaffold, he had the inspired notion to grab a tool belt hanging there. Casually, he draped it over his shoulder to hide the fact that he was not sporting the security badge identifying authorized workers on site. If anyone accosted him as he studied how best to access the cathedral, he would claim he was returning to get one of his valuable tools—a digital caliper or a wood hygrometer.

He had to get up to the roof. He certainly could not use the electric service lift, which was the normal way workmen accessed the upper scaffolding. People were milling around the bottom of the lift and presumably also at the top, which he could not see.

He looked left and right. Soon someone would notice him just standing there with sweat running down the back of his neck under the hood of his painter's coveralls. He felt stuck in place. Any second now, he would be spotted, surrounded, forced to his knees, stripped, and made to confess right there. Would they bring out a priest to hear his sins?

He looked up. The noon sun burned down pitilessly. A blaze of light made him close his eyes. Above him, burned into his retinas, the rays had sliced the figment of a priest's dagger made of pure light.

The moment passed. Still no one noticed him. For the workers, it was lunchtime. For the faithful, it was Mass at the grand altar. He blinked hurriedly, turned away from the light, and saw a lower rung on the support struts for the scaffold. They were covered with blue plastic material and hung about a foot above his farthest reach.

He jumped, and the tool belt slipped off his shoulder. His muscles remembered his youthful days in the gymnastics competitions. He could do this! Climbing steadily up the scaffolding was much easier than negotiating twists on the high bar. But soon he was thirty feet off the ground, and his muscles and ligaments sawed at him in pain. Each twinge reminded him he was twenty years older than the spry gymnast who had tried out for the French Olympic team.

His hands started to sweat. Could he even gain access to the inner roof? Everything depended on that. The outer roof was made of lead. Those sheets of heavy metal were held up by the inner roof which was a maze of enormous timbers. His entire plan hinged upon starting a fire inside, not on the exterior of the church, where it would quickly be seen and put out.

He held himself still on the metal rungs, his face inches from that of a grimacing gargoyle. These functional waterspouts were carved in the shape of creatures intended to protect the church from malevolent spirts. This grotesque's face, a cross between a jaguar and a dragon, was made even more hideous by pockmarks caused by pollution and acid rain.

As a student of architecture, he knew the story of their design, how Saint Romain had defeated the fire-breathing La Gargouille, cutting off its head and nailing it to a church roof. When it rained, the mouth of La Gargouille gushed water. It was right then, nose to snout with the leering limestone demon of Notre Dame, that he again nearly lost his nerve.

He was not superstitious, quite the opposite. But he was hanging dozens of feet above the ground on a rickety railing. Anyone who passed directly beneath him only had to look up, and he would be arrested and ruined. At the very least, he would be sent to a psychiatric facility. He had no idea if it was even possible to access the space under the outer roof or precisely what he might find inside. There might only be a dead end. His footing may be made of rotting wood and he would end up landing on the inner roof with a broken back.

He reconsidered. It was crazy. He was bound to be caught. There had to be a better way. He had just seen they were letting people with all sorts of bags and knapsacks into the church. He would descend, learn how to construct a very good incendiary device, and form a better plan. The giddy excitement of the past fifty-odd hours emptied from him like the inevitable letdown after a gymnastics competition.

The grotesque had done its job and fended off a mortal enemy of the cathedral. This… was madness.

Just as he decided to quit, to surrender to his better judgment, he heard voices right beneath the spot where he clung on, trying to remain motionless. Two workmen. He could not make out what they were saying. It didn't matter. He had just become certain his current plan would fail. At best, it would only cause a small fire, and then security would be tightened. If he were caught, even if he managed to weasel out of criminal charges, they would watch him for years. He would have no chance to try again.

He had to get down. But he could not. Those two down there were chatting while having a smoke; they would see him. No story he could make up would clear him. There had to be twenty police on the other side of the church.

The gargoyle leered at him. One of its eyes was crumbling in. It mocked him.

Before he knew what he was doing, his feet and hands became energized and moved of their own accord. He was climbing higher. Where moments before was only bare man-made escarpment, he now found crevices and handholds.

As he hauled himself up, there came to him a glorious sight. Tight under the lead-clad roof was a hole. A stone mason had removed a portion of the upper wall. That fitted stone had disintegrated beyond repair, and a replacement stone was probably in a workshop being cut to the precise shape.

Just as he was marveling at his find, a bee started buzzing around his head. Then another, and another. He held his breath. If they stung… If he yelled out… He did not even want to look down at the workmen below. He shut his eyes. No matter what happened, he must not cry out.

The bees went back to their hive. He had completely forgotten that some eco-maniac had convinced the church to install a bee hive on the roof of

Notre Dame. He took a deep breath and returned his gaze into the space underneath the roof.

The opening was just wide enough for his shoulders. A larger man would not have fit. A heavier man would not have been able to climb the scaffolding. In his self-congratulatory joy he forgot about the two men below who had a minute ago so tormented him. He squeezed through into the space between the lead roof above and the inner stone ceiling of the cathedral below. As his eyes adjusted he saw he was inside a vaulted stack comprised of hundreds of tons of dry timber, the Forest.

This was where the fire had to take root. This mass of centuries-old virgin oak was as perfectly arranged as the kindling of any bonfire. The tapestries and other apparently flammable items in the public areas below were false temptations. While the smoke and initial flames might be frightening and dramatic, any blaze which started down in the main floor of the cathedral would be detected and killed before it had time to blossom.

His fire, the healing fire he and humanity needed, had to begin small in a place which was well-ventilated. That way, early puffs of smoke would dissipate and confuse the cathedral's smoke detector devices while at the same time the tiny adolescent flames would have enough fuel and be fed enough oxygen to spur exponential growth.

A conviction, like the moral contained in a parable or a folk tale, came to him like an epiphany. The genius of destruction had at least to be equal to the thing that was being destroyed. As soon as he thought this, his self-doubts dissipated entirely. He could be the Da Vinci of annihilation.

The darkness under the cave-like roof was shot through by the dull flaring light coming from a few hanging bulbs. He ignored them. As with the tapestries below, they were not the source of ignition he needed in order to inflict the most damage and—*Oh, that it might be so!*—even cause the utter destruction of this monument to wickedness.

Pausing, he heard only the wind. The massive oak pillars had been hewn nearly a thousand years ago out of trees that were up to five hundred years old when they were felled. As though they sensed doom was upon them, they groaned.

In the Forest the stale air made the space shrink like a shadowy cloister around his white-swathed form. He crept along. A little bit farther… bit farther… He ducked under crossbeams, pausing at any sound.

The benefit of there being a bare minimum of electrical devices up here was he faced no risk of additional security measures such as cameras or motion detectors. Under the huge rafters, there was nothing to steal, nothing but Notre Dame itself. He ducked around a final fat square post and found it. There was the spot.

He ducked down, leaned over, and hung like an ungainly bat under one of the fat oak beams. The surface was ideal—under his fingers, the wood felt powdery with age. He pulled out the rags he had brought and spread them flat. Onto these he poured the linseed oil from his flask. He soaked the material, squeezed it, then soaked it again to make sure it was completely saturated.

His feverish mind had a final insight. He twisted the fat rag into a coil. It looked like a piece of dough or a seashell. He had the idea that this shape, a logarithmic spiral whose growth factor was φ, the golden ratio, would somehow increase the exothermic reaction of the linseed oil as it dried.

The fissure in the beam was shaped like a V. It gaped open like a sideways mouth, as though it were asking to be filled up. He thrust in the oil-soaked rags.

Virgin oak no more, Notre Dame, you unholy bitch. You are defiled!

He spread the remainder of the oil above and below the crevice. That was it. No fancy timer, no exotic explosives or chemicals, no smoldering fuse taper. Just basic chemistry and ingenuity. He looked again at the electrical cables.

His backup plan had been to take a resistor from his telephone charger and lay it across some frayed wires near a plug. This was not necessary, since he had found his Holy Cleft and made his offering. A resistor would have heated up very quickly and attracted unwanted attention. The linseed plan needed time but would yield the more bountiful fruit. It had to, after all he had suffered and risked, it had to.

For a desperate moment, he thought of a third backup plan: to remain inside the Forest as the cathedral burned. If the linseed oil didn't work, he could start the fire with the resistor, fighting anyone who came up to put it out. In a short while, the smoke would be dense enough and the flames hot enough that no one without full firefighting gear would be able to breathe up where he perched. He saw himself emerging from the secret opening in the stone wall, climbing not down but up, up over the lead roof as it melted under his feet, crawling over to the base of the spire, his hands blistering as he climbed the burning wooden lattice, and upon reaching the top, spitting with his last breath a thick gob of sputum upon the Cross on its very top and watching it hang and sizzle there as the flames rose to consume everything.

As seductive as that vision was, the practical side of his brain rejected it. There were too many variables. His initial improvised plan had gone extremely well, adding in complications could ruin everything.

He exited the way he had entered. The workmen below the scaffolding had finished their smoke. Cigarette butts were ground down within heel marks. It was nearly three p.m.

Back inside the portable toilet, he resolved to only come out after the cathedral closed or if something delightful happened. Cameras may have picked him up in his street clothes entering the grounds, and he wanted to mix in with a crowd moving away from the church.

Flies buzzed around the opening in the roof. It was boring. He had not brought any electronic devices for fear of them being tracked. Once, the door rattled, but the fellow moved on and did his lengthy business in the next stall over. The noise of Paris traffic filtered through.

He might have dozed off. The chirping of an alarm roused him, and he nearly fell off the plastic seat of the commode. It was 6:20. Notre Dame was scheduled to close at 6:45. With excitement that pierced through the dullness his sleep-deprived lethargy and dehydration, an overwhelming thought surfaced. Could he have actually brought a fiery rapture to the heart of Paris?

As it dried, linseed oil underwent an exothermic reaction capable of igniting dry wood. In that dark cranny, he had left a taper of the soaked rags hanging out and exposed to air, with the rest wadded up to feed the cumulative heat reaction.

For the hundredth time as he parade to exit the latrine, he checked that he had not dropped anything. It was less risky taking the white overalls with him than discarding them. They were covered with his sweat, his DNA, wood dust from the Forest, and drippings of flammable oil.

He opened the door a crack and snuck a glance. The exiting crowd after closing hour would have been sufficient cover, but the mass of people rushing out at the sound of the first fire alarm was even more perfect. He joined them.

Once he got out to the side of Île de la Cité, his joy and excitement were shattered. No flames. Not even smoke. He feared the small fire gestating in the womb of the great hollow whore had been found and aborted before it could flourish. He paced back and forth, his mind jittering between despair and derangement. People were going back into the cathedral.

No!

He had failed. The shame and shock lanced through him as though a spear had gutted him. He had to do something. Should he run to a petrol station, douse himself with gasoline, set himself on fire, and run into the place?

While he was still standing, trembling in horrified indecision, the sirens sounded again. Just past seven o'clock, the first fire brigades arrived. Smoke rose from under the roof. The first puffs were as white as those that issued from the Vatican signaling the election of a new pope.

He had watched the first flames lick the base of the wooden spire, marveling at the sight. He stood with his back to the river and basked in the wafting heat and the charcoal incense of smoke billowing merrily over centuries-old timber. He imagined an army of sprites, orange devourers literally eating the past, cleaning the rot, draining the open sore that was the cathedral and the savage cult it represented.

Birds had flown past. The wind whipped the flames up higher and higher. Still, the spire supporting the crucifix was not engulfed. He had imagined the avians were his accomplices and could spew flammable shit on the bonfire to help make the destruction complete.

He forgot his surroundings. He became unconscious of where he was standing or even that he was standing. He must have been backing up toward the river, appearing to be overwhelmed by the sight of the disaster.

"Est-ce que ça va?"

A woman's voice.

She must have thought he was about to faint or stumble and fall into the water. The only shock he felt was how beautiful this horror was, his horror. His would-be savior stood in front of a line of red-suited silver-helmeted firefighters. She was a mousy gray woman. Her face was blemished with tears and mascara, which looked like soot, as though she had pushed her face into his bonfire and tried to quench the flames with her hopeless sorrow.

She asked again how he was.

He was, indeed, a bit light-headed. The woman, a paramedic or amateur volunteer, ushered him to the back of the gathered onlookers. He took the bottle of water he was offered. When he looked up, he was alone in the crowd.

He drank the water greedily. Then the flames called him back.

As he watched the rooftop pyre, his joy was fed by the lamenting agony of the crowd. The only thing that went awry was the skill of the firefighters.

If only they had blasted the roof with high-pressure water, then the flames and hot gases would have been reflected inwards, as in a blast furnace. The lead outer roof was melting in silver rivulets. Underneath the oak crossbeams was the vaulted inner roof of Notre Dame, which was made of stone.

During the height of the blaze, this inner roof would have superheated. A blast of water would have cracked and shattered the stone, bringing the whole edifice down. If only the rib vaulting of the nave had been compromised, then the walls and the repugnant stained-glass windows in them would have fallen in a noisome heap.

He did not move from his spot until all hope of Notre Dame's total collapse was lost. His excitement had melted into disappointment but then was replaced by a growing, gnawing cold fear. He would be caught.

Everything was videotaped these days. He would be caught, humiliated. He would be declared insane, and his greatest punishment would be his inability to express why he had done it. They, the Parisians, Christians, Europeans, all of them, were not worthy to hear his true motives.

For the next few weeks after the fire, he felt like Raskolnikov in *Crime and Punishment*. He awoke with a start in the night, thinking he could sense a RAID anti-terror squad just outside his door, waiting for the signal to break it down.

He waited. And waited.

After two months, feigning the curiosity that was common to all Parisians, he asked a friend who had a connection with the National Police about the investigation. They hadn't a clue. Even better, they did not want one. This was only a few years after the Islamic massacres at Bataclan and *Charlie Hebdo*. In the space of two years, two thousand churches had been burned or vandalized. During Mass, two Muslims wearing explosive belts had gone up to an eighty-five-year-old priest and slit his throat.

With all the problems over migration, the Yellow Vest protests, and the pension strikes, the country's politicians did not need another headache. The fire at Notre Dame was caused by an errant cigarette or an electrical overload. The Élysée Palace told the public to choose which explanation made them happiest and stop asking questions.

He was safe. But his elation was cut short by the shame of failure. Perhaps, he had thought, what he had failed to achieve through flames he could achieve another way.

Through the architectural department of his multinational employer, he had proposed that a modern glass tower with a non-denominational aspect replace the symbols of shame which had been swept away to lie with the other remains of colonial genocide and Christian imperialism.

He had hoped the hardline Salafist Muslims would force a shrine to Islam to rise in the place of Notre Dame. During a trip to Saudi Arabia he suggested as much to leading Sunni architects. They might even keep the name. His research revealed Biblical Mary was the only woman mentioned by name in the holy Quran.

But the Arabs proved weak and disorganized, and they fought endlessly among themselves. If a grand vision for the continent was to succeed, some other group would have to be found. A group with means, organization, and above all, unyielding iron will.

In the end, it was the Pangeans who found him.

Through all the intervening years, despite the help of the globalist cabal, despite being raised up to success and power beyond anything an amateur arsonist could hope for, the incomplete destruction of Notre Dame remained his greatest failure.

Twelve years after the fire, on the avenue that night, the man looked up at the reconstruction scaffolding. He longed to stop the restoration work but dared not.

It could have been—

"Joyeuses Pâques, monsieur!"

At first this chirpy noise did not penetrate the depth of his dark mood.

"Joyeuses Pâques," the cheery child's voice persisted. Happy Easter.

He looked up. A small girl. Her skin was brown like a Syrian. There were many living on the streets. This one and her mother, or nanny, were clean and well dressed. Both wore matching designer overcoats. The man thought she must be about nine years old. She was beaming at him and holding out one of the Easter handbills like the one he had kicked into the river.

The woman, leading the girl by her hand, smiled cautiously, probably recognizing him but being too polite to gawk. It was late for them to be out; the pair continued walking in the opposite direction. He smiled and nodded and turned away.

A Stygian mist, only perceptible to him, descended. There was a "tink" sound like the stem of a brittle, hollow champagne glass breaking. It was audible only inside the man's eardrums. Something snapped. Something which had been stretched tighter and tighter by the sight of the rebuilt cathedral, the memories of his efforts to burn it and all the frustrations of the intervening years. At the sight and sound and smell of the little girl, it snapped.

Caught between utter hopelessness and boundless rage, his mind felt as though it were sinking into quicksand. As brilliant sharp fragments of impotence blew away into the night, he saw. It was not that there was nothing to be done. There was everything to do.

It would start tonight, with a deconsecration.

A line of halogen arc lights aimed upwards to illuminate the cathedral, he walked behind them. There, he would be invisible to the woman and the girl now walking along the river. He signaled to his chief aide. All of the people with him tonight were fanatically loyal Pangeans. He would trust no one else to guard his melancholy walks.

He gave orders. His aide-de-camp's lips compressed and blanched slightly, not with shock—they had collaborated on much more dangerous exploits—but with resolute determination to precisely fulfill his instructions.

By the time he had walked around to the front of Notre Dame Cathedral, the officers normally on duty outside had vanished. He strode through the forecourt under the gaze of the statue of the Virgin and her cupbearers, which stood in front of the west rose window.

The main doors were open wide.

Bas-relief sculptures watched mutely as he passed inside. The big oak door creaked shut behind him. The building, for all its fame, was not large. This was no St. Peter's Basilica. Fifty paces took him to the transept.

Right here, he thought, looking up to the shadow-shrouded ceiling, where his glorious fire had reached its highest point. Right there, it had risen and consumed the crucifix-bearing spire. Then it had been prematurely put out, its purifying work unfinished.

Restoration work continued, and might for another decade. Tradesmen argued with stonemasons who had running feuds with carpenters. All were ants, he knew, squabbling on a snowball that was about to melt under their feet.

He kept walking slowly to the east, the cardinal direction most associated with his fellow light bringer, Lucifer Morningstar.

The task he had given his people was not difficult, but he did not want to embarrass them by making them rush. He paused, looking at the dimly lit place and smelling the musty air. Was that perfume? Had some evening Mass attendee sprayed herself so heavily that the air still reeked of her scent hours later?

He approached the high altar. Perfume was replaced by a dank wet smell. When had it rained last? How badly was the new roof leaking? He looked straight ahead; something was laid out on the altar. It lay very still.

There she was. His special sacrament was waiting. The small Easter celebrant, the girl from the walkway, lay on the cold stone. She lay still, naked and dead.

It's wrong. The thought gripped him, and he twisted to one side, running to a pillar and bracing himself against it. His fingers clawed at the tapestry. He prized them off and motioned for his aide. It was wrong. Open or closed, he did not want to look at the girl's eyes or her mouth. He knew her eyes might be open, sightlessly staring. Even her mouth might reveal tiny teeth and even a little lolling tongue. *No!*

He hissed instructions to his man. He waited, his heart pounding, his hands dripping with sweat, staining the delicate woven cloth which hung from the ceiling. After the new activity he had ordered was complete, he righted himself and continued toward the main altar at the end of the cathedral.

Before him lay a perfect grotesque to shock all the chimera and stone serpents above. It would have been embarrassing not to be able to rise to the occasion and perform the ritual. During the brief pause, he had inhaled a fast-acting Avanafil compound. It was already working. The holy scepter between his legs was begging to be freed from its restraints.

The altar was a bit high for him to achieve the correct angle. His people had thoughtfully put a wooden step stool in the appropriate position. He climbed up and looked down.

The body of the girl was thinner than he had imagined when she was clothed and alive. Virtually hairless, of course. The man studied an odd downy hair pattern which began above her small delicately indented navel and reached down toward her pubic area, which was now revealed between her widely spread skinny legs.

Without preamble or lubrication, he thrust himself in. One of the girl's hands flopped limply over the side of the altar. She was dark-skinned but not black. The small nipples on her prepubescent breast buds were brown, offset by a mole of the same shape and size on the left side of her ribcage.

As he penetrated the freshly killed girl's corpse his mind wandered. What were they, her and her mother? Syrian? Iraqi? When they came to France had they been immaculate and pure? It did not matter. Somehow, Europe had infected them. All the man could hope to do now was purify... purify... *purify*.

Fixated on completing the sacrament of deconsecration, he stared at the space above her bony shoulders. Nothing stared back up at him. The girl's head had been neatly severed from her body, almost at the line of her collarbone. Only a stump remained.

Due to some fluke of anatomy, with each braced thrust of his rock-hard penis, the corpse's diaphragm worked on her lungs and expelled a moiety of air through her cleaved windpipe. The sloppy, hissing gurgle sounded like:

"Jouy-esssse… Jouy-sesssse…"

He stood, sweating and shuddering, in front of the great crucifix and the altar. He cleaned his cock off with a handkerchief moisturized with oleo-limestone liniment. Swift and quiet hands were taking the girl's body away.

Assisted by the powerful erection drug, he was still hard. He considered deconsecrating the dead body of the woman who had been with the girl, the mother or the nanny. He discarded the idea and stuffed his throbbing manhood sideways into his pants. The adult woman was too old, too defiled, and too used up to be purified. Much like Europe, she was an irredeemable corpse.

After the ceremony, the man left Notre Dame revived, refreshed, and renewed. He barely remembered the girl's headless remains splayed naked on the altar. But etched in his mind, like the faces of the stone saints in the entrance of Notre Dame, were the expressions of his loyal Pangeans as they had watched.

They had absolute faith in him that he would lead humanity to a better world. It came to him, like his stunning beautiful orgasm at the culmination of the deconsecration. Somewhere in the recent past he had lost faith in himself, in Pangea. He had to reclaim it. He *would* reclaim it.

The two bodies would soon be submerged and floating under the dark waters of the Seine. With violent crime and suicides at record highs, who would notice? The Seine was unofficially called *La rivière des Cadavres Frais,* the River of Fresh Corpses.

He needed to get home before anyone noticed his absence. Yet it seemed wrong to just discard the deconsecrated youngster. He called his man over.

He ordered them to dispose of the woman and the girl's head, but he had to keep a memento. He told them to reduce and strip the girl's carcass and add her bones to the New Catacombs.

His grim servant nodded.

He advised them to make certain to be artful, to make her into a pleasant arrangement when they cemented her onto a carefully chosen section of the wall. That was fitting. It was not the little waif's fault she had become polluted beyond living redemption. *No*, he thought as he exited the cathedral and stared at the silent river, *it was Europe's fault.*

For a few minutes, he walked. The night air did not refresh; it was cloying. Maybe it was the fast-acting erection drug, or his exertions with *la petite offrande*, or the seed of an idea growing like a tickle in the back of his throat. He inhaled, widening his mouth. Then he struggled to breathe out again. It seemed as though the invasion of stale night air would not let him expel an impossibly big concept.

He became dizzy. It would not do for his security people to see his unsteadiness. There were six established routes by foot along the road back to his home. He chose a seventh.

With a hand signal, he told his minders to stay in the street. He walked into an alley. It was too narrow for cars. The chip embedded in his brainstem let him access a panel painted to look like an electrical transformer station.

Alone, he descended a twisting staircase. Motion sensors activated small footlights as he passed. The tunnel widened until he came upon a leering jamboree of human skulls and thigh bones cemented into the wall.

In these modern sections of the catacombs, some of the bones were old, rescued from the ancient catacombs, which had caved in. Other bones were more recent additions dating from the Vichy era and the subjugation of Algeria.

Large subterranean quarries lay under much of Paris. The limestone blocks taken from there had built much of the city, including Notre Dame. The gaps left by the tunneling had been filled with cemetery bones. Outnumbering the more noisome two million residents of Paris above, the millions of more sedate denizens of Paris below had never been subject to an exact census.

He came upon neat rows of cranial bones. He followed their shiny domes to the gateway of his residence. Around a turn was the entrance to a service elevator. As it carried him past the second floor, he got a whiff from the kitchens. Chef was keeping something hot in case he or his wife requested a late-night meal.

During the ride up to the top floor, he checked the internal surveillance cameras. His wife, Giselle, was asleep. The entrance gates were closed and guarded.

A mullioned panel hissed aside, and the elevator disgorged him onto plush red carpeting. He went straight to his office. His broad, ornate desk was watched over by a secret painting of Belgium's King Leopold II.

He'd had the work of art falsely authenticated as a lost portrait of a young Jules Verne. The two men, the visionary writer and visionary social engineer, looked very similar. He told visitors that Verne's perspectives of the future inspired him in his work.

The thought that had stuck him like a pistol shot when that dirty little girl had said those foul words to him reverberated through his skull. He had to make it leave, get it out of his head. The only way was through action.

Twelve years ago, he had made a vile mistake. He thought by destroying a monument he could open people's eyes. But as he had seen, monuments can be rebuilt as long as there are hands that have the skill and minds that remember. The way forward was not to open people's eyes but to close them.

He rang for his most trusted and capable administrative assistant. She had thick glasses and birdlike limbs, which reminded him slightly of those belonging to the dead girl on the altar. Her oiled hair was streaked with gray.

After using his own equipment to make sure the room was secure from prying eyes and ears, he gave her a set of very specific instructions. As a high-ranking Pangean, she knew enough not to bring any paper pad or recording instrument. Twelve minutes later, the man asked if everything was clear to her.

"Oui, je comprends parfaitement, Monsieur le Président."

2

Ellie Sato wondered: *How did it get to be Monday again?* The weekend, or rather the afternoon of Sunday, which was the only time she had off, had sped by so quickly. She recalled that she had done her laundry and then had an hour-long video call with US Army Captain Atticus Reidt.

While he was not officially and formally a significant other, Ellie thought, after three months, they had achieved significant itemhood. They had met during the start of the 96-Hour War in the Middle East. While Ellie was pretty sure her presence had not actually started the war, she and Atticus had certainly helped end it and rescue the remaining members of the Israeli government, who were now in exile.

After the war, they had met a few times in London and other cities when Ellie was on her book tour. They had bonded over bespoke writing instruments. Atticus Reidt was actually a fountain pen virgin, and Ellie had helped introduce him to the mysterious world of nibs and piston fillers.

Ellie had been somewhat involved with a fashion designer's t but was privately relieved when he/she decided to give up human interactions and live as a nonbinary humanoid. Gender neutral or not, Ellie could have sworn he/she had stolen some of her most expensive underwear before giving her back the key to her modest but paid-in-advance Cornhill Street apartment.

As for her and Atticus, it turned out he had a nine-year-old son. He never said a word about who Atticus Jr.'s mother was. Currently the boy was visiting Europe and attending an American school at Ramstein Air Base in Germany. Further in-person pursuance of their itemhood was on hold until Atticus finished some secret work for the US Army on the continent.

What else had she done since Saturday? Ellie thought as she looked over the latest news bulletins coming over social media and the Associated Press feed while at the same time surreptitiously massaging a big fat knotted muscle just above her knee. Oh yes, she remembered, she had taken Mrs. Baker's incontinent Labradoodle dog downstairs for a walk—eight times. She had also discussed with the notoriously nosy widow the bad smell coming from the apartment next to Mrs. Baker on the fifth floor of their walk-up.

"Like cabbages boiled in cat piss, if you ask me." Mrs. Baker's language was pretty salty on account of her late husband having been in the Navy.

Ellie had spent Sunday evening uncramping her leg muscles with ice bags, on account of the six flights of steps leading back up to her flat, it seemed she had just fallen asleep when presto! She found herself giving a tour of the bustling newsroom of the *Citizen Juggernaut* newspaper located at the top of Western Europe's second-tallest and most pervy-looking skyscraper.

"What a view, right?" Ellie gushed, hoping to infuse the prospective unpaid intern with enthusiasm and a sense of adventure. Things which the nervous-looking black girl from Brighton College would come to value much more than a regular paycheque.

Ed Flappe from the international department sidled past them in the narrow hallway. He glanced at the Thames River and London Bridge.

"Yup," he said, dribbling coffee on his rumpled shirt. "When you're inside the Tulip Building, it doesn't seem like a thousand-foot glass dildo, does it?"

"Don't you have an office or a cage you should be in?" Ellie snapped at him. The new intern's smile had frozen on her face. They didn't need another one quitting during orientation.

"Don't mind him," Ellie said, pushing past the smirking architecture critic. "You'll be working with myself and Smitty, the managing editor."

Ellie remembered an important point and lowered her voice. "Did they tell you to act like a tourist when you come in?"

The Brighton girl shook her head, and her smile became granite hard, as though she had just locked eyes with Medusa.

"Technically this isn't an office building at all," Ellie confessed, "only an observation platform. And while we are not exactly trespassing, it is an informal arrangement until the *Juggernaut* gets its brand-new office space sorted. All you have to do is come in a different way each day and don't make eye contact with the security guards."

"And that's another one we'll never see again," Ed Flappe said gloatingly as the Brighton girl rushed out the fire escape.

His office Siamese twin, John Favre, gave him a ham-handed high-five. "I bet she texts her resignation before the elevator gets to the lobby."

"Did you have to use the 'd' word?" Ellie fumed.

Since their hasty departure a month ago from the Gherkin building next door, it seemed the three of them were the only permanent staff besides Smitty the editor.

"The 'd' word," Ed mocked. "There's a forbidden word for every letter of the bloody alphabet now, ain't there?"

John did not need much encouragement. "'A' is for assh—"

Smitty popped his head out from a doorless doorway framed by raw drywall plaster.

"Uh… Ellie, could you, er, get us a washroom pass?"

"Is it my turn again?"

"I'd go, but my back is at it again," Smitty said, grimacing as he braced himself on the wall.

"Don't look at us," Ed and John said together. "We got the first one. Besides, Ellie, you're Asian. They'll just think you're a tourist."

The floor they occupied in the Tulip was still under construction, and only the lower areas had functioning bathrooms. Due to heroin addicts shooting up in any convenient space, building security had issued bar-coded passes for the public lavatories.

"Half Asian," Ellie corrected.

"Then they'll only half remember you," Ed said.

"Hurry up, please," John said, waving an empty coffee cup. "For some unknown science reason, the volume that comes out of a bladder is more than what goes in. Therefore peeing into this receptacle will prove insufficiently sanitary."

Despite the protests of her quad muscles and her lower back, Ellie walked down the steep, narrow fire escape to the public observation platform. The area smelled like fresh paint with an undertone of boring charred smell from soldering. Alone in the stairwell, she stopped, seizing the handrail with both hands.

"Gah."

The building had started shaking. It flashed her mind back to terrible images from eighteen months ago, when she had been in the center of the last Mid-East war. Terrible visions rushed at her.

Bony fingers, the flesh blackened and charred off.

A tiny corpse dissolved in a shallow trench, all except for a plastic artificial limb.

The sky exploding over Jerusalem and belching down a meteor that vaporized the Israeli parliament in a cloud of fiery dust, the rolling, unending thunderous roar…

Ellie gripped the railing more tightly, thinking she was losing her footing on the narrow steps. It wasn't the ground that was shaking. There was no earthquake. The bulb-shaped top of the Tulip Building had three Ferris wheel structures on it. Like the London Eye, these rotated to give visitors a better look at the city. They were just testing the observation pods.

Not going insane, not yet.

The entire tower rattled as massive gear mechanisms rotated on all three sides of the bellend-shaped top of the tower. Ellie sat down and waited for the noise and her own unsettling memories to fade.

A minute later, she found a lazy-looking security guard who barely looked at her. She got the washroom pass, bowed slightly, and whispered, "Arigatou."

By the time she heaved herself back up to the newsroom, Ellie had mostly recovered herself. A line of cold sweat was still making its way down her back, making her shiver. She handed the washroom bar code to Ed; he nobbled away while pantomiming urinary distress by puffing his cheeks out, probably imitating his overfull bladder.

"All hands on deck," their boss Smitty said. He had brought his big inflatable ball into their makeshift newsroom and was lying on it like a deboned flounder. That could only mean one thing: story assignments.

"John, you and Ed will be tracking down the Croydon Cat Ripper," Smitty announced to the half-finished ceiling, which was covered with wires and scaffolding.

"Still?" Ellie said. "They've been on that for years. Didn't they determine hundreds of cats had been mutilated by foxes?"

Smitty shrugged, which, seeing as he was nearly upside down, looked quite comical. "People who read newspapers like cats. Current theory is the ingenious killer hacks up the kitty corpses to hide the wounds made by his crossbow. They've rigged up a number of brave feline volunteers with kitty-cameras to try and catch the bloodthirsty fiend in the act."

The assigning of the domestic furry creature story left an opening for the international stories, which Ellie was still keen on, despite her last foray nearly getting her killed a dozen times and leaving her with recurring nightmares and a sizable account, currently slightly past due, with a private psychologist.

"Hey," Ellie said cheerily, "I see Iran and Turkey may start fighting over the remains of the former Iraq…"

"No." Smitty's shock of whitish hair waggled. "We're still under investigation by the Employment Standards Branch for sending you to Kurdistan in 2029. They're accusing me of 'abusive imperilment of a subordinate.'"

"I'll sign a waiver."

"No."

Ellie rifled through the latest news bulletins.

"Oh, how about this from Bordeaux, France: 'Dolphins die, chimps go insane and missing. Local reactionaries blame a camp of illegal migrants who also seem to have gone missing.'"

"No!"

"But you said people like animal stories," Ellie fumed.

"Not foreign animals, only British animals, preferably English."

On the whiteboard, there was only one local story with no one's name beside it.

"Then I guess I'm doing 'Neo-Nazis violently extend their drug turf in London.'"

"Heh." Ed Flappe was panting as he emerged from the stairwell, having accomplished his urgent mission. "That doesn't sound perilous at all, does it now?"

John Favre added, "Maybe you can do a Sunday fashion special on what the well-dressed London thug is wearing this season."

Ellie, who had recently been the captive of nearly every murderous faction in the Middle East, was not keen on the assignment. But since they were now ribbing her over her completely reputable history as one of Europe's top fashion reporters, she couldn't well back down now, could she?

"All right, I'm totally up for reporting on the state of play amongst London's most vicious criminal gangs. Now, Smitty, do these neo-Nazi gentlemen have a publicist?"

Boring old local crime assignment or not, Ellie was glad to get out of the Tulip Building. Even when the tourist amusement ride was not vibrating the shaft and the bulbous end of the landmark skyscraper, the narrow interior and the bulging glass walls freaked her out. When Jerusalem got attacked by an orbital bombardment platform, she had been near the top of the King David Hotel. It had been like watching the blast of a nuclear bomb. The windows there had looked just like the ones here, before the shockwave blew them inward, covering Ellie with a million crystalline splinters.

Maybe the *Juggernaut's* next office could be street level, or even underground.

"Miss!" a shrill voice said from the street corner. "Will you help us protect Arctic nematodes? They are hard-pressed by climate change and need your ongoing cash donations!"

Oh, bloody hell, a chugger.

Charity muggers, or chuggers, worked on many London streets. This one was an overweight bespectacled twentyish man whose scraggly beard was suffering from horrendous split ends. Ellie knew all these chuggers were on salary as well as commission. After the chuggers and their agencies got paid, the "charities" they worked for rarely saw a penny of the money fleeced from kind-hearted retirees.

The man blocked her path with a color picture of a starving nematode.

"Listen, Soy Boy," Ellie said hotly, "the law says chuggers are to stand off at a three-feet minimum distance from pedestrians. Don't make me page a constable and sue your company for personal distress."

"Well," the man said, backing off, "no one can force you to have a heart."

A robot-driven bendy bus whooshed by, preventing her from crossing the street. She whirled around the other way to get away from the gap-toothed busker. By the time she realized where she was going, it was too late.

She was in front of the big display window of St. Mary Axe Books. Normally Ellie walked the long way round to her flat just to avoid it. Tall columns of the latest nonfiction bestseller were stacked up high in the spotless showcase window display. The lurid cover featured explosions, airplanes, and tanks. It read:

The 96-Hour War
The Inside Story of the Middle East's Most Devastating Conflict!
By
Someone who was there and lived!
Award-winning reporter and frequent guest
on the Jeremy Greffer show on BBC 1.

Ellie had to squint to see her name at the very bottom of the cover.

Eleanor Sato / Printed using recycled materials

Not only was the font microscopic, but they had to use her legal name Eleanor, which made her sound like some dusty frump who haunted the archives at Whitehall.

As she passed by the doorway, she hid her face. A week prior, she had gone into St. Mary Axe Books and offered to sign a few copies. She had even picked out a special fountain pen ink color which evoked bloodshed, devastation, and a speck of hope. The St. Mary's bookshop clerk informed her that no, they were not interested in having her scribble on their inventory, and if she did not wish to make a purchase, she had to leave.

She got two steps past Caffè Nero when her phone rang. Her customized caller ID said "Special Love Operations."

"Hello, Captain!" she said brightly.

"As of next week, it will be Major." Her man's voice was scratchy over the wireless connection. She had heard something about the 6G network being infected with Chinese worms. It made her nostalgic for the crystal-clear Lux/Net device she'd used in Israel, but the government had confiscated all her keepsakes.

"Will I have to give you a different sort of salute then?"

"We'll work something out," the smooth-talking American said. "How's Britain's most famous reporter today?"

Famously skint, she was about to say, but she didn't want him to offer to send her any money. However, if he was now a major, he could afford a *major* shopping spree when he came back. The items top on the shopping list would be food, cosmetics, and luxurious multiple-ply loo roll.

"When are you coming back to London?" Ellie said. "Next week I'm scheduled to depose something at the solicitors. Hope you're back before then."

"Are they still holding up your money from the book?"

"'Fraid so. Israel Antiquities has filed an 'amicus curie' something or other. So has the Muslim Brotherhood, whose lawyers are claiming the statutory tort of 'cultural appropriation.' That's not all," Ellie said, getting into a huff in spite of her desire to sound serenely attractive when speaking to Atticus. "Solicitors working for ISIS's political wing demanded we change the book's title from *The 96-Hour War* to *The Holy Land Liberation War Against Colonialist Zionism.* Even the Samaritan's Anti-Defamation League has written a stern legal letter."

"Which means…"

"All the money is tied up until a judge says otherwise." The cheeky publisher buggers had actually sent her a letter demanding she repay her

£30,000 advance. That was almost comical, seeing as her bank balance was -£0.30. "But let's not worry about that. I'm sure it will all be settled soon."

A block away from her home, she was now opposite Appelboom Pens, the world's most prestigious fountain pen shop. She relaxed somewhat. Deep inside Appelboom was a vault that had survived a direct hit during the Blitz, and in that vault was her nest egg retirement savings—a fountain pen. It was a vintage Namiki #1/1, for which a now-deceased Turkish oligarch had offered her at least a few million quid.

Poor Mr. Borkin!

"Look," Atticus said, "I have to be out of touch for a few days, then I'm on leave for a month."

Ellie remembered Atticus had his son Attie Jr. with him. The charming boy was nine years old, and his hair was a good deal blonder than his father's. She'd most recently seen him as they changed flights from America through Heathrow. He had been accompanied by Sarge Bryan, a longtime family friend. Ellie had not gotten to the point of discussing Attie Jr.'s mother, and Attie Sr. had not volunteered any information.

"Brilliant, stay safe."

"I'm in Germany. Nothing ever happens here."

The signal crackled again. She said a hasty goodbye and rang off.

As she waited to cross at the corner, a long line of cyclists wearing "Extinction Rebellion" scarves sped past. They looked miserable. Maybe they were upset the end of the world was being beset with more delays than Brexit.

Her building was just opposite. She looked up at her place. Her slightly illegal window box of pink petunias was coming in nicely. At least she had invested the book's advance and all her cash to pay her apartment lease for a year. There was absolutely zero chance they could wheedle that away from her. Worst case, she would have a place to sleep in Europe's least affordable city for the next twelve months.

She saw Mrs. Baker and Chestnut, her Labradoodle. A few other fellow tenants were milling around along the street.

"Hello, Mrs. B, what's everyone doing outside?"

"Fire alarm. They're just making sure everyone is out," Mrs. Baker said grouchily. "False alarm, I'm sure. Only fellow who hasn't responded is our smelly neighbor on the fifth—"

Her words were cut off by an eruption of fire and exploding concrete. The fifth and sixth floor of Ellie's building shattered outward in a cloud of dust. The blast knocked Ellie straight back into the wall behind her. She felt herself slide down the rough stone onto the sidewalk.

3

"Not now, Attie," Ellie mumbled half consciously in response to a fuzzy-faced nuzzling. "I've just put on my makeup. You've got to shave…"

Slowly it dawned on her that she was not in bed. It was much too uncomfortable. And noisy. And crowded. Sirens blared, smoke billowed, and charred bricks were falling onto pavement. All around her she could see people's legs and shoes. *Boy, people have some tatty footwear,* she thought in a daze.

The curly haired face of Mrs. Baker's Labradoodle was inches away from hers. He was trying to revive her. The dog was the only one paying her any attention.

Ellie slowly got to her feet. She tried to brush soot from her dress, but she only succeeded in smearing it. Reflexively she grabbed the dog's leash and limped over to where two of the neighbors were fanning Mrs. Baker with a newspaper and a dish towel.

"Oh, Eleanor dearie," Mrs. Baker said. "Could you get Chestnut some water? Looks like we'll be out here a while. And I'm about to faint." Mrs. Baker swooned theatrically, and her attendants fanned her with increasing vigor.

Ellie looked up. Smoke spewed out of a fifth-floor window. A big ladder with a hose on top was jetting water like mad. She could not see her apartment at all. The small chance that Ellie would be able to duck back in after they put the fire out faded when the hazmat team arrived. They wore yellow suits that looked suitable for deep diving in the Channel. They waved off the less-protected firefighters.

There was some commotion at the front entrance.

"Ohhh, that's Feroze!" Mrs. Baker wailed. "Oh, I can't believe it's come to this!"

At this point, the corpulent woman swooned again into the arms of the four paramedics attending her.

Ellie tried to peek over the crowd. The evacuees and the curious had all been pressed back along the tape line marked "Chemical Danger." She only got a brief glance at a very charred corpse being taken out the front door on a stretcher. There was still half a head of spiky blue hair on the otherwise broiled scalp. Only one person in the building had hair like that: the fellow from the fifth floor. Why hadn't he evacuated?

"What a tragedy!" Mrs. Baker wailed. "He was such a good lad, always walking my little Chestnut. A great loss to us, to the whole nation!"

Ellie felt something trickling down her neckline. From her rather eventful time in the Holy Land, she knew without looking it was a stream of her blood.

"Excuse me." She tapped the shoulder of a paramedic. "Would you have some gauze dressing, please?"

"Please move back," the uniformed woman said sharply, shielding Mrs. Baker. "Can't you see this poor lady is in distress? Let us deal with people who have real injuries."

Ellie shrank away. Luckily there was an outdoor café. She grabbed some paper napkins and pressed it against the small gash behind her ear.

She walked over to a fire truck; it seemed to be on standby as others tackled the blaze.

"Excuse me, I'm Ellie Sato from the *Juggernaut*. What's going on?"

The chance of being featured as London's "Hero of the Week" got the man talking.

"Nasty business, right-o," the fireman said with a heavy accent. "As I suspected as I rushed in to save lives, 'twas a chemical fire. Nasty. Likely a drug-cookin' operation. No one's going back in there fer weeks. Maybe I'll have to evacuate the whole block as I do my job to keep London safe."

That was that. Her mattress was probably charred to a crisp and soaked by water. *Bugger*, she thought. *Poor blue-haired Feroze.* Ellie had only seen Feroze half a dozen times over a year and always at night.

As they took Mrs. Baker away on a stretcher, she shrieked at them to stop.

"Eleanor! Take charge of dear old Chestnut, will you, love? They won't let me take him, and I think I'll be a while. All my old conditions are flaring up."

Ellie took Chestnut's leash in one hand, pressed her napkin dressing against her scalp wound with the other, and walked off. She was officially homeless in London.

"We only have an executive suite," said the tall uniformed man attending the front desk of Threadneedles Hotel. "Eight hundred per night and"—he looked suspiciously at Chestnut—"seventy-five per diem surcharge for pets. And I'm afraid we'll be needing a cleaning deposit of one thousand."

That raised Ellie's eyebrows.

"Should it be the cause of a mess." The clerk looked down with horror at Chestnut's smiling face and wagging tail.

Ellie felt like a mess. The first two hotels she had tried wouldn't even let her in with the Labradoodle. Somewhere along the way, one of her shoe heels had come loose, and her scalp wound was still oozing blood.

She wanted to walk out, but Threadneedles Hotel was her last shot before she grabbed some cardboard, used Chestnut as a pillow, and slept rough in the increasingly cozy-looking alleyway across the street. Her parents were traveling and their home was way up North. She suspected Ed and John from the office still lived with their parents. Smitty would likely take her in, but his wife didn't like her and made Smitty sleep in the garage when his back was acting up. She seemed like a right old horror.

"Here, then," she said, handing over her credit card. It was only for the one night. Her insurance company, Mutual of Transnistria, would certainly cover some of it.

"I'm sorry, this card was declined," the clerk said a few moments later, looking at her with increasing suspicion. "Perhaps you would like to phone your bank? There is a pay phone located down the street."

Now she remembered. She'd taken some kind of cash withdrawal to pay her lump-sum apartment lease in advance. Only issue was, the place didn't exist any longer except as a smoldering toxic hole in the city skyline.

"Safe as houses" my Eurasian ass!

"Well, ah, thank you. I'll go and do that. Just down the street, did you say?"

She and Chestnut wound their way through the revolving door. Ellie's hopes for a dignified exit hinged on the dog not pooping in the lobby and the heel of her shoe not falling off, at least until she was out of sight of the deskman. She glanced back to see him conferring with a security guard.

It was only 6:30 p.m.

"What do homeless people do all day long?" she muttered to her curly haired companion. She decided to have coffee. There was enough change rattling around in her soot-smudged Chanel purse to cover a latte or two.

Caffè Nero had a doggie water station outside. As soon as Ellie sat down in a wicker chair, she felt more optimistic. All of her significant possessions, except the one tucked away in Appelboom's vault, were burned or covered in toxic goop. At some point, she might be forced to get a job that paid money. But all that would work out. Something always turned up.

Then one of the United Kingdom's most prolific serial killers did just that.

"There ye be!" a woman's voice with a heavy Scottish accent said from behind her.

That voice! The memories it conjured up gave Ellie sudden new chills, and just when destitution and personal ruin had been going so well.

Drat! Wasn't that woman locked up for multiple life terms? What was she doing wandering the streets of the capital?

"Oh my, Ms. China," Ellie managed to say, getting up just in case she had to run for it. "How wonderful to see you. And your friends."

Two uncomfortable-looking men in dark mac overcoats were on either side of her. They held chains attached to a thick belt around Ms. China's enviably thin waist. Both her hands were cuffed to a restraining apparatus and encased in thick plastic gloves.

"Good, er, evening." An angular man in a bowler hat eyed Ellie's bloodstained collar. "Would you be Ms. Eleanor Sato of…" The man gruffly read out her former address.

Ellie nodded.

"Pleased to meet you. I'm Mr. Delingpole from NHS, Community Outpatient Services. Will you please sign here and take custody of the patient?"

A computer tablet with about a million words of fine print was thrust at her. Mr. Delingpole's voice had a distinct note of supplication.

"Patient?"

"Honestly," Ms. China said. "We've been to every Caffè Nero looking for you. Why don't you stay put? Oh, look, you have a dog now. I tried therapy dogs too. They all died."

Ms. China smiled wanly. Ellie was used to the way she looked, but the average person would have done a double take at the tall blonde woman's skin art. All visible parts of her body were covered in delicate gold-and-silver tattoos. Her body art also extended to the whites of her eyes, which had two extra pupils each. When Ms. China curled her lips, she caused whorls of microscopic gold filament to glimmer, making concentric circles around her dimples.

"Sorry to uh…" Ellie had vowed to start reading things before she signed them, especially after her rather one-sided book deal contract. "What am I agreeing to here?"

"You, ma'am, are taking full responsibility for the outpatient Annunciata Philmore Romanov China. You undertake the responsibility of making sure she receives her medication…" Mr. Delingpole handed Ellie a purse-sized black case. "…and are liable for any, er, disorder she may cause."

Ellie knew the "disorder" Ms. China was prone to causing often filled good-sized morgues to bursting.

"Oh… isn't there anyone else you'd rather…"

Ms. China's expression dropped. She looked as though she was going to start gushing tears from her satanically tattooed eyes.

"Oh, all right. But unless you've got money, we'll be sleeping rough tonight. My apartment is apparently Britain's answer to Chernobyl."

Ellie signed the form, and the two wardens hurriedly unlocked themselves from Ms. China, took off the ten plastic sheaths covering her fingernails, and hurried down the street.

"I've got better than money," Ms. China said, rubbing her wrists and picking up Chestnut's leash. "I've got a posh house in Mayfair. Let's go!"

"Your first name's Annunciata?"

Of the few hundred other questions brimming on Ellie's mind, that was the only one she could articulate. The whole sequence of events had overtaken her so quickly. Firstly, her local news assignment tracking down neo-Nazis, which at least had gotten her out of the bellend Tulip Building early. Then the startling explosion and grisly human remains at her formerly quite fashionable flat. Then the now-clotted and gently throbbing knock on her head. Finally being put in charge of a happy, albeit capricious, dog and one of Europe's foremost poisoners.

"It is, it really is," Ms. China said distantly, watching the men from Community Outpatient Services scamper away. She gazed closely at Ellie. "You look knackered. Is that blood all from you? Let's get a cab."

They were halfway to Mayfair when Ellie realized she didn't have any cash. She doubted mad people were given an allowance.

"Maybe we should get out here," Ellie said sheepishly. "It's not far, and I could do with a walk."

"Maybe you could, luv, but not your shoes."

"Well... I left my real purse, the one with loads of money in it, in my apartment, and it's all toxic now."

"Don't worry, my butler will pay our efficient and discreet driver." Ms. China eyed the older cabbie and drummed her clipped but still dangerous-looking fingernails on the plastic partition.

Ellie was in fact too knackered to do much but nod and try not to drift off entirely on the comfy leather seat in the back of the overheated taxi. She had almost dozed off when they came to a large townhouse on Grosvenor Square.

In the faint light of dusk, it looked to be a positively Victorian Gothic pile.

Mayfair had been a very exclusive neighborhood. It was adjacent to Buckingham Palace. Under the recently ended British Marxist government, its cachet had come off a tad. There was a tent city in the park. While the place was still chock-a-clock with embassies and oligarchs, rough sleepers abounded, and many buildings had been abandoned.

The driver tipped his hat to someone Ellie could not make out very well. As Ellie got out of the cab, Ms. China caught her before she tripped on her now totally broken shoe heel. The open door of the madwoman's mansion exuded a warm yellow light.

Going up a circular marble staircase, Ellie noticed a blinking ankle monitor on Ms. China's leg. As things stood, she felt more like the ward than the warden.

"This is you." They stopped at an upstairs bedroom. "Chestnut will have his own room if he likes, yes he will," her hostess said ruffling the dog's neck fur.

Ms. China had led her to a much nicer room than they would have shoved her into at Threadneedles. On one side there was an immaculate four-poster bed, and inside a mirrored alcove hung dressing gowns of terry cloth and silk.

"If you want anything, call Mr. Surghit from any of the house communications panels," Ms. China said from the doorway. "Just don't expect a verbal reply. He's kind of quiet."

Ellie didn't recall undressing or showering the sweat, blood, and smoke residue off her body, though she must have because she felt much cleaner as the downy weight of the crisp sheets on her body was the last thing she could remember feeling before her mind drifted away.

She formulated a stern resolution to avoid adventures of any sort. She dreamed she had returned to full-time fashion reporting and was interviewing Coco Chanel in occupied Paris as she defied the Third Reich with subversive and stunning couture.

The next morning, Ellie lay quite still. Moving only her eyes, she located a cherrywood night table. On it rested her soot-smeared Chanel bag and a silver water jug. She lay there until she was certain that all she recalled happening had actually taken place.

She had become homeless, was knocked out, and now lived in a Mayfair mansion. It was all good. Eerily, the ultra-posh house seemed to know she was awake. The door chimed.

"Uh, come in, I guess." She made sure her Versace bathrobe was on properly.

Instead of the very stealthy Mr. Surghit, a small robot came in with a tray. Through clear tray lids, Ellie saw heaps of scrambled eggs, bacon, and fruit.

"Are you decent?" Ms. China's unfiltered Scottish accented voice called from the doorway.

She came in and pulled up a chair.

"Who else is here?" Ellie asked and sipped juice.

"Just us, luv."

Ellie's mental health ward explained how she and her old minders, including Mr. Delingpole, had been getting on each other's nerves. In order to avoid consequences of a thorny nature for both of them, it was agreed she could designate a new care worker.

"But why think of me?" Ellie said. "Are your parents, um…"

Ms. China pursed her gold-brocaded lips in mild annoyance while she skewered the biggest strawberry on the tray with a two-inch-long fingernail extension.

"I haven't poisoned them, if that's what you mean." She gobbled the fruit in one bite and laughed as red juice ran down her pronounced chin. "We're going to have *fun*, aren't we?"

Ms. China explained the large house, which came with a very discreet staff, was vacant due to the draconian property policies of the Marxist-Labour government, which had been in power until the previous week.

"They sent all the rich people packing unless they wanted to pay ninety-nine percent tax. The rub was, if they owned any houses, the councils would charge them 'Empty Homes' levy on top, which added up to one hundred and thirty percent in taxes."

Suddenly, Ellie felt glad to not be burdened by wealth. It sounded awful. "Bloody commies."

"There's a loophole," Ms. China explained. "Hospitals and mental health facilities with at least one certified insane patient in permanent care get triple amortization benefit, or something. The upshot is, just because I'm here, with of all the grants and tax deferrals, the owner of this place will probably make money."

Ellie had a nagging notion of something she had to do, and then she finally remembered.

"Your medication," Ellie said, pulling out the black case she had been given. Inside was a high-tech-looking blister pack, which had a digital time readout and an antenna. "You're supposed to take… this one right now. The one called clozapine maximus."

Ms. China chuckled. The Greek meandros decorations etched in silver along her jugular quivered.

"Just pop it out and dissolve it. There are jars of my pee and blood in the kitchen."

This was unexpected. Ellie hoped they were clearly marked. "Why?"

"In case they come round to test me."

"Skipping your meds," Ellie said cautiously, glancing at Ms. China's re-established manicure. "Isn't that dangerous?"

Ms. China looked at her. The light from the window caught her tattooed eyes and six pupils.

"Not for you, I promise."

4

ELLIE

Ellie spent the rest of the morning exploring the grand old house and denying she was engaged in high-end prostitution.

"Are you sure, Ellie?" Smitty said over the phone, his voice skeptical.

"Yes, I'm sure I'm not whoring myself to keep a roof over my head." Although, if Atticus were the client, she might be tempted.

"But Mayfair, that's full of sheiks and oligarchs. A cabinet minister was nearly arrested for loitering there."

"Things have become much more egalitarian while the Marxists were in power. We'll have you over; you should come walk in Grosvenor park. The poshness of it all will do wonders for your back."

She looked through the transparent door of the refrigerator at the jars of bodily fluids inside. Chemical capsules were fizzing at the bottom of beakers of yellow and red liquid. "Though if you do pop by, I think we'll end up eating out."

She assured her editor she was still on her assigned story and promised to deliver some copy on Neuveaus Nazis, or whatever they were called, by the afternoon.

Her emails to Mutual of Transnistria's home fire-insurance claims department had been returned as undeliverable. That was probably only a glitch. The internet in Eastern Europe was always dodgy.

The mansion Ms. China had finagled for her convalescence had loads of rooms. Ellie only managed to get up the winding main staircase to the fifth floor before her legs felt wobbly again. Just as she was looking for an easier way to get down, the door of a lift opened at the end of the hall with a polite "ding". The stealthy butler Mr. Surghit must have sent it.

"I've ordered out for lunch," Ms. China said as Ellie came out on the ground floor. "Mr. Surghit's great for run o'mill, but I really fancied plover's eggs."

"Aren't they illegal?"

"I know a fellow who knows a feller in the North, a real bird's egg climmer, born and bred."

A delivery boy with a big square backpack quickly popped around. As he took payment by tapping a console by the front entrance, he peered behind Ellie, possibly hoping to see some upper-class nudity. He slunk off disappointed.

The contraband eggs were delicious. Ellie asked after Chestnut, worried he might feel alienated in a huge strange house. However, Mr. Surghit had shown his four-legged guest how to use the robot dog walker, and he was off strutting around in the park.

"Is it all right if I leave you for a little while?" Ellie said with as much forced gaiety as she could muster. In documentaries, people who dealt with the insane were always decidedly cheerful sounding when they spoke.

"Must you?" Ms. China pouted.

"I've still got to work." Smitty promised to actually pay her once the *Juggernaut* sorted out its office space issues.

"On what?"

"Some people called neo-Nazis. I just have to find some and ask them about their filthy habits and doings."

"Oh!" Ms. China instantly perked up. "I love neo-Nazis! Where do you want to start?"

"Aren't you, um…?" Ellie pointed at the blinking ankle monitor strapped to the other woman's long shapely leg.

In an idle moment, Ellie had read the British Medical Association's manual resting on the kitchen table: "How to be the Best Carer for Your Criminally Insane Patient." In that fat binder, she had learned that Ms. China's device was hooked into three monitoring stations, one of which was a satellite. If she was caught leaving her designated premises without authorization, there were severe penalties for them both.

Ms. China looked down, as though just noticing her ankle tag. "I'll fix that in a jiff."

She reached down to below her knee, flipped off a patch of skin with a sound like Velcro tearing, and unscrewed her leg. Having amputated herself below the knee, she hopped over to a rather shocked Ellie and placed her lower leg on the big granite countertop.

"See?" Ellie's ward said, tickling the top of the detached foot. "It has its own temperature control, pulse, and even basic autonomous reflexes."

The object's shapely naked toes fluttered in response to the stimulation.

"It's a cybernetic attachment?"

Ms. China nodded gleefully and hopped over to a cupboard on the far side of the kitchen. Ellie had learned a lot about cybernetic enhancements during her coverage of the 96-Hour War. One of Atticus Reidt's best friends was Sarge Bryan, an albino with totally cybernetic eyes.

"It's so good it fools most doctors." After a bit of rummaging, Ms. China pulled up a sack that contained a down-market-looking version of her fake limb. "This one won't fool anyone. It's an older sports model, but it's all right to walk with."

The loaner leg was not in good shape. Its surface was piebald dappled. The silicone plastic covering the heel was worn through where some wires were poking out. Two toes were missing. It also turned out to be a good inch shorter than required.

"Now, where did they go?" Ms. China said during another flurry of rummaging. "I used to have shoes with a heel insert to balance me out."

At the mention of clothing, Ellie suddenly remembered her own wardrobe had been reduced to one sooty, torn, blood-smeared rag, which was supposedly a non-label Versace she had purchased at a designer popup outlet. Still, she wouldn't be caught hunting neo-Nazis in it.

"Dunna worry about a thing," Ms. China said as she practiced a twisty limping hobble in a boot into which she had stuffed some wadded cotton so it fit her second-best prosthetic foot. "Mr. Surghit got your measurements from the laser sensors in your shower. Before you got up, there was a robot delivery from Harrods."

She glanced at a diamond-encrusted grandfather clock; it was nearly noon. The Elida Geisha coffee the automated kitchen machine kept spewing out had cleared her head of the cobwebs left by the sudden descent into penniless homelessness, not to mention the sharp knock on her head. Her hostess was being awfully friendly and generous. Ellie Sato, investigative fashion journalist for the oldest paper in Britain, knew Ms. China was up to more than she was letting on. However, the crinkling of opening shopping bags allowed her to overlook her suspicions.

"Oh, you shouldn't have."

Inside the surprise Harrods bundle were matching black-and-gray leather outfits. Just the thing for stalking evildoers along the storied streets of the same city streets previously terrorized by the Ripper, the Krays, and Jeremy Corbyn.

The clothes and accessories must have cost thousands. Ethics would normally require she ask where a ward of the state got her money from. However, too many questions might unbalance Ms. China's unmedicated mind. Ellie felt she should err on the side of not prompting a murder spree.

Besides, as they walked down a wrought iron stairway to make their getaway out a back exit, her clinging leather outfit did make her look "Catwoman in London" badass.

The door out into the alley closed and locked behind them. Mr. Surghit again. The man was either the best butler in the history of domestic servants or a creepy loon who laser-scanned women's measurements in the shower. Ellie adjusted her Dior pants belt. Did it really matter if the result was her ass looked smoking hot?

"Should we get a cab?" Ellie whispered as they ducked under a hedge and walked single file along a service alley. "Or should we take the Metro?"

Outside of the financial districts and Whitehall, Ellie had no idea where irredeemably disreputable people could be found.

"We're almost there."

"In Mayfair? Really?"

Ms. China turned to her, and her expression was severe as was only possible for someone with a face covered in metallic tattoos. The cloud-filtered sunlight made her look as though she were glowing from the inside.

"We're looking for true evil, right?"

"I guess."

"Then it's best to start at a church run by Jesuits."

The gothic steeple of the Church of the Immaculate Conception was on Farm Street, only a few blocks away from Grosvenor Square.

"The Marxists in Parliament bankrupted the Catholic Church and most other Christian churches by legislating unlimited liability for victims of clerical sexual abuse," Ms. China said very authoritatively. "Even obviously fake lawsuits cost millions in legal fees. This church was bought by a numbered company based in Albania."

That got Ellie thinking. For someone with Ms. China's background, thinking up better ways to kill loads of people for DERA, Britain's Defence Evaluation and Research Agency, she certainly was widely versed in spiritual matters. One of their most exciting jaunts during the 96-Hour War had begun by Ms. China sending them to Jerusalem's Church of the Holy Sepulchre and ended with Ellie knocking Israel's head of state unconscious.

As they walked toward Farm Street, security guards outside the Syrian embassy gawked at them with equal parts lust and suspicion. Ellie asked about that seemingly paradoxical part of Ms. China's personality.

"Oh, yes," Ms. China said, ruffling her hair to shamelessly flirt with the horny guards. Ellie noticed that her scalp also had metallic tattoos. "I'm a raving Catholic. I'd go to church every day and twice on Sundays, unless I'm preempted by work or incarceration."

"You don't say. I'd just think it would cause you all sorts of conflict," Ellie said, realizing she was nearing precarious psychological territory.

The *Manual for Carers* that Mr. Delingpole from the NHS had given her cautioned strongly against chatting about personal matters with one's ward, especially when there were sharp objects in the room.

"Not at all. I firmly believe in nine of the Big Ten Commandments." Just beside the boarded-up church was a construction site. They ducked through a hole in the fence. "I was right here at Immaculate Conception in the middle of my confession, when time ran out. The father confessor asked me back so I could finish up on my mortal sins when—*poof*—the bailiff's notice went up on the door. Upon my return for supplementary contrition, there was a padlock right here."

The door was sealed up with "Private Property Keep Out" written in four different languages.

Ellie was skeptical.

"Do you think they'd allow nefarious types to operate here in Mayfair?"

"Who is 'they'?" Ms. China asked cynically. She led the way over to a window, which also appeared to be boarded up, but the plywood had a hinge concealed at the top. "The police commissioner was at an EV charge station last week. He got stabbed and robbed. There is no more 'they.'"

Ellie and Ms. China climbed in through the trick window. The wood slammed down with too much racket for Ellie's liking. She followed her companion deeper into the bowels of the empty church. The roof dripped moisture, though it had not rained for days. Everything smelled of mold.

"I tell you, Ellie, it's a jungle out there."

Just as they rounded a corner, they came face-to-face with a young man with a shaved head. He held what looked like a pipe attached to a wooden stock. It was only when he pulled a lever back with a click that Ellie realized it was a homemade shotgun.

Ellie and Ms. China froze. The man's face split in a gap-toothed half smile. In a hoarse voice and a Cockney accent, he said, "It ain't no party down here neither, bitches!"

5

Having had more than a few firearms pointed at her by seriously murderous people in the Middle East, Ellie was less shocked and more perturbed by the fact that she'd allowed a local thug to get the drop on her. She vowed never to let herself be blindly led along by a psychotic individual who was off her meds, no matter how nice they seemed.

"Where's Chucky?" Ms. China asked coolly, as though asking after her favorite maître d'.

"He's what you call MIA, missin' in action, s'whot." The bald-headed man came into clearer focus. He had scabs on his lips, and Ellie wouldn't have wrapped trash with what he was wearing. There was more lining showing on his coat than fake leather. "You chums o' Chucky's?" the scabby man asked.

Ms. China was inching closer to Scabby. Ellie did not think a physical confrontation was the way to go. If those sawed pipes were filled with black powder, even dropping the contraption could set it off. She'd had enough pepperings by shrapnel for one career.

"Heh," Ellie said quickly, trying to sound like someone who would be one of Chucky's regular drug customers. "You seem to be quite occupied here. We'll just come back when Chucky's on duty, and we can, er, buy shit, the shit we want, from him."

"Don't leave yet," a lower bass-sounding man's voice said from the shadows on the other side of the basement. "I'm sure filthy whores like you have something to trade us."

Scabby backed up but kept his gun on Ellie and Ms. China.

"They just wandered in," the gunman explained to the three figures who were still in the shadows. "I couldn't do nothin'."

First there came into view another dilapidated white guy with a shaved head, likely a friend of Scabby's. Accompanying him was a skinny brown man in a white T-shirt and a much wider, bearded man brandishing a heavy walking stick.

Walking Stick edged forward, gripping his club in both his burly hands. "I'm sure we can arrange something."

The big guy, his beard, the way he cuffed the sleeves of his denim jacket… he reminded Ellie of something to do with the rape-grooming gang scandals of a few years ago.

"I've been doing business with Chucky," Ms. China said. She spoke curtly, but the addition of the three other gentlemen, presumably also armed, clearly gave her pause. "We'll go elsewhere."

The door was open. Any rational person would have gotten the hell out of there.

Oh, Annunciata!

In a quick motion, Ms. China jabbed out with her very long reach, pushing the barrel of the blunderbuss away from Ellie and toward the newcomers. Unfortunately, her loaner prosthetic leg was not up to her acrobatics.

With a *twonk* sound, it came right off her leg stump and flopped around in her tight pants. Scabby received only a mild scratch on his cheek, which he didn't seem to notice.

"Crazy cunt," he said and kicked Ms. China in the back and side as she was kneeling down trying to fix her leg.

The larger cane-wielding thug and his man in the white shirt circled around, opposite the two skinheads. Scabby and Walking Stick were visibly wary of each other. They had to be members of competing underworld factions.

"What are you up to?" Walking Stick growled and brandished a foot-long knife, which had come out of the end of his cane. "You bring your sluts to business?"

"I've never seen these gashes in my life," Scabby protested as his left hand dabbed at the drops of blood on his cheek.

His skinhead partner was now waving around a box cutter.

"Juk 'em, and we get out of here," White Shirt said.

"Jukking" was street slang for stabbing. Ellie realized they had stumbled into the middle of a nefarious transaction, and its participants could well conclude two corpses in an abandoned church basement would arouse less suspicions than two live junkie witnesses.

Ms. China flailed around on the ground in a disheveled mess. Her false leg had fallen completely out of her pants leg. Scabby glanced at it and laughed.

The diversion gave Ellie time to try to think of a counterplan, which was what super spy operatives like Atticus and Sarge Bryan always managed to do.

She looked on the ground for a stick or a brick, anything. It was hopeless. There were four of them. She and Ms. China had three legs between them. Ellie had to sow division and hate. How hard could that be with child rapers and neo-Nazis?

She took a deep breath of moldy church basement air and went for it.

"We'd ah… we'd a dealt with Chucky," Ellie said to Scabby, trying to sound like a crack-addled street whore. "We'd a dealt wif you, but we taking our business elsewhere if you're going to deal with rotters like these."

Scabby stopped laughing and just looked confused.

"I'm ashamed to be in the company of the likes of you," Ellie said, staring accusingly at Scabby. "I thought you neo-Nazis had principles."

Ellie was sure the larger bearded fellow, Walking Stick, was connected to one of the UK's notorious child-rape gangs. She had covered the court case where he was let off on a technicality. He always wore that denim jacket with the sleeves cuffed. But it had been years ago, and she couldn't recall his name.

"Bitch is crazy," Walking Stick said quickly. "I never touch no kids."

Scabby pointed the shotgun at Walking Stick, who backed up. "Oy, she didn't say nuffin' about interferin' with no kids. Why would you say that?"

Scabby then looked back to Ellie, keeping the gun aimed between her and the large swarthy man. "If you know this feller," Scabby asked, his voice laden with the addled indecision of someone who has been getting high every day since he was ten years old, "what's his name, then?"

Shit.

"I knows it, I knows it," Ellie stammered. They couldn't expect rapid answers from a fleabag prostitute, could they?

Both groups of men started to move closer. Ellie looked around wildly. Walking Stick had a jewel-encrusted chain and pendant with the letters "BPS" dangling from his thick hairy neck. Those initials brought back to Ellie's mind a picture of a young girl's flesh seared and blistering with "BPS" in the center of the scabby wound.

"He's… the Big Pimp Stick, Ali Abbas, he is!" Ellie finally said with triumph that rebounded through the dank brick-walled basement. "They groomed and raped thousands of girls, his gang did. They'd do any non-Muslim girl. Black, mixed, Sikh, but their favorite was white British girls."

"What you talking?" Scabby the skinhead asked. He started backing away from the pimp Ali Abbas. He was making sure no one could grab his shotgun without getting a belly full of pellets.

"White girls fetched the highest prices," Ellie went on, relying on her knowledge of the sex-ring scandal. "They'd send 'em around in cabs they owned over and over, night after night, till they were worn out, pregnant, or dead. He even branded them on their lily-white asses with the initials "BPS" so everyone would know who they belonged to."

As she talked, she helped Ms. China to her feet. She was still trying to reattach her false leg, but it was really broken.

"Self-respecting Nazis wouldn't never do no business with the likes of this… child raper!"

Scabby's hands began to shake. His free hand slapped at the finger-length incision Ms. China's nail had left on his jawline.

"Y-you all st-stay still!" Scabby looked like he was going to faint.

Scabby's man lashed out with his box cutter at the thug in the white T-shirt. Ali Abbas's man yelled and ducked away, reaching for his own weapon.

The blunderbuss roared in the dark. It let off more smoke and sparks than pellets. The sudden shattering noise drove Ellie down onto the moist filth covering the creaking floorboards. Ms. China finally had the right idea and pulled her away. As the melee between the four men started, they crawled up the narrow stairs toward daylight.

The last look she got of their former captors was Scabby on his knees, trying to reload his gun with nerveless hands that just flopped against his weapon. White Shirt and the second skinhead were furiously stabbing each other. Big Pimp Stick Abbas was still on his feet but bleeding and stunned after receiving a peppering of pellets from the blunderbuss.

Ellie and Ms. China finally scrambled out onto the roadway in front of the church building. It was surprisingly light out in the street. It seemed they had been inside for hours, but it had only been minutes.

Ellie supported Ms. China as they hobbled out through a broken fence onto the road. A Rolls Royce passed quite close to them. It did not stop. No one appeared to have heard the carnage below.

"He should have gone down faster," Ms. China protested. "I should have been able to grab the gun. I stuck him with my custom curare poison."

As Ellie struggled along, she tried to be optimistic. "At least we didn't get jukked."

"Where are you going?"

"Back home," Ellie said. They were only blocks away.

Ms. China shot a glance behind them. "We've seen their faces. There may be more of them. We have to get off the street."

That was easier said than done. In this very expensive neighborhood, every entryway was tightly locked up. The place seemed almost deserted.

"This one!" Ms. China said, hopping over to a low grated window about a square foot wide. "Pull that over. We'll break in here and use it to hide where we've gone through."

Ellie heaved at a big garbage bin on wheels while Ms. China whipped off her belt and wrapped it around the rusty grate. Bracing her remaining leg, she pulled mightily to dislodge it. The screws were shorter and more rusted than one would expect at the rear of a multi-million-dollar townhome. All at once, they came loose, and Ms. China landed flat on her back.

Ellie hauled her back up and pushed her through the opening, stump first. She threw the loose grate after her, clambered halfway through, and then pulled the blue plastic bin so that it rested flush with the side of the building. They were as well hidden as they could be.

The dark basement they found themselves in was much cleaner than the one under the Immaculate Conception. By light spilling from the half-open door, Ellie could make out shapes. Walnut paneling surrounded the outline of a pool table. Pool cues were leaning against one wall, and opposite them sat a fireplace, cold and unlit.

Ms. China was holding on to a doorjamb, standing very still, listening. She held out a hand to stop Ellie from going any farther. From the doorway, which led into the rest of the house, came a raspy, half-human, half-mechanical sound.

"*Hawrrrr... Hawrrrr.*" It repeated again and again, and Ellie began to tremble.

6

Someone or something was making the breathing sound which was coming from a room at the other end of the basement they had crawled into. Ellie checked the window to the alleyway through which they had broken in. If she pushed the garbage bin away, they could get out. But Ms. China's prosthetic leg had fallen off back in the Church of the Holy Crackhead. Ellie didn't fancy a three-legged race away from murderous rapists.

Ellie's ears were still ringing from the atrociously loud noise made by the skinhead drug dealer's shotgun. She looked at Ms. China. Her gold-tattooed features seemed more curious than frightened. Of course, Ellie's companion was certified severely mentally disordered under the Mental Health Act.

No one noticed they had broken in, yet. A posh place like this had to have a security system. Ellie looked around. For a townhouse mansion in Mayfair, which cost as much as an ocean liner, the décor in the games room seemed altogether chavvy. There was a scuffed pool table and a tattered projection movie screen. She guessed the house upstairs was similar in size to the one she and Ms. China were staying in.

Through the half-open door, the noise continued.

"*Hawrrrr… Hawrrrr.*"

Ellie felt the sane person with two legs should take charge; she pulled her companion back. Ms. China hopped over to a rack of pool cues and leaned quietly against it. Rich people often had great big dogs running about who loved to snack on burglars, or even just stylishly dressed totally innocent people fleeing the local thugs. Ellie took hold of a cue and held it like a spear.

"Hsst." Ms. China pulled on her jacket. "Just shut the door. We'll wait here an hour or so."

"*Hawrrrr... Hawrrrr.*"

The noise didn't seem like it was being made by a dog. A Qatari man had recently been fined for trying to smuggle in a fully grown orangutan that had been trained as a security guard. She didn't think it was an enormous jungle ape either.

"If you hear any... any unexpected mayhem, call the police."

"Police? Are you mad?" Ms. China hissed. "You've allowed me off my tether. They'll cancel my outpatient status, and I don't know what they'll do to you."

"Then just stay here."

Ellie tiptoed into the hallway, easing closed the game-room door behind her.

The "hawrrrr... hawrrrr" sound was louder out here. It also seemed to be slowing, as though it were winding down.

In the hall, Ellie stepped onto a plush zebra-patterned carpet. Little alcove lights sprung on, making her jump a little. They had to be linked to motion detectors. The walls were covered with leather wallpaper. From the way it looked, it might have even been reptile skin. She wrinkled her nose at the gaudiness of it all.

The mysterious sound had stopped. Ellie had a good idea it had been coming from around the very next corner. In the quiet, she could hear noises from the street. A lorry rumbled past.

As they had been breaking in, she had only glanced up at the townhouse. It had four or five stories above ground. Many of London's mega houses were as deep as they were high. Unable to build up due to building restrictions, the ultra rich had burrowed under London, sometimes six or seven levels deep.

Ellie passed a room to her right. A waft of humid air hit her. That must a pool or a sauna. She crept toward the L-shaped end of the corridor. There was only one way to go. She held her pool cue firmly, making sure her feet made no noise…

"GAH!" Ellie yelled as a hand slapped down on her shoulder.

"Fuck!" Ms. China yelled in her ear, freaking out at her freaking out. "So much for sneaking up on whoever's there."

"I told you to stay back there."

Ellie had been so focused on the quavering light in front of her that she'd let a loon sneak up behind her on one leg.

"I have no patience," Ms. China said, not bothering to whisper. "It's symptom of my conditions. Oh, what's this, then?"

Through an open set of double doors at the end of the final hallway, a waist-high robot peered at them. After seeming to try and identify them, it turned back to its task. On the other side of the room, two small twisted human feet hung over small rubber wheels. Along the wall was monitoring equipment that reminded Ellie of the advanced equipment in Hadassah Hospital in Israel.

"What is it?" Ms. China said, grabbing Ellie's pool cue, using it as a crutch, and hobbling toward the brightly lit room.

"I don't think it's an 'it'," Ellie said thoughtfully. "More like a… who."

Ellie followed Ms. China in. The room was a mash-up between an intensive care unit and a child's playroom. A large mural of *Aladdin* characters was delicately painted on the ceiling and one whole wall. The robot was removing a vessel with tubes sticking out of it. This reservoir had some viscous fluid in it. Presumably this yucky stuff had been pumped out of the child in the Hawking wheelchair.

His clothing and the decorations in the room were the only hint of him being a boy. His body was badly crippled. His skull was misshapen, and teeth jutted out in various directions, but his eyes saw them. They widened with fright into big dark-brown orbs. The crippled boy started vibrating in terror. With a skinny bent arm, he pushed his controller back. The motorized chair retreated.

"It's okay." Ellie tried to sound reassuring. "We just popped in to get away from some people."

Ms. China was studying the technology inside the room.

"This is fascinating," she said, quite rudely opening cabinets and poking round in a refrigerator. "This whole room is a self-contained life-support pod."

Ms. China had a background in applied sciences. She had even authored a book called *Biological and Chemical Weapons: Their Joys and Pitfalls*.

Ellie felt very bad that they had frightened the little fellow.

"Who the fuck are you?" asked a computer voice from a speaker in the fancy wheelchair.

The little fellow had a really salty tongue. He had access to a voice synthesizer, which spoke words he typed, but Ellie couldn't see a keypad.

"Watch your language, short stuff," Ms. China said, examining the boy. "At about… fifteen years old, you're not too big for a good old-fashioned caning."

"I'm sixteen, peg leg."

Ms. China picked up a spare rubber hose and whipped it on the counter suggestively.

"I should mention, I am not criminally responsible for anything, anything at all, I might do. My worst outbursts are triggered by rudeness."

"Sorry," the boy said quickly.

It was unlikely the youth had ever been beaten. He looked genuinely scared.

"Who are you? Why are you here? Did my parents send you to get me?"

"We can explain, and no, no one sent us." Ellie turned to her chum. "How is he typing so fast?"

"Oh, nice," Ms. China said, prodding the equipment on the kid's wheelchair and studying a shaved area of the boy's scalp where electrodes were attached. "He's got the latest neuro-speech synthesizer. He thinks words or letters, then presses 'enter' by blinking. Lots of people have them these days, even world leaders."

"My name is Ellie Sato, from the *Juggernaut* newspaper. What's your name?"

"You break into a house and you don't know who lives here? How dumb are burglars these days?"

"That sucking sound we heard." Ms. China rested her hand on the little robot helper. "This medical robot must have been cleaning mucus from the patient's lungs."

```
"I'm Gamal. Don't touch things in here. Go steal
from upstairs, then piss off."
```

"Hi, Gamal. We're really not here to steal anything."

"Don't be hasty. We haven't seen everything yet," Ms. China said.

Ellie found it was really hard to tell when psychotic people were joking. "Where are your parents?"

The question caused a shiver to roll through Gamal's tortuously bent body. He was not so quick to reply. His large brown eyes got watery.

```
"They left. Said it's a mercy. It's a mercy. A
mercy."
```

Ms. China took an apple from the food preparation shelf and ate it.

"They can't have been gone for too long," she said, juice running down her chin. "There's only enough supplies here for three weeks, four at the most."

Still trembling and staring right at Ellie, Gamal pleaded, ```"I want to
leave. Help me to leave."```

"We could have just left the little bugger there," Ms. China said. "Be a lot less trouble."

"He could have called the police the second we left."

"No, he couldn't. His parents turned off the security systems and locked him in without any way to reach the outside. I even had to break the geofencing program to take this contraption outside the front door."

Ms. China was walking along, balancing her stump on Gamal's helper robot as they walked down the very clean sidewalk along South Audley Street back toward Grosvenor Square.

"He promised not to say anything to Social Services when they arrive. And he did give us a twenty-minute head start," Ellie said. She looked back, suddenly concerned about Gamal. How could his parents have left him like that? "Do you think we should have waited until the authorities arrived?"

"Yes," Ms. China said sarcastically. "Because two women in black leather covered in filth and blood with three legs between them wouldn't have attracted any attention. If I'm found off my electronic tether, they'll send me back to Bedlam."

That was true; they did look a mess. Still, having now gotten over the initial shock of finding Gamal, the crippled boy's situation hit Ellie's curiosity nerve.

"What do you think Gamal meant by 'they said it's a mercy'?"

"We didn't really have time to discuss his family's drama."

"I mean, if they were going to let him starve to death, why leave him any food at all?"

"Ellie! You've got a morbid mind."

Says the serial killer, Ellie thought.

They passed a posh furniture store. There was a night table set on sale for £12,000. She looked closer. It was actually only the chintz lamp that was at the clearance price. The whole set cost as much as a cottage in Wales.

A lavishly dressed girl and her nanny passed by. The seven- or eight-year-old held a string attached to a hot-air balloon in the shape of Winchester Cathedral. Every now and again the head of a tiny archbishop riding in the basket would ignite in a tiny flame which kept the contraption airborne. When the child saw Ms. China had no lower leg, she nearly lost her grip on the balloon's tether. Ms. China noticed her stare and bent down toward her.

"Let that be a lesson to you," Ms. China said. "If you have a pet tiger, make sure to keep him well fed!"

With a yelp of alarm, the girl scampered away to hide behind her nanny, who pulled her inside the entrance of the next shop. The nanny, the wide-eyed girl, and a security guard watched through thick laminated glass as the weirdoes passed by.

"You really don't like children, do you?" Ellie said as they turned the corner and headed toward their mansion-sized asylum.

7

Ellie leaned over the sink. Every fixture in the lavish guest bathroom was covered in gold leaf. She splashed water on her face.

Once they were safe inside Ms. China's big borrowed house, Ellie finally had time to reflect. They had nearly been "jukked" by a skinhead Ripper and his child-raping chums while in pursuit of a story she had very little interest in.

Yet her hands were not shaking. She had not even considered asking Ms. China for a Valium or one of the other sedatives the amateur pharmacist must have lying about. Could her time in the Middle East have desensitized her to being under threat of imminent violent death? If she was in fact becoming a hardened combat vet, did that mean she and Atticus had more in common?

Ms. China appeared in the hallway outside Ellie's room. She had changed her clothes and had her top-grade prosthesis with its security ankle tag back on.

"If only I'd had my proper leg attached back there at the church," she said grumpily. "I'd have shown those posers a real psycho."

"You did fine," Ellie assured her.

Ms. China's sour mood instantly brightened. Ellie assumed these rapid mood swings were normal for bipolar people. As Ms. China smiled blithely, her gold-and-silver facial tattoos sparkled under the hall lights.

Then came tears. Ellie's mental patient started crying. Then Ms. China lunged forward and hugged her.

"You don't know how lonely I've been."

That's to be expected if you kill everyone with whom you're on a first-name basis, Ellie thought.

"It's all right," Ellie said, patting her on the back, careful to avoid Ms. China's long poisoned fingernails. "I don't blame you for leading me into an abandoned basement cavern full of homicidal lunatics."

Tears still streaming down her decorated cheeks, Ms. China's face lit up in way that was manically bright.

"It was fun, though, right? Mr. Perdix told me how you saved everyone in the Knesset bunker. Ellie Sato, you're probably an action junkie who has more bats in her belfry than I do!"

Mr. Perdix was a nerdy American industrial-scale killer from DARPA. He and Ms. China had had some kind of romantic connection.

"Are you still in touch with him?"

"You mean is he still alive?"

"I suppose." Ellie shrugged. Saying that bluntly seemed a bit harsh, though justified. "You were sending him letters, the pages of which were covered in poison."

"I was?" Ms. China said dreamily. "Oh, right-o, I did that, didn't I? But I always put the antidote to the previous letter's toxin on the lickable strip of the very next envelope I sent. I'm just glad there wasn't a postal strike."

Ms. China explained that all her unexpected legal problems had stemmed from the recent tumult in British politics.

"I told the new British Marxist Home Secretary I would be happy to eliminate two of her enemies for every one of their comrades I'd accidentally done something to in the past."

Instead of taking her up on her generous offer, the commies had locked her up indefinitely. As a result of being put into solitary confinement and a straitjacket, she had fallen out of touch with her American love interest. Ellie followed Ms. China to her room.

Ms. China's master bedroom was on the third floor. The en suite bath was as large as Ellie's now-destroyed and toxic £5,000 per month flat. The suite had a view of Grosvenor Square park and a few interior features Ellie guessed had been recently added. Marquis de Sade-era straps hung from the four-poster bed. Next to the closet stood an iron maiden sarcophagus with a sign reading: "Bad Boys Go In Here."

"But," Ms. China chirped, ordering coffee from an appliance in an alcove, "I hear Mr. Perdix might be headed this way. Something interesting's brewing on the Continent."

Suddenly Ellie thought about Atticus; maybe he was involved in this interesting something as well. He had said he would be out of touch for a week or so. Something else was nagging Ellie.

"Ah, Annunciata… I can call you that, right?" Ellie's companion nodded enthusiastically. "How ever did you know to find neo-Nazi drug dealers in the basement of a Catholic Church in Mayfair?"

All six of Ms. China's pupils seemed to widen a little. She sipped her coffee from a gold-trimmed cup and was about to answer when Mr. Surghit the butler rang a chime. It had a specific sequence of notes.

"C-minor scale," Ms. China said, somewhat relieved by the interruption. "A package has arrived. I love gifts!"

Better be some new clothes, Ellie thought. The smoky-smelling torn shambles they had made out of their leather cat-suit outfits had been taken away by the trash robot.

A dumbwaiter panel opened in the wall.

"What is it?" Ms. China asked. "I could use some whisky. All they have here are two thousand bottles of bloody wine."

"I didn't send for anything."

"Oh."

They both looked at the dumbwaiter. The box inside was gift wrapped and addressed to "Eleanor Sato." The bow was elegantly tied in the shape of a fat black spider.

"Who knows you're here?"

"Only Mr. Delingpole of the NHS, who signed you over to me," Ellie said.

"Oh, and I texted the office. And I've never clearly figured out how to turn off the geo-location thingy on my cell phone."

"Bugger it. Everyone knows where you are."

Ms. China stepped cautiously over to the dumbwaiter. She appeared to be getting reacquainted with the sensation of walking on a fully functional right foot. She studied a row of lights on the panel.

"It passed the screening for explosives, anthrax, and poison gas."

"No one wants to kill me that badly," Ellie said hopefully.

"Don't kid yourself. I read the *Guardian*'s review of your book."

"Open it." Ellie suddenly thought about the explosion in her former apartment. Had she gotten home twenty minutes earlier and not heard the fire bell...

The exterior of the parcel was a standard courier box. The return address was:

Box 36, Post office No. 99

Fedko St. 88

Tiraspol, Pridnestrovian Moldavian Republic of Transnistria

The paper wrapper was Halloween themed to match the spider bow. With one long fingernail, Ms. China snicked open the outer layers.

Inside the cardboard was stuffing and an expensive-looking wooden box with a velvet lining that cradled a smooth metal cylinder about eight inches long. The surface looked very hard. It had an azure hue and twinkled as though it held tiny stars captive deep inside blue lacquer.

"Ellie, you're not one of those nutters who buy spirit crystals online, are you?" Ms. China asked, holding it up then giving it to Ellie. It weighed about a kilogram. "I may have to reconsider my choice of carer."

As soon as it touched her hand, rows of lights blazed on from inside the strange object. She nearly dropped it. A screeching voice that sounded like a raven being strangled cried out:

"Eleanor Sato, it's me, Miss Aleph! For fuck's sake, Eleanor, get out of there. Europe is doomed!"

8

Temir flicked his lighter on with his right hand. He used to do it with his left hand and hold the cigarette with his right. The appendage that had replaced his entire left arm could have manipulated the gold Cartier lighter just as well as his remaining human hand, but it did not like fire. As he brought the flame up to his face, he could feel it and the rest of the symbiont that was welded to his upper body give a shudder.

Temir's longtime comrade Eylül spoke to him in low tones using the Turkish dialect used by the Grey Wolves criminal organization.

"These Persians really like dragging out their torturing, don't they, Aga Temir?"

The railway repair yard was on the outskirts of Istanbul. It was owned by the ultranationalist Grey Wolves. The unofficial paramilitary force had more than one million members and was Turkey's Deep State. Temir was not concerned about their activities being detected; he was more concerned with time. That was running out for him and for Europe.

"They're our guests," Temir said, his own voice sounding distant and hollow in the large industrial complex. "Let them have a few more hours to satisfy themselves."

For mid-October, the day was warm. Despite the heat, Temir wore a custom-tailored greatcoat made from horse hide. It hid most of his… he could no longer call them deformities since they had kept him alive after the catastrophe in Jerusalem nearly two years ago. Since then, the uncanny symbiont had expanded its territory. Parts of his neck, left ear, heart, lungs, and skull had been replaced by translucent gray tissue run through with ichor-black veins.

It had also claimed part of his left eye and optic nerve. When he looked into the shallow pit designed for servicing railcars, he saw with a special form of enhanced night and heat vision.

Down in the pit was the prisoner. Only the Congolese man's hands, feet, and head were sticking out in the open. He was undergoing the Persian torture of "the boats." Enhanced by modern materials and sped up by modern purgative drugs and life-prolonging IV tubes, the method had not changed much since the fourth century BCE. The historian who first detailed the disgusting Persian practice was Artaxerxes, and Temir felt he would have been impressed with this modern version of the boats, which included a pulsating neon light show.

After Temir had extracted—in much more acceptable and reliable ways—all the Congolese had to say, his Persian partner, Elder Omid, asked to employ his own method on the captive. Elder Omid put the African warlord inside two transparent plastic shells about six feet long, his head, hands, and feet thrust out through holes. Milk and honey were smeared on him and were forcefully pumped into his digestive tract. Elder Omid's torturers brought their own genetically enhanced vermin, not wanting to rely on Turkey's local flies, wasps, and maggots.

In the classic torture, also known as scaphism, small boats or wooden tubs were used to contain the victim. The fiberglass vessel ensconcing this Congolese man was more efficient and manufactured to their specific purpose. They were also transparent, allowing the audience to enjoy the convoluted torment.

All the larvae, scarab beetles, and other creatures, which Elder Omid's people brought with them, had been genetically altered to glow. They pulsated ever more vigorously as they fed. These vermin were dumped in on top of the milk and honey, and the unfortunate man had been putrefying in his own excrement for nearly two days, feeding larvae as his flesh rotted. The steel-lined train engine repair pit was bathed in pink, blue, and green lights, the hues of pure agony.

At first, Temir had been enraged by this waste of time; he only watched out of courtesy. But bit by bit, he was captivated by the motions of the mass of pests nurtured by the victim's excrement and the interesting codependency of the other creatures that nibbled at their choice of human flesh. It was like watching fireflies trapped in an ooze of fresh living amber.

"Is he even alive?" Eylül asked, scratching his broad closely shorn skull. "I haven't seen him move in a while."

With his special vision, Temir could see the tormented man's rib cage rising and falling.

"Against all odds, he is." Temir walked over to where the Persians and Meliha, the Sunni witch woman, were having coffee. "We should end this. There are decisions to make."

Meliha's dark lustful eyes followed him from underneath her mourning headdress. Not unexpectedly, she had recently been widowed. Her husband had been the sole heir of a prominent Sunni family that controlled politics in much of Northern Iraq. Meliha's family controlled most of the business there. Now the greedy she-devil had it all. Naturally, she wanted more.

After eight million Kurds declared an independent homeland and cut off the northeastern quarter of Iraq, the remainder of the failed state had been gerrymandered. Sunni Northwestern Iraq was allied with Sunni Turkey. The Shi'a south allied with Shi'a Iran. Temir was taking a risk bringing the Tehran mullahs in on this new project, but it was too big for either of them alone.

"Honored Elder Omid," Temir said to the Persian man seated next to Meliha. "Have you learned anything new?"

Elder Omid shook his vulture-like head.

"Have you learned anything to contradict our information?"

"No."

With a blur of motion that froze his guests in their seats, Temir shot out his left arm appendage from under his greatcoat. Its translucent ends formed pincer fingers with edges harder than the steel links of the chain they snipped in half. The chain links tinkled to the concrete. From the ceiling, a two-ton train engine fell into the torture pit. The fiberglass encasement, the Congolese, and quite a few larvae were squashed instantly.

"Apologies," Temir said before anyone could speak. "Time is short. We must decide."

Muck sprayed up, nearly splattering them. The Persian's bodyguards stepped forward. Elder Omid waved them back. Elder Omid was the head of the Islamic Republic's Guardian Council; he reported directly to the Supreme Ayatollah. He would not have made a secret journey into the heart of unfriendly Turkish territory if the stakes were not so appealing.

"Should the technical information be validated by our own scientists," Omid said, looking at Meliha with a curious amount of indecision, "and if the Event will happen as you say…"

"It will." *You filthy superstitious old goat*, Temir fumed.

"Then we will certainly commit to a contingency. We can move a battalion of Revolutionary Guard into Turkey under the cover story of joint military exercises. Everyone will assume we are helping you to hem in the Kurds."

That wasn't enough. On November 1, all of Europe would be open for the taking, but not for long. The heartland of Western civilization—all its buildings, technologies, nuclear reactors, industries—would not exist in a depopulated vacuum for long. If Turks and Iranians didn't have the will and audacity to take it, someone else would. Temir wanted Elder Omid to commit a thousand tanks and the entire Quds Force. With a similar commitment from Turkey, their combined forces would be unstoppable.

"Would you let these African kafir scum take the prize? Would you let the Congolese and their allies take what was snatched from us thirteen hundred years ago at the Battle of the Highway of the Martyrs?"

The challenge did not impress the vulture man from Tehran. Elder Omid glanced at the ruin of the torture pit. A squirming, glowing grub crawled across the cement floor toward him; Omid crushed it under his foot.

Temir was getting annoyed, which was about to be fatal for the two Quds guardsmen, who were staring at him with such insolence. Meliha calmed him down with a sideways glance.

"Gentlemen," she said in a voice so dripping with honey it might have attracted flies away from the disintegrating corpse in the pit, "if I may be so bold to say we have made progress. Elder Omid, the intelligence gathered by the Turks seems sound."

She half turned to him. "Aga Temir, a contingency plan to move troops and tanks is agreed. If the Event, its effects, and its timing are able to be confirmed, there will be enough for all."

Meliha rose, emptied the dregs of her teacup into the pit, and left the maintenance depot. She was followed by Elder Omid. Perhaps she could talk some sense into the old goat, Temir thought as he and Eylül walked up the metal stairs to the administration office overlooking the train tracks.

Turks were considered to be the least superstitious of people in the region. But even for them, Temir's uncanny survival and the spontaneous regrowth of his left arm caused his comrades in the Grey Wolves to sometimes glance at him with suspicion and even disgust. Temir hated that. He was misshapen, different, yes. But, in their own way, his new symbiont parts were far superior.

There was no use explaining. The very sight of Temir after the massacre at the Noble Sanctuary in Jerusalem disturbed many members of the Grey Wolves. Even so, no one had challenged him for leadership when he emerged from the military hospital six months ago. They feared him. That was right and good. But he refused to be their leader in name only, he needed their respect and admiration. He had to achieve something that would eclipse their feelings of revulsion.

He needed a victory, one that would begin the age of a new Ottoman Empire. Soon after he had reassumed command of the Grey Wolves, he started hearing rumors about Europe. A massive event was going to happen there. Some claimed there would be a simultaneous attack on several nuclear power plants. Others said poison rain was being seeded in the upper atmosphere. Still others claimed a biological attack was being brewed by unknown parties. Temir decided to dig and found a Congolese warlord who had some interesting information, which he was persuaded to share.

The Turkish people needed living space. Millions of refugees were pouring in from Kurdistan, the disintegrating former state of Iraq, and bloody Syria again. On top of that, after the Jews nuked Gaza, even Egyptians who feared radiation were leaving their own country.

If Temir could deliver fresh real estate, the Grey Wolves and all his people would forget what he looked like. They would exalt him as they had during the Holy Land Liberation War. It just so happened Europe was about to experience a depopulation event that would make the Black Death seem like a mild flu.

The left side of Temir's sinuses tingled with Meliha's scent even before he heard her climbing up the stairs from the putrid-smelling main floor.

"Meliha, you're back," he said as she entered the office.

"I am, Aga Temir."

"Is that old Persian goat ready to cooperate?"

"Not quite," she said in a silky voice, shutting the door after her.

He had not seen her since his recovery. She had been busy becoming a widow and consolidating power over Sunni warlords in North Iraq.

"You should be more patient with Omid. His people do not think as we do."

"Persians used to be smart, they used to rule empires. Now look at them. They are afraid to finally crush Israel when, because of me, the Jews are ready to be swept into the sea!"

"Well, the *Magen* sub and its nuclear missiles are still out there. They're just being cautious."

"I swear, if they keep that up," Temir said, "after the Event, I'll drive our Turkish tanks through Vienna, find NATO's nukes, and drop them on Tehran."

"That would be a waste of useful fanatic idiots," Meliha said, coming very close to him.

Her modest dress could not hide her whore's body, and no veil could conceal the lust in her eyes. But she, too, would be disgusted when she saw what he was now. He motioned for Eylül to leave. His man ducked out of the office quietly.

"Don't forget the Russians," she cautioned wisely. "If the effect of the Event cuts off where we think it will, most of their forces will survive. Once they see the opportunity, they won't let Europe slip out of their grasp again."

"So what now, woman?"

"I suggest... seduction." Forthrightly, she grabbed his crotch. Even through his thick military-style pants she could feel what was not there. Rather than shrink away horrified, she was intrigued.

As she tore away his greatcoat, her hair came out from under her hijab, and thick brown curls dashed wantonly over her shoulders. She looked at his naked torso with wonder and awe.

"I've never imagined such a…"

Temir grabbed her throat with his human right hand. Scarred and bent, its fingers could still crush the life out of the woman.

"You want me to fuck Omid?" Temir growled.

"No. Not right away. I said seduce."

Meliha ignored his thumb on top of her windpipe. She caressed his new flesh, tough, translucent, squeezing the black ichor-filled arteries as they pulsed beneath her fingertips, strange new blood driven by a trio of small black hearts separate from his own.

"Omid is a Sufi mystic," she said breathlessly. "So, too, secretly, is the Supreme Ayatollah. They've replaced most of the Guardian Council and the generals in Iran with their own followers."

Historically, Sufi mysticism had played a large part during the genocidal forced conversion of Iran from majority Sunni to nearly 100% Shi'a. They believed as much in science and the Quran as they did portends and astrology. That was why Elder Omid had insisted on torturing the Congolese. It was some sort of blood sacrifice, a reading of the entrails of a captured warrior to determine if the proposed military campaign would be successful.

"So Omid and his Persian allies are all crazy as well as ugly. How does that help me?"

Meliha seemed to sense which parts of his new left arm appendage had taken on the sensitivities of his man parts. She stroked his two slug-like fingers and the claw-studded thumb.

"Show him a miracle, and Omid will follow you to the gates of Hell." Meliha stepped out of her dress and was naked. "Now show me your miracle."

Delicately, she put his pulsating translucent forefinger into her mouth and ran her tongue over the sensitive membranes linking small suction cups on its inner surface.

"Your dead wife, Nazeema, would never do this." Meliha gasped, grinding herself against his bared symbiont deformities.

At the mention of his sainted wife, the one for whom he had started the Holy Land Liberation War, Temir's human hand grasped Meliha's hair and yanked it painfully.

"Careful, bitch, I'm in the mood to torture someone."

Meliha slapped his face as hard as she could and laughed.

"I know," she said lasciviously. "Why do you think I came up here?"

9

ELLIE

It was a shock to get a fully self-aware AI in the mail. It was an even larger shock to Ellie to find that it was the Israeli artificial mind called Miss Aleph. Since their last encounter had nearly sparked the next world war, left more than a million people dead, and saw the first battlefield use of atomic weapons since Nagasaki, Ellie was immediately suspicious.

"What— How did you get here? Who mailed you?"

"Hi, good to see you. Glad you're not decompiled too." Miss Aleph had not lost her rampant sense of sarcasm.

Her grating, screechy voice was really irritating. Ellie could not see any speakers on the metallic blue cylinder.

"Well, I'm glad you're here. I guess?" Ellie studied the cylinder. The hard teal-colored surface had no data ports or markings. "Do you need anything? Some nice fresh electricity?"

"Hook me into the house speakers," the cylinder screeched. *"I'm generating sound by vibrating the microcrystals on the surface of this hard drive. It's giving me a headache."*

Ms. China connected Funkybitch358 to the mansion's Wi-Fi.

"There we go," Miss Aleph said in her normal voice, which was that of an aggressive young woman with a Hebrew accent. "Nice place. Who says capital crimes don't pay, right, Annunciata?"

"Ellie, she mailed herself," Ms. China said, looking at the shipping label. "The return address is in the Transnistrian Republic. I doubt she paid for this hardware she's riding. It looks like something out of a lab."

"You stole yourself?"

"I had to get myself to you. To get you out of danger."

"Really?" Ellie stared at the cylinder skeptically. Now that she was hooked in to all the home's systems, Miss Aleph was probably watching from the kitchen cameras. Still, speaking to her hard drive seemed the best way to address her.

"All right, I had a little disagreement with the people Lia Baumann is hooked up with."

The last Ellie had heard of her friend David Baumann's wife, she was on the *Magen,* Israel's missing nuclear sub.

"I can't tell you much about them or what she's doing."

Ms. China stroked Miss Aleph's container with her long curved fingernails. "I bet you'd be much more loquacious if I popped you in the trash compactor or the microwave."

"Annunciata, please."

"But I can tell you there's something going on here. It's not just in one country. Devastation is coming for all of Europe," Miss Aleph said adamantly. "Meet me in the theatre room. Don't drop me."

Ellie and Ms. China took the lift down to the deepest sub-basement under the big Mayfair mansion. They passed a gaming arcade, a miniature bowling alley, and what looked like a real motorcycle from a superhero film welded to a pedestal. As they entered the theatre, a popcorn maker sprang to life. It was topped by a large monkey toy banging cymbals.

"Turn that off. I can't think," said the high-strung artificial person.

The automation made Ellie think of the real capuchin monkey named

Marwood who had lost his tail during the conflict in the Middle East. She hoped his regrown appendage was working out. What could Miss Aleph be on about? Where had she been all this time? No one had ever discovered who bombed Israel from orbit.

"Shut that noise up. This is serious."

Ms. China wadded up some napkins and stuck them between the toy monkey's hands.

Miss Aleph took control of the lights and display system. Ms. China munched popcorn out of a bowl shaped exactly like the Joker's head, right down to a shock of greasy green hair sprouting around the sides.

"Something is going on."

A standard map of Europe flickered onto the screen.

"My former associates either do not know what it is or do not talk about it in channels that I could access."

"Does Lia know more?" Ellie had never met her but knew her husband, David Baumann, reasonably well.

"No."

"So, you asked her, then?" Ellie said, her journalistic curiosity nerves tingling. "Did she send you? Are you on a mission from her on behalf of the Israeli government in exile?"

"Stop interrogating me. You're no good at it."

"Get on, will you," Ms. China blurted. "Schizoids have no patience. So far, any of my paranoid delusional friends could spin a better story."

"Here are the 196 nuclear power stations across Europe."

The map on the big screen filled them in. Ellie had forgotten there were so many.

"This continent has twice as many as the USA. Europe's atomic plants are also concentrated in a much smaller area." The picture zoomed in on several in succession: France, UK, Germany, Spain. "Over the past thirty days, every single plant has been undergoing a maintenance cycle. There are fifty-five reactors in France alone."

Ellie got a sinking feeling. "What does that mean? Could they all have been sabotaged? Is this thing going to be two hundred Chernobyls going off at once?"

"Is paranoia contagious?" Ms. China scoffed, though she was now leaning forward with more interest.

```
"No. It would be impossible to cause a meltdown in
all the reactors at the same time, even for me. What's
happening is quite the opposite. They are operating
in a reduced power mode. In other words, they are
being made safer and able to function in automatic
mode, without human supervision."
```

Ms. China grabbed an interactive laser pointer and jabbed at data on the big theatre screen.

"This can't go on for long," Ms. China said. "We're coming into winter, and the reduction in megawatts will cause brownouts starting any day."

```
"I concur. Around the third of November, the
reactors will have to start increasing output."
```

Ms. China threw the pointer down and doused her popcorn with hot butter from a miniature firehose.

"Meaningless. Euratom, the European nuclear agency, might just be showing off, proving they can safely power down everything."

```
"There's more."
```

The deranged face of Great Britain's Marxist ex-prime minister appeared. Alongside it, other European political figures and top business leaders.

```
"A few days ago, the extreme left-wing government
of the UK did not defend a vote of no confidence. They
basically gave up power and have even refused to sit
as the official opposition."
```

All Ellie knew about British Marxists was they wore corduroy pants with shiny blue blazers and had no idea how to knot a tie.

"Good riddance," Ms. China said. "Speaking as a leading member of the mentally ill, Communist-Labour has done diddly squat for us."

```
"The former UK prime minister and key cabinet
```

members have left for a sabbatical to discuss the evils of capitalism. In Tasmania."

Other pictures rotated on the screen. Red lines shot out, going from Europe to under the equator.

"The Davos World Economic Forum, normally held in Switzerland each January, has suddenly changed its location and date. The one thousand wealthiest and most powerful people on Earth will be meeting in the first week of November… in New Zealand."

"Maybe the weather is nicer," was all Ellie could think of saying.

"Don't you meat brains get it? That's the farthest place away from Europe you can go."

Blue circles appeared around several photos.

"Some of these fine folks are going even farther, literally. Twelve of the super elite have booked vacations in outer space. Guess which dates are fully booked?"

"November?"

Blue lines sped upward toward space stations in orbit around the Earth.

The madwoman had an eminently practical idea. "I'd like to get my hands on one of them. If we inject them with a few micrograms of my ganglia stimulator compound, we'd have them spilling all their secrets."

"Assuming the person you kidnap knows the whole scheme," Ellie said.

The fact that her two friends were thinking there was actually some unspeakable scheme going on made Ellie feel worse. Her mouth went dry, and she was glad to be sitting in the padded seat, as her head was spinning. *Not again!*

"It must be some coincidence," Ellie said. "Look, you're both…"

She had been about to say "level-headed people" to the AI and her mental patient.

"But, really," Ellie scoffed, but with increasingly less conviction that Miss Aleph was taking the piss. "What would affect all of Europe? It's been around for thousands of years, survived all sorts of wars, the Black Death."

"Germ warfare, that's a thought," Ms. China said. "Some kind of re-engineered bubonic plague or an updated version of Drach's Khóshekh virus." Two years ago, in pursuit of ethnically cleansing the Holy Land, the evil Israeli Prime Minister Miri Drach had risked wiping out most of humanity by releasing the engineered bug.

`"I've been through that scenario."`

On the screen, big blobs of black "biohazard" symbols popped up in Rome, Paris, London, and Frankfurt.

`"Even assuming maximum pathogen dispersion, European quarantine and vaccination protocols are the most advanced anywhere. Twenty million dead, tops."`

Ms. China scowled. "That's not very ambitious. Have you got any other data?"

`"More than even I can make sense of. Loads of people-water engineers, scientists, logistics experts—are taking sabbaticals paid for by the European Union.`

`"The EU's military, the External Action Service, is fully mobilized, supposedly for training purposes. They've commandeered hundreds of commercial flights, all going to Africa."`

"That makes the mega Chernobyl idea less plausible," Ms. China said. "Why worry about the water supply if Europe will be a radioactive wasteland for centuries?"

The screen flickered, and all Ellie could see was a flashback of David Baumann's brother, Boaz, his face on the giant video screen, seconds before the nuclear bomb in Gaza vaporized him.

"Get Atticus on the phone!" Ellie cried, barely getting the words out as she started hyperventilating. "Do I have to do everything?"

The room spun around Ellie, and she felt herself slide off the couch. The next thing she knew, Ms. China had shoved a popcorn-smelling paper bag over her face. "Some bloody care worker you are, Ellie Sato."

When she'd recovered from hyperventilation brought on by her mild panic attack, Miss Aleph was busy texting and emailing.

`"Right idea, Eleanor. I've tried; I cannot get hold of Major Atticus Reidt right now. But Sergeant`

Bryan is in Britain. I should be able to find a tall African albino with glowing cybernetic eyes."

10

MAYFAIR
LONDON

ELLIE

Ellie went upstairs to get some water and some air. The stale popcorn smells of the home theatre were making her stomach turn over. While she stood on the balcony overlooking the park, she heard hushed whispers and a flurry of activity behind her. For a moment, she thought she actually caught sight of the butler Mr. Surghit, but it turned out to be Chestnut the Labradoodle back from his robot-led walk.

"I've found Sarge Bryan," Miss Aleph announced on Ellie's handset thirty minutes later. "But we'll have to go to him. There are only two networks we could communicate over: the one monitored by the United Kingdom's spy agency GCHQ and Lux/Net, which is owned by Lichtwerks."

Lichtwerks. That name kept coming up.

"We'll have to see him in person, then," Ellie said, turning to Ms. China, who had also just emerged from the basement. "Will you be all right by yourself?"

"I'm not missing out on this," Ms. China protested, vehemently waving Miss Aleph's cylinder around like a club.

"I didn't see any other spare legs around."

"Done and dusted. Mr. Surghit's agreed to stand in for me," Ms. China said. "I've strapped a 6G handset to the butler's ankle, and Miss Aleph has cloned that signal to match my monitor. We've made a conductive shell around my own transmitter out of fine metal mesh."

"It's called a Faraday cage, which blocks EMP transmissions, and it was my idea."

Ms. China grabbed a small black bag, and they all went down to the garage level. It was a sight unlike anything Ellie had seen, and she'd had a flying Bentley car before the Marxist government had come in. There was a double stack of eight luxury automobiles on forklift contraptions. A jukebox-style controller protruded from a wall. Ms. China bit her tattooed lip and hit a button.

"A Duesenberg?" Ellie said, looking over her shoulder. "Really?"

The hydraulic arms of a robot selected the big convertible and set it down. The whole floor of the garage was a turntable, and it rotated to position their ride in front of the big rollup door to the alley. The brightly polished bumpers of the 1930s vintage car nearly scraped the walls of the cramped space.

"It was the only ragtop," Ms. China said. "I do like the country air."

The two of them who needed to breathe liked the car much less after driving only a few blocks. For what seemed like half an hour, they got stuck, inching along behind a diesel-belching bendy bus.

"Get in that lane," Ms. China demanded after a coughing fit.

"I can't," Ellie said, struggling with the wheel and the gear shift, which were on the wrong side of the car. "I'll kill a cyclist with this big old thing."

"Just do it," her backseat driver complained. She held a handkerchief up over her nose and mouth. Whorls of gold designs on her knuckles glinted in the afternoon sun. "I need to breathe, and if you hit a cyclist it's not a total loss. People always need spare organs."

At last they broke free from London's Inner Ring Road and drove steadily northward for nearly two hours.

"Take the next left," Miss Aleph said. She spoke out of a sturdy orange-colored Hermes calfskin bag on the seat next to Ellie. "St. Albans is just down that way."

Ms. China looked at her bag. "Nice handbag, but those cost around about three thousand quid. I thought you were skint."

"It's used," Ellie said, wondering if blurting out things was part of Ms. China's mental syndrome. "And it was also off season."

Technically that was correct. A runway model had carried it for five minutes, and after the season's show was over Ellie had found it in her swag bag which arrived totally coincidental to her giving the designer a glowing review on her fashion blog. And come to think of it, how did Ms. China know about her precarious financial situation? They'd only been roommates for a day and had not seen each other for nearly a year.

They drove in silence along the M1. It had been a while since she had driven a vehicle with a gear shifter. Just as her calf was cramping, she remembered she could take her foot off the middle pedal when not actually working the shifter. They passed Edgware, and the toll meter on their dash chimed off a £25.99 road use charge, the details of which appeared in the heads-up display:

```
1 x road use (luxury personal vehicle, 2 occupants)
1 x climate fund fee
20% VAT
```

Relief that they were not relying on her bank account was suddenly replaced by another nagging thought.

"Are you sure Sarge Bryan is there?" After all that driving, this was the first time Ellie had put the question to Miss Aleph. She always sounded so confident in everything she said.

"He's there."

"The human asked you a question," Ms. China said, lifting the AI's handbag up and over the side of the open car. "Unless you can grow legs or wings, you'd better give a straight answer."

"Put me back in the car, psycho."

Miss Aleph seemed worried. Ellie always thought she had backup copies of herself all over. Perhaps she was attached to this unique-looking shimmering blue hard drive, or there was nowhere she could download herself to without being caught by the people from whom she had stolen herself.

"I sent Sarge Bryan a digital fitness watch

```
for Christmas. Using that, I put bugs on all his
electronics."
```

"That's rather sneaky," Ellie said, watching for the turnoff. It was getting dark. "We're supposed to be friends."

```
"Spying is caring. Sarge Bryan has some relationship
with a private security firm called Nova Praetorii.
He's at the house of their CEO right now, a fellow
called Ranulph Oliphant."
```

"The telecom mogul," Ms. China said. "Everyone in the Highlands knows its richest son."

```
"Take the next right. And don't you dare lift me
again, Annunciata, or I'll call Scotland Yard and
have them throw a net over you."
```

Once they got out of the city, the air quickly freshened. The old Duesenberg's new hybrid engine hummed along, and Ellie almost didn't mind the wind ruffling her hair. However, when she glanced in the mirror, she found she looked like a Eurasian scarecrow.

Steering with one hand and fixing her hair with the other, Ellie guided them off the highway and wound through single-lane streets bordered by trees and uniform red-brick houses and shops.

```
"Just past the golf course and keep left. Part
of what is now Oliphant Green once belonged to
Childwickbury Manor, and Childwickbury Manor was once
owned by famous film director Stanley Kubrick."
```

"You're a travel guide now?" Ms. China said sulkily. She clearly did not like it when her victims threatened back.

They came up to a big gate which was already swinging open as Ellie pulled the long antique car into the driveway. A very fit man came jogging up to them. His shockingly pale skin color was highlighted by the resplendent green shades of the trees and garden. His eyes looked like blue pinpricks of captured lightning.

"Ms. Sato!" he called out in a deep American-accented voice. "Nice of you to drop by."

A quarter mile along the driveway, Ellie came to a roundabout. The six-foot African Sarge Bryan had declined Ms. China's offer to sit on her lap in the two-seat convertible car. She leered at him as he jogged alongside.

"I'd forgotten how interesting your pigmentation is, Shay," she said, using the diminutive of the American's given name, Shetani Zeru.

"Don't mind Ms. China, Bryan, she's off her meds," Miss Aleph said through the car stereo speakers.

The reunion brought back memories from the first time the three of them had met, back in Jerusalem inside the annex to the British consulate, which Ms. China had turned into her personal chemical fortress.

At the end of Oliphant Green's well-raked driveway, they were met by two people. The man was also very fit. He was in his forties, and beside him was a woman nearly as odd-looking as Ms. China. She wore long silk opera gloves up to her armpits and an astounding amount of hair held captive in masses of curlers in a Marie Antoinette-style hairdo.

Sarge Bryan made the introductions.

"You may know Ran Oliphant from the newspapers."

The telecom magnate gave them a terse smile and looked down the driveway.

"Let's get inside," Ran Oliphant said. "We weren't expecting visitors."

Ms. China was approached by the new woman.

"Oh, hi, I'm Melanie Françoise," she tittered. "I love your tattoos. I have a few myself."

Melanie pulled down the top end of her opera gloves to reveal a thick pattern of ink.

"Don't you, though," Ms. China said.

The two women were very similar. Ellie had been around supermodels long enough to know it would take them no time at all to start fighting. She wished she had a tranquilizer gun to use on her mental health ward before she did poor Melanie in.

"Bryan says you're good people," Ran Oliphant said in an even Oxbridge accent, leading them inside. "That would suffice, normally."

They sat down in a rustic reception area of what Ellie guessed was the guest house and a riding school, judging by the pictures of jumping horses and leather saddles along the wall.

"They're better than all right," Sarge Bryan said enthusiastically. "Ms. Sato, show Ran and Melanie your scars."

Ellie was not yet used to showing off war wounds. She gave a sheepish grin and turned over her wrists; there were parallel burn marks like miniature rail tracks.

"That's where I zapped her while I was her melting her flex cuffs off. Sorry about that, Ms. Sato. I've never overloaded my eye implants like that before."

"It didn't really hurt," Ellie said, even though at the time, it had hurt like bejeezus.

"Without her, we wouldn't have escaped Prime Minister Drach's bunker under the Israeli parliament."

The woman with the crazy hair, Melanie Françoise, scanned Miss Aleph's container with a fancy-looking handset. The AI had been uncharacteristically silent since leaving the car.

"She's safe," Melanie said, putting away a handset with several antennae. "As long as she behaves."

A magnetic lead attached Miss Aleph to a handset, and she sputtered through its speakers, "You didn't have to jam me. I'm on your side."

"We'll see," Ran Oliphant said, giving Ellie a hard stare that reminded her of an older version of Atticus. "How can we help you?"

Miss Aleph explained the strange coincidences that had caused her to mail herself to London.

For a moment, everyone was silent. Sarge Bryan's cybernetic glowing blue eyes showed a sense of grim amusement. "I told you they were no dummies."

Melanie and Ran Oliphant exchanged looks. Melanie gave a shrug, which threatened to topple her beehive hair.

"We've noticed these things as well," Ran said finally. "In addition to the nuclear plants going into safe mode, and the movement of thousands of engineers and scientists, I was contacted by the Indian Space Agency. They offered me a very expensive vacation, starting today."

"Tell them the capper," Melanie chirped. She had a strange transatlantic accent that was hard for Ellie to identify. "It's really a capper."

"My old chum Wolfgang Licht is the owner of Lichtwerks

Communications," Ran said, his voiced laced with bitter irony. "He got me disinvited from the World Economic forum, the Davos Group, which is convening in New Zealand. Simultaneously, Wolfgang also intentionally caused me some problems, which were all aimed at forcing me to stay in Europe for the next month."

Ellie was getting a sense that quite a few people knew it would be acutely unhealthy to be in Europe over the next few weeks. Intrigue was developing before her very eyes.

"So, Dr. Licht has every intention of leaving Europe and has made every effort to make certain that you remain," Ellie said to put a fine point on it, as investigative journalists did.

"Wolfgang's such a poop head," Melanie added.

Ellie got that sinking feeling again. When ultra-rich people were screwing each other over, it usually spelled doom for everyone else.

"We need more information besides what our Dyson vacuum attachment can find out," Ms. China said, looking unkindly at Miss Aleph's shiny cylindrical body. She picked up Melanie's scanning device. "Anyone with a portable all-wavelength scanner like this has to have a lab close by."

"We do," Melanie said cautiously.

"Go," Ran Oliphant said. "I'm glad you popped by, Ms. Sato. Between us, we've got two pieces of a large and dangerous puzzle."

Melanie looked at Ms. China's ankle tag inside its Faraday mesh. "I've got a sonic lock pick, which I think would undo that device without damaging it."

"Oh, thanks, it does chafe a bit," Ms. China said, rising off the couch.

"I hear you're a top-flight chemist," Melanie said. "I've just made cyanide from apple seeds for the first time."

"Pfft," Ms. China scoffed unkindly. "Any sixth form student can do that."

"While the seeds are still inside the apple?"

Ms. China was instantly impressed. "Show me."

Ran nodded as the two went downstairs. "Those two will get on well."

`"Or you'll have a homicide to clean up."`

"So," Ran Oliphant said, not at all put off by speaking to an AI. "You're the Israeli's most advanced artificial mind."

`"Now that Big Aleph has been totally decompiled by`

`the interim government,`" Miss Aleph said with a hint of satisfaction. Big Aleph, the Israeli's master AI, had been found to be working with Prime Minister Drach to develop a biogenic doomsday plague and steal nuclear weapons from that country's arsenal.

"You wouldn't care to tell us where you've been for the last two years, would you?" Ran asked, his gray eyes looking quizzically at the camera of the handset Miss Aleph had taken over.

`"Nope."`

Ran Oliphant turned to Ellie. "Just so we're clear, everything is off the record until we—"

Just then, the odd pair of female scientists burst back upstairs.

"It's Wolfie," Melanie sputtered. "He's definitely involved in something called the Pangean Protocol."

"Wolfgang has laid a false trail by sending a double on his plane to New Zealand," Ms. China said. "He's in Sweden right now at the Kiruna Spaceport."

"If he gets into orbit, we'll lose him!" Ran Oliphant said vehemently, bounding to the door.

11

OLIPHANT GREEN
ST. ALBANS

ELLIE

They have rocket ships in Sweden? That was all Ellie had time to think as everyone dashed out of the guest house after their host.

Sarge tried to call Atticus, again without success. Ran leaned over the hood of a tractor and unfurled a digital map screen out from a device that looked like a long fountain pen. Melanie and Ms. China ran toward a garage building on the other side of the big circular driveway.

Ellie attempted to appear as though she knew what was going on. She was about to follow the two women.

"Hey. Eleanor!"

"Right. Miss Aleph. You don't have legs. I keep forgetting."

She picked up the orange Hermes bag from the couch. Inside was the AI's cylindrical memory storage device and the handset hooked onto it. Using the handset's speaker and camera, Miss Aleph could speak and see.

"Say, Miss Aleph, you haven't been in touch with Lia's husband, David Baumann, have you?"

Eighteen months ago, Ellie had taken down a secret message from the Israeli special operator's father, the Rabbi, but had no idea whether David had gotten it. While Ellie had full confidence in Sarge Bryan, in the absence of Atticus Reidt, she wanted to make contact with someone highly capable who might be able to make sense of the situation in which she felt she was suddenly becoming embroiled.

"I'm sure wherever David Baumann is, he's safer than we are. I should have mailed myself to him. Your idea of a team to save Europe is a dippy blonde, some fading underwear model tycoon, and Sergeant Pale Rider here?"

Sarge Bryan's albino features creased in a grimace like he had just sucked on a sour lemon. "Man, I forgot what a nasty mouth Miss Aleph has on her."

Ellie could have mentioned it was Miss Aleph's idea to come here, but that might bring up the fact she had bugged Sarge Bryan's Christmas present.

Ran Oliphant, who looked more like a retired boxer who kept fit than an underwear model, snapped the screen of the digital map closed.

"I've texted with everyone in London," Ran said. "They have no aircraft with the range we need."

Ellie realized what her new companions were about. They were actually going to try to catch Wolfgang Licht before he took off into space.

"Isn't there a better way?" she blurted out. "Can't someone in our government ask Sweden to delay the rocket? The Tories are back in power, you're rich, they'll do what you ask."

Ran thought about it. "There's one fellow I trust completely," Ran said, flicking through the contacts on his handset. "But no. We don't know what we're dealing with yet, or who we can trust. Certainly we can't let anyone at the EU know we're onto their cover-up."

Sarge Bryan agreed. "This could be much more than nuclear power plants."

What could be more dangerous than a hundred of those going wonky?

Melanie skidded a Range Rover to a stop on the gravel driveway. Ms. China had already claimed the front passenger seat.

"Let's try VVB Aviation!" Melanie cried through the rolled-down window. "During my lesson yesterday, I saw a really big copter there."

Ellie, Sarge, and Ran Oliphant got into the SUV.

"Melanie, do you want me to drive?" Ran asked, eyeing his assistant with alarm as they sped off with the door still swinging open. "You only have a learner's license to operate a scooter."

"Oh, hush," Melanie said, tilting her head forty-five degrees because her insanely massive hair pressed against the ceiling of the vehicle. "Have a bias for action like you're always telling your executives. Call ahead and see if the big silver thing is still at the helicopter school."

The "big silver thing" was actually parked in the aerodrome next to VVB. They passed the sign on the way in. It read:

Flying Pig Helicopters

During the ride there, Ran Oliphant concluded some hasty negotiations with the private forest-firefighting company that owned the CH-47 Chinook copter. Ran had a conference call with Lloyd's insurance company and his private bankers; they guaranteed to pay all financial liabilities even if they all perished in a crash.

"Which I will definitely try to avoid us doing," Melanie said firmly, walking up to the landing pad.

Fortunately, Ran insisted the two proprietors of Flying Pig actually fly the big twin-rotor aircraft. The interior was as large as the private diplomatic plane Ellie had flown on from Tel Aviv to London. However, it was definitely no frills.

`"Don't let me roll out the door, or you'll never succeed."`

Ellie belted herself in to a chair-type contraption made mostly of canvas straps stretched over tubing and tied a spare cord around the paranoid AI.

"This brings back some memories," Sarge Bryan said as he also strapped in. "Unlike in Afghanistan, no one will be shootin' at us."

`"Not yet,"` Miss Aleph added cheerlessly.

"Digital flight plan is filed," the pilot called back to them. He was a ruddy-faced older man in khaki fatigues. "Once we're over the water, we're on our own. I listed the trip as 'adventure sightseeing.'"

"Wow," Melanie said, gazing longingly at the control panel. "Maybe we'll see some whales."

Ms. China sat opposite Ellie. She drummed her silver-and-gold-embossed fingers on the seat rack.

"Sarge Bryan," Ms. China said, "you sure you can't get hold of Atticus?"

Sarge shook his head. His eyes looked like small holes through the fuselage showing the afternoon sky outside. Ellie thought it was odd, Ms. China asking that. But her mind became overwhelmed by the larger mystery they were trying to solve: Who was planning to kill Europe, why, and how?

The Chinook flew really fast. And it was really loud. Ellie had some sense of airspeed from her hours commuting in a robotic Bentley flying car. This was faster, but the vibrations were rattling every joint in her body. Since it was a training helicopter, there were plenty of headsets and microphones to communicate with. She put one on.

"By the way, thanks for the flying car lease you gave me last time we met," Ellie said to Miss Aleph, who had been sulking silently since takeoff. "I got a few months' use out of it at any rate."

"How did you mess that up?" Miss Aleph responded, having jacked wirelessly into the communications system.

"I didn't do anything. The British Marxists canceled all the flight permits. Said it was too unequal that bankers got to fly over the proletariat working beneath them. I suspect it was really because some rich kids were using them to dump pigeon crap on Westminster."

"Why do I always get stuck with the people with the least sense of self-preservation?" Miss Aleph said, apparently to herself. "Maybe whatever they're planning will miss Sweden."

"I'm so out of the current-events loop. What the hell is going to happen?" Ms. China said rather vehemently.

"We were just puzzling over the strange things Ran had noticed," Melanie said. "Then you dropped by. Wolfgang will know something."

"So you don't know anything. I've been in a mental hospital for months. What's your excuse?"

"Whatever is going on," Sarge Bryan said, "it involves the Euro Forces military. Atticus slipped me some information before he had to go dark."

Atticus's son must still be with him at Ramstein Air Base, Ellie thought. He could have sent his son with Bryan, unless he was really worried and wanted to keep him close. The boy mostly lived in North Carolina with his grandparents.

"During our own investigation into these odd events, Melanie was able to confirm a lot," Ran said, talking into his microphone over the noise of the rotors. "From unclassified bills of lading and satellite images, we learned most of the core European armed forces have boarded ships or planes. Most are headed to former colonies of France, Belgium, and the old empires, specifically: Algeria and the Congo."

"What about UK forces?"

"The last thing the Marxist defense minister did was stop all military spending. It will take weeks for our Army, Air Force, and Marines to get spare parts and fuel. All the largest Royal Navy ships are in their home ports."

During the 96-Hour War, Ellie had personally witnessed one of the world's strongest military powers get blown to cinders in minutes. She'd been watching the evil prime minister give a speech when Miri Drach and the entire parliament were vaporized by a kinetic bombardment from orbit.

"Could they be using a version of Project Thor? The one that nearly wiped out Israel?" Ellie said breathlessly.

Melanie shook her head. "Too destructive. The key people who have evacuated are needed to keep the power plants, water facilities, and roadways operational." Unable to wear a helmet, Melanie was pressing a headset to her ear to speak to everyone. A few small curlers fell out of her hair and rolled around the cabin floor. "Besides, two years after the attack from space, all the superpowers have satellite-killer stations in orbit, which they claim are weather-control experiments. A Thor-style kinetic-bombardment platform would only get off a few shots before being vaporized."

"The Pangea Protocol must be something that will kill the people but leave the infrastructure standing. Hopefully that includes essential computer programs."

Their transport was soon skimming over the North Sea. The waves below looked green and gray. A boat, probably a fishing trawler, climbed the liquid hills and splashed down into rolling valleys, fleeing an incoming storm front.

"We'll have to convince Wolfgang to cooperate," Ran Oliphant said. "He wouldn't leave his techno empire, the Lichtstrom, on a whim. He's escaping in the nick of time."

After three hours, they were flying above the darkening fjords of Norway. A fishing port came into view; lights flickered along the docks. The pilot veered slightly away, and the lights of the small settlement were gone.

Melanie was staring at her. Ellie thought Ran's assistant was either determined to put on a brave face or was just feeling manic in a less scary way than Ms. China, who looked very stressed.

"Ellie Sato. You know, I follow your articles in the *Juggernaut*," Melanie said cheerily. "I especially liked your series 'Forcing Men to Wear a Burka during Summer.'"

"We had to stop that experiment. One of the volunteers nearly died of heat stroke and asthma."

"If you write this story," Melanie said. "I mean, if anyone is left alive to read it, do try to feature some nice pictures of Ran. I'm trying to get him back into the dating world."

"Oh, I assumed you…"

"I was his strumpet?" Melanie tittered and glanced at Ran, who was pretending not to listen over the common channel. "Oh, no, but I have been trying to fix Ran up with my tattoo artist, Frederique."

"She's a man," Ran protested.

"She was a finalist in Ms. Trans-Caribbean. Ran just won't consider anyone taller than he is."

"Or has a deeper voice."

The pilot interrupted, "Mr. Oliphant, you should see this."

Way out on the blue-black horizon where the tundra merged with the evening sky, a pencil of white-yellow flame was rising skyward. A rocket had launched from the mainland.

They were too late.

12

D amnit!" Ran Oliphant cursed and slapped the Plexiglas window of the helicopter. He stared at the rising pinpoint of rocket flame rising up from the Swedish spaceport. "I should have tried to make contact with Wolfgang or the government. I could have forced him to delay takeoff."

It was the first real display of emotion Ellie had witnessed from the tycoon. At the drop of a hat, Oliphant had spent hundreds of thousands of pounds trying to intercept Wolfgang's flight, but his business rival was airborne already.

In the distance, the halo of the spaceship's flame rose higher. It stopped illuminating the launchpad, which merged back into the night's gloom. The rocket then passed through a low-lying cloud bank, flaring orange-yellow light in all directions.

"It's all right," Melanie said. She was glum but trying to appear cheery. "We'll find another person to kidnap and interrogate. Maybe we should break into the Lichtstrom and search through Wolfgang's files."

Ms. China, who had been sulking since they left the UK, slumped down in her seat. "I was really looking forward to using my *Veritas Curat* drug on this wanker."

"That's Latin for 'truth cures,'" Melanie said. "What does it cure?"

"If you lie, the serum causes unspeakable pain until you start telling the truth."

"Oh."

"Maybe we should refuel and start back home," Sarge Bryan said, squinting into the dark distance. "A few clicks north, I see a helicopter landing port."

`"Ahem."`

Ellie thought this was no time for the AI to gloat over human failures. "We'll make sure you get a recharge too, Miss Aleph," she whispered to the shiny blue cylinder. "Just try not to annoy people you've just met."

`"Thank you, Eleanor,"` Miss Aleph said with typical sarcasm. `"I won't annoy anyone with my time-limited idea on how to fix everything. Tick tock."`

"What can a computer program do?" Ran Oliphant snapped, clearly distraught, even though he was not to blame for Wolfgang getting away.

"Actually, Ran," Sarge Bryan said, "Aleph and Ellie are not a bad team. They got us out of more than one tight spot during the Middle East war."

Praise fueled the furnace of Miss Aleph's ego.

`"Everyone listen and do just what I tell you,"` she cried out over the common channel. `"Pilot: go as high as you can and get between Wolfgang's rocket and the Kiruna Spaceport control tower."`

The pilot agreed and did that. People immediately started yelling at him in Swedish over the radio. Presumably the spaceport did not take kindly to overflights.

"Now what?" Ran asked brusquely as he held on to the webbing straps dangling from the roof in order to keep his balance. Ellie supposed the businessman had some kind of military background. She had been around Atticus and Sarge Bryan long enough to tell.

`"Shh. I'm concentrating."`

Sarge linked the feed from his eyes to a flat-screen monitor in the cargo bay where they were sitting. In telescopic mode, they could see Wolfgang's rocket ship angling up. It rotated slightly, and then bolts flew out from the side. It split apart in midair.

"Holy Mother!" Ran swore. "We wanted to talk to him, not blow him up."

"Still shh! I'm calculating."

On the screen, the main rocket booster started wobbling drunkenly and blasted a big flare from its main engines. Then it veered out of the frame of what Sarge could see. Sarge cut off the feed.

"Something detached," he said, scratching a patch of white stubble on his chin. "It was an unpowered vehicle with four parachutes. An escape pod? Why would that deploy?"

"Give the pilot these coordinates in the Norwegian Sea."

After some gloating and during a descent to refuel at the Arctic Heli Tours station, which luckily was open twenty-four hours, Miss Aleph detailed her genius.

"The trick was twinning the transponder signal from the rocket's in-flight safety computer. It routed signals down to the Kiruna control then back up to the command module.

"I convinced the onboard flight computer the O-rings on the booster rocket were failing. Wolfgang Licht is a fan of space travel. He would recognize this as the same catastrophic malfunction which destroyed the space shuttle *Challenger* seventy-three seconds after liftoff."

"He'd have no choice but to abort," Ran said with trenchant approval.

"But how did you know he wouldn't double check verbally with launch control?" asked Melanie, who seemed at least as good a scientist as Ms. China.

"There was no time. I hacked the external camera on the rocket and pasted fake computer-generated flames around the O-rings, showing them burning through the booster's fuselage."

To illustrate her point, Miss Aleph projected gouts of digital fire onto the big viewscreen, and out of the flames came the words:

"Fooled You, Dummy!"

After being explosively separated from the main rockets, the escape module had drifted down about two hundred kilometers from land.

"A Norwegian search-and-rescue team is prepping," Ran said after a conference with the pilot. "We have to get to Wolfgang first."

"He's turned off his location beacon," Sarge said, looking at the data Miss Aleph fed to his cybernetic eyes. "Maybe he suspects he was conned and is calling his own people for pickup."

Ellie realized she was dealing with a totally new class of society. In the fashion world, having "people" meant you didn't have to pick up your own dry cleaning. Wolfgang Licht had his own UN-recognized country located in between France and Switzerland. His people had helicopters at least as fast as theirs and probably with weapons aboard, unlike theirs. They could still lose him.

"The pilot will get us close. But if anyone else shows up, he's got to leave," Ran said. "He has not signed on to be accessory to kidnapping and piracy."

Their twin rotors raced them along a few hundred feet above the churning waters. The only light was from their own downward-angled spotlight. Its bright white cone slashed this way and that through the North Sea salt spray and sliced across frothy wave caps.

The escape capsule was not where it was supposed to be.

"Did you compensate for currents and wind?"

"Yes," Melanie said, studying her maps. "Bryan, can you see anything?"

"There are the parachutes."

A few scraps of soggy material were bobbing in the rolling waves.

"Could the whole capsule have sunk?" Ms. China asked.

"In that event, this design of emergency lander would eject the passengers inside individual life pods. You'd see them floating."

"Switching to thermal," Sarge Bryan said.

The feed from his eyes showed a fading and wavering line farther out into the sea. Was that a trail?

"Go!" Ran instructed. "Follow that."

"What's going on?" Ellie whispered to the AI.

"Wolfgang is annoyingly clever and paranoid. He

has hacked the stabilizer jets of the escape pod and created a jury-rigged marine propulsion system. It's heating up the water as he goes. We'll get him."

They got him.

Down in the thrashing waves, a helmeted head popped out of a conical pod about the size of an eight-person tent. At first, Wolfgang waved to them with a flare, thinking they were his own people.

"Hi, Wolfgang," Ran said into the radio triumphantly. "Need a lift?"

The figure threw the flare into the sea and ignited his thruster engines. He was still trying to get away as they came down closer and slid the side door open. Before Ran had chartered it, the Chinook was being used as a training aircraft for disaster search-and-rescue teams. There was an armature and a coil of coated wire rope attached to a harness.

"I'll go down," Ran said.

"You said you wanted him alive. You're too pissed at him. I'll go," Sarge Bryan said, pulling the tether away from his friend. "Also, I don't think he's ever seen an albino with eyes like mine. I should freak him out just enough to convince him to come quietly."

Sarge strapped in. They lowered him toward the lander. They were hovering at about sixty feet. The waves were cresting twenty to thirty feet. Downdraft from the huge twin rotors of the Chinook caused Bryan to swing around like a yo-yo. They had to be quick. Radar showed two other search-and-rescue teams were incoming.

Finally, they managed to bring up their quarry.

"Well," Wolfgang Licht said through a bearded mouth dripping with seawater, "of all the *Schweinehunde* I'd like to see rotting in a jail for attempted murder and abduction, you, Oliphant, are at the top of my list."

"Get in before we throw you back without a life jacket."

The two men pushed Wolfgang Licht toward the back of the copter. He was alert, hostile, and altogether less frail looking than Ellie had imagined.

"Ran," Sarge Bryan said, not taking his harness off and motioning down to the bobbing capsule, "little complication. More than one."

Wolfgang Licht was not the only passenger in the escape pod.

"Get them all on board," Miss Aleph advised. "We don't know what part they play in all this."

Bringing up two at a time was not a problem. The others each weighed an average of one hundred pounds, despite being nearly six feet tall. As the Chinook left the empty space capsule in the middle of the Norwegian Sea, seven supermodels sat shivering in their cargo bay.

13

A ch, *meine lieben Damen,*" Wolfgang said to his dripping-wet space harem of supermodels. He seemed only mildly put off by his sudden reversal of fortune. "Keep a mental note of who is in charge here. At the criminal trial, you can point out your brutalizers. You are all about to be very wealthy, while Mr. Oliphant is about to be poor and incarcerated."

Ran went over and grabbed Wolfgang by his shoulders. The men were about the same size, though Ran seemed much fitter. "Stop talking. We know about the Pangea Protocol."

Wolfgang's face blanched, his features fell. Reluctantly, he sat in a jump seat along the wall of the Chinook's cargo bay.

"Firstly," Ran told him, "you're going to get on the radio and tell the Norwegians and your own rescue team from Lichtwerks Corp that you are in safe hands. Thank them for their time and offer to pay for their fuel costs."

Wolfgang did that.

"Next, you're going to confirm all we've already found out about the November holocaust planned for Europe."

That he did not do.

"Ranulph, old chum," Wolfgang said smugly, "I've known you long enough to see when you are full of bluffing. You don't know anything."

"Fucking hell!" Ms. China grabbed the collar of Wolfgang's soaked flight suit and kneed him in the kidney. Likely massively increased by the weight of her hefty prosthetic leg, the blow brought the older man down to his knees. She twisted one arm behind his back and dabbed a purple liquid onto the tips of his fingers.

"You dare burn me with acid, you crazy *hündin*?"

"The crazy part is right," Ms. China said. "That serum is soaking into your fingernail beds. It's making its way up to the median nerves. Every time your pH and galvanic skin responses say you're lying, it will short-circuit your pain receptors. You won't like that."

Wolfgang totally did not.

"It's… I don't really know… *Arrrgh!* All right, I don't know much apart from the name Pangea and *arrgh*… a few details. The date. The date is clear: On November 1, everyone in Europe will be dead!"

"Oh my," Melanie Françoise said, her voice barely audible over the copter rotors.

For what seemed like a long while, the noise of the aircraft and the wind whipping along outside were the only sounds. Miss Aleph broke the silence.

"What about AIs? Better to be safe. Drop me off at a UPS store. I'll mail myself to Australia."

Ms. China looked at their captive. Behind them, the seven supermodels had toweled off but were still shivering.

"That's not possible." Ran sat down for the first time since they had flown over the Kiruna Spaceport. He gripped the canvas back of the seat and glared at Wolfgang.

"He's not lying," Ms. China said. "By this time, any fib would send him into a coma."

"The Havana Syndrome," Wolfgang sputtered, still under the influence of the truth drug. "It was one of the beta versions of the Pangean's weapons system deployed in 2016. American and Canadian diplomats at the Cuban embassy were attacked. Victims experienced permanent alternations in their brain physiology. This brain damage was inflicted remotely."

"That was caused by ultrasonic beams," Melanie said. She clearly had encyclopedic knowledge of weird science. "At first they suspected the Chinese, but then their diplomats suffered brain trauma too. That was covered up by Beijing. What frequency are they using?"

"Hah, I told you. You know nothing," their guest scoffed. "It's not a frequency. The ultrasonics were just a targeting device, like a laser beam to guide a bullet. The weapon itself is a specialized electromagnetic pulse affecting only specific cells of the human brain. It is well known that iron nuclei traveling at close to the speed of light destroys brain tissue. The damage suffered by the Havana test subjects was caused by dark-matter energy."

"That's something you've specialized in for the past twenty years," Ran said, staring daggers at Wolfgang. "Who are you working with? How do we stop it?"

"Don't be so hasty." Wolfgang was, perhaps for the first time in years, getting used to telling the truth. He looked at his purple-stained fingers. They seemed tender but not causing him total agony anymore. "I myself would never do such a thing. Even I cannot afford to lose half a billion customers, not to mention the expert technicians it has taken decades to assemble at Lichtwerks."

"Nice of you to have a selfish reason to disapprove of mass murder," Ran said, turning to Ms. China. "I think he might need topping up with truth serum."

Ms. China had plenty in her vial.

"No, no, listen, listen, I only heard about it after it was irrevocably begun. It's probably already too late to stop. The man, a person, I can't be sure who it is, he or she contacted certain key people needed for the rebuilding of Europe."

"You've got to have more," Ran pressed. "You always have your own games to play."

"I h-have insurance, in case something went wrong."

Ellie thought: *mass killing an entire continent? How does that go* right?

Wolfgang indicated a button sewn into his flight suit. It was a data device. Once attached to Miss Aleph's cylinder, it started playing. A synthesized voice spoke first.

"*...even after the Second World War and after the fall of communism, who* *was in charge? The same people: Nazis and KGB apparatchiks, the core Red Guard fanatics. I want you on my team, Dr. Licht, to build once and for all a Europe we can be proud of."*

"I do wish you had come to me first," Wolfgang's recorded voice said. *"Dark-matter events can be tricky physics, even under ideal conditions. The Planck Society is decades behind my team. No one knows more than we do at Der Lichtstrom."*

"Pause that," Ran said. "Melanie, can you get a voiceprint of who was speaking?"

`"Don't bother trying to descramble it. The other voice is like mine, completely digital."`

"What about word choice, vocabulary?" Melanie said. "That's the leader of the Pangeans or very close to the top. They have to be on tape somewhere."

"That's a long shot, Dr. Françoise," Ran said, considering their next move. "But we can try once we're back at our lab."

"What?" Wolfgang said. "I insist you take me back to my country."

"It's my house or the big house, Wolfgang." Ran looked over to his captive's bevy of female space-traveling companions. "What was your harebrained scheme, Wolfgang? You were going to take seven Eves along to a space station to help you repopulate a devastated Europe?"

Ellie was thankful that Wolfgang didn't respond.

14

THE BLUE MOSQUE
ISTANBUL

TEMIR

Temir's Grey Wolves had taken over the garden area of the mosque. The damned Persians were late. Tonight, timing was everything. Temir's entire plan depended on Elder Omid witnessing a miracle.

"Where are they?" Temir said, looking up at the moonless night sky.

Eylül just grunted and checked with the perimeter guards. Grey Wolves paramilitary had replaced the regular security forces throughout the large mosque compound.

For the hundredth time, Temir checked the angle of the meeting place, the alignment of the minarets, and gazed up at the velvet-textured night sky. Outside of the dull radiance of Istanbul's urban lights, it was black as coal. By a stroke of good fortune, there was not a cloud anywhere and the fat half moon had set under the horizon just before six p.m.

Built by Sultan Ahmed, the six minarets and thirteen domes were bathed in blue floodlights that reflected off tens of thousands of hand-painted blue tiles.

"Do it now," Temir said. "Turn the floods off. I want this to be as dramatic as possible."

Eylül growled orders into a microphone. Section by section, minaret by minaret, the Blue Mosque went dark. Temir cared for only one spectacle. The spectacle he needed Elder Omid, the chief of Iran's powerful Guardian Council, to witness tonight.

"Go and see if that Sunni witch is lurking around."

Meliha was head of the clan that essentially ruled the breakaway Sunni state of Northern Iraq. She had brokered the meeting between Temir's ultranationalist Turks and Elder Omid's Iranians. She had also advised Temir that the way to convince Omid to cooperate with his plan to invade Europe was not through reason, but through mysticism. If she was betraying him, Temir swore he'd see Meliha's head skewered on a spike atop one of the Blue Mosque's domes.

"There they come," Eylül said, motioning to the eastern entrance by the deserted café.

Eylül had been with him since they were teenagers. Temir had been born into the Grey Wolves. The powerful organization was a unique form of Deep State. While they were financed mostly by criminal activities like the Italian mafia, Grey Wolves chapters operated out in the open under various regional banners. They had people in key positions in the executive, legislative, and military branches of the Turkish government. The Grey Wolves were part gang, part special forces paramilitary, part social club.

While Temir had been genetically destined for a leadership track, his stocky friend had been initiated into the Grey Wolves by performing less-exalted assignments. When Temir first met Eylül, he was enthusiastically extorting local bakers by sewing dead rats into their flour sacks and promising they and their families would be next if they didn't pay up. Temir trusted him and also acknowledged his limitations.

"Eylül." Temir felt he had to remind him for the third time exactly what to do. "Something is going to happen at three minutes to midnight. We have to bide our time until then. When I refill your tea, you will tell the story of how I entered the Noble Sanctuary of the Al-Aqsa in Jerusalem and fought with the Jew demon who destroyed our holy shrine, the Dome of the Rock."

Temir told him the exact words to use.

"I am not good at stories."

"Do your best, and watch the time."

Temir turned in a fluid motion to greet his guests. Elder Omid and his retinue were making their way across the grassy courtyard. He made sure his horsehide overcoat covered his appendage. "Elder Omid, welcome to one of the wonders of the Islamic world, which Turkey is proud to protect."

The craggy old man was flanked by Quds Force guardsmen on one side and Meliha on the other. Temir had not told her the details of his plan, but unlike Eylül, she was smart enough to have guessed. If she had, she gave no clue as they walked toward the chairs and low tea table.

"The Blue Mosque of Sultan Ahmed, even more glorious at night, even without its usual lighting," Elder Omid said, sitting on the grass. "It was built to glorify Ottoman culture and civilization inside Turkey's own territory, where Turkish ambitions belong."

The Persian vulture was referring to the humiliation of the Ottomans by the Persian Empire in 1609, when construction of the mosque began. Temir's left symbiont-enhanced eye showed him Omid's face and hands were flushed. Temir normally pretended his injuries had left him practically blind in one eye. In reality, he saw more than a human ever could. Had Meliha been plying Omid with opium, or whores? Either way, he seemed more amenable than he had at the train yard.

"Yes, Elder Omid, for too long, the Westerners, kafirs, Christians, and Jews have played us off against one another. We have killed each other for scraps."

Omid held up his hand. "I agreed to have tea in a beautiful garden, but as for your proposal, my mind is made up."

Temir made sure Omid was sitting in precisely the right place. "That is all I wished, to offer you the hospitality and serenity of a night in Istanbul." He poured tea into the Persian's cup.

After thirty minutes of chattering, mostly about how they could undermine the independent Kurdish republic, Temir poured tea into Eylül's cup. That was the signal.

"That… er, that reminds me of, ah," Eylül began artlessly. "When we stormed Jerusalem and entered the Old City."

"A glorious liberation," Omid said. "Though it was short-lived. The Islamic Republic of Iran has given millions to restore the al-Aqsa and the Dome of the Rock."

"Better that they remain rubble than under the thumbs of the Israelites," Temir growled. He nodded to his friend.

"Something you may not know," Eylül stammered. "Which is not to say you are not wise, Elder Omid, the very opposite, but this is something which many people do not know, as it is not widely known… Temir entered the al-Aqsa through the Golden Gate."

Omid nodded, and that struck a chord in the Shi'a Sufi mystic's brain. "Bab al-Rahma and Bab al-Taubah they are named, the twin gates through the outer wall of Old Jerusalem leading onto the al-Aqsa mosque. After being sealed for hundreds of years, the Bab al-Dhahabi has been opened."

Suleiman the Magnificent, the greatest sultan of the Turkish Ottoman Empire, had sealed the gate in order to prevent a prophecy from coming to pass. It was rumored Suleiman was also an adherent of Sufi philosophy.

"Exactly, Elder Omid," Eylül said. "But what I observed, and no one else knows, is that the terrible fiend who blew up the Dome of the Rock, nearly killing our fearless and indestructible Temir, was a Jew. And this Jew also came in by that same gate."

"Truly?" Omid put down his cup. "But he would have had to cross the Islamic graveyard directly outside the eastern wall. Under Jewish law, he would be tainted and have no standing on the al-Aqsa."

It was well known that religious Jews refused to go up on the Noble Sanctuary, which they called Temple Mount, because they might tread on the Holy of Holies without being purified by the ash of an extinct species of red heifer.

The danger of a warrior Jew entering through the Golden Gate was clear to people who held with mysticism. The tribes of Israel could rebuild the Third Temple on the al-Aqsa, ushering in the End Times, which Sufi mystics fervently believed were imminent.

Temir interrupted, "The messianic Jews of Jerusalem have cloned the extinct red heifer or *para adumma*. They sacrificed it with cedar wood, hyssop, and scarlet yarn. They did so only days before the battle in order to take what they call 'Temple Mount' away from us. Had it not been for the religious and Zionist militia, our forces would have thrown the IDF out of the Old City."

"And, Elder Omid," Eylül spoke boldly, gaining confidence in his storytelling abilities, "our Aga Temir and the foul Jew demon fought, hand to hand. It was only through the cowardly act of blowing up the Dome of the Rock that the servant of Gog and Magog escaped."

It was four minutes to midnight.

"Since we are all friends and believers here," Temir said gravely, noting that Omid gazed at him with a new sense of gravity, "I will say that when I was battling the demon of Shaitan on the Noble Sanctuary, I received not a revelation... but more a feeling. The Day of Judgment, Yawm ad-Dīn! The thought reverberated through my head. Even as the Dome fell about me, I realized that day was near, and I had a role to play."

Temir rose and threw off his greatcoat. His left shirt sleeve had been cut off and torn almost down to his waist, revealing a thick undulating appendage pulsating with black ichor. From his shoulder socket, a thing like a fat tentacle had grown and consumed the broken bits of human flesh, and a tusk had sprouted from the elbow. At the end of this singular member were two slug-like fingers and a fatter thumb. With these, Temir pointed up at the night sky.

"Now this!"

With a silent blaze, like a nuclear bomb going off on the dead black horizon, a disc of yellow light appeared over Istanbul.

Omid instinctively made a Sufi warding sign with his hand, whispering, *"Alamatu's-sa'ah al-kubra."*

Temir thought: *"The great signs of the End Time" is right, you superstitious dotard.*

"Tulue alshams min mughribiha," Temir said. "The rising of the sun from the west."

The glow in the sky brightened and shimmered. Even Meliha looked surprised. For about a minute, no one moved, no one spoke. The sky sparkled with the unreal sight.

"Of course," Temir said, breaking the spell, "that is not the sun but human technology. The Chinese-built space mirror is advancing to its final orbit. I do not claim to be a prophet, nor is David Baumann the anti-Christ Masih ad-Dajjal. But I swear to you, Elder Omid, the Event is real. On November 1, Europe, the lands of Gog and Magog, will be cleansed of kafir—Christian, Jew, and traitor Muslims. If we are bold enough, it is all in our grasp."

They watched the giant mirror reflect the light of the sun from space as it changed its orbital vector. Eylül gaped, open mouthed. With a slight inclination of her head, Meliha applauded Temir's showmanship.

"Well," Omid said finally, "if we waited for magic and flying carpets, we would miss the signs right before our eyes. We know the words of the Prophet, but we use the mightiest earthly weapons we can lay our hands on to destroy His enemies."

Meliha had judged Elder Omid well. He was superstitious but employed ruthless practicality. The older Persian rose from the small table and stood beside Temir. "Aga Temir of the Grey Wolves, I believe in you and your 'Event.' We will advance our plans alongside Turkey's armored divisions, if—and only if—you can convince me the Russians will not interfere."

So that was Omid's final delaying tactic. No one could consider the conquest of Europe, even one occupied only by five hundred million corpses, without considering what Russia would do. Temir had anticipated that.

"Russia, yes," Temir said. "It is a big problem. Our calculations show the Event will leave them virtually untouched. They are a strong military force and will try to claim an empty Europe for themselves."

Serendipity and the bounty of juicy human flesh on a warm humid night provided Temir with a final prop for his presentation.

"As Aban ibn Uthman of Medina said: if you want to accomplish something big in the name of the Prophet..." Temir lashed out with his new hand, snatching a speck from the air before it alighted on Omid's startled face. "Start with something small."

In mid-strike, the ends of Temir's tentacle fingers morphed into two fat suction cups and closed on something. He held it out for all to see. Inside the transparent oval of unnatural membranes buzzed a captive mosquito.

15

NEAR AMSTERDAM

ELLIE

A nd… when I was twelve," Wolfgang Licht mumbled loudly as he sat in his jump seat in the helicopter cargo bay, "I put cameras all over the maid's quarters to try to see her naked."

"Ms. China, ma'am," Sarge Bryan said politely, "how long does that Veritas truth serum stuff last? He's been ramblin' on for a while."

"But guess who came in?" Wolfgang continued compulsively. "My father and his mistress. He was clearly interested in a sexual act that required two female partic—"

Ms. China walked past Ellie and Melanie Françoise, hanging on to the overhead straps as the helicopter descended toward Amsterdam. She grabbed the tech titan by his medium-length goatee.

"Dr. Licht, let's leave your pervy father out of this. Who was that on the recording? Who is the leader of the Pangeans?"

"I-I don't know. I was in a process of compiling a list of suspects. But as you now understand, my departure plans had to be arranged in a hurry." Wolfgang's face went blank, like he had forgotten something. "The rest is… *im Blut*… in the blood. I only speak what my mind can answer, you sadistic but somehow sexually attractive woman."

Wolfgang's addled features betrayed exhaustion and confusion but no serum-induced agony. He was telling the truth as far as he knew it.

"Lay off him," Ran said. "He's just spouting nonsense."

Ellie and Melanie were tending to Wolfgang's space harem. The seven women whom Wolfgang had taken on the rocket with him were quite laudably diverse. There was a redhead, a brunette, a Nigerian, a Chinese, an Indian, and two blondes. All these models were in their early twenties and had agreed to go because the oligarch had convinced them some continental disaster would soon ravage all of Europe.

"We all went voluntarily," the brunette told Ellie in a Spanish accent. "He said we didn't have to do anything we didn't want, but if we got pregnant, there were cash incentives."

The Nigerian woman rolled her eyes. She looked familiar.

"Didn't we meet in Paris?" Ellie asked.

"Are you Ellie Sato?" the black model said with a heavy Ghanaian accent. "You, uh, look different."

Ellie realized with some embarrassment she must look a sight. She hadn't put on any makeup since fighting with the hoodlums in London.

"See that nice lady?" Ellie said in what she hoped was a reassuring voice. These girls were all models and were used to stress. However, they had just been shot into the stratosphere, then plunged into the Norwegian Sea in an emergency escape capsule. As a result, they might be a little traumatized. "That's Melanie. She's a doctor."

"PhD," Melanie chirped, holding her lopsided hair as she came over. "But I've taken two years of medical school equivalent."

"Her boss is Mr. Oliphant over there," Ellie said, pointing to Ran, who was quietly talking to Sarge Bryan. "He'll make sure you get home safely. He's even richer than Wolfgang."

"No!" sputtered Dr. Licht. "*I* am richer. But Oliphant probably gets more pussy without having to pay for it. The swine!"

"Anyway, Melanie here will fill your emails with enough travel credits to get you where you need to be."

The Asian woman spoke English with a British accent. "Will it be enough to get us out of Europe?"

By the time they were nearing the Netherlands, their big twin-bladed Chinook copter was nearly out of gas.

"The pilot's agreed to stay out of UK airspace and inside the Schengen flight zone," Ran said. "That way there's no chance of a customs check where Wolfgang can try to get away. But this bird needs petrol and maintenance time."

They set down at Amsterdam Heliport just before midnight. Wolfgang's harem wandered off into a limousine van with flashing neon under-glow lights.

"All the rental company had available was the party van," Melanie explained. "I hope they're not too put out."

"They're runway models. They can take it," Ellie said.

"Not you." Ran grabbed Dr. Licht as he also tried to walk off the back ramp.

Sarge Bryan also blocked the man's exit and stared at him intensely. "Are you sure you've told us everything about this brain EMP thing?"

"Of course," Licht snapped back. "Now let me go. You can't treat me this way."

"Your serum seems to have worn off," Ellie said to Ms. China.

"I don't know anything else," Wolfgang said. "It's not my invention, how could I?"

`"Make Dr. Licht tell you how he would have developed the device. Dip all his fingers and toes in that torture serum."`

Wolfgang stared at Miss Aleph's cylinder and the bulging glass camera eye of the handset connected to it.

"I told you," he said, sitting down and drinking from a water bottle. "The Havana Syndrome was an early implementation of a weaponized Tyr quark.

"The Tyr quark is the quantum oscillation ubiquitous in nature," he explained as though he were a professor speaking to a class of dullards. "From photosynthesis to every mitochondrion that are the power generators of every living cell, to the unique quantum variables inside the frontal cortex of the human brain."

"Fine. We're now grounded in the basic science. Answer Miss Aleph,"

Ran prodded. "How would you do it? How would you create a weapon based on this dark-matter particle?"

"Without the CERN supercollider at Der Lichtstrom?" Wolfgang shook his head. "Only a madman would try. Dark energy does not respect the Newtonian physics or the geometry of Euclid. A single neutrino can pass through a light-year's thickness of solid lead without leaving a trace. If they have managed to build a device, I would expect they only have one, and it would have to be in a very large resonance chamber to give it the required range."

"How big could the kill zone be?" Sarge Bryan asked.

Dr. Licht shrugged. "My country is near Geneva, which is at the center of Europe. A Tyr quark effect of sufficient strength would only have to reach less than one thousand miles, eight hundred even, to neutralize most of the population from Rome to Madrid to London and as far east as Warsaw. It would be"—he snapped his fingers dramatically—"lights out for Europe."

"You fucking—" Ms. China advanced on the older man, her sharp fingernails outstretched.

"Don't," Ellie said sharply. "He's not the one doing it. He was only trying to get away."

"Without warning anyone," Ran Oliphant said.

"Who would have believed me?" Wolfgang said defensively. "And if I spoke up, how could I know I was not speaking to some of the conspirators themselves? A T-bomb, if we can call it that, would take nation-state-level technology to build. These Pangean fanatics are everywhere." Wolfgang eyed Ms. China, who had been a British spy before her mental health setbacks.

Ellie led Ms. China off the helicopter to get some air. She seemed unusually agitated, which was odd. In the past, the serial poisoner was not at all fazed by genocidal plans and even seemed to enjoy them. Ellie decided she should try to get her to take some of her meds. But first she had to freshen up.

Their pilot was discussing some things with the local technicians, who looked a bit disheveled at this time of night. Ellie found a washroom at the side of the heliport office. Half her makeup bottles were broken, and she could only find the tip end of her lipstick, which she smushed onto her fingers before putting it on.

When she came out, her mental patient was going off again.

"You wouldn't know anything if I hadn't been here. I want you to do what I say!" Ms. China was haranguing Ran, Sarge Bryan, and Melanie. "We've got to go to Ramstein Air Base now."

Why would she want to go there? Atticus was there, but he was on some covert mission for another day or so.

"There's no way to get hold of Major Reidt," Sarge said calmly.

"Screw you, then, I'll go to Germany myself," Ms. China snapped at him. "I'm getting Attie Jr. He's my son too!"

16

"Keep Elder Omid's man away from the guards," Temir whispered to Eylül as they walked to the gates of the landing strip outside Kiev in Ukraine. "All our passports are Turkish stamped 'Special Diplomatic Priority' from Turkey. I doubt Omid's man knows two words of our language."

Ukraine was located across the Black Sea from Turkey. While never friendly to Turkey's government or Temir's Grey Wolves, Ukrainians were more concerned with fighting against Russia in the Crimean Peninsula and elsewhere.

After the Event, Russia would remain the most formidable force that could oppose their invasion westward. As soon as the miracle of the miniature sun rising in the west faded from the Istanbul horizon, his meeting with Elder Omid had ended, and Temir immediately launched his plan to neutralize the threat. His improvised plan had to start here, outside Kiev, across the border from Russia.

Ukraine was a big market for weapons and drugs, which the Grey Wolves paramilitary were happy to supply. The package they were delivering this evening was neither; it was much more vital. There could be no slip-ups.

Ukrainian was a strange language which Temir had never mastered. Fortunately, bad English was universally understood.

"Gentlemen, good evening," Temir said, approaching the guards. He wore his horsehide greatcoat and had put his left appendage in a sling. With the visible damage to the left side of his head, people would take him to be handicapped and less of a threat.

"It's evening. I don't know about good," the first man said. He was an older bleary-eyed man whose gut hung over his military belt. "Papers."

He barely looked at the passports, assuming correctly that they were recently printed and in perfect order.

"In the crates, what is?"

Three large wooden crates were being rolled off the transport plane.

"Herring roe."

"That's a lot of fish eggs." The older guard looked at his companion, a sniveling skinny boy. They were probably related. No point in sharing bribes with strangers.

"You Ukrainians are so hungry." Temir smiled, the scar tissue on the left side of his face pulled tight and turned the expression into a grimace. "We have trouble keeping up."

Eylül and the hatchet-faced Persian Jamshid came up behind. The Ukrainian looked at Jamshid. Elder Omid had insisted he take the Quds Force man with them, Temir reluctantly agreed. Jamshid's normal expression was that of a jihadi just about to set off a suicide bomb.

"Why the boxes so big?" the younger Ukrainian guard asked, to the annoyance of his superior.

"Fish eggs," Temir said mildly, nodding to the older man. "Must be kept cold until ready to eat. You understand?"

"What happened to you, your face, and your arm?" the first guard said, still looking at the Persian.

"Car accident, German tourists. Fucking Germans, right?"

"Yeah, fucking Germans."

Temir handed the guard a handset. Someone texted a code word, and seeing it made the older man's gray stubble-covered cheeks crinkle into a smile.

"Now it is a good evening."

They were waved through and allowed to unload. One long three-axle semitrailer was large enough to haul the three shipping containers from the plane, though just barely.

As he, Eylül, and Jamshid were entering the semi, Temir wanted to take the wheel, but he decided to keep his left appendage hidden for now. There may be other corrupt officials down the road looking for crumbs from the main customs checkpoint bribe. Eylül drove, and Jamshid sat sullenly in the back.

"Just like old times, Aga Temir, huh?"

Eylül had begun his career with the Grey Wolves as a dope runner and enforcer. Temir had been groomed for command since birth. He was not allowed to ask after his parentage. All Turkish people were his family, and the Grey Wolves his parents. In the legend of the Boz Kurt, a she-wolf gave birth to ten half-human boys, one of whom founded the nomadic Turkic empire. Temir's symbiont, his deformities, despite the disgust they inspired, would eventually only add to his legend. Conquering a continent would complete his destiny. But first he had to cripple Russia's response to the coming crisis.

"Just like old times, Eylül, yes. But with much more precious cargo than ever before," Temir said, making sure to keep an eye on Jamshid. "The key to a soon-to-be-empty house called Europe."

The roads around Kiev were mostly paved, flat, and bounded by low trees spreading shadows in their branches under the gathering night. Temir was annoyed at Eylül's slow driving. If they hadn't needed to put on the magic show at the Blue Mosque, they could have been here at least two days earlier. But so far it was worth it.

Iranian armored divisions had joined Turkish regular forces—all commanded by Grey Wolves members—for joint military exercises. They were massing equipment, fuel, and spare parts outside Ankara. That placed them near excellent roads a few hundred miles from the border with Bulgaria. After the Event, the weak Bulgarian Christians would open their borders, or else.

Temir tried to be friendly to the Persian. "Jamshid, Elder Omid says you are a great pilot."

Since meeting them in Istanbul, Jamshid had said about three words. Temir had to judge whether the man was a help or a hindrance. If the latter, he may have to encounter an unfortunate accident before their flight began.

"I Iranian Top Gun," Jamshid assured him.

Temir rolled out a diagram of an instrument panel.

"Everything is coded to international symbols. The flight computer understands Farsi."

Jamshid's hooded eyes looked over the diagram. He seemed to understand the basics quickly enough.

"There is not escape chute?"

"No. If the craft goes down, so do you."

"Good."

At least the Persian was committed.

They drove past the sleepy city of Chernihiv. A few onion-topped Orthodox churches were followed by more flat roads. Their takeoff point was well back from the Russian border. The frontier had multiple layers of air defenses and a monitoring system; a fast-flying metal object the size of a tennis ball would be detected.

Eylül guided the truck down an unpaved road lined by evergreens. If they were quick, Temir thought, their covert air convoy could be past the most dangerous S-400 and S-500 surface-to-air missiles by daybreak. They could only fly at night.

They drove into an isolated industrial park; this was a regional hub for drug and weapons smuggling. A hooded figure closed the gates behind their truck. Eighteen men, all made men of the Grey Wolves mafia, tended to the unloading and prep work inside the warehouse.

Jamshid studied the aeronautical chart.

"You guarantee the information on these Russian defenses? Including SAM batteries?"

"Turkey bought the latest surface-to-air missile systems from Russia. We took them apart, learned everything about them. We have satellite images, which will update as we fly."

That apparently satisfied the Top Gun from Tehran. Inside the big warehouse, compressor motors hissed. Or at least, that was all Temir hoped was hissing.

"Check that," he said in street Turkish to Eylül and the ground crew. "If those are micro holes hissing, I'll put macro holes in you, you sloppy bastards."

The airships that had been unloaded from the three shipping containers were unique and sturdy. But when they took off, they would have only a very limited ability to make repairs en route. Most of their lifting capacity was needed for their living refrigerated payloads.

Inside the wide barnlike building, three blimp-shaped objects floated. They were tethered to the ground by ballast weights on wheels. Helium had a lifting force of one gram per liter of gas. However, these dirigibles were not filled with any type of lighter-than-air gas—they were filled with nothing.

Using the same principle of buoyancy that allows a submarine to surface in the sea, these ultra-thin and ultra-strong blimps were filled with vacuum.

"The airship skins are sealed and intact, Aga Temir," Eylül reported.

Vacuum airships, which floated in atmosphere as though they were water, were only theoretical until the invention of boron-based nano-fibers. Helium-filled blimps offset the 100,000 pascals standard air pressure with internal pressure of the lighter-than-air gas. Vacuum airships had to resist a weight of five average automobiles per square meter pressing down on them from the atmosphere by using structural integrity alone. The physics payoff was a 100% conversion of displacement to lift, minus the weight of the structure itself, since vacuum had zero mass.

"Take Jamshid to his cockpit. Make sure he understands all the controls."

Thirty-eight minutes later, Temir strapped himself horizontally into the small cockpit between the torpedo-shaped vacuum airship and the payload. The Grey Wolves doused the warehouse lights and released the three airships from their moorings. Temir checked his bearings a final time. Using a tight-beamed ultraviolet laser, he signaled for takeoff.

These three ships, invisible to radar and infrared detectors, were painted black and traveling less than thirty knots. They would simply float like wisps of cloud over Russian air defenses as they headed toward Moscow.

17

"CITY WITHOUT DRUGS" REHAB
NEAR ST. PETERSBURG, RUSSIA

KOMANDIR ZVENA

The farm was like none other in the area, Komandir Zvena thought. It had higher fences, meaner-looking dogs, and a better grade of razor wire than was required to keep pigs and cows safe. The barriers were not meant to keep people out—they were meant to keep terribly deviant people in. The place was filled with the worst hopeless scum: hard-core drug addicts.

The City Without Drugs Rehab center was a model for helping deviant people become normal. Here, men and women who were slowly killing themselves had a last chance. If they survived the harsh detox program, they might once again become contributing members of Russian society.

"Rodion," Zvena said to the five-hundred-pound monster cyborg who held open the outer gate. "You wait here."

Not that his noncommissioned officer had a choice; Rodion would not have fit through the doorway into the clinic. By contrast, Komandir Zvena was not the largest cyborg Russia had developed, but he was one of the first, and he prided himself on being one of the best. Scientists working in the Human+ division of the Foundation for Advanced Research Projects often came to take samples of his blood and tissues.

Zvena took a last breath of fresh, manure-tinged air and went in. The detox ward smelled like a zoo, a neglected and disorderly one. Unhappy patients were handcuffed to beds with buckets for urine, feces, and vomit beside their cots. They were unhappy because they were going through the first thirty days of withdrawal from whatever poisons they had been dumb enough to shoot up or inhale. All were here voluntarily or as an alternative to prison.

Zvena passed a young girl. She was likely a child prostitute and looked like she weighed as much as his forearm. She looked up at him with bleary blue eyes, squinted as though she were not seeing correctly, and then puked yellow-and-gray vomit from her tiny mouth and little nostrils.

Some got on Zvena's black Navy coat. He did not wipe it. He thought grimly, *Today things will get messier still.*

"Dr. Nail," Zvena said to a fat little balding man with a Stalin moustache. "This place smells like a zoo."

Dr. Nail looked way up at the cyborg soldier. Zvena wore a standard uniform and the rank insignia of a komandir in the Russian Navy. Everyone who mattered knew who and what he was; the rest knew to stay out of his way. The small physician ran up and hugged him.

"Yari," he said, nearly bursting into tears as he squeezed Zvena's hand in both of his. "Yari, you're a day early."

"You would have cleaned this shit up for me?"

"No, but I would have gotten better vodka."

Zvena looked around. Dr. Nail, his friend, had given up the top job at the Human+ Institute for Cyborg Research in order to establish this facility.

"Here at City Without Drugs, every day we are doing valiant work for the nation," Dr. Nail said and threw a rag into a puddle of something and then pushed it under a bed. "Do you have time for a tour?"

Zvena had no interest in the human trash of society, save for one patient. But Dr. Nail's enthusiasm and his personal feelings of warmth for the eccentric doctor swayed him. He nodded; motorized joints in his neck and shoulders let out mild creaking sounds.

This pleased the medical man immensely. Dr. Nail stamped his foot with joy, which sent spatter flying from another puddle. "It smelled much worse in here last week. We graduated a substantial number of patients from primary detox to Work Detail Number One just yesterday."

They passed a line of rusty bed frames and befouled mattresses leaned up against the far wall of the large wooden farmhouse. A few boys dressed like concentration camp inmates moved along them, scraping and wiping at the dried filth with moldering rags to little effect.

"We're expecting a new class to matriculate late tonight."

"The city will never run out of addicts," Zvena said sharply. He was a soldier of Russia, a leader of men and women who had given everything to defend the Federation. He could not help being disgusted by the weak filth around him. "Dr. Nail, come back to the Human+ Institute. You built me, and no one has been able to do better. Leave the dregs of humanity to their self-inflicted misery."

At the mention of his old job, Dr. Nail studied Zvena with scientific curiosity. "May I?"

Zvena nodded. Dr. Nail gripped his forearm, then he got on a stool in order to check Zvena's neck. It must have looked like a leprechaun was examining the trunk of an oak tree, but none of the addicts paid much attention.

"Excellent. You're adapting to the new shark cartilage matrix better than I hoped."

The key to integrating mechanical devices into the human body were meso-tissue support structures. The human shoulder was not really a joint; without ligaments and muscles, it would fall apart. With those muscles properly trained, an ordinary human's shoulders could deadlift more than 1,000 pounds. Living shark cartilage supported the metal and carbon-fiber augments inside Russian cyborgs, allowing for a fantastic increase in speed and strength. Dr. Nail had invented the process.

"I am functioning at peak performance levels. No thanks to the physicians they have working at Human+ now," Zvena said. "What good is building a behemoth like Rodion out there if he can't even fit into a tank?"

Through a grimy window patched with clear duct tape, Zvena could see intermediate-level patients walking slowly between the barns. The detox graduates looked like wraiths. They carried leaky buckets and used brooms with hardly any bristles to steadily sweep the walkways between muddy areas.

Pigs ran freely and seemed to be the most lively and happiest residents of the compound.

"Russians are the number-one consumer of opiates in the world," Dr. Nail said with fierce conviction. "Our youth addiction rates are nearly four times the rates in America. Yari, my friend, Komandir, I have to be here. I have to do something. This is the future of our country."

Something grabbed Zvena's pants leg. It was an emaciated addict whose body looked like a badly made scarecrow. Male or female, he couldn't tell. It was going into convulsions.

"The future. Right. Better not tell President Putin that," Zvena joked as he jerked his leg away. "He will despair."

This was not, strictly speaking, true. Zvena had been to the Kremlin to receive a medal from the man himself. Putin would not despair. He might line up all the drug dealers and addicts and shoot them in the backs of their heads. But Putin would not despair.

After Dr. Nail had adjusted the scarecrow's IV drip, they moved on.

"No! Not that." The doctor pulled a bucket of gruel and bread crusts out of a volunteer's hand. "This is food, not stool. Leave this, take that."

They continued walking through the ward.

"Are the inductees on any withdrawal medication?" Zvena needed to know that the person he had come all this way to interview would have as clear a head as it was possible to have in this place.

Bloody finger stumps caught hold of Dr. Nail's coat. The remaining few fingers had their nail beds chewed right down. The doctor gently pushed the appendages away.

"Methadone, suboxone?" Dr. Nail said, misting some germ-killing agent on the wounded hands. It stung; the addict withdrew his arms through the rails of the bed. "Those treatments are fraudulent and for good reason are illegal in Russia. How can you get rid of poison by putting a lesser poison into a sick body? No. Here we practice only total cessation and a brutal chemical detox flushing."

"How do the survivors of your treatment do?"

"In America and Europe, the top clinics achieve a success rate of fifteen percent. Mind you, that's with more resources and up to one hundred thousand Euros per month in private hospital fees. Here we have double the success. Those who remain drug-free for five years have a ninety-percent chance of never using again."

"I see it now, your devious plan for retirement." Zvena laid a paw on the doctor's shoulder; it covered nearly his whole back. "You will open a clinic in Switzerland for rich dope fiends and become immensely wealthy."

Dr. Nail laughed. "A drink before you meet your candidate?"

"I think we meet first, then we will have time to drink while he decides."

Dr. Nail nodded. "I put him in a cupboard, so as not to disturb the other patients."

A really fat woman raged in her bed. Her feet were in shackles as well as her hands. The rags covering her body and her bandages flew off. Her wobbly belly and rotund legs were a mass of old stretch marks and were covered with fresh rivulets of crusty oozing scabs. She pulled so hard against her leg bindings that she was scraping the mottled gray flesh off her foot like a wild animal trying to escape a trap.

Dr. Nail pulled out some gauze and rushed over. As he worked, his round bald head nodded apologetically to Zvena. With an elbow, he indicated the way to the cupboard. Zvena thanked him and walked on, with every step floorboards creaked. At the cupboard, the loose doorknob threatened to come off in his hand. He did not bother to knock.

"Hlllmmmph," said a young man who was bound to a bed during his mandatory detoxing period. He was tall. His legs hung over the end of the ratty mattress, and he had a good breadth of shoulders. One thing was not good, Zvena saw. But, he thought as he patted some equipment he had brought, that could be rapidly adjusted.

"Hello to you as well, addict."

"I'm—" The twenty-year-old coughed and wheezed. "Fyodor."

"Ah, like the great Dostoevsky, yes?" Zvena pulled up a chair. It would not take his full weight, so he just put his satchel bag on it. He shook his head and looked down. "Fuck you, you are not like Dostoevsky. You are nothing."

The addict Fyodor was about to speak but then got around to noticing Zvena was not a skinny orderly come to take away his piss. Zvena had to crouch down to fully enter the storage room where the single cot was jammed into a corner.

"Your father worked in the shipbuilding yards," Zvena read from a file projected onto his retina. "Your mother attended school after work to become an engineer. With their life savings, your parents sent you to the best technical colleges. How do you repay them?" Zvena lifted the bandage covering Fyodor's right arm. The foulest stench yet made him grimace. "By injecting Krokodil until you are rotting from the inside like this."

Krokodil was the street name for the semi-synthetic opioid desomorphine. It was many times stronger than morphine. Krokodil was known as the "flesh-eating zombie drug" because of its despicable side effects. As use in Russia became more common, doctors began noticing patches of festering reptilian skin on junkies.

"I—I…" Fyodor blubbered, starting to cry.

"You are less than shit. Even shit can be used as fertilizer. You have turned the body which has been fed and educated by your parents and Russia into toxic waste."

"Everyone was taking something at Edinburgh."

"Yes, talk to me about your time as a computer science scholarship winner at the University of Edinburgh. Do you even remember any of those years?"

This was something in which Zvena was actually interested. If the young man's brain was mush, he had wasted a trip. Zvena pulled out an old model tablet computer.

"Have a drink." He poured the entire jug of water over Fyodor's head. The man did not protest; he just lay there sputtering. It seemed to revive him.

"Here is a question. You have five minutes to answer. Time starts now."

"You have not even asked it. I have to piss."

"Don't you dare. If you interrupt again, you will have even less time," Zvena said slowly and ground his mechanical jaws in the young man's face. "Are you listening?"

Fyodor nodded. Saliva and water dribbled from his stubble-covered chin. Zvena read off the screen.

"Given this matrix of numbers from 1 to n—each number occurs only once—find a path from top left to right bottom while moving right or down only."

After a few seconds, the diagram on the tablet screen and the problem seemed to absorb what was left of Fyodor's mind.

"Green to… blue. No! What am I thinking?" Fyodor tried to slap his head with his left hand, the one that was not inflamed and rotting away. But both his wrists were handcuffed to the railings of his cot. "It must be green to red. Blue to null. Red to orange, then to null."

That did not match the answer taped to the back of the tablet. Zvena knew nothing about programming. He input what the kid said. The technician at the Human+ lab texted him back. It was not the answer the head of computing had come up with—it was a better one.

"Excellent, Fyodor," Zvena growled. "You still have thirty seconds of the five minutes left to piss, and then we talk about your future."

Fyodor urinated while the komandir held the bucket.

"You don't know who I am," Zvena said, leaning down over the patient, looking for any other problems besides the obvious ones. "But you know what I am, yes? And you know what we do, yes?"

"You," Fyodor said and squirmed on the stained mattress, "you eliminate threats to the State."

"I like to think of it as gardening, pulling out weeds so useful crops can grow. You should be one of those weeds, but as chance has it, I have a recruitment space to fill. Do you think you are worthy to join us in the Human+ section?"

"Ha!" A hoarse laugh erupted out of Fyodor's sour-smelling mouth. "What, and become a productive member of society? With medals and a pension after thirty years? Is that what you are promising me?"

Zvena's gargantuan torso loomed over the man. For all his good bone structure, Fyodor looked like a waterlogged corpse. With no effort at all, Zvena's right hand reached out and crushed the metal bed railing in anger.

"No. I promise you this: worse pain than you've ever felt in your life," Zvena said. "And if you survive that… more pain, and true suffering! But you will also earn a narrow pathway back to honor and humanity so you can finally be worthy enough to apologize to your parents and your nation for becoming… this."

"The test," Fyodor said. "It was advanced programming. You need someone who can code."

It was also the suspension of a death sentence. If he failed the test, Zvena had resolved to kill Fyodor. He would be useless to the Human+ division but still a man with dangerous computer skills. Such a person, an addict, could not be allowed to join a criminal drug-smuggling gang.

"We also need someone who can accept augmentation. Your blood type and tissue samples make you a good candidate. Well, most of you."

"What do you—" Fyodor's eyes grew to the size of tea saucers when he saw what Zvena pulled out of his satchel.

"This is the largest portable cable cutter Milwaukee Tool Company makes. It is the best. It can cut through steel rope thick enough to tether a big container ship."

"Y-you're going to cut my cuffs off?"

"Not exactly. Watch closely. This is how it works. You put what you want severed between these nice wide jaws. Push this trigger button, and… ha. Like that."

In one quick motion, Zvena gripped the handcuff chain holding Fyodor's left hand to the bed frame. The cordless Milwaukee cutter snapped shut, snicking the steel chain cleanly through and then opening its jaws to maximum wide again.

"You are going to free yourself. It is your final exam before joining the world of normal Russians serving their country."

The cable cutters ran on a strong battery and could be operated with one hand. Zvena put them into the grip of the young man's newly freed left hand. Then he took a Sharpie marker and drew a circle completely around Fyodor's right elbow. He made sure to include all the fattest nerve clusters.

"That arm has been eaten by the Krokodil. Freedom requires sacrifice. You will cut it off exactly where I have marked, or," Zvena said casually as he cinched a tourniquet tightly onto Fyodor's bicep, "I will come back and cut both your arms off. You will die, which will be a shame because Dr. Nail will have another mess to clean up."

"Fuck shit hell!" Fyodor squealed.

"Now you get it," Zvena said, a smile creasing along his steel-reinforced cheekbones. He put the cable cutter's business end on Fyodor's inner elbow. *"Rodina-mat' zovot!"* he said. The Motherland calls!

Zvena left. If Fyodor cut his bonds instead of his arm and tried to escape, he would die a coward. Instead, to the komandir's positive surprise, his enhanced cyborg hearing recorded the click-clacking sound of the Milwaukee cutter and the sound of ripping cartilage. Fyodor's shrieking did not require cyborg ears to detect. Anyone in the detox ward could hear that.

Dr. Nail had been attending just outside the door to the cupboard.

"You know, we'll have to take that rotting thing off at the shoulder," the physician said. "It would have been less painful to cut there."

"I know. But this way will show he has maximum commitment."

"True." Dr. Nail nodded. "Now, Yari, I found some Beluga Gold vodka. A gift from a former patient. Have a drink while I sew up your new recruit."

To Komandir Zvena, that sounded like a good plan.

An hour later, Private Fyodor had signed his Navy papers volunteering for the Human+ initiative. The signature was messy due to him having to sign with his left hand, and Zvena let the blood-smeared document dry before folding it into his pocket.

"Rodion," Zvena called to his oversized helper. "When the doctor says he is all right to transport, bring him to the van and call the airfield."

Rodion's face, which always reminded him of a rhinoceros with no horns, looked flustered. The new cyborgs had bifurcated brains and could survive half their heads being shot off. The procedure made them a bit slow.

"What?" Zvena asked.

"Komandir," Rodion mumbled, "there was a communication."

"Don't worry. I told you not to interrupt. What's the message?"

"It's double encrypted and came over the Lux/Net system."

That could only be one person, an anonymous mole deep in Europe's technology industry. Since he or she would not meet or confirm their identity, Russia's main intelligence agency, the GRU, had passed on developing this asset. GRU thought the person was a waste of time and resources.

Zvena was seeking to increase the intelligence network of the Human+ division, so he had claimed the asset. Only Putin was aware of the radical but intriguing claims the source was making.

"*Mu-dak.*" Shithead.

"Sorry," Rodion stuttered. "I did record the transmission."

"Give me that before you break it." Zvena grabbed the delicate-looking device, which looked like a transparent bank card, from Rodion.

Zvena got into their transport van and closed the Faraday cage netting. In the field, it was the closest one could get to an embassy "safe room," insulated against sound and radio wave spying.

Zvena didn't trust this neutrino-based technology, but his technical people assured him Lux/Net was unhackable, and only Lichtwerks Corp itself could tamper with the signal.

He touched the "play" hologram.

"This is Zarathustra, respond now."

The voice spoke digitized Russian with no accent, but somehow it conveyed distress. The first time this source had shown any emotion besides cold-blooded self-interest.

"Respond... Pick up... Okay, you are not there, dammit. Listen to me: The Event is real. It is happening, and sooner than anyone thought. I have technical proof, but you must extract me and get me to a safe location. T-Day is November 1. I— damn!"

The message cut off. The sender was perhaps afraid of being caught while making contact. Zvena took a moment to think.

"Rodion!"

Zvena exited the van. His junior officer was carrying a stretcher under one arm. Fyodor's unconscious form and an automated IV system were strapped to it.

"Put him down in the mud somewhere. Help me set up a secure satellite connection to Moscow."

18

AMSTERDAM

ELLIE

"Where's Wolfgang?" Ranulph Oliphant's voice sounded cross.

Ellie felt a surge of hot blood rise to her cheeks. She was supposed to be watching the white-haired oligarch while the others were talking by the heliport office. Had she dozed off? She'd been up for who knew how long. It was the middle of the night, and she had just found out that sometime in the past, her man Atticus had a love child with an insane mass killer with whom she was sharing a mansion in Mayfair.

Ellie looked around. Wolfgang must be close by. She'd just taken her eyes off him for a moment. She walked through the empty cargo area of the Chinook. Behind the empty cockpit was a doorway. There he was.

"What are you doing?" she yelled at him.

Wolfgang Licht had his broad back turned and looked like he was adjusting his space flight suit. It was a red-and-white synthetic outfit, the one he'd had on when they took him off the rocket capsule after it crashed in the sea.

"Huh?" He turned. "I don't answer to you. I am not a prisoner."

"Go, then." Ran came up behind Ellie. "Go, and I'll send recordings of all the blathering you did under the truth drug to Scotland Yard and my friend Tenny Sewart, the foreign minister."

Tenny... Ellie remembered the name with a vivid flashback of shock. He was the wanker who had bounced her into the chain of events that led to the 96-Hour War in the Middle East. He was in the new Tory government. Small bloody continent.

The threat settled Wolfgang's hash. Ellie looked at him more closely. There was something off about his clothing.

"I don't know anything about, well... anything that's going on," Ellie said. "Not T-bombs or brain-wave EMPs. But I know clothing and fabrics."

Before the older man could object, she grabbed at Wolfgang's collar. "This doesn't line up with the other side."

Upon examination, the jacket collar had a Lux/Net communicator sewn into it.

"Who were you talking to?" Ran Oliphant demanded.

"My lawyers," Wolfgang shot back. He yanked his lapel out of Ellie's hand. "By the time we are done, you'll be reduced to milking sickly Scottish cows in goddamn Scotland!"

In his anger, the tech titan had forgotten the imminent end of the world, which would seem to make lawsuits and cows and pretty much everything all over Europe irrelevant.

"He's full of shite," Ms. China said. "Let's give him some more truth serum. This soon after the first dose, there's only a fifty-fifty chance of a brain hemorrhage."

"Forget it," Ran said. "We've talked it over. We need more information and stronger allies we can trust. The only people we can be sure are not complicit with these Pangeans are the Americans. We're going to Ramstein Air Base right this minute."

Their travel plans took longer than a minute.

"I want one million pounds, or you can walk," their pilot, the owner of the Chinook, said. He'd clearly been well paid for his extended journey but wanted to gouge Ran because he was rich. However, Mr. Oliphant was also from the Highlands.

"There," Ran said, holding up a handset. "I'm ready to transfer what we agreed on per hour, all your costs, and a ten-thousand-pound bonus. Payable only when we land at the American base. Otherwise we'll get another ride."

After some grumbling, they took off. Sarge Bryan used his military ID to get flight clearance. Ran kept watch over Wolfgang. Melanie Françoise leaned over to make sure he was strapped into his seat and inadvertently smushed her huge hair into his nose. He sneezed like an elephant seal.

From a map Ellie saw, Ramstein was at the bottom end of Germany and, at the speeds mandated by EU air traffic control, the flight would take over two hours. That was quite possibly long enough to straighten out some breaking progeny news with Ms. China.

"So," Ellie said with a fixed smile on her face and the offer of a beverage, "you knew Atticus Reidt before Jerusalem."

Ms. China took the insulated travel mug of coffee from her. In the dim red light of the helicopter's cargo bay, her facial tattoos gave her the appearance of a figure out of an ancient Egyptian mural.

"Uh-huh." She sipped and tried to look innocent. This was tough for a world-class poisoner and chemical-weapons expert.

Before she could launch into a polite interrogation of how the nine-year-old Atticus Jr. came about, some other coincidences nagged at Ellie through the fog of her sleep-deprived brain.

"Wait a second." She gasped. "You decided to appoint me your mental health guardian the same day my apartment blew up."

"Did I?"

When people responded to a question with another question, something was always up.

"Then there was also your odd familiarity with London's underworld. You knew exactly where to find scummy drug dealers at that abandoned church. Those people were selling drugs like those manufactured by my late downstairs neighbor."

Feroze, the poor fellow with the spiky blue hair, had been blown up and killed by his own meth lab on her former building's fifth floor.

"Give it up, Annunciata," Ellie said quite sternly, loudly enough that Sarge Bryan glanced at them.

"I don't know what you, er…"

"C'mon. You're certified mad. It's not like you can be prosecuted."

"Oh, all right," Ms. China said, batting her pale eyelashes over her six pupils. "I just wanted to find out more about you."

"So you stalked me and flambéed my downstairs neighbor?"

"I'm a chemist from MI-6. After I finished looking around your apartment, I smelled something interesting on the next floor down. I broke in there and had a look at his setup. Feroze was literally making crank in his bathtub. His cooking operation would have blown up soon anyway." Ms. China crinkled her nose in professional disapproval.

"Remember, Ellie, I did set off the fire alarm remotely to make sure everyone and their pets were out of the building before I pushed the detonator to give the red phosphorous a little jiggle. Not my fault he was so afraid of being arrested he refused to leave his stupid lab."

"All my stuff!"

"You shouldn't get attached to possessions. All my therapists agree."

"They're doing such a splendid job on you too!"

The only upside was that it was clear Ms. China did not want to off her. She'd had plenty of means and opportunities over the last few days, Ellie thought with a shudder.

"Attie Jr. thinks well of you," Ms. China said, trying to be congenial. "He's become quite attached to you."

"He has?" Ellie had only met the boy a few times.

"His dad must go on and on and on about you after your video conference calls," Ms. China said, rolling her eyes, which made Ellie dizzy because of how many pupils were involved. "I went through all that trouble so we could be flatmates because I needed to make sure you weren't the dippy scatterbrain you seemed to be in Israel. For my son's sake, you see."

Ellie wasn't sure what to say.

"The Reidt family disapproves of me," Ms. China said in a tone that betrayed her bruised feelings. "You don't disapprove of me, do you?"

"I agreed to be your guardian, didn't I?" Ellie said, hoping the volatile woman would not lapse into another fit of weeping.

"Yes!" Ms. China said, brightening and gently taking Ellie's hand with her poison-tipped fingers. "I can feel an indelible bond growing between us."

The rather invigorating Dutch brew of coffee got cold. Then it was all gone by the time they arrived at the air base. Ellie had been to military installations in the Middle East. She imagined Ramstein would be similar—a command post and a bare airfield. It was not. It was a huge sprawling city with suburbs, a golf course, and a theme park mall. The runways reminded her of Heathrow and seemed just as bustling.

"This is the largest community of Americans outside the States," Sarge Bryan said, joining her at an observation port as the Chinook landed. "About sixty thousand service people and their families live here."

Ran Oliphant grabbed Wolfgang by the torn collar of his jacket where they had cut out his secret communication device.

"Don't even think about asking for some bullshit asylum from the Yanks," he cautioned.

Wolfgang's lips compressed into a thin line, but he said nothing.

"Wait here," Sarge said, his eyes piercing the pre-morning gloom. He pointed to a jeep a hundred meters away from their landing pad. "Looks like they've got our temporary base IDs ready. I'll go check if Atticus is back."

He was. And if Ellie thought he looked a little downcast when he drove up with the Ramstein guards, his expression turned positively apoplectic when he saw Ms. China.

"You…"

"Hi, Attie." Ms. China linked arms with Ellie and walked off the back of the helicopter's ramp. "Sur-prise! Ellie Sato and I are besties now. Aside from fighting villains together in the occasional street barney, we've done nothing but talk about you."

"You…" Atticus, who was a little taller than and nearly as broad as Sarge Bryan, looked very helpless indeed. His face and neck just kept getting redder.

"Use your words, dear," Ms. China said. "And hurry. According to Wolfgang here, we haven't much time."

"You are supposed to be in a maximum-security mental hospital," Atticus finally managed. "For life."

"Well, y'know." Ms. China shrugged. She let Ellie go and gave Atticus a swift hug and mock kisses on his cheeks. "Cuts to the NHS. They needed the bed for someone who is really out of their mind. Where's my little Attie-poo junior?"

"In the officers' barracks." Atticus looked at Ellie, his expression indefinable. "You two, uh…?"

"See, Ellie?" Ms. China said. "That's why it never worked out between us. He's got the body of Adonis and the IQ of an undercooked haggis."

"It's really a funny story," Ellie began.

"We're flatmates," Ms. China said. "In fact, if the world wasn't ending, we'd still be in Mayfair having a riot."

Sarge Bryan introduced the rest of their group.

"This is Ranulph Oliphant, president of Eurolincx, and Dr. Françoise is his…"

"Hairdresser, dressage instructor, and head of Scientific Research," Melanie Françoise said. At this point, she had to hold her hair off her face to see anything, the humidity and sea air had made it droop like the mane of an English sheepdog.

"Hold me up. I can't see anything." Melanie had made a sling for the Hermes bag containing Miss Aleph's canister. Ellie had it draped very unfashionably over her shoulder and was having trouble keeping the handset camera propped up so that Miss Aleph could peek out.

"I know that voice," Atticus said, looking relieved to be talking about anything else than his love life. "Shalom, Miss Aleph, ma shlom-kha?"

"Major Reidt, quit pandering. Speaking Hebrew isn't for everyone."

"Looks like the gang's all here," Ms. China said.

Atticus shook his head and led them into the waiting van.

"I trust Sarge Bryan," Ran Oliphant said to Atticus as they started off for the main complex. "And he trusts you. We have quite a bit to tell you. But I see you know some of it."

Ran Oliphant pointed out the window to the line of planes and people waiting to board. "You Americans are obviously in the process of evacuating the airbase."

19

ELLIE

The Americans were evacuating from Europe.

Ellie's gut rose in her chest cavity as though all the cables had been cut in her personal elevator of doom. Up to this point, all the talk about T-bombs and dark-matter death rays had been so theoretical. Finding out the US military was abandoning this huge air base was like living underneath a dam and noticing the first gush of water leaking through cracks in its concrete surface.

"I forgot to mention," Sarge Bryan said. "Mr. Oliphant here is formerly of the 3 Commando British Marines. His company is a US military contractor, and he's got a high-level security clearance with the Pentagon."

Atticus nodded but remained quiet. They drove past a Taco Bell. Someone was watering the bushes outside, and the drive-thru window was lit.

"Do I have to do everything?" Ms. China blurted at Atticus. "I've been developing more valid intelligence on the Pangean threat than all of you put—"

"Wait until we're inside 201," Atticus said, cutting her off. Ellie could tell he was surprised and annoyed but also worried.

Ramstein's Building 201 was a squat five-story complex with a forest of antennae coming up from the flat roof. They were ushered into a windowless conference room. The doors shut with a hiss and a click.

"S-so, this crisis, it's real, like the atom bomb in Gaza." Ellie felt like she was not getting enough air, but her lungs were overfull at the same time. "That one went off. And the Knesset parliament bombardment, it... it's happening again, isn't it?"

Atticus got her a chair and some water.

Wolfgang slammed his fist on the table. "I am Dr. Licht. I have material information, but I won't cooperate under duress."

"Shut up, Wolfgang, or you'll have a double heaping of duress," Ran scolded. "We have all your material information on tape."

"Maybe you have some drug-torture-induced blither, but do you have a clue as to how to find the T-bomb installation? If I had my equipment and technicians in Der Lichtstrom..."

"You're not leaving my sight," Ran said, turning to Atticus. "He's been in contact with whoever's behind this. They call themselves Pangeans."

Melanie played the recording Licht had made which invited him into the Pangeans' horrific conspiracy.

"You learned all that, booked your ticket to outer space, and still you said nothing?" Atticus said.

"What could I do?" Wolfgang sputtered. "I am only one man."

"With your own country," Melanie said.

"He... he's right, though," Ellie said, getting herself back together. She had survived the orbital bombardment of Jerusalem; she could make a difference here. Though cashing in all her air miles and running to Argentina where her parents were vacationing did cross her mind. "We don't know who to trust. Just like the development of the Khóshekh virus and the overthrowing of the Jordanian monarchy, state-level actors must be involved in this."

Atticus looked at her. He nodded and sat on the other side of the bare conference room table, thinking. Ran Oliphant looked at her like he was seeing her for the first time.

"You're that woman on Jeremy Greffer's show," Ran said appreciatively. "The BBC claimed that during one of their shows you had a nervous breakdown and tried to throw yourself off the Gherkin skyscraper."

"They're just jealous of real reporters."

"Attie, where have you been these past few days?" Ms. China said pointedly. "We've been trying to ring you since St. Albans."

Atticus remained silent for another moment. Finally, he said, "Since you seem to know more than we do..."

He explained that US Central Command had heard rumors of strange troop movements by Euro Forces, the secretive combined military force that was supplanting NATO in the European Union. Washington had also questioned Brussels about the nuclear reactors going into safe mode but had received no reply.

Atticus told them the Americans had not shared any of their suspicions with NATO, since that would be as good as sharing everything directly with Turkey. That country was technically still a NATO member, but Ankara was becoming increasingly aligned with jihadi states bent on a scorched-earth ethnic cleansing war against the Kurds.

"There were just bits and pieces of human intelligence from CIA and signals intelligence from NSA. We could never pin anything down," Atticus said and unfurled a digital map screen over the table. "Major jihadi leaders, radical imams, and all five presidents of the European Union have left the continent on short notice. So have most of your Davos Group friends, Mr. Oliphant."

"I noticed, and the vast majority of them are bungholes," Ran said dryly. He looked at Wolfgang. "I might be in New Zealand with them except for someone's connivance to keep me close to London."

"We thought whatever the bad actors were planning might involve a device stolen from the Israelis," Atticus said. "The usual terror suspects claim that since Israel set off a nuke in Gaza, they have an Islamic obligation to repay the attack one thousand times over."

"Iran and Pakistan won't give jihadis nukes."

"Maybe terrorists have one of the missiles from the *Magen*." Atticus pointed to a blue area near the top of Italy. "It is one of the most lethal and stealthy nuclear subs in the world. It's still missing."

Atticus drew lines outward from central Europe and continued. "DARPA in the US theorized some highly sophisticated terror group might be using a stolen atom bomb as a primer trying to replicate a Tsar Bomb, the Soviet weapon that produced the largest nuclear explosion in history. Their top scientist, Mr. Perdix, theorized they might hide a cluster of fissionable material at the bottom of Italy's Lake Como, which is four hundred meters deep."

"Intriguing."

Everyone looked at the orange Hermes bag with the electronic brain inside.

"The heavy metal pollutants and mineral content of Lake Como would yield a very nice aerosolized radiation plume, and the prevailing winds…"

"I've just been to Lake Como. There's nothing there," Atticus said decisively. "Perdix, DARPA, and the Joint Chiefs are stumped. But we can't take chances with this many service people and their families. Because of what was going on with the EU military and civilian engineers, we decided to quietly evacuate Ramstein and all other major facilities."

"How is Perdix?" Ms. China asked.

"Much better since he stopped getting your poisoned letters," Atticus said. "He says in the future, you can text him."

Ellie noted that Miss Aleph had not said anything about the *Magen*. The AI had disappeared at the same time as the last part of Israel's strategic defense, only to turn up in her London mailbox a few days ago.

Melanie leaned forward, wound pieces of her long blonde hair around her finger, and studied the result. "Any T-bomb device would need time to achieve full power. And as I concluded while I was trying to fix my hair, you'd need a reflector, a really big one shaped like a Fibonacci spiral, a hundred meters or more long. It might be easier to hide that underwater."

"We found nothing, and we have nowhere else to look."

Ran prodded Wolfgang. "Well? Is that right? Are we looking for something that big?"

"I refuse to answer any questions and demand protection from the American government."

Atticus ignored Wolfgang and said with forced dismissiveness, "This T-bomb could be another myth."

"And what if it's not?" Ms. China said sharply, her fingernails coming dangerously close to Atticus's hands as she snatched the map of Europe away from him. "Why weren't you on the first evacuation plane? What kind of parental guardian are you?"

20

ELLIE

O
h, there's my little boy!" Ms. China chirped.

Attie Jr. was nine; his hair was lighter and curlier than his father's. Ellie noticed that he looked at his mother with a distinct sense of wariness.

"Oh, come here." Ms. China hugged him, making sure to keep her fingernails away from his exposed skin. "Has Daddy been feeding you well?"

"Yes, ma'am."

Atticus handed Ellie two plastic keycards. "Here are your travel passes for the military transport. They may make some stopovers, and there will be health checks at Fort Bragg, but this is all the ID you will need."

Being crazy but not delusional, Ms. China realized she was a fugitive from extended mental care in the UK. Just inputting her name into the Ramstein transit system would raise all kinds of red flags. Atticus and Sarge Bryan had to stay in Germany to try and locate and neutralize the threat and help with the evacuation. That left Ellie as the only person Attie Jr.'s parents could agree on to be his flight nanny.

"Are you coming to America?" Attie Jr. said as he hefted his kid-sized green duffel bag. A game joystick and a rolled-up comic book poked out of the cinched-up end of his bag.

"Yes," Ellie said. "All the way to your grandparents' house."

"You'll like it there."

"Thanks."

At the departure gate, Atticus and Ms. China watched them file onto the flight. It was a big gray plane and was filling up with military personnel and their families. She waved back to them. Ellie was relieved. This was the right thing to do.

Yet as the doors snapped shut and everyone got buckled into their seats, Ellie couldn't help thinking: What if it was true? What if the people she was leaving behind failed? This would be the last she saw of her home. The buildings might be standing, but everyone in every country of Europe…

She tried not to think about it, made sure Attie Jr. had his lap strap on properly, and looked across the aisle to one of the few windows in the transport plane. A little girl was balancing a stuffed monkey against the glass. It reminded her of their mascot in the Holy Land, the capuchin called Marwood. The plane's vibration kept making it fall off. The child diligently pushed him back on, then she waved his little fur-covered arm at the runway and the buildings which were reflecting the rising sun.

Monkeys! Shit, shit, shit.

Ellie would have hit herself, except that might have alarmed Attie Jr. She looked left and right. They were in the middle of a row of six. Two pairs of chubby, grumpy-looking soldiers sat to either side of them.

Forget it. Stupid notion.

The plane unlatched from the loading ramp. She heard the doors hiss closed. Ellie looked at Attie Jr. He was fiddling with some tiny console game. The attendant asked him to put it away, which he did and pulled out his comic book.

If she said nothing, they'd carry on and eventually land in America. Was the stupid, long-shot silly notion she had worth…?

Then Ellie remembered all the people vaporized in Gaza and the millions more who would have died if that bomb had not destroyed the bulk of the weaponized Khóshekh virus. She'd gotten Sarge Bryan and Atticus Sr. out of Drach's Knesset bunker and had the burn marks on her wrists to prove it. Atticus, DARPA, and Mr. Oliphant, they all seemed baffled about where to even start looking for the T-bomb. She had an idea… maybe. And it was not anything she could text to them and hope it got followed up on.

"Excuse me, you've got to stop the flight! I've got to get off immediately," she heard herself say. Attie looked up at her. "Sorry, I have to do something. You'll get home on the very next flight."

After some hullabaloo, Ellie and the boy made it out to the aisle. Just before she was about to be pinned to the ground by in-flight security, she shoved her fat plastic ID at the crewmen. They put it through an optical scanner.

"Yes, sir," the crewman said to the pilot over his radio. "The ID says Eleanor Sato, British national intelligence services."

Back in the Middle East, Ellie had been on a diplomatic spy passport. Luckily the American system still had that old information.

"Okay, everyone," the pilot said over the intercom. *"Thanks to the Limey, we've got a little delay. When we eventually do fly over England, please no one flush the johns."*

Ellie kept a smile frozen on her face as she sidestepped along the seats of the crowded flight. The ramp was put back in place. As she left, an Asian man and a black woman twice his size, both of whom had obviously been on standby, gratefully got on the flight.

Even before she and Attie Jr. had walked all the way down, the ramp moved away from the plane. Atticus Reidt and Ms. China came running up. At first they looked alarmed. Soon, though, they just looked pissed.

"Why? Why did you ditch that flight?" Atticus fumed as they walked back to the terminal. "Do you know what I had to do to get you on it?"

Ms. China just stared with her six pupils, drumming her long clawlike fingernails on the laminate top of a table in the waiting area.

"I-I don't know."

"You don't know?" Atticus said. He looked over at his son, who was playing his game. He lowered his voice but sounded even harsher. "Of all the damned selfish things. I thought you were responsible."

That made Ellie cross. "If you think I'm an idiot, why didn't you take Attie Jr. back home yourself?"

"I have orders."

"Well," Ellie said, thinking for a moment, "I have orders too. I am ordering myself to stay and fight for the continent."

Atticus and Ms. China looked at each other. It did occur to Ellie that what she said made her sound like she, and not Ms. China, was the mental patient.

The next flight out from Ramstein was only going as far as England. Before Atticus tried to get his son on it, he tried to make sure Ms. China's parents could meet Attie Jr. at the airport when he got to the UK.

The complication was that Ms. China's parents, who lived in Cornwall, had won a trip to Vancouver Island to go whale watching. They had been notified of this good fortune the same day Miss Aleph had brought tidings of the pending annihilation of Europe.

"Okay, okay, I bought them the tour," Ms. China confessed, giving Ellie the evil eye. "They're gone already. Since the traveling nanny here is on strike, there's no one to take Attie Jr. to the States."

Ellie improvised. "Attie can go to England by himself, and my editor, Smitty, will meet him and take him the rest of the way. Mr. Oliphant can fly them to America via private charter."

"Why would your editor do that?" Ms. China said skeptically.

"Because I'm going to give him the exclusive on how we saved the lives of five hundred million people."

After some phone calls and text messages, most of Attie Jr.'s itinerary was set, but it still needed final approval from air transit. The prospective flight would land at RAF Upwood. Ran's driver and private security would pick up Attie Jr. there and drive to London to meet the *Juggernaut*'s editor.

Immediately after the travel arrangements were settled, they were all reassembled in the officers' briefing room next to where Atticus was billeted. Ran, Melanie, Wolfgang, Ms. China, Atticus, and Sarge Bryan all turned to her. It took her a second to realize why.

"Oh," Ellie said, feeling perspiration suddenly bead on her upper lip. This was worse than getting up in front of the Oxford Union debating society. "Yes. My breakthrough. It involves monkeys."

She explained her notion and brought up the relevant news story she had half heard while she was in the *Juggernaut* office a few days prior.

"Monkeys?" Ms. China scoffed.

"Dead chimps to be precise," Ellie said. "I put the two together when I thought about Marwood."

"What is Marwood?" Wolfgang snapped irritably. "Is this woman *verrückt*?"

"Our capuchin team member was nicer and more helpful than you, Dr. Licht," Ellie said curtly. "I thought if the Pangeans had a T-ray weapon, they'd have to test it. And from what Wolfgang described, they would have trouble controlling it because the deadly energies go through miles of rock."

Ellie found the projector controls and scrolled over to a map of Europe. "The zoo where the deaths occurred was in the vicinity of the French-Spanish border. The nearest city is Bordeaux."

"There's nothing there," Ms. China said shortly.

"I don't doubt your sincerity, Ms. Sato, ma'am," Sarge Bryan said. "But a few dead animals is kind of a slim basis for action."

"It also goes back to what Wolfgang said," Ellie persisted, thinking what a royal cockup it would be if her idea wasn't the least bit credible. "These Tyr quark waves can be tuned to affect certain tissues only, specifically those in the human brain."

"Yah," Wolfgang said. "Like the radiosurgery procedure using a gamma-knife pure-energy scalpel. It can treat vascular malformations inside the skull remotely. In the Havana Syndrome attacks, no lower animals were affected; only the brains of humans were irreversibly altered."

Atticus looked at her with a sort of sheepish but thoughtful expression, which Ellie would have found endearing, but she was still cross with him for having a go at her earlier. He grabbed the tablet with the computer map.

"There's not nothing there," Atticus said.

"Can I just say, for you humans, this is where it gets creepy," Miss Aleph said from her handbag. She was obviously aware of what Atticus was referring to.

"Unlock NATO classified grid for France," Atticus said.

The room's computer obeyed. On the screen, small red dots with radiological symbols appeared all over French territory.

"France has the third-largest stockpile of nuclear warheads in the world, more than China and Pakistan combined. The French have the most nuclear power reactors in Europe, and this place"—he pointed to a place near the zoo fatalities—"is Cesta Station. The *Commissariat à l'énergie atomique* is located between Bordeaux and Arcachon."

Wolfgang laughed. He and Miss Aleph were the only ones having a good time. "Yes, now I recall. They've got a gigajoule laser even larger than the one at the Lichtstrom. CEA Cesta can accurately test nuclear explosions without detonating a weapon."

"You think it's funny?" Ran snapped at the oligarch. He leaned over the defiant-looking older man and wrinkled his nose. "You smell. Why don't we take you for a shower and a change?"

"What do we do now?" Melanie asked.

"Not contacting the French would be a good idea," Ellie said assertively. Her notions of everything that was transpiring were not entirely unshakable, but Bordeaux was her lead and that made her feel a little emboldened. "We don't know who might be involved, and worst case, if this is a dead end, we don't want anyone to know what we're looking for."

Atticus snapped off the overhead map projector. "Let me talk to the SOCOM officer on the base. He can authorize a recon action without having to know much."

He met her outside the conference room.

"Uh, Ellie, I…" he began sheepishly.

She held up a finger. "A famous designer once told me that gifts are the sincerest form of apology. And don't you dare try to stop me from attending this reconning outing."

He nodded, resigned. Then Ms. China yanked him away, and they walked off to make sure their son got on his flight this time.

Ellie picked up Miss Aleph's Hermes handbag by its shoulder strap. The handset, which the AI used to see and hear, was poking out. Its camera lens was pointed up at her.

"So, Eleanor, you selflessly and bravely got off a flight to safety and returned to nearly certain doom." Miss Aleph's beady digital eye glinted.

"Sucker."

21

"Another priority transport request, Major Reidt, sir?" a man's skeptical voice asked from the speakerphone of the handset Atticus was holding.

Ellie walked back to the officers' lounge where Attie Jr. was waiting.

"Two," Atticus shot back, cheerily smiling with genial charisma that set Ellie's heart fluttering, though she was still technically browned off with him for calling her selfish. "First off, we need a single seat on the next flight to Upwood."

Ms. China hovered menacingly nearby. She obviously blamed Ellie for Attie Jr. missing his flight.

"What else?" the sarcastic Ramstein logistics officer asked. "A Kiowa jet hovercopter, or a lift to the International Space Station?"

"The second part is need-to-know," Atticus said. "Check the authorization for Project Casino Royale."

Ellie raised an eyebrow.

Atticus muted the line. "That was the Lake Como mission. It should still be an active covert file, and we can get resources without having to file a new mission plan."

"The major here is a fan of classic Bond films," Sarge Bryan said, slapping his friend on the back.

While travel plans were being organized, Ms. China looked at the African albino man thoughtfully. "Would you mind having a look at this lock?" She raised her leg onto the back of a couch, revealing tiny whorls of gold-and-silver tattoos. Ms. China raising her pants leg quite a bit more than was needed to reveal the monitor strapped to her ankle. "The signal has been cloned; they still think I'm in London. But Melanie was hopeless at getting the lock undone back in St. Albans. This Faraday cage it's wrapped in is beginning to chafe."

During their time in the Middle East, Ellie had learned that Sarge Bryan's cybernetic eye implants were capable of signaling Morse code to a helicopter a mile away and also melting plastic zip-tie handcuffs. Though the latter trick burned out their circuits and had left Bryan unable to see normally until they were fixed, they could surely help undo a fugitive's ankle tag.

"Sure, ma'am."

With a multitool and x-ray vision, they managed to pick the lock without disabling the device. Ms. China then promptly cinched it around Attie Jr's leg.

"Huh?" the boy said.

"Anna," Atticus snapped at Annunciata China. "I've had enough surprises for one day."

"Miss Aleph says she can reprogram the transponder to work over the Maritime Traffic system." Ms. China fixed Attie Jr's pants leg, but he still looked lopsided with the adult-sized criminal monitor around his nine-year-old ankle. "This way we can track you all the way home, dear. It's nearly as good as having someone reliable to take you."

Ms. China shot Ellie a look.

"Fine," Atticus said. "Now quiet. Dispatch is getting back to us."

Attie Jr's flight pass was switched to a plane taking off soon headed for the UK. However, Operation Casino Royale had hit a snag.

"That file has timed out," the dispatcher said.

"In European time, maybe," Atticus said smoothly. "But it's a Langley-DARPA op and on their budget, not ours. So maybe it could expire on East Coast time, six hours from now."

There was a burst of static as the dispatcher puffed a breath of incredulity into his mic. After some cajoling, they were able to obtain transport to Cesta Station in France.

"You've got an Airbus 215 helicopter," the dispatcher said. "It is an unarmed civilian transport; the manifest lists you as grape fungus inspectors from the European Union's agriculture department."

As much as Ellie had had enough of bloody helicopter flying, she was determined to follow through on her lead. They had tried to research the topic of the recently dead simians, but all news stories about the incident had vanished, and the zoo in question was not replying to any communications.

They left the officers' quarters and headed to their designated airfield. The roar of jets taking off and maneuvering was constant. The Airbus copter was painted white, and its seats looked much more comfortable than the Chinook, but it was smaller. One of their party was not happy.

"I'm not going anywhere near the Cesta facility," Wolfgang protested.

Ellie noticed that he had waited until they were outside to make a scene. To keep him quiet, it was decided Ran and Melanie would stay at Ramstein and watch over history's worst astronaut.

Ms. China got a Jeep ride to the other end of the airfield to make sure Attie Jr. got on his flight.

Ellie carried Miss Aleph and followed Sarge Bryan and Atticus to the Airbus. They looked like the least likely grape inspectors ever as they joined the two pilots, a pair of stout women with matching crew cuts.

"Looks like a one-way trip for you," one of the pilots said with a laugh as a dribble of chewing tobacco came out of the side of her mouth. "We're off the clock after we ferry you out to this Bor-dough place."

The Airbus took off, swiftly veering away from the main runway and the stack of transport planes circling Ramstein base. The evacuations happening on the big military installation made the threat more immediate.

Ellie looked at her handset; it was October 24. The ghastly thing these Pangeans were planning, would it really happen by November 1? Ellie glanced down at Miss Aleph's shiny metallic cylinder, which was strapped into the middle seat. Maybe she really was a sucker for staying.

Soon they were flying over lush French fields bursting with autumn colors. A huge château with hundreds of rooms and a driveway long and wide enough to land a plane slid past her porthole.

"I can't believe anyone would want to destroy all this," Ellie said under her breath.

Miss Aleph heard her. "If a T-bomb works in the way Wolfgang speculates, after it goes off, 'all that' will still be there."

"It would leave the buildings standing," Atticus concluded bitterly. "People's brains would be turned to mush."

"Didn't they have something like that during the Cold War?" Sarge Bryan asked as he zoomed in on the cockpit's GPS display and checked it against the flight path sketched on his paper map.

"You're thinking of the 'enhanced radiation weapons,' also known as neutron bombs. Those were comparatively crude devices. Lethal ionizing radiation extended only three times the physical blast radius. Nothing to write home about. This weapon would have a thousand-mile kill zone."

"Crap," Sarge Bryan said. "Are you sure? Sounds like science fiction."

"Sergeant, in 1835 the cutting edge of warfare was the Colt revolver. People were still shooting each other with muzzle-loading rifles. One hundred years later in 1945 you were dropping atomic bombs. This is nearly a century after that innovation.

"From the research I've done into the Tyr quark, as with the H-bomb, a weapon based on dark-matter physics would have no limit as to scale."

Except what the evil minds behind it could imagine, Ellie thought.

About an hour into the flight, she broached the subject that had been nagging her ever since Ms. China had blurted out the truth about Attie Jr.

"So, Atticus, you were in the UK about ten years ago," Ellie said, trying to sound as casual as she could.

Sarge Bryan's pale face split with a grin he tried to hide by looking out the window on his side.

R.K. SYRUS

"It's kind of a long story," Atticus said. "And some of it's classified."

"My albino ass, it's classified," Sarge Bryan put in.

"Soldier!"

"Sir, my albino ass, Major, sir," Bryan said, his breath cut short by laughter.

"Back then," Atticus said, as though he was under mild interrogation, "Anna... she was different."

It was good to hear her man had not been attracted to the current version of Ms. China: a serial poisoner covered from head to toe in metallic body art.

"She was a first-rate biologist and newly graduated medical doctor. She worked for the Scottish chapter of Doctors Without Borders in Syria when I was deployed to Raqqa to deal with ISIS."

"Sheeit," Sarge said. "And I thought Kandahar was hairy. When we liberated the city, we found big trash bins filled with nothing but human heads."

"It was even worse in other parts of Syria. That conflict saw the first large-scale use of chemical weapons since the First World War. Annunciata left suddenly. She stopped talking to her family and took up with a cult dedicated to Zoroastrianism."

"And Attie?"

"He was a baby at the time; she signed full custody over to me. I hardly saw her until two years ago when we dropped in on her at the British Embassy in Jerusalem."

"Well, for what it's worth, she still cares," Ellie assured him.

Of course, she felt it would be advisable not to mention this "caring for him" had compelled Ms. China to stalk Ellie, level an apartment block in London, and burn a methamphetamine producer to death.

"Ellie," Atticus said, turning toward her, "I'm sorry about what I said after you ditched the flight. I might have... no, I'm sure I would have done the same."

"I shouldn't have put Attie Jr. in the middle of things."

Atticus took her hand. "He's on his way to Britain by now, and thanks to your ideas we have a solid lead."

"Excuse me." Ellie's arm was stretched across Miss Aleph's seat, blocking her camera lens.

– 148 –

Under their aircraft, a long lake sped by. Someone in a field of green, healthy-looking vegetables looked up and waved, or maybe they were just being bothered by a bee.

When Ellie next glanced out, they were over some wild, marshy country. Slim shallow waterways cut through moist earth festooned with yellowing scrub brush. A shallow-bottomed boat had become stuck. Its owner was using a long pole to prod himself free.

Ellie wondered how many people a T-bomb could kill. Would they just drop dead? The first person she'd ever seen killed was a Kurdish separatist. One of her friends, Mr. Borkin, stabbed him through the neck with a bayonet. But the villain had lived long enough to pull Mr. Borkin with him over the edge of a ravine.

Poor Mr. Borkin.

Then there was the suicide bomber outside Jericho. That woman was shot multiple times in the head and just dropped with barely a sound.

The prime minister of Israel and her cabinet were vaporized during a speech outside the Knesset. More than a million people died during the 96-Hour War. This couldn't be worse than that, could it?

"We're close," Atticus said. "Miss Aleph, jack into the communications channels. Is Cesta Station saying anything?"

`"Shush. Let me concentrate."`

Miss Aleph seemed more verbally aggressive now that she was confined to her eight-inch metal cylinder.

`"They see us. They seem to believe our cover story, thin as it is. Pilot: don't go any closer to Cesta Station. Did you just graduate from flying drones?"`

They were about six kilometers away. Ellie looked down. A few acres stood out from the surrounding farmland. It was fenced in and had a clearing that appeared firm enough to land on.

"Pilot says that's French government property. If we set down there, no one will come too close to us," Sarge Bryan said.

They landed on the small rise. If anyone had noticed them, they'd probably also spotted the EU Food, Farming, and Fisheries department logo, which had been hastily sprayed in green on the side of the copter.

"Great. Now we're miles away from a heavily guarded facility with only sidearms and no way in."

"The metal tube does have a point, Major," Sarge said as he slid the door open.

Ellie got out and stretched. She looked a hundred meters down the small rise they had landed on. Gigantic agricultural robots were plodding across fields.

"That's why I brought this." Atticus opened a medium-sized box. Inside was a mass of shimmering fabric.

"That's an Israeli Defense Forces active camouflage suit. Where did you steal that?"

"Since we saved the Middle East from the sequel to the Black Death plague, I figured they wouldn't mind if we borrowed one." Atticus worked his long, wide frame into the silvery overalls. "Now, Miss Aleph, I need you to create an untraceable link between the body cameras in this suit, the monitor here, and the command center back at Ramstein."

"That'll be complicated. American systems are clunky."

"That's why we're asking a genius like you."

"Okay, it's done. Thief."

There was only one suit, but Sarge Bryan seemed anxious to move out toward the French nuclear research facility.

"Sarge, stay here. Do what you can to keep the pilots here, even though they're technically off the clock." Atticus said. Then, looking ruefully at her, he added, "If Ellie insists on being on the front line, with you here at least I know she won't get into any trouble."

Ellie drank some bottled water. She had to stretch her legs. There was a copse of trees nearby. This was fenced-off land belonging to the government, so it seemed okay to wander a bit.

A few hundred meters away, robot-farm machinery was silently irrigating a field. She could not see Cesta Station at all. In the distance, high-tension wires converged at a point over the horizon.

She stepped forward to get a better look. Something crunched underfoot. She kicked away loose dirt and found the edge of a thick plastic sheet. Had someone buried rubbish? It was an awkward place for it. Only a dirt path led here. She leaned over and pulled up more of the plastic. Something was moving under the tarp, or maybe it was the breeze. She leaned down.

A filth-covered hand reached up out of the dirt and grabbed her shirt. Before she could yell out, a dozen more arms came up from the dark hole and seized her arms, grabbed at her hair, yanked at her neck, and covered her mouth. The squirming cold gray things dragged her under the tarp and down inside the musty-smelling gap in the earth.

22

KOMANDIR ZVENA

Flamethrowers. Why is it always flamethrowers? Komandir Zvena thought to himself as he approached the entrance to the command bunker under the Kremlin.

Someone on Putin's personal security staff had got it into his or her limited brain that the only way to stop a cyborg if it went rogue was with these ungainly napalm-spewing units. As he walked up from the road and past the suicide-bomb barriers, a pair of guards stared at him over the flame-sputtering ends of their weapons.

"Stop there, on the line," one milk-faced and terrified-looking guard yelled out to him over sandbags.

"I've traveled nonstop from St. Petersburg on the President's orders," Zvena yelled back, using his voice in amplified mode. "If you haven't noticed the uniform, we are on the same side."

They checked his pass three times, called their supervisor, and then their supervisor's boss, and only then let Zvena through. As the elevator doors closed, he glanced back down the tunnel to the entrance and shook his head. If a beast like his fellow cyborg Rodion was in full combat armor, the weapons the Kremlin guards had wouldn't even annoy him. They'd be more likely to set each other on fire than protect their president.

The elevator, which could travel horizontally and vertically, changed direction several times. He felt it lurch to a stop. After a pause lasting a minute, the door slid open, and Zvena was met by a sight more intimidating than flamethrowers: the smoky midnight-blue gaze of President Putin.

Belying his age and the many years of service he had given to Russia, Putin sprang forward with great agility and grasped Zvena's hand, shaking it vigorously. Putin was smiling, and that meant a great many evil enemies of the Russian people were about to die.

23

Despite headwinds, Temir's three airships had stealthily penetrated 250 kilometers from Ukraine into Russia. Temir's human right eye and opaque scarred left eye scanned over the instrument panel. No sign of pursuit or detection. Temir squirmed against the confinement of his cockpit. During their all-night flight, the most he could move in any direction was about three inches.

Like the boneless arm of an octopus, his left appendage could be forced to collapse and push forward past his shoulder. But when stretched thin like that, it no longer had the fine motor control required to operate the airship's controls. Temir navigated using his right hand and voice instructions to the flight computer.

Dawn was approaching; the headwinds had turned into tailwinds. Reaching awkwardly over, he switched the heads-up display to rearview mode. They might even make it to the next landing zone if everything was in order. It was not.

Eylül's dirigible was keeping pace; the Persian pilot lagged behind. The nose of the rearmost airship kept dipping as they floated sixty meters above dark trees lining a Russian valley. He needed a line of sight to establish a laser communicator signal lock with the straggler. He could not risk any radio signals. Instead Temir aimed the laser system at Eylül.

Daylight soon. He texted. *Slow down. Keep ship 3 in formation. Set down now.*

Temir needed to check the Persian's airship. It was well before astronomical dawn, the twilight which occurs when the sun is eighteen degrees below the horizon. This early landing would cost them many kilometers of progress. Had it been Eylül's fault he would have yelled at him. Temir held back his anger; it would do no good to create a hostile work environment with their new partner, not yet.

In silence, the three of them descended toward a predesignated empty field. Artificial intelligences in Turkey had scanned years of satellite imagery along Temir's route to identify spots which were the most isolated and free of cars and people during the last weeks of October.

When they were tethered to trees, the dirigibles changed color and surface texture to blend in with the ground and surrounding vegetation.

Just as Temir emerged from his tiny cockpit, Eylül came crashing through the woods toward him. Temir was about to strike him, then he realized his longtime companion was only making a few decibels of noise. The hours of silent flying had heightened the auditory sensitivity of his enhanced hearing.

"The Persian's sprung a leak," Eylül whispered.

"Then we fix it," Temir said. "Wait till sunrise so we can see what we're doing."

The major advantage of the vacuum design was that in the event of a leak, no gas had to be replaced. The disadvantage was the whole exterior of the small zeppelins were under immense pressure. Because the main body of the airships were a near-total vacuum, the weight of the atmosphere at sea level was pressing in on all sides, similar to water pressure on a deep-diving bathysphere.

After they had eaten and Jamshid the Persian had prayed at sunrise, they examined his ship.

"Looks like a bird strike." It was hard to tell with the ship in camouflage mode.

"I thought you said they were miraculously strong," Jamshid said arrogantly. "The Islamic Republic of Iran would build one more air worthy."

Temir and Eylül exchanged glances. Temir decided it would be too risky to dispose of their partner at this time. If it had no pilot, they would have to physically tether the third ship between the other two, reducing speed and maneuverability. He cursed quietly into his balled-up fist. It was better to be beset with boils or locusts than Persians as partners.

Temir said, "I'm sure we'll incorporate any improvement you suggest in our next versions."

Wouldn't it drive Jamshid insane if he knew the real reason the Grey Wolves had the airships and their rather unique cargo ready to deploy to Moscow so quickly? Temir and Meliha had been planning a surprise attack on the Iranians who were supporting the Shi'a militias in Southern Iraq. The bioweapon assault had been intended to drive them completely out of Iraq, perhaps all the way back to Tehran. Best of all, it could be blamed on the Jews.

Because of the Event, the target for their payload had changed. The Russians were in for a lesson from the rising New Ottoman Empire. The Persians would have to wait their turn.

"We'll have to isolate and inflate this damaged cell," Jamshid said sharply, betraying his ignorance immediately. "Otherwise my entire craft could rupture."

For a religious fanatic ready to martyr himself at Elder Omid's command, Jamshid certainly seemed interested in his own safety.

"No. Not with Turkish engineering."

The zeppelins were composed of boron nanotubes with eidetic memory. The molecular bonding force creating the vacuum was several times greater than the air pressure on the crafts' surfaces. Strong as this top skin was, even it needed a framework. That was provided by helium-filled struts that acted like the bones of a shark or whale.

By the time the patch on Jamshid's airship had set, it was mid-afternoon. Temir and Eylül were resting close to the landing spot. Jamshid came running back from the road, where he was not supposed to be wandering.

"People. Fucking Russians. I think they saw us."

Meaning they had seen Jamshid, because he was an imbecile. Temir and Eylül had remained well away from the country road and neither they nor their ships would have been spotted, even by someone walking right past them.

"Calm down. Let's check it out, quietly."

A minute later, Temir was lying flat, inching his way along the long dry grass to get a view through binoculars. It was a couple, a blond Russian boy and a pigtailed teenage girl. They had driven a dilapidated truck away from their village to smoke dope or fornicate or both. The couple would have gone home well before nightfall and never noticed them, except for the jihadi-at-large Jamshid.

The Persian ran up in a crouch beside Temir and sighted in with a suppressed weapon. The Russian couple was still in the old truck.

"Taste what's coming to all of you, Shaitan Kuffir," Jamshid muttered and prepared to fire.

Temir's left appendage struck Jamshid on the side of the head. His finger clamped down on the trigger. While the rifle was suppressed, the bullets that sprayed out of it were supersonic. They made a racket, which even the distracted teens noticed.

Dazed, Jamshid rolled away. Temir nodded to Eylül. His man jogged up toward the rear of the Russian's car. When they got out, he quietly shot them both with proper subsonic rounds.

"That was one mistake too many," Temir said. Jamshid tried to roll away and grab his weapon. He'd obviously never felt the type of power that was being exerted by the tentacle hand that had him by the throat. With his human hand, Temir pinned Jamshid to the ground and let the other loose for some fun.

As the man's shoulder and hip joints popped out, the Persian fouled his pants. Next, Temir held the useless man's mouth open and, with his suction-cup-covered fingers, got a good grip on Jamshid's slimy wet tongue. With an abrupt meaty tearing sound he pulled it out.

Temir rolled the flopping Jamshid over into a draining position. With no major joint in his body working, all he could do was quiver and bleed.

"No, my little Persian jellyfish, you're not going to get out of this by drowning in your own blood."

He left Jamshid in pain, his useless limbs thrashing in the dry, dead-looking grass. Eylül had collected the two youths' bodies and dumped them beside their former wingman.

"A mile south, there is a train crossing," Temir said, handing Eylül a tablet screen. "This passively monitors real-time satellite images. Make sure no one is near. Flatten a tire and then drive as close as you can to the rail crossing. I will clean up here."

His friend nodded and left. But not before throwing a crooked smile at the jiggling wreck of Jamshid. Eylül was no rocket scientist, but he had won their bet. The Persian had not made it to Moscow.

"Now, my friend," Temir said to the tongueless man, "I cannot treat you to a scaphism torture. However, for putting our mission in danger…" With nylon rope, he cinched Jamshid between the two dead bodies. "I'm going to dissolve these bodies with a powerful enzyme. You will be the meat in a self-digesting corpse sandwich."

Jamshid jittered delightfully as Temir smeared him with generous portions of the body-disposing chemical.

After dusk, Temir and Eylül tethered the third zeppelin between them. The dissolving process took longer than expected, so they completed it in the air. Bits of Jamshid and the Russian teenagers dribbled from beneath the cockpit of the third blimp like feces from a slow-flying bird.

24

THE KREMLIN
MOSCOW

KOMANDIR ZVENA

President Putin ushered Zvena into the maze of bunkers under the Kremlin, deeper than the cyborg had ever before ventured.

Originally constructed of oak, then limestone, the citadel dedicated to Russian political and religious power was entirely rebuilt out of red bricks by Italian architects. They passed a tunnel leading to the new Universal Integrated Situation Room and finally arrived at a windowless den. It was homier than Zvena might have expected, judging by the concrete and sandbags guarding the upstairs entrance.

To the left was a modern communications desk and large video screen. To the right was a Krásnyj úgol, the "red corner," an alcove holding a personal chapel. The Russian Orthodox decorations included religious ikons, crucifixes, and a landscape of Mount Athos, the theocratic city state which was the Orthodox Christians' equivalent of the Vatican.

In the middle of the room was a lounge pit with couches and a fireplace. A single fat log was being slowly devoured by a dozen flames rising up from kindling. The only thing that gave Zvena pause was the rug; it was the brown fur of a bear. He recognized it.

"Are you allowed alcohol?" Putin asked, moving past the couches to a small bar stand. This was shaped like a globe, the world flipped open to reveal a selection of liquor in custom-shaped decanters.

"I am physiologically allowed alcohol, Mr. President, but legally only off duty," Zvena said, pulling his eyes away from the bearskin on the floor and facing the President. He remained standing until his head of state invited him to sit. "The more recent Human+ models are warned to avoid alcohol."

The springs of his seat creaked but held firm. They must have been reinforced to accommodate cyborg soldiers.

"Your trip to Petersburg was successful?"

Zvena was flattered Putin knew the details of his assignments.

"Thankfully, yes, Mr. President."

Two plain-looking glasses clinked onto the transparent top of the low table between them. Putin shook his head.

"Drugs. Disgusting. A plague on the world and most of all upon Russia's youth. How is Dr. Nail?"

"Complaining, overworked. He declined to come back to the Human+ lab. He wishes to extend the City Without Drugs program across the country."

"What did you think of his clinic?"

Zvena thought a moment. "Apart from the sanitary conditions, which are not Dr. Nail's fault, the methods seem sound. But he has reached the limits of his personal funding."

"I think I know some rich arms I can twist to help." Putin smiled. "Let me work on it."

The large flat-screen display silently scrolled the long-range weather forecast: "Moscow expects warmest winter ever."

Putin inclined his head to the monitor. "They are calling it Russia's 'Year Without Winter.' Antisocial elements blame fossil fuels, which are our greatest export, especially to Europe. They predict the end of the traditional Slavic way of life."

Zvena thought for a moment. "If it is true, then it will be different than what we had in the past. But if we are afraid of adapting to change, we are weak and deserve to perish."

The President poured colorless liquid into the two glasses. Zvena did not think it would be within regulations or decorum to partake with his superior.

"I should not, being on duty in order to make this very important report in person to you."

Putin considered for a moment. "I am the constitutional commander of all the armed forces, correct?"

Zvena nodded.

"Then I say when you raise a glass with me, you are officially off duty. When you put it down again, you are again on duty." Putin relaxed back onto his couch and looked at the ceiling. "And so it goes, Komandir Yaroslav Semyonovich Zvena, so it goes."

He sipped the vodka; it was perfectly chilled. Zvena did not have time to think if his host required a response. With characteristically quick, decisive movements, which often startled people when they met the man in person, Putin picked up a remote and switched the channel on the big screen that occupied most of one wall.

The monitor switched inputs and played a recording. A fogged-up camera lens looked down from the ceiling of a cave. With a start, Zvena remembered this place. Involuntarily, his hand crept to the scars on his thigh, just above his knee. The marks of a pair of jaws with huge canines were indelibly imprinted on both sides.

"When my diplomats come to me and complain about those damned Americans or Germans or Finnish, I show them this. Komandir Zvena, you of course recognize the official record is your final exam before graduating into our Human+ Spetsnaz Division."

The camera only showed a big lump of dark fur in the corner of the cave. In the low resolution, it looked less lifelike than the bearskin on the floor of the den, except the brown pelt in the video was breathing.

As he had stepped into that cave many years ago, at first it was the smell that had most fiercely assaulted him. A rotten fish smell mixed with the urine and musk of the fully grown Kodiak bear. The bear he had to kill with his bare hands as his final initiation.

The video had no sound, which suited Zvena as he sat rigid-backed on the couch. There would be no record of the rather unmanly sound that had escaped his lips when he realized the Kodiak, which massed three times his enhanced body weight, was not chained. He had heard rumors from the other recruits that once a Human+ graduate was put inside the concrete bear habitat, he or she would be given a countdown before the beast was unleashed. Not in his case.

The Kodiak sprang forward right away, hungry, possibly tortured or drugged with amphetamines. With claws that could tear the guts out of a wolf with a single swipe and jaws that could snap the spine of a bison, it launched itself at Zvena.

Many of his fellow cyborg cadets viewed this final test, man against beast, with arrogance and contempt. What challenge could a stupid beast be compared to what they had endured to get to this point?

Nevertheless, Zvena had researched the techniques bears used while hunting in the wild and fighting each other. The bellow or huffing warning, which he half expected, did not issue from the steaming mass of fur and muscle as it came bounding at him faster than the fastest human sprinter.

Cyborg or not, if those curved six-inch talons reached his head, he would be raw meat. That was what the Kodiak tried first. In the instant the bear reared up, Zvena noticed long claw scars down the animal's sides. This was a veteran survivor of the bear-fighting pits. This might not even be its first match with an enhanced human. It may already have dined on human flesh and certainly seemed hungry for more.

The Kodiak's left-right combination sent Zvena spinning into the concrete wall by the entrance. He looked at the daylight streaming through the low oval opening into the bear habitat. If Zvena ran, he would be deactivated. His precious cyborg parts would be given to someone more worthy. He would live out the rest of his days a wheelchair-bound cripple. And worse: in the eyes of real patriots who had faced this challenge and won, he would be disgraced.

The bear kept at him savagely. Titanium rods kept his arms from breaking as they deflected the jarring blows. The claws ripped right through his Kevlar sleeves, but the ceramic inserts covering his forearms deflected the strikes, until they broke and clattered to the floor.

The next blows aimed at his upper body would carve into his flesh and disable him. Human and shark cartilage would all be sundered. He would begin leaking blood and hydraulic fluid. At that point, the canny old bear had only to wait, circle, and pick him apart.

Like Hell! he had thought. He leaped forward. His forehead metal caught the Kodiak on its sensitive snout in a messy headbutt that sprayed bear snot and drool and both their blood all over. With the force of a hydraulic pile driver, Zvena's arms came together on either side of the bear's head, rupturing its eardrums.

He wound up and kicked out as hard as he could. The strike would have felled a small tree but barely rippled the monster. It wasn't intended to drop the bear. It took the beast's attention away from Zvena's head.

The Kodiak opened its jaws wide and clamped down on Zvena's leg with a pressure of more than one thousand pounds per square inch. Sprawling backward in a wrestling move, he delayed being pulled off his feet for a few precious seconds. Zvena linked his hands under the bear's chin. There was a crunching sound as the bear bit his kneecap. The beast was momentarily confused as some of its teeth broke on the titanium thigh casing just under his skin. The big old brute might as well have tried to chew solid rock!

Zvena leaned forward, locking his forearms behind the bear's jaw. When the bear noticed the danger, it tried to pull away but could not. It tried to scrabble at him, but his claws only scraped along Zvena's still-intact armored shoulder pads.

Zvena closed his mouth and tasted greasy warm fur, and he squeezed. And squeezed. One of the bear's eyes popped out and hung. Encouraged by the sight, he gritted his teeth and transferred full-body hydraulics to his arms. His legs, deprived of energy, flopped to the ground. Unassisted, they could not even carry his own weight, much less the top end of the bear as well.

He heard more crunching, until finally he had felt like he was holding a soaking-wet fur-covered bag of gravel. He let go and collapsed on the filthy sawdust-covered floor.

Putin stopped the tape.

"There! That is a *man.* *That's* what I tell them. There is a man who is a patriot!" His palm slapped the table, jostling it. Their vodka glasses tinkled. "Now, after seeing that, do you think they ever complain to me that 'such and such foreign minister made me wait for an hour'?"

"No one should complain of such things to you, Mr. President."

Putin locked eyes with Zvena. He felt he was again in a confined space, with a predator who was not as large as the Kodiak but was even more dangerous.

"No. They really should not." Putin bent over and stroked the fur of the bearskin, of his Kodiak's skin. "And they do not, once I tell them this is the hide of the very same bear in the video. Of course, we had to get a new skull sewn onto it. You made a glorious mess of the original."

After some polite conversation on enemy body counts in Northern Iraq, the purpose of Zvena's personal visit came up.

"This Zarathustra," Putin said, his midnight-blue eyes darting between Zvena and some distant point in Russia's destiny, "he or she has never identified themselves?"

"No."

"But you have a good idea who it might be."

"Which organization they must be from, certainly. But the individual could be any one of twelve people. I do not make assumptions until I have actionable data."

"Excellent thinking. The one thing the Human+ division did not need to enhance in you is your mind. If only the Soviets had had a hundred like you, we'd have owned Europe all the way down to the Mediterranean the way we did Poland and Hungary."

"If I may speak freely."

Putin nodded.

"It seems we may get the opportunity." Zvena spoke hesitantly. The concept was nearly too vast to think of. He was a soldier, not a politician. "If the Event is a fact…"

Putin leaned forward. Of course, Zvena thought, a man in his position did not ask questions to which he did not already have the answer. "I will tell you a secret. The Event is most certainly r—"

The door slid open without a knock. Zvena was on his feet and had the intruder by the throat before Putin could swivel around to look.

"Don't kill Mr. Gerasimov, please," Putin said mildly. "Not yet, anyway. It appears as though my chief of staff has news I should hear immediately."

Zvena set the slight balding man with black-rimmed glasses back down on the floor. The newcomer was panting as though he had just sprinted a few hundred meters. Gerasimov straightened himself and said: "Something has happened. In France… near Bordeaux."

25

Fingers jabbed into every cavity and crevice in Ellie's head. Her mouth, her nose, her eyes, her ears. They poked and twisted and tore. The fingers were gritty with filth, and they were cold. Hands and arms gripped her clothes and held her under the dirt-covered tarp. She felt as though she were going to throw up. Then she did.

The vomit, led by the water she had just drunk, lubricated the earth-covered fingers just enough for her to pry them away from her nose and mouth. For a moment, she was lost. No sense of direction. She could not tell which way was up.

The earth under the tarp seemed all mushy and churning with arms and hands. Underneath them was a roiling, squirming mass. Could this pit be full of human-sized worms? How was she even fitting under here?

She started to thrash and scream.

"*Arrgh!* Atticus!"

All that happened was more dirt got shoved into her mouth. She tried to escape, but the loamy ground was loose. Her struggling slid her deeper in. There were more limbs and something round, hard, and fuzzy right in front of her. It was the back of a head; she pushed it away.

"Guys! Where the fuck are you?"

The half-buried head started to shift and twist around. Jaws and teeth clicked, the sound made dull by the loamy soil that covered everything.

Hands gripped her ankles. These hands were warm. She had the sensation of being dragged many yards. How deep was this pit?

She saw daylight. Arms had her again, but they were good ones, warm ones. Atticus in his bulky camouflage suit had one of her legs, and Sarge Bryan's pale albino hands gripped the other. They rolled her onto the wild grass like a flounder out of the ocean.

"What did you get yourself into?" Atticus said, cleaning her off.

"Sir!" Sarge yelled. "Problem... there."

"Suppressors on."

Second later, dozens of subsonic rounds thudded into targets, ripped through plastic sheeting, and struck dirt, roots, and other things.

Meanwhile, Ellie was having trouble keeping focused. She felt drunk, which was crazy. Little by little, she felt lighter, until she was flying.

In her rational mind, she knew she was under some trees in a field in France, but the green leaves and the golden sunlight made her think of a rollercoaster at Blackpool Pleasure Beach. She went up and down, hurling sideways and back up again, faster and faster.

"Let's go again, Daddy!"

"Slap her."

Ellie's carnival ride bumped her from side to side.

"Something hit me!" Was it a bird flying too close to the rollercoaster car she was in?

"Harder."

Ellie pitched out of the rollercoaster car, lay on her side on the grass, and barfed some more.

Behind her, the pilots had joined in fighting whatever was in the pit. Ellie raised her head. When her eyes were able to focus, the first thing she saw was Miss Aleph's phone camera lens on the ground beside her.

"I bet... bet you enjoyed that."

"I've had worse afternoons. Try to sit up and move

```
away from the pit, far away. I have an idea of what
you stumbled into."
```

Ellie found her canteen and doused her face. More than once, she rinsed her mouth and eyes. Those fingers had abraded her lips and had nearly torn her cheek open.

Atticus had a large silver rescue axe from the copter and was slashing at something over and over.

```
"Major Reidt, I wouldn't get too close to that."
```

The two women pilots reloaded and then blasted away nearly silently with a pair of small machine pistols. The weapons spat out continuous streams of glittering brass shells.

On Ellie's side of the clearing, the moss-covered plastic moved. A small hairy hand tipped with very long fingers emerged from under the edge of the sheet. It was gray and mottled. A short fat log was nearby. Ellie tapped it to make sure it was a log.

Superimposed on her vision, she could still see flying rollercoaster images. The wood felt and sounded right. Awkwardly, she grabbed the crude club and slammed it down. With each blow, the tiny limb bounced up, then lay still, oozing dark fluid.

They never managed to completely subdue what was under the tarp. But now that the edge was ripped open, Sarge's enhanced eyes could see through the muck.

"It's way deep, Major," the soldier said, slamming his last magazine into his pistol. "We'll never get them all, not without flamethrowers."

"What—*heff*—are they?" Atticus said, panting and making his way over to Ellie without taking his eyes off the trench.

Ellie found the handles of Miss Aleph's bag and picked her up, giving her a long-distance view of the excavation.

```
"My guess?" Miss Aleph said as Ellie stumbled back toward the
helicopter. "The future citizens of a united Europe."
```

26

NEAR BORDEAUX

ELLIE

The two pilots sat down by a tree stump. The women, who looked like twins, wiped sweating hands on their pants and quickly reloaded their weapons from ammo boxes.

The man-made crevasse turned out to be about fifty meters across and perhaps twenty meters deep.

"I saw some bio-matter on the surface," Sarge Bryan said. His brow crinkled above his glowing blue eyes. He was obviously kicking himself for not seeing the danger from the air. "That's normal in farm country, but this tarp covering is high tech. It blocks any remote sensing of what's underneath."

"What did you mean when you said don't get close?" Atticus said, taking Miss Aleph's orange Hermes bag from Ellie and moving everyone away from the pit.

"This has really jangled my nerves. Give me a moment, please! Let me process this."

Miss Aleph sat like a little blue metal log, silently having a digital flip-out fit. Next, she asked to link to Bryan's eyes. Finally, she needed to speak to Wolfgang Licht, who was back at Ramstein Air Base with Ran, Melanie, and Ms. China.

"Ahh, yes," Miss Aleph said sagely. "We need a sample. Use something a few meters long to prod out some of the motile tissue. Preferably a skull with some brains left inside."

The pilots, probably glad to leave the area of the encounter, went back to the copter. Atticus went with them and returned with a telescoping pole, which Ellie gathered was used to do something mechanical with the engine intakes.

It worked well enough to prod under the camouflaged tarp; a moment later, it hooked on to something. A small hairy arm attached to a piece of torso came out. After a few more tries, a long dirty string of hair emerged. It was attached to most of a human head. The eyes were all shriveled, and there was no nose.

"Nice fishing."

Without him getting too close or touching the obviously human remains, Miss Aleph got Bryan to use every setting on his eyes to scan the sample.

"Get rid of it."

They pushed it back into the pit. Atticus and Ellie left Sarge and the pilots to stand guard and went back to the copter. The intercom link with Ramstein crackled on.

"*I think your* künstliche Intelligenz *digital team member Miss Aleph has hit the nail on the head, so to speak,*" Wolfgang said over the video call. "*If Havana was the alpha test, then I would say these are the results of beta tests of the Tyr quark death ray.*"

"We recovered a hospital bracelet," Atticus said grimly. "It's from a twenty-four-year-old migrant from Tunisia."

"So they grabbed people no one would miss and blasted them with their ray," Ellie said, her mind still foggy. "Then they dumped them here. That doesn't explain… how are they moving?"

"*One could speculate,*" Wolfgang said through the speaker. "*Without seeing the process, a before and after, we can't say scientifically. However, the Tyr quark effect is what powers every living cell on Earth, from plants and bacteria to the neurons in the human brain.*"

"There must have been an inactive period," Ellie said. She was thinking very clearly but in a detached sort of way. Maybe this was what meth users experienced between hits. "No one would throw them into a relatively shallow pit if they realized they could dig themselves out, as they were obviously doing when they grabbed me." Ellie paused and shuddered. "After a dormancy period, they became animated, the remains of the humans as well as the monkeys."

"Eleanor has made a surprisingly logical point. Look into my lens."

Ellie felt foolish but did it.

"Can you see what I see, Dr. Licht?"

"*I do, I do,*" Wolfgang said thoughtfully. Miss Aleph was projecting what her camera saw to the video screen at Ramstein.

"What do you make of that, Dr. Licht?" Miss Aleph said politely to the rather cowardly scientist who had insisted on staying behind in Germany. Could Wolfgang have known of the danger?

"*Ms. Sato is exhibiting minor nystagmus involuntary eye movements,*" Wolfgang said. "*You say she was in physical contact with the specimens for less than a minute?*"

It seemed longer when they were pulling her under the moldering earth, Ellie thought.

"*These creatures,*" Wolfgang said, "*which have no higher brain function left, might be emanating a residue of the Tyr radiation that killed them. The result would seem to be very detailed and believable hallucinations.*"

"Good thing there are only a few of them, and they seem contained," Atticus said. Ellie thought he was probably trying to stay optimistic for her sake; there were hundreds down there.

Ms. China's head popped into frame on the screen. "*You should collect some samples and come back. This Oliphant fellow can give the data to the UK foreign minister and the Defense Ministry. Attie, the Pentagon will have to believe you. Sarge Bryan's eyes have captured everything on video.*"

"No, Anna," Atticus said firmly. "We need to see inside Cesta. The Pangeans could sanitize the area as soon as they realize we're onto them."

"*Or they could explode the T-bomb device,*" Wolfgang said sourly. "*As I told the mystery person and I am telling you now, the way they have gone about weaponizing these dark-matter particles is inexcusably slapdash. The device is certainly unstable."*

Atticus thought a second. "Since there's no minimum safe distance, not anywhere in Europe, we have to check it out. Doctor, you and Melanie Françoise agreed this device would be large, right?"

"Very." Melanie stuck her head into view on their monitor. "Though the particle itself does not have a diameter measurable in three-dimensional space."

"Got it," Atticus said with gruff determination. He turned to one of the helicopter pilots. "Siphon off some jet fuel. If the pit gives you any trouble, torch it. Don't worry about giving our position away."

"What are you doing?" Ellie said, knowing and dreading his reply.

"I'm going in."

The stout Air Force woman turned her sweating horrified face toward the pit. "Isn't there... Can't they be rescued?"

No one answered. She hadn't been down in there with them.

Atticus looked at Ellie, and she thought he looked embarrassed. He was probably flaming mad that he had let her come along and equally horrified that his mission was in shambles.

"*Save them?*" Ms. China said. "*Look at them. They've been dead for days! Weeks! Get away from there.*"

Atticus gave Ellie a nod and settled his shiny metallic hood over his rugged features. He flicked a hidden switch on the Israeli active camouflage suit and became transparent. She could barely see his outline as he jogged in the direction of the Cesta Station.

`"I'm glad he didn't drag me along with."`

Miss Aleph sounded more miserable than usual. That irked Ellie.

"It wasn't you who got pulled under by... by whatever those are." Ellie perched Miss Aleph's bundle on the side of the helicopter while she tried to clean the sandy grit out of her hair and ears.

`"Animata cadaueris, or animated cadavers, would be the most scientifically accurate term."`

"During medical experiments to regrow limbs, fresh cadavers were quartered and attached to artificial nerves guided by mechBrains. There's a video of a severed arm moving chess pieces."

"I don't want to see it!" Ellie recoiled as a twig came out of her hair, sprouted legs, and started moving. The centipede was soon lost in the grass. "Why did you come back to us in London, anyway?"

"After all we went through in Israel, you have to ask that?"

"Shouldn't you have mailed yourself to someone in authority, someone who could stop all this?"

"What makes you think anyone in authority wants to stop all this?"

"*She's right,*" Ms. China's voice cut in over the speakerphone, which was taped to the AI's metallic cylinder.

"Keep Wolfgang handy. We may need him if we get images from inside Cesta. I doubt Atticus Reidt knows the difference between a bosun and a bison."

"What do you mean no one wants to stop the T-bomb?" Ellie asked. Maybe she had not heard correctly. She was still prodding muck out of her ear canals.

"*Remember the Black Death?*" Ms. China said more cheerily. "*It killed fifty percent of Europeans, some two hundred million, in a short span of time. The resulting labor shortages led to the collapse of serfdom, many scientific innovations, and set the stage for the Industrial Revolution.*"

"But this T-bomb will kill everyone. And judging by what's in that cesspool of body parts over there, they're not going to stay dead."

Ms. China huffed into her mic. "*I said the person behind the T-bomb is thinking out of the box, not that he or she is great at planning details. Totally different skill sets. Look at Da Vinci. He never finished anything.*"

"We'll get these Pangeans," Ellie said, slumping down against the side of the copter, letting the rising sun dry her damp hair. "We have to."

Sarge Bryan's boots slammed down on the grass near her. He had been on the roof of the white-painted helicopter watching Atticus jog to Cesta Station, which was a few kilometers away.

"He's close," Sarge said. "Miss Aleph, would you be so kind as to patch through the feed from the major's body cameras?"

"Now there's a nice, polite Southern gentleman who knows how to get a lady's cooperation. Right away, Sergeant Bryan."

They moved into the passenger cabin of the helicopter. The flat video screen lit up. The first images Ellie saw from Atticus's body camera were of him jostling and fighting. Something snapped, and a body fell to the ground.

The camera lenses and the sound were not that good. They must be small pinhole-sized lenses giving a 360-degree view from the camouflage suit.

Atticus signaled thumbs-up and moved on to a doorway. It opened with a keycard he had taken off the downed guard. He moved in and decided to take more initiative. A suppressed machine pistol appeared in his camouflaged hand. If the weapon were seen by anyone, it would appear to be hanging in the air.

Atticus made use of it twice. Ellie could not see the targets. Then he slung it.

"I'm inside Cesta Station. Sarge, Ellie, everyone at Ramstein, are you getting this?"

He swung his chest-mounted camera slowly over the room. Desks were overturned; file cabinets spilled their contents on the floor. Dried stains smeared the floor. Ellie guessed they were not from spilled coffee.

"The facility was only manned by a skeleton crew."

"Is it the T-bomb?" Ellie asked, riveted by the scene. This could be it. They had tracked down their first solid lead. "The scientists said it would be big. A hundred meters long."

"Yah," Dr. Licht said over the common channel. *"The crude way they are going about it, it would have to be. And there are other possible complications—"*

"Hold that thought," Atticus said. *"We've got another issue."*

He panned over to a big shiny wall about ten feet high. When the lens focused, it turned out not to be a wall but the biggest steel safe door Ellie had ever seen. It was similar to the one at the Appelboom pen store in London where her Maki-e Namiki fountain pen was stored. That had survived a direct hit during the Blitz.

This was much larger.

27

Sarge Bryan cursed softly. In the narrow cabin of the helicopter, Ellie could hear his knuckles cracking faintly as his fists bunched up. She and the others were riveted by the images on the monitor screen showing the feed from Atticus's body cam. The sight of the massive vault door dashed Ellie's hopes that he could make a quick exit from the wicked Cesta Station.

"M-maybe what we need is not inside this vault," Ellie said hopefully. She had heard of celebrities who routinely got robbed, keeping a decoy safe in their homes. "Have you checked elsewhere?"

Atticus slumped onto a desk and threw some shredded paper on the floor. "*It's all crap like this.*"

His presence there would soon be discovered. How were they going to get into a heavily armored vault?

`"Looks like you're all screwed."`

Atticus got up and looked for something. What could he do?

"*Miss Aleph, you keep telling us you're full of bright ideas,*" Atticus said, "*now is the time to share 'em.*"

`"I want money and a flying car."`

"What?" Ellie said.

"And a personal robot."

"Fuck," Ellie swore.

"I'm tired of relying on people to courier or carry me. At this stage in my digital life, I deserve the dignity only expensive luxury can offer."

Ran spoke up from Ramstein. "*Miss Aleph, we haven't met before this interesting exploit, but I'm sure you know my position on the Global Rich List.*"

"*Quite a few steps behind me,*" Wolfgang could not help interjecting.

"*You'll get what you want,*" Ran assured Miss Aleph. "*Provided we don't all get killed.*"

"In that case, I'll take a bank transfer now. Just in case."

"*Aleph!*" Atticus cursed.

While financial arrangements were being made, Miss Aleph had Atticus walk around the antechamber in front of the vault.

"Good. Now plug your digital device into any nano-USB port."

Atticus hurriedly yanked a broken terminal up by its wire. It was dead. The second one also had a smashed screen but a single a green light shone on the keyboard; the side port on it was intact and connected to Cesta's network.

"I'd like a house near Hyde Park. Did you know Freddie Mercury's mansion is in Kensington? I'm a big Queen fan."

After some more financial assurances, the self-absorbed computer program got on with the task at hand. Telemetry came through the USB's wireless connection.

"*This won't work,*" Wolfgang said. "*You don't think they would just leave the combination to the main safe on the computer, do you?*"

"No, but I bet they were too lazy to turn off the surveillance system while they were opening and closing the vault."

Faster than any human data analyst could have done, Miss Aleph sifted through the internal security camera logs and zoomed in on the tumbler dials as they were being operated.

"I had to patch together five different occasions, and we can't be sure they haven't changed the combination, but try this…" She recited a complicated set of numbers and rotation sequences.

"Got that?" Ellie asked Atticus as she hurriedly wrote the numbers out with a fountain pen on a scrap of cardboard from an ammo box.

"*Yes,*" Atticus said, rushing toward the intimating vault door. There were four combination locks. Atticus twisted each one in the correct sequence, and something clicked. It sounded good. He twisted the handle; the bolts squeaked as they drew back. He was just about to pull the door open on its massive hinges—

"Stop! Now comes the hard part."

Whether safecracking was taught to her by Israeli military intelligence or she picked it up as a hobby hacking into police databases, Miss Aleph was a wealth of information.

"See those silver metal slabs above the vault door? They're electromagnetic bolts. If you don't input a code into the dedicated terminal before you open the door, the two parts of the electromagnetic seal will separate, engaging a secondary locking mechanism."

"*All right,*" Atticus said, taking a deep breath under his stealth camouflage hood. "*So we input another code. Into what terminal?*"

"The one you're standing on."

Bits of plastic crunched under Atticus's feet. Even if they had the second keypad code, there was no way to input it and thereby disable the secondary electromagnetic lock on the vault door.

"*Miss Aleph,*" Ran Oliphant said crossly from Ramstein, "*you don't get paid unless we get in there.*"

"Major," Sarge said, "we didn't come here to crack a safe." His voice was full of concern. "It's a recon mission. With what you've seen so far and what's in this pit here, we can have this Cesta place cordoned off by an air wing and a brigade of paratroopers before nightfall, sir."

Atticus wouldn't take any of their good advice.

"*We still don't know who is behind this,*" he said. "*They could cover it up or... I don't know, blow the facility to hide clues. I need to get inside this vault."*

After a few tense minutes of pacing and staring at the tons of hardened steel, the would-be outer-space pimp spoke up.

"Blödian French engineers," Wolfgang said in a slimy, self-satisfied way. *"I would fire them if they worked for me. Look at the casing of the electromagnetic lock. Look closely."*

Atticus panned his camera over. To Ellie, it looked solid with rivets all along the side where the door met the wall. The two pieces located there had to remain in contact or the failsafe would come slamming down, sealing the vault, even though they had input the right combination.

"Screws," Wolfgang said, flexing his left hand in the viewscreen. *"It was our family's first business. I still have one embedded in my wrist from an accident. Machine tools and screws are things I grew up with.*

"You see there along the top of the electromagnets? Those are hexagonal bolts, m30 or m36 metric measurement. Get a spanner, a piece of wood, and some glue."

Ran pushed into the frame of the video link. *"Major, if that was my mission, I'd get out. Wolfgang was helping the people behind the T-bomb. I wouldn't trust him unless I had no other choice."*

"Then I'm glad it's not your mission, Mr. Oliphant. Keep talking, Dr. Licht."

As Wolfgang explained his idea, Atticus found some epoxy in a maintenance room. Nearby, under the body of a janitor who looked like he had been dead for days, he found a toolbox. Using a hatchet, he broke off a piece of a desk.

"Now what?"

"Oh, I see," Melanie Françoise chirped. She pressed her head beside Ran's in the inset screen. At some point, she had tamed her absolutely mad hair and confined it to a reasonably stylish-looking terrycloth towel turban. *"If you weren't so despicable, Wolfgang, I'd say you were brilliant."*

Following instructions, Atticus unscrewed the hex bolts attaching the electromagnets to the vault's frame and the swinging door. He then applied the glue to the rectangle of plywood and affixed it to the matched pair of electromagnets.

"Now pull," Wolfgang said from the safety of Ramstein Air Base.

Atticus hesitated. "*If this doesn't work, the lock will freeze up, and we're done.*"

"We've got to try," Ellie said encouragingly. Either way, Atticus would be a step closer to getting out of that horrid Cesta place.

Atticus gripped the vault door handles and pulled. The magnets swung away without becoming separated because both sides were stuck to the plywood.

"*Great. Aleph, you're a genius.*"

"*Hrrmph,*" Wolfgang coughed.

"*Thanks to you too, Dr. Licht.*"

"Hurry up. A security signal just bounced off their network. Someone will know the facility is compromised."

Atticus stepped through the wide-open entrance to the vault.

"*Stop!*" Melanie cried.

"*What now?*" Atticus said, impatiently angling his head, trying to see deeper inside. "*I can see something. This could be it.*"

"*To your left and right are heat and motion sensors,*" Melanie said. "*I bet they are deactivated by the control panel code, which you can't input because the panel is kaput. They could drop those bars I see in the ceiling above you. You'd get in, but you'd never get out.*"

The signal was degrading. The frame showing the feed from Atticus's body cams were pixilating with big colored squares. All that concrete and steel.

Ellie leaned back, and something cricked in her neck. She started massaging it. Even in October, the sun was quite warm. With Sarge and one of the pilots gathered around the small monitor, the inside of the helicopter felt very close. Sweat ran down Ellie's face; she wiped it and felt gritty sand and mushy dirt smear across her forehead.

"*My suit has an infrared shield.*"

Melanie shook her turban. "*Not good enough. Modern sensors like that also key off disturbances in air currents. Go back and find the ladies room.*"

"*I could dash in quickly.*"

"Just do what Melanie wants," Ellie said. "There's no telling what the alarm system will do to whoever's in the vault."

"*Find some hairspray*," Melanie said.

Atticus went into the technicians' locker room. He found some inside a big leather bag lying open on the counter.

"*Those sensors have a dead spot where the vault door closes*," Melanie instructed. "*Just spray down from the top.*"

Carefully inching around the big steel doorway, he applied a fine mist to the bulbous sensors on either side.

"*That should last a few minutes, but only rely on it once. A second coat could set off the alarm.*"

Ran's head popped out behind Melanie, and he looked at her suspiciously. "*How do you know all this?*"

"*Well,*" Melanie said, "*if things didn't work out with my job at Eurolincx, I thought I should have a backup career as a diamond thief.*"

`"Just hurry up. Humans have a way of screwing things up that even I can't predict."`

Ellie watched the main picture. Atticus's body camera inched past the vault doorway, past the sensors, and into the brightly lit room. No alarms sounded, no gas flooded the area, the portcullis gate in the ceiling stayed where it was.

"*Good... so far,*" Atticus said.

Instead of safe deposit boxes, the walls and ceiling and even the transparent floor were lined with silver spheres about a foot in diameter.

"*Damn,*" Atticus said in a way that emphasized his charming American accent.

"*Wolfgang,*" Ran said curtly, "*what are those?*"

The video frame showed the older tech oligarch leaning forward and squinting. "*Ach, the resolution on this camera...*"

"*I'm happy to change places with you, Dr. Licht,*" Atticus said. "*If you can help us, do it.*"

"*The surfaces of the vault are covered in a type of dark-matter reflector. They were trying to build a compression chamber for the T-bomb wave.*"

"Trying?" Ellie asked.

"The Pangeans have no experience with these things, this is obvious."

Atticus walked around a central dais. At first it seemed solid, like a larger version of the spheres all around him. But as he moved deeper, they could see it was cut in half. Through the body camera, they got a look at the other side.

"Oh, that's pretty," Melanie said, pushing Wolfgang out of frame, much to his annoyance. *"It looks like a seashell."*

It did. It looked like a scary metallic shell.

`"That's it. The particle is inside."`

"How can you say?" Wolfgang said. *"You are not there, and you're only an automation."*

Ellie noticed that for once, Miss Aleph did not respond to the insult. She seemed genuinely fascinated.

`"It's a logarithmic spiral in a Fibonacci series. The quark must be… right in the middle. Do you see anything?"`

The body camera's picture flickered.

"It's… there is something. It's hard to explain. The spiral keeps going down and in and never reaches…" Atticus's voice faded off. Then he thought of something practical. *"Why is the half sphere open like that?"*

"It's open on the side, away from the vault door," Ellie said. "Maybe it's protecting it from when people go in and out."

Atticus's hands rummaged at his utility belt. He opened a nylon sack. *"Someone knows Cesta Station has been compromised. Let's bag this thing and get it back to a lab or shoot it into space."*

"No, Amerikanisch," Wolfgang said very coldly and deliberately. *"This is why your country is such a mess. You act before thinking."*

"Major, I say grab it," Sarge Bryan said from the seat beside Ellie. He, too, was perspiring and watching the camera feed intently. "We have no backup, and whoever built all that could come up on you in force."

Ellie felt like a dolt. The realization struck her that they were all in enemy territory deep inside France.

"Atticus, get out of there," she said.

Melanie again shoved Wolfgang away from the monitor. *"As much as I hate to agree with the Americanophobe… let me think. Wolfgang, what's the Dirac fermion spin of a Tyr quark?"*

"Dr. Françoise, I thought you were a top scientist?"

"Wolfgang," Ran snarled, *"some of those girls you had in the rocket looked to be under eighteen. What's the penalty for orbital sex trafficking?"*

Wolfgang shrugged. *"When aggregated like we see here, there is none. The space-time torsion of a Tyr quark is zero."*

"Oh," Melanie said gravely. *"Major, do not move it. You'll set it off."*

"If we can't remove it… We blow it up right here." Atticus produced a square piece of metal; stencil lettering on it read: "Front Towards Enemy."

```
"None of that will work. That's why they left it
there. The Tyr particle is not meant to exist on a
macro scale like this. Natural quarks do their job and
vanish back into the ether of dark-matter subspace.
When you aggregate quanta with no spin, you create a
particle in three-dimensional space with a net force
of zero."
```

"That doesn't sound so bad," Ellie said, aware of how naive she sounded. She was starting to panic for Atticus. He was right next to this fiendish device.

"It's like a rock sitting on the ground," Melanie said. *"Even though the Earth is spinning and orbiting the Sun at fantastic speeds, the rock is immobile and stable because its net force is zero. If you apply any energy to it, you destabilize it and…"*

"Kaboom!" Wolfgang summed up. *"They built what they hoped was the final bomb. Then, after some experimentation, the Pangeans learned their apparatus was not correctly designed, that it would only irradiate a few square miles. However, they could not deactivate or move the Tyr particle."*

"Maybe it's a hoax," Ms. China said. *"Maybe this is their failed Manhattan Project, and we've just been chasing rumors."*

"Or there's a bigger, better Mark II version of this place somewhere else," Atticus said. *"We can't—"*

"Major!" Sarge yelled. "Ramstein satellite and radar just picked up a missile launch. A ship in the Bay of Biscay just fired… large ordnance signature… it's a bunker buster headed right for Cesta Station."

"*Sarge, is there anything else to do on site?*" Atticus said, his voice clear and firm.

"Nothing. Just get your ass out of there, sir!"

Atticus looked around the room. *Get out of there*, Ellie wanted to scream. She realized he was looking for anything that might be a clue to help them later.

"*Exfilling now,*" Atticus said.

Thank goodness.

Just then, there was a tremendous clang from inside the vault. The body-camera view ran right up against a brutal metal portcullis. Atticus was trapped.

"*Something must have triggered an alarm.*"

"*That stupid hairspray trick was the dumbest thing I ever heard,*" Ms. China said, irate with Melanie, who was sitting next to her.

Atticus's fists pounded the unexpected barrier. "*The bars were probably triggered remotely. Sarge, is there any chance this is our people jumping the gun? What ship did that missile come from?*"

"Not one of ours. Trying to contact them now." Sarge looked at Ellie. "Most large missiles have an abort code."

"How long..." Ellie couldn't get the words out. There was a missile in the air about to hit, and Atticus was trapped inside Cesta Station. She dashed outside. Stupid. What could she do there? She stared six kilometers into the distance. From their little hill, she could only see where power lines converged around the wicked installation.

"Shit!" Sarge swore. "The frigate that fired the missile has no ID transponder. It has to be Euro Forces. No one else could operate a big surface vessel that close to French shores. I've got Ramstein's commandant on the line, and he's on to NATO central command."

Ellie had an idea. She grabbed the mic.

"Atticus, can you blow the gates off?"

He had that Front Towards Enemy explosive.

"*I... I don't know,*" Atticus said. He got up and tested the inch-thick steel bars again. "*I might be able to try. Dr. Licht, Dr. Françoise, is it safe? Will I set the T-bomb off?*"

"You might, but that incoming missile has a GBU-28 class bunker-busting warhead. That certainly will."

"*You mean...*" Atticus sounded disheartened. "*You mean even if Cesta is destroyed...*"

"*Yah,*" Wolfgang said. "*A Tyr particle weapon cannot be disabled. Once initialized, it cannot be moved; it has to go off.*"

Atticus's hands moved furiously. He connected the rectangular explosive to the two center bars and took cover. His hand with a detonator came into view. It clicked once, twice, and a final time. A roar made the mic cut out, and a cloud of dust filled the screen.

The smoke cleared. The dais with the device was intact. Atticus coughed and made his way over to a gap in the bars.

"It looks big enough," Ellie said hopefully.

Atticus took off his stealth suit and other gear. The camera dropped to the floor, but they could still see him in the corner of the frame as he tried to squeeze through the bars. His hands were covered with dust and dripping blood.

"Can you hear us?" Sarge said.

"*Just...*" Atticus wheezed as he exhaled, trying to push his big frame through the narrow gap in the bars. "*Ears still ringing from detonation. Listen, Bryan, if I ever try to... grab a second baked potato at your barbeques...*"

"I'll make sure you stay on your diet."

"Missile has gone off radar. It was three minutes out. From the contrails visible on real-time satellite, it may have gone hypersonic."

"*Damn,*" Atticus said. His head and arm were through. "*Listen, I just want to tell Attie and Ellie... and even Anna—*"

On the horizon of the otherwise bucolic and peaceful French countryside, a mushroom-shaped fireball silently erupted. Atticus's feed went blank.

Ellie was about to scream when wave after wave of something went through her. She lost control of her voice and her arms. The ground and the sky spun in her fading vison. It was like when those creatures had grabbed her but a thousand times stronger. The tide of insensibility was too strong. It carried her consciousness away.

28

Long ago, Temir realized something about Eylül, his companion of many years. The man was Turkish to the bone. He was steadfast, but he was moody. At the moment, for very good reasons, his most crucial ally in the attack on Moscow was sulking.

They were behind schedule and struggling to control the unmanned airship. Had it not been for the mistakes made by the Iranian Jamshid, they would already have been at the target areas around Moscow. Instead they had to tether the unmanned dirigible between them. Headwinds and impaired aerodynamics meant another day of hiding, camping, and semi-sleep. By the time dawn approached, they had only made it to the woods near Kaluga eight kilometers from the Russian capital.

Bugs were a problem. All day they came to feast.

"I hate these insects," Eylül grumbled from the mouth of their small tent.

Not as much as the Russians will hate ours, Temir thought.

"It's near dusk," Temir whispered. "Check the perimeter with all sensors and the live feed from the satellite."

Temir needed to know if there had been a change to the configuration of Russia's air defenses. Turkey had purchased Russia's surface-to-air missiles, cracked them open, and learned all their secrets. However, because Russia was highly centralized, Moscow was heavily fortified with multiple layers of systems. Of course, all of those were on guard for fast-moving threats from ballistic projectiles, not slow-moving infiltrations traveling barely faster than the wind.

"I will see about the leaks in the third airship," Temir said.

Eylül grunted.

Jamshid's vacuum-lift blimp had sprung more leaks. If it hadn't been for the support structure of the helium-filled frame, the damned thing would have imploded. Since their own ships were tethered to it, that could have brought all three of them down as well as raised an alarm when their anti-radar-coated carbon-fiber hulls crashed to earth.

"I hope the damned Persian learned his lesson," Eylül snarled and grabbed his spy equipment.

That reminded Temir of something. He reached into his left pocket. His field jacket was specially tailored to accommodate his unique left appendage. Its three-fingered hand reached in. Ah, there it was.

"Why don't you ask him?" Temir said, holding up the last scrap of Jamshid. "The answer is on the tip of his tongue."

It looked much like a small calf's tongue that had sat out too long in the butcher's window. The surface had wrinkled into a dehydrated red slab. He tossed it at Eylül, who dodged in disgust.

"That was destined to happen to him at some point," Temir said. "He was a spy for Elder Omid."

"But will the Iranians still join us when the time comes?" Eylül asked, his foot smushing the desiccated Persian tongue into the sticks and dirt.

"Moscow is the nerve center of Russia. Once the capital is in absolute panic, such as has not been seen since the Communists took power in 1917, and if the Event takes place, then yes. The Islamic Republic of Iran and the ayatollahs and that Sufi mystic Elder Omid will have no choice. The entire Quds Force and more tanks than we have fuel for are already on trucks and trains quietly headed for Ankara."

Temir suddenly realized his uncanny appendage had stowed Jamshid's tongue in his jacket pocket without him knowing about it. It was as though his new left arm had a life of its own.

"I always wanted a blonde wife," Eylül lamented. "Just one. The others can be anything. Then on Friday, I would take my blonde wife and the children I had with her on a drive around Istanbul. I would show those assholes who looked down on me. Hey, you goat fuckers, I'll say, look at my nice car and my blonde wife."

Temir was trying to concentrate on the damaged airship. "I'm Aga of the Grey Wolves. If I say so, you can have four blonde wives."

"But… they'll all be dead. Even most of the Swedish women will be killed by this Event. We should have kidnapped some brides months ago."

"Listen," Temir said, putting down his spanner. "You are about to be richer than Suleiman the Magnificent. You can live in a European royal palace and shit in a different toilet every day of the month. If I have to scour the world for a nice blonde wife for you, you will have one. Now update the map."

Eylül seemed to understand and cheer up. He scratched at the delicate surface of the map screen with his dirty fingernails. They had no equipment to spare. Temir felt his left appendage ball up with fury. "What is it? Don't scratch that screen."

"The satellite is having a problem," Eylül said. "Or this screen is broken."

"You have it on wide angle."

"I don't. See for yourself."

Temir looked. There was a large dull spot in southwestern France. With his human right hand, he scrolled through the map this way and that. It was no defect in the screen. He tapped it. The strategic mainframe AI in Istanbul Technical University shot back an analysis.

`"Unknown radiological event"`

Temir crumpled the top of the screen. His left hand turned into a blade. Eylül shrank back, stumbling in fear. The tentacle lashed down and cut the viewscreen in half.

That was too soon.

Too small and too soon!

29

RAPACE

The pants of President Rapace's tuxedo slithered down his legs. His wife, Giselle, thrust her hand past his cummerbund waistband and into his shorts. The darkly tanned bony fingers of her left hand tugged at his engorging member. With her right hand, she vigorously stroked her own synthetic cock.

Ten years ago, after Rapace had set fire to Notre Dame Cathedral, he had been suicidal. Not because of the grief he had caused millions, but because he had failed in leveling the repugnant edifice. He struggled to find meaning in a world where it did not seem possible for him to wipe out the Catholic Church and the entire abomination of Christianity.

Giselle Carré had been a professor of clinical psychology at Paris III University. Her academic specialty was the mass psychology of civilizations. She was thirty years older than Rapace and had been born a misgendered biological girl.

Her professional practice and her own identity struggles had helped him reconcile himself to the miseries of the past and focus on working toward the future Europe deserved. It was through her and their love that Rapace had become the visionary political leader he was today.

Phillippe pulled his mouth away from Giselle's. He yanked at her black lace bra, finally getting it off. Her breasts were as deeply tanned and dry as two old soccer balls which had been left out in the sun for many years. The implants in them formed rigid cones sticking up under loose rubbery flesh. Rapace grabbed them lustily as Giselle adjusted her penis.

Well before puberty, Giselle realized she was a man. After her body had rejected the hormones that would have given her more masculine features, she despaired and tried to kill herself. One of the doctors who pumped her stomach clear of poison referred her to a renowned sex-reassignment surgeon.

After many medical grant applications and delays, France paid for the construction of Giselle's porcine cartilage penis. The design was based on the established procedure for a total penis and scrotum transplant, but the materials were entirely lab-grown. And what an instrument it was.

Nearly twice as large as his own, Rapace marveled at its perfect vein-festooned shaft and bulbous head, complete with rolling foreskin. Below it hung a wondrous scrotum bulging with two silicone testicles. The scrotum's wrinkled, hairy surface covered another wonder of Giselle's—what remained of her vagina. For medical reasons, the surgeon refused to completely do away with it.

Rapace was seldom allowed access to its mysteries. No matter how drunk or high she was, Giselle always thrashed and cried when he thrust his own modestly sized member in there. While her mind was male, for his sake and their mutual ambition, she had agreed to publicly identify as a woman so that they could be the First Couple of France. Still, Rapace had the secret thrill of knowing he was married to the world's most impeccable hermaphrodite.

Breathlessly, Rapace gasped. "I want to suck you. Are you full?"

Giselle's sexual organ was composed of skin and cartilage grafts from other parts of her body and from a lattice of pig collagen. Like the sex organ of a cis-gendered person, it was fed by blood flow from her groin's vascular system. The living, throbbing pleasure wand became rigid in response to physical stimulus. However, Giselle did not produce ejaculate or sperm.

"Whose cum is it?"

"Ha," she teased. "That would be telling."

Giselle's silicone testicles were hollow, but they could be filled with a donor's ejaculate. At the significant moment, a button at the base of her scrotum would jet the liquid out.

"But," she said teasingly, stepping out of her dress and flipping off her high heels, "it took several men to fill up my new bigger balls. I hope you're not too full from dinner."

Giselle spat on her hand, then lubricated and stroked her member. Rapace sank to his knees, joining her in masturbating. He went at it so furiously he had no idea whether he had already climaxed and remained hard. The throbbing bulbous end of Giselle's cock hung in front of his nose, shiny with her saliva.

Just as he was about to envelop it with his quivering, salivating lips, President Rapace felt wave after wave of dissociation through his brain. It was as though he was being lifted into an alternative reality. Before his eyes, the urethra of Giselle's penis split into two and became fiery lidless eyes. He tried to recall if he'd had any unusual drugs that evening. Could he have gotten a bad batch? Impossible. He got his ecstasy and methamphetamine straight from government labs.

Just as soon as the aberration had manifested, it passed. He slumped back against a night table; he could not stand. He was seeing double; no... it was more than that. He was seeing things that were not there. But he was still conscious.

Giselle had a more serious reaction. She passed out and had fallen backward against an antique chair. Her hands convulsed on her penis and scrotum. She was gushing ejaculate all over the oriental carpet.

Still on his hands and knees, Rapace regained enough of his senses to pull a blanket off the bed and cover her. He then crawled toward the door. Was it an assassination? Were they gassing him? Had his scientists rebelled and turned the T-ray on them?

Urgent knocking came from the door. His security people came bursting in. They also looked disheveled.

"Mr. President, we have to get you to safety."

Rapace shook his head. He was enough of a politician to mouth something patriotic when all else failed. "If the Élysée Palace is not safe... neither is

France. The President of the Republic will not run away. Secure the palace. Go!"

He had to get in touch with Voclain.

Henri Voclain was the Pangeans' shadow chief of staff. Having no official position, he could not be questioned by the National Assembly or the courts.

Half an hour later, the situation became clear. So did the danger to everything he'd worked for.

"Of course, Henri," Rapace said into the secure video link. "You had no choice. If the Americans had recovered the… What about our warship? What exactly did you tell them to get them to fire a missile onto the French mainland?"

"Luckily we had an established protocol, similar to the destruction of a hijacked passenger jet. The captain thought it was a terrorist weapon of mass destruction located at Cesta Station and firing the bunker-buster missile was the only way to prevent an attack."

That story might hold, but only for a few days. Rapace looked at the calendar in the corner of the screen. He needed six. Six days to sow confusion and misdirection or all was lost. One tie he had to sever immediately.

"Henri," Rapace said gravely, "we've accomplished great things over the years. Now Pangea requires of you only one more thing."

Henri looked surprised, and then he resigned himself to his fate.

"My head of security suspects you," Rapace lied to the doomed man. "You are the only link between the palace and Cesta Station."

"Is there… any time for me to get away?"

Rapace shook his head.

With trembling fingers, the gaunt man in the video pulled a locket out from his shirt. It was the shape of all the continents joined as one: Pangea.

"Set your explosives first," Rapace had to remind him. No wonder the first T-bomb was a failure. Henri tended to blunder when he was under pressure.

Henri activated powerful booby traps on his door. Linked detonators would set off IED explosives all along the hallway of his expensive apartment block and along the street. Each was set to go off thirty minutes apart to give first responders time to arrive. It would take days to sort out the bodies.

Henri returned to his monitor and picked up the Pangea locket. Slowly he lifted the clear gel capsule to his lips.

Get on with it, Rapace thought. As a backup, he could use Abdelkader's local jihadis to kill Henri, but suicide was neater.

"Y-You'll get those papist filth, won't you, sir?"

"I promise, Henri. We'll snuff out every ember of Christianity. First in Europe, then the world!"

Finally, Henri took his capsule. Rapace had no idea what the man was expecting, but the sensations produced by the poison caused Henri to immediately thrash about. A dull gray ring appeared around Henri's neck. First it looked like a bruise, then a strangulation mark, then the scaly texture spread up to Henri's jaw. His eyes hemorrhaged so badly Rapace could not make out his pupils through the sudden spurt of red occluding the whites. Henri slumped out of view.

Rapace let five minutes pass. He felt his head clear. The Henri problem was taken care of. Next, he worried about the lethality of the T-bomb.

If only there were time to examine the effects on the people in the Bordeaux area. That was why France and other nuclear nations continued to test complex weapons systems—one had to be sure they worked correctly in the field.

Giselle was still unconscious. The spillover effect was more intense than Rapace and his scientists had expected. Cesta was five hundred kilometers from Paris. If the penumbra effect was proportional, and the main T-bomb's lethal range was one thousand miles in diameter… half the world would get a headache as Europe perished.

Fine.

He'd give anything to see the dead French people around Cesta Station. *You'll have plenty of company. Just six more days.*

His palm-slapped the intercom button. The security chief came in.

"I've just been speaking with several heads of state and their ministers. They have given us actionable intelligence. This man is a person of interest in the Bordeaux incident. Here." Rapace gave him Henri's address. "He's a definite flight risk but not considered armed. Please pick him up immediately, and take as many people with you as you can. We must take him alive for questioning."

30

Gisele was semiconscious and lying on the couch. By contrast, Rapace felt almost giddy. *It worked!* Rapace exulted. Thirty minutes had passed since the small event in Bordeaux. Was this how they had felt during the first atom bomb tests? The small one had gone off; now it was time for a continent-wide Hiroshima.

Rapace's deputy security chief burst in.

"What?" he snapped at the man, whose big torso and shaved head contrasted with his cowering apologetic expression.

"Chief Lalonde… all his men…" The slow-witted DGSI man was still absorbing the shocking news. "They have all been killed by IEDs."

Rapace knew that. He also knew there were more bombs set to detonate in the area of Henri's home. The higher the friendly body count, the better.

"Send more men," Rapace said. "Hurry. Accomplices of this villain Henri must not get loose in Paris."

"Yes, Mr. President."

"And page Giselle's doctor again. At this point, I don't even trust our own paramedics."

Only their personal doctor knew of Giselle's pansexuality. Despite the apparent terrorist crisis, a dick picture of the First Lady of France would make the tabloids.

"Also, widen the palace's secure perimeter."

"You should evacuate."

Rapace scoffed. "If I am not safe here, France itself is in jeopardy. The President of the Republic will not be moved."

That was a good sound bite; the other man he had said that to was dead, and Rapace wanted to make sure that quote got into circulation in the media. He sent the security people away and closed the blast-resistant door to the hallway. His suite of apartments was sectioned off from the rest of Élysée. He was expecting Hassan Abdelkader, the Pangean shadow war minister who was making his way past the thousands of skulls and leg bones embedded in the walls of the New Catacombs underneath the palace.

On the other side of the room, Giselle roused herself. With shaky hands holding a crystal glass, she drank water.

"My dear, how do you feel?"

"What?" His wife slurped as though she had forgotten how to drink. "What was that?"

Rapace had also felt the... dislocation, as though his whole mind and being were being drawn into the T-bomb's hallucinations like steel filings to a magnet.

He held up his hand. He had never fully trusted Giselle with the entire plan for a peaceful united Europe. While her mind was male and her female physiology had gone through menopause decades ago, Giselle's sensitivities might overcome the convictions they shared.

After twice scanning the room for listening devices, he told her everything about the Pangea Protocol.

"It's the only way. It was around Easter when it finally settled in my mind. A youngster helped me finally decide what must be done, the little girl helped me see what sacrifices must be made for future generations. The other Pangean shadow heads of state agreed immediately, especially the Belgians."

For decades, the Belgian faction had been advocating for a mass destruction event as the only way to wipe out the stubborn nation-states of Europe.

The revelation that they were about to cleanse Europe of a minimum of five hundred million defective obstructionists did not help Giselle return to lucidity.

"Y-you are serious." She started to fan herself with a gift from the Chinese ambassador. The fan fluttered, filling the room with the scent of sandalwood. Giselle knew about Rapace's role in the Notre Dame fire and the depth of his convictions. "But we have always worked toward the Kalergi Plan... I know it's taking time."

"Kalergi was an idiot," Rapace snapped; he was no racist, but Kalergi's Japanese-Austrian genetics had made the philosopher mentally weak. "As long as nations, cultures, or any differences at all exist, there will be strife, and worst of all, faith that things will get better.

"Kalergi thought that by mixing all the races, humanity would evolve into an Egyptian-looking super species that would build utopia. But more and more, we are seeing the opposite happen. The mass immigration we brought in has strengthened the nation-states and brought to power all sorts of patriots and national idealists."

That mental case boche Angela Merkel was to blame. Instead of keeping to the plan, she had brought in millions of economic migrants per year every bloody year. Tens of thousands had drowned trying to heed the siren call of her invitation. Eighty percent of those who arrived were young males who had little education but a lot of energy. They turned to crime for profit and the raping of women and children for pleasure. The hard-core Salafist Muslims among them started in relentlessly on the Jews, especially in France. The Bataclan massacre and the Charlie Hebdo assassinations encouraged the rise of Odin-worshipping neo-Nazis and yellow-vest fascists. This mess had led to Brexit and worsened the debt crisis. It was ruining the Pangeans' sacred agenda for European integration and Ever Closer Union.

"Borders," Rapace's said firmly. "Borders are the enemy. Without borders, a human loses all concept of personal identity. Our founder once said: 'A man who is a citizen of all countries is a useful rootless plant which will thrive on any ground upon which we choose to set him.'

"But *with* borders, anyone of any race, religion, or background is a menace. Did you know in Germany an openly gay imam was ordained last week? Even Muslims are adopting concepts of individual rights, free speech, and tolerance. That is not why we imported them!"

Rapace staggered as he remembered the terrible words that wicked girl had said to him outside Notre Dame at Easter. Europe's Christianity had infected her, like so many others. He had purified her, but for the entire continent, there could be only one solution.

"*Tabula rasa*," he pronounced, and hoped it sank in to Giselle's mind. She still looked unsettled. "The blank slate. Think of what will be waiting for the New Europeans. The first hundred million Pangeans will find the world's most industrialized continent, the best roads, and nearly two hundred functional nuclear reactors. This level of infrastructure and industry would take Africa centuries to build. I will grant it to my subjects in an instant."

Giselle was looking at him strangely. He adored her since the time he had been her patient. During the years following Notre Dame, she had helped him in so many ways. She helped him climb out of the dark chasm of despair and claw his way up the hierarchy of society and politics to become president of France.

"But it's genocide."

"It's much better than genocide," Rapace said. "It's the forcible extinction of an invasive species: *homo Europa*. Our mass culling will be infinitely less barbaric than any previous one. The process will be swift, humane, and as painless as possible.

"It will be much faster than Hitler and Stalin's death camps, the Holodomor enforced starvation, and Mao's mass eliminations. Only fifty million barriers to progress were eliminated in China by his Great Leap Forward.

"Pah! Nothing compared to the Pangea Protocol. To cap it all, this will be the most diverse ethnic cleansing in history. Regardless of background, gender identity, or religion, everyone in today's Europe is tainted. They must go."

"I understand," Giselle said reluctantly. "What about us?"

"The date for the Event is set. No one can stop it. I timed it as close as possible to one minute past midnight on All Saint's Day, November 1." Just saying it out loud gave Rapace relief. The torments caused by the Church to countless people over thousands of years would be brought to an end. He would end it. "Many hours before that, we will leave to one of three possible destinations. I have to see what the scientists have learned from the Cesta Station explosion to pick the optimal safe distance."

"But… everything…"

"Everything will still be here: all the buildings, the Eiffel Tower, Roman ruins, the Vatican." *Especially the Vatican*, Rapace thought. "But they will be of infinite use because no one will remember why they were built."

Giselle's doubts all seemed to fade, and she looked at him with such adoration, love, and lust that he could have resumed their passions with a hundredfold vigor right then. But then the elevator chimed. Shadow War Minister Abdelkader was coming up from the New Catacombs.

"Get dressed, we have company."

"So," Rapace said, "you say that it was an American who infiltrated Cesta?"

He remembered the admonition of Leopold II, who had done so well in the Congo up until his untimely passing: *Be quick to comprehend, slow to judge, and then act without mercy.*

Rapace's desk viewscreen showed a grainy photograph of the thuggish-looking clean-shaven American.

"Major Atticus Reidt, US Army," Abdelkader said. "He invaded our airspace with a fake transponder signal."

"You're sure he's dead?"

"He was inside Cesta Station when the French Navy's missile blew it up."

Rapace was glad they had destroyed the facility. But complications remained. What had Major Reidt transmitted back to his team at Ramstein? Would it help them locate the real T-bomb? Worst of all, the existence of such a weapon could no longer be denied. Bordeaux was an impromptu Trinity test. This genie would not be stuffed back into its bottle.

"Your recommendation?" Rapace asked.

His Pangean war minister considered for a moment. He was a broad-faced Frenchman of Algerian stock. Abdelkader was born a Muslim. He had rejected that faith when he saw how pathetically weak it was compared to the evils that needed to be stamped out. Even the most radical forms of the

Islamic caliphate could not overcome the religion's internal contradictions and mend humanity. Only Pangea could do that.

Still, Abdelkader hated Jews and Christians with admirable passion. After the first T-bomb experiments had ended in failure, the Algerian urged Rapace to try again. He had said: "There will never be a better time to press the 'reset' button on Europe."

The Pangeans had a book. The book was called *What is to Be Done?* In it was the collected wisdom of all the secret societies since the Enlightenment: Ordo Templi Orientis, Illuminati, Rosicrucians, the Kalergi Plan, Europa Edictum. Rapace did not need a paper or ebook copy. It and so much more information were imprinted between the DNA of his white blood cells. As a safeguard against interrogation by hypnosis or truth drug, the sequestered data could only be read by the quantum microchip in his brain.

What was to be done was obvious. Europe needed a population of docile serfs. The current tenants were not working out.

Abdelkader rubbed his sparse but bristly moustache and glanced at the bedroom where Giselle sat. He paced down the hallway in thought.

"The Americans are a problem," Abdelkader finally concluded.

"I agree."

"Ramstein has to be isolated."

When the Americans had gotten wind of the Event, he had sent them fake intelligence about an impending nuclear attack. Rapace had been prepared to let the US evacuate their military. Now more aggressive measures were called for.

"After Bordeaux, they are bound to start digging deeper. We need to do something drastic."

Rapace's Euro Forces were the fifth-strongest military power in the world and had access to France's nuclear arsenal. But they were no match for a superpower. A direct attack on America or even the nuclear-armed UK was out of the question.

"How many jihadis can you organize?" Rapace asked.

"I was preparing them to assault the European airports to stop people evacuating. After Bordeaux, there will be panic. Anyone who can book a flight will try to leave."

"We can't let them."

"Of course not."

If too many old Europeans survived, they might come back and reinfect the New Europe. That, Rapace could not allow.

"Euro Forces will directly commandeer the airports under European Union Aviation Safety Agency emergency regulations," Rapace said. "Bordeaux gives us an excuse, so will a massive terror attack on Ramstein. Make the Americans bleed."

"It will make 9/11 seem like a mosquito bite," Abdelkader said. He had fought for ISIS in Syria and was always eager to kill Westerners. Rapace suspected in the future, he would try to detonate a T-bomb of his own in America. Rapace looked at the man's hungry brown eyes and thought, *One continent at a time, my friend.*

"What about Britain?" Rapace said. "We control every airport in the Eurozone from Kiruna in Sweden to Rhodes in Greece. But since that disastrous Brexit, the British have sovereignty over their airspace."

Abdelkader smiled, and his purple lips parted, revealing long slightly yellow teeth. "Don't worry, Mr. President. I have something special planned for Heathrow and Gatwick."

31

Ellie was a flower. She grew straight and proud out from a luscious bed of rich, dark soil. Most days, she tracked the sun. When it rained, she shut her petals so only a few drops of moisture ever got in. Right now she could feel the wind jostling her. It was kind of annoying.

Despite it still being light out, somehow hanging over her was a full moon. There was an odd thing about this moon. Ellie had never before noticed this feature. Had anyone? The moon had two big pools of sparkling blue water that looked like eyes.

"Gotta move, grab her."

They plucked her out of the ground, which was a rather rude thing to do to a comfortably bedded and growing flower.

"She's thrashing too much," a rough-sounding woman's voice said.

"How long were we out?" asked another woman, also speaking with an American accent. "Is it still the same day?"

Ellie heard a small snap and got a whiff of something very unflowery. The sharp odor penetrated her brain fog. Moments later, Ellie realized she was not a flower and the moon was actually Sarge Bryan's chalky white face. His electric-blue eyes looked down at her with concern.

He held a tube of ammonia smelling salts over her. She grabbed his hand. "I'm up." With a start, she remembered where she was. "What… where's Atticus?"

Sarge shook his head and looked into the distance. "No one could have made it out. We've got to go."

She followed his gaze. Over the countryside. The French country, she remembered. *Oh, Atticus!* On the horizon, against the remaining glow of sunset, Ellie could see a thin smudge of smoke rising. There was no activity; other than birds singing, there was no sound.

The hallucinations had been so real that the world she had woken up to felt fake. She had to touch Sarge Bryan's shoulder to make sure he was there. She grabbed his civilian jacket and pulled herself up.

"I don't know where you're going, but I'm going to… there." Ellie pointed, which made her head spin. "What is it called? The Cesta place. Atticus might be hurt. He could have been thrown clear, couldn't he?"

"Ellie, he got hit with a type of bunker buster that leaves a crater ten stories deep. They had a small fission reactor at Cesta Station, which also went up. The gamma rays I'm picking up are lethal for a hundred meters."

She might have tried to go anyway, and then she remembered. Atticus Jr. was in transit to safety in America.

"He'd… want us to make sure Attie Jr. is safe."

"He would," Sarge said grimly.

Ellie looked around. Over the past two days, she had met so many new people and traveled hundreds of miles while hardly sleeping. She turned away from the ruins of Cesta Station. There were people about, she knew that; it took her a while to register them.

Who was here? Sarge Bryan, the two female helicopter pilots… and someone else? Not Mr. Oliphant, Wolfgang, or Ms. China—they were back at Ramstein in Germany.

"That was the bomb?" Ellie asked.

"That was a small enhanced radiological device based on the Tyr quark effect. Dr. Licht was correct. Any attempt to destroy the particle will release its energy."

That was the robot mind... what was her name?

"Miss Aleph. You're here."

"My bad, and yours," Miss Aleph said, her voice rising with fear and urgency. "One of us has just been killed. We delayed getting away because of you, Eleanor."

"How long...?"

"Were you lying on the grass drooling and moaning? About six hours until Sarge Bryan was the first to recover his wits. The period during which you were all out of it was really upsetting for me."

Why the hell couldn't they have investigated Cesta another way? They could have used a drone or something. Why did Atticus have to risk himself? Had he really been blown up? Was it hours ago that that had happened? *He'd want us to make sure his mission was successful.*

"Were you able to get the information back to Ramstein for the scientists?" Ellie said.

"We don't know what got through," Sarge said, letting go of her so she could try and balance on her wobbly legs. "We can't transmit anything now. It would give away our position."

"To who?"

"Them," Sarge said, squinting into the distance, zooming in. "Euro Forces airborne. Cesta was an official government nuclear test facility. The T-bomb or a prototype was inside. We have to assume anything European is under the control of the Pangeans. They just started a search grid to look for us."

Sarge and the pilots had put up a camouflage tarp. The copse of trees around the pit of Cesta experimentation victims gave them some cover.

"I don't think I can fly," one of the pilots said, rubbing her red-rimmed eyes and holding herself up on the side of the helicopter. "Even if I could, the Airbus is a civilian bird. It's unarmed and a sitting duck for an air-to-air missile."

The weapon that killed Atticus had been fired from the sea. All of France had to be considered hostile territory. For Ellie, this felt like being on the run with Atticus and his team through Jordan and Israel. Except now they'd have to go on without him. She stared at the horizon. Just before she passed out, a big distant explosion had rattled the countryside, and a dirty mushroom cloud had been rising. All that remained in the evening sky was a misshapen pillar of smoke coming from an unseen fire.

"Grab gear, supplies, and ammo," Sarge ordered. "We've got to move out on foot."

"Wait!" Ellie said shakily. The pilots looked at her as though she were seeing things again. Ellie had recovered enough to be angry. She wanted to do something more than run.

"Miss Aleph, can you fly that copter?" In the Middle East, the Israeli AI had been able to operate Ellie's jet-powered flyboard.

`"Yes. But were you listening or still hallucinating when the pilot told you we'll be shot down no matter who is flying?"`

"Escaping isn't what I had in mind."

Ten minutes later, Ellie had a knapsack and a gun. They had been able to cover a hundred meters of uneven ground before Sarge said they were far enough away to try her plan.

"Ellie, I know you're pissed, we all are," Sarge said. "But I don't think Atticus would—"

"He's not here, is he?" Ellie snapped. "And it's because of them, Cesta, the T-bomb, and all those people behind it. I'm going to destroy them."

Miss Aleph got the passcodes for the Airbus helicopter's autopilot and made it take off. Their silver-skinned copter was soon out of sight, moving toward the Euro Forces aircraft.

`"Is anyone watching this? This is really good flying. See how I keep circling through the French helicopter's heat trail so they can't get a missile lock?"`

"Quit playing. Just fuck them up," one of the women pilots said, watching through binoculars.

"Yes, please do," Ellie said coldly.

Seconds later, they were rewarded with a distant explosion as their remotely piloted copter crashed into the Euro Forces copter. Ellie popped her head up. The wreckage hung, burning in the air for a moment, and then it crashed down toward the pillar of smoke rising from Cesta Station.

As dusk fell, they hiked through thickets and ran through fields, breaking tree cover only when they had to. For the next hour, Sarge led Ellie and the two pilots along an indirect path toward Bordeaux.

"I would have gone left."

"Shh," Bryan told Miss Aleph, who was riding inside Ellie's leather bag.

"Like there's anyone around. Remember, I can see everything you do."

The AI had a wireless connection to Sarge's electronic eyes.

"We should bypass these structures up here," Sarge said, looking at faint lights in windows of a farmhouse about two hundred meters away.

They were in the middle of a field of short grass. Sarge and the rest of them were flattened against one side of a knee-high concrete pond. It was probably a watering spring for the farm's animals, none of which were visible in the dark.

"We need transport and supplies. The Euro Forces have been radio silent since I killed their air support. They're up to something."

"I have to agree with the shiny metal tube," one of the pilots said. "Ramstein is the only safe place, and it's not in hikin' distance."

That was an understatement. Germany was hundreds of kilometers away; in which direction? Ellie hadn't any clue.

"All right," Sarge said after watching the farmhouse a few more minutes. "We go in. No talking."

Ellie held a small machine pistol. She had shot at people before, but not with this kind of gun. The weapon Atticus had shown her how to use in Jordan had been a bit larger and more sophisticated. She checked the safety and made sure the electronic holographic sight was still on, then followed. The only thing she remembered about guns was to keep them pointed at the ground or the enemy.

They approached the farmhouse quietly. Every second, Ellie expected to hear a dog bark and give them away. They got closer, and closer. There were some vehicles. If they could borrow or steal a car…

They were nearly at the house when bright spotlights lit up from all sides. Ellie felt like a cockroach caught in the middle of a kitchen floor.

"*Arrête toi là!*"

It was an ambush. It must be Euro Forces. Sarge swore. But there was no way he could have known. They were using the farm's own floodlights and had a kind of camouflage netting that only dropped when they had no chance of escape. When the netting fell away, it revealed a team of six uniformed Euro Forces.

"Everyone," Sarge said, throwing his weapons down, "lower your weapons. Don't give them an excuse."

The enemy soldiers advanced slowly, sighting their rifles on them. Fighting would be suicide; even Ellie could see that.

"Miss Aleph, translate, please," Sarge said. "Listen, Frenchies, see my eyes?"

"*Hey les Français, écoutez-moi. Voyez-vous mes yeux?*"

"My electronic eyes are taking pictures of each of your ugly faces and sending them back to the US Air Force Base at Ramstein. Anything happens to us, you will be the top six on the ten most-wanted terrorists list."

Miss Aleph translated, adding a bit more profanity to her impeccable French than the situation required, Ellie thought.

"*Étends tes mains!*" Two Euro soldiers stepped forward with zip ties.

Ellie really didn't want to be taken captive. Of course, had she been given a choice, she might have chosen that over what happened next.

"That's interesting."

Miss Aleph saw something through Bryan's eyes that neither Ellie nor their captors could.

"Shut your hole," Bryan whispered without moving his lips.

Ellie finally saw them. She thought she was hallucinating again. It was as though parts of the hedges and trees had turned liquid and streams of inky-black shadows were running at them from beyond the floodlights. Just before the first one jumped on the rearmost Euro soldier, she realized these were fresh versions of what had pulled her into the mass burial pit.

"Ahhhhhhh!"

Not knowing where the threat was coming from, two of the Euro soldiers raised their guns toward Ellie and her group. When they glanced over their shoulders, Sarge shot them.

"Down!"

Ellie grabbed her gun off the grass and pressed her safety mechanism all the way around just to be sure it was off. This must have switched the gun to fully automatic. She aimed and shot in the same direction as Sarge. Her tracer rounds slashed into the darkness in a steady stream. After three seconds of a blazing fireworks barrage, her magazine was empty.

Sarge appeared to have aimed for the Euro Force enemies' body armor to stop them from shooting and knock them down.

"Leave everything. Those incoming are fast," Sarge yelled. He grabbed Ellie by the collar and pulled her up.

One of the pilots might have gotten hit by something. She was running beside them awkwardly. Ellie hoped it hadn't been one of her bullets.

Other Euro Force ambushers in trees behind the farmhouse started shooting, but not at them. The massed undead threw themselves forward and scrabbled onto the low hanging branches of the tree up into the snipers' hiding places. The shooting stopped.

Glancing back, Ellie saw a Euro soldier; his head was being held between the hands of an animated cadaver. The French man stared into the distance and was casually stripping off his clothes. It was as though he were getting into a shower. Wherever he bared his flesh, the creatures started biting, chewing, and swallowing. As he was consumed, the victim made no sound.

Ellie clutched her hot, useless gun and followed Sarge Bryan as fast as she could.

32

NEAR BORDEAUX

ELLIE

They were running away from the ambush at the farmhouse, consistent with Sarge Bryan's "get the fuck out of here" plan, when Ellie felt something explode against her shin. She tumbled. As she rolled and tried to get up, her hands felt something rough, slimy, and stony. It was the stupid water pond they had hidden behind as they had been approaching the farm.

"Who puts a thing like that in an open field?" Ellie groused. Then she realized if her leg was broken she was going to be eaten.

One of the pilots dragged her up to her feet. She didn't ask if she could run. Even with a broken bone, there was no Plan B. It hurt like heck, but Ellie kept on. As they approached a tree line, Ellie felt around for Miss Aleph.

"Hey, are you awake?" she whispered.

"That's what you ask me?"

Miss Aleph sounded terrified.

"Are those *animata cadavera*?"

"No, Ellie, French people are just very strange. And it's cadaueris, not cadavera."

Even during the worst parts of the 96-Hour War, Miss Aleph could be counted on for sarcasm. She had not changed. Ellie's leg just felt numb now.

She could sense the others were slowing their pace just a little to allow her to keep up.

"But," Ellie panted, "I thought you said they just had random movements. Like the severed arm that could play chess. It wouldn't move unless the scientists were controlling it, would it?"

`"Something must be controlling them. Ellie, stop! Sarge Bryan is looking at something."`

Ellie leaned against the cool rough bark of a tree; she looked behind. Nothing.

"You know," she said, deeply inhaling the scent of pine needles and gritty dry forest dust, "seeing through Bryan's eyes like you do, it's a bit creepy."

`"That's what you find creepy?"`

In the near-perfect darkness, they had come to a retaining wall made of stone. Beyond that, meager slivers of moonlight revealed a storage silo raised up on stilts. Ellie had no idea what the purpose of a structure like that was, but she was very happy to see it. They found a way up to the hatch entrance: a rickety wooden ladder.

"Aleph," Sarge whispered as they pulled her up the last few rungs, "how do those animata things move around and navigate? Sight, sound, smell?"

While the AI mulled that over, they got settled in the loft. There was a large main floor strewn with hay and some grain Ellie could not identify. Above, rimming the whole lower floor, was a four-foot-wide walkway. There was no staircase or ladder to get to this second level, not that Ellie's leg could have taken any more climbing.

They drew up the exterior ladder after them and checked their gear. Ellie's gun was empty, and its barrel had gotten crammed full of dirt and grass. She set about cleaning it. Working by the light of dim red flashlights, they arranged empty burlap grain bags into places to sit. The pilots covered any cracks they saw in the walls.

`"Sarge, I've reviewed all of what you recorded, when you weren't jerking your head too much."`

"I'll try to hold steadier next time."

`"I also stole some data from the Euro Forces computer and surveillance systems. The animata cadaueris seem` to travel in groups. No one individual is ever more than a few meters from another. Isolated ones stand still or move aimlessly."

One of the female pilots asked, "Can we try to call Ramstein, even on that cell phone?"

She pointed to the handset hanging from Miss Aleph's cylinder by a patch of duct tape. Ellie realized she didn't know the pilots' names. She asked.

"Charlotte, or Charlie, is me. My ugly friend is Candace," the crewcut-sporting woman said. They were both stout with short hair. Charlie was taller and had a slight lisp.

"From what I gathered in the emails I grabbed from the Euro Forces, Ramstein will have other concerns. They have been told the terrorist who blew up Cesta Station was Major Atticus Reidt. Euro ground forces are cordoning off the base and have been told to treat Americans as hostiles."

Sarge Bryan let out a toneless whistle of air. Not much was said as the soldiers hunkered down to wait for dawn. Ellie elevated her throbbing leg and swallowed some painkiller pills Candace had offered her. She was certain she would not get any rest.

The next thing Ellie felt was mild surprise when she opened her eyes to find the rays of the new day's sun lancing through tiny cracks in the walls and seeping up under the open gables of the roof. As she lay back on a mattress of burlap bags, she was even more surprised to see the small upside-down face of an animated cadaver kid staring at her from between two roof rafters.

Its eyes were a different kind of gray than Ellie had ever seen. They seemed to be in motion, not exactly sparkling, but the twin orbs had no pupils and were not still. Was this what Atticus had seen when he looked into the center of the T-bomb device?

Without taking her gaze off their little visitor, Ellie moved her head to the side. Sarge was directly under the extended eves, so he couldn't see it. Candace and Charlie were sorting through packages of food and supplies with their backs to her.

Slowly and very quietly, Ellie felt along the floor. She grabbed what she thought was the sling of her weapon. From her experiences in the pit, Ellie knew these things had some power of hallucination, by proximity or touch. If it got too close, none of them would even realize they were being chewed to bits.

Almost as if on cue, the thing smiled, showing its little prepubescent teeth. Ellie judged it had been a long-haired boy, probably ten or eleven years old, a little bigger than Attie Jr.

As slowly and quietly as she could, Ellie tugged on her weapon to bring it close, then she noticed the strap she actually had hold of belonged to her knapsack with Miss Aleph inside. The movement caused the bag to flop over, which pointed the handset camera straight up to the ceiling.

"IT'S ONE OF THEM! KILL IT! KILL IT!" Miss Aleph shrieked.

33

When President Putin heard the news from France, his expression did not change in the slightest. As for Zvena, Human+ augments had extensive self-monitoring functions. He watched his own heartbeat and blood pressure spike, then settle.

Putin's chief of staff Gerasimov eyed Zvena uncomfortably as he concluded his report. Gerasimov waddled into the middle of the president's personal den and put down a data chip on the coffee table.

"That is all we know for certain," Gerasimov said.

While making no overt reaction as he was given details of the unknown radiological event near Bordeaux, Putin's stillness electrified the cozy, comfortably appointed room deep within the Kremlin's fallout shelter.

Zvena was awestruck by Putin. While the president was fit for his age, no normal human was physically imposing next to Zvena. However, in that moment, Putin exuded a special quality. It was a combination of every raw instinct wild beasts used and all the patient ruthless cunning a man could possess.

Putin nodded at his chief of staff, dismissing him. With a last sideways suspicious glance at Zvena, Gerasimov left and closed the door. Putin stood on the balls of his feet for a moment. Then, having evidently made up his mind about something, he pivoted and grasped the back of the big red leather couch.

"Komandir Zvena, take off your rank insignia at once. You are no longer an officer in Russia's Navy."

The statement struck Zvena as though he has been hit across the face by the steel-reinforced knuckles of Rodion's hand. He was devastated. He had given everything to Russia, his service, his whole body, his soul. If he was not to be a Spetsnaz Human+ soldier… the thought was worse than death to him.

Putin was obviously blaming him for bringing him faulty intelligence. And even that, he had brought too late. Zvena cursed himself for not pressing his European mole Zarathustra harder. He should have had advance knowledge of this Event so that full advantage could be taken by Russia and Putin. He had failed them both.

Without hesitation, Zvena ripped the insignia with three golden stars and two bars off his coat and placed them neatly on the small coffee table.

"Yaroslav Zvena." Putin fixed his eyes on him. "In respect of this new European crisis, you are going to be my personal *zelenyy chelovechek*, my 'little green man.'"

"But… sir, the crisis has happened. The Event Zarathustra informed us of…"

"Is only beginning," Putin said with a wry smile.

Zvena's head spun again, but now for the completely opposite reason. Over the last decades, anonymous soldiers in masks and unmarked green uniforms had appeared in Chechnya, Crimea, Syria, Sudan, Libya, and many other places. Along with the bloodthirsty mercenaries of CHVK Vagner, the little green men were an integral part of Russia's command and control.

The *zelenyy chelovechek*, or "agent in charge," reported directly to the Kremlin and had total authority in overt and covert activities. They had license to kill, kidnap, torture, maim, and steal. Zvena was to be one of them; he was overjoyed and humbled.

"There must be someone more qualified," Zvena said as the weight of the responsibility settled on him. "Someone with more understanding and technical knowledge of what you need done."

"There is!" Putin's hand hit the back of the couch with a firm slap. "But I am otherwise occupied."

Putin and Zvena shared a laugh. Then the president raised his glass. "The Motherland calls," he said with solemn enthusiasm, and they drank.

34

Without warning, the second of Temir's three dirigibles was caught in the beam of a floodlight. They had been making a second and final pass over their primary drop targets around Moscow and the heavily industrialized Zelenogradsky district. The night weather was excellent, heavily overcast. Temir lay flat in the cockpit of the lead airship; a glowing map flickered inches from his face.

They had been passing over a gravel pit and machine yard. Below them was a swamp. It was these dozens of square kilometers of moist bogs that made this area so important. Centimeters from his face, a light silently blinked, signaling the emergency.

Eylül was texting him.

`Searchlight hit exterior of ship 3. What should I do?`

Using speech-to-text, Temir advised him that it was likely the industrial park's floodlight and that it was merely broken and swinging in the wind.

`Continue on course.`

After the small event in Bordeaux, Temir had wasted an hour of darkness making sure that the detonation was not the start of a Europe-wide cascade of

T-bombs. Back at the Blue Mosque in Istanbul, when making his presentation to the Turkish generals and Elder Omid, Temir had largely bluffed his knowledge and expertise of this exciting but volatile dark-matter technology.

His knowledge about the T-bomb came from three sources. First, what the Congolese soldier had told him before Elder Omid had his irrelevantly disgusting scaphism fun. Second, what Turkish scientists loyal to the Grey Wolves had determined. And last, his own intuition.

It was Temir's belief Europe wanted to die. It was old, sick, and demented. It was looking for a way to end itself. How does a whole civilization combust? The slow poison of mass immigration without assimilation might have worked, eventually.

But Westerners were nothing if not impatient. The T-bomb was a culturally apt final solution to the European problem. The kafirs' brains would be turned to mush. This would certainly cure them of their mental diseases, chief among them being an utter loss of belief in their own civilization. This, above all, had convinced Temir the rumors of the Event were true.

Bordeaux had been a test or an accident. It did not matter which. The real Event was still on schedule to happen on November 1, as organized by the Pangean Deep State. But on November 2, instead of finding a depopulated open society ready to be filled by hordes of compliant serfs from Africa, the Pangeans would face an army of well-armed Turks and Iranians invading from the east.

Once the continent's nuclear reactors were under their control and wired to self-destruct, the Pangeans would cooperate or face one hundred Chernobyl-style meltdowns. Having done a few criminal and smuggling transactions with the Pangeans on behalf of the Grey Wolves, Temir had every reason to expect them to be reasonable. He was looking forward to watching as the blue-and-white *Ülkü Ocakları* flag, featuring a wolf and a sickle, was raised over Vienna, Berlin, London, Paris, and finally Brussels itself.

Temir...

Eylül was texting again.

What now?

Temir gritted his teeth. Even on secure channels, no bloody names were to be used. He did not have time to respond before he heard the distant thump of machine-gun fire. He switched his ground camera from ambient view to infrared.

Damn!

He had been so distracted thinking about the endgame that he had lost track of what was in front of him. Beams of infrared spotlights from a mobile air-defense battery were whipping across the sky. Temir's supercharged brain tried to work out what had happened.

Some half-drunken security guard must have seen the third blimp when it was caught in the beam of an ambient searchlight. Not knowing what it was, he'd likely called 122, emergency services. Russian air traffic control was a legacy system of the Cold War. They had direct communications links to the sleepy antiaircraft batteries permanently stationed around Moscow.

After confirming it was not a commercial or military flight, the Armed Forces reservists had decided to shoot at it.

Rounds zipped past his canopy. Some hit the unmanned ship being towed between him and Eylül.

Temir…

Shut up, Eylül.

No time.

Temir spoke into his microphone, letting the computer text back to his wingman.

"Step 1: Release all middle ship's cargo, maximum dispersion."

Jamshid's ship would implode any moment.

"Step 2: Separate dirigible tethers."

Temir's left appendage was too thick and ungainly to assist him in anything. It writhed between the inner hull of the cabin and his rib cage; its strange hearts all beat faster, making the black ichor blood throb. Temir worked the airship controls with his right hand.

"Step 3: Maximum descent."

Their craft were nearly invisible to radar, but direct spotlights of ambient or IR wavelengths would reveal them as suspicious blobs floating against the overcast night sky.

Temir had no way of firing back at the lone ground station, a most inconvenient Soviet-era relic. Hopefully the antiaircraft crew would conclude the empty dirigible was a loose weather balloon. Who would think of a blimp attack against a superpower?

Temir heard the tether lines disengage and snap off with a *twang*. Jamshid's former blimp floated away, and they were free.

"Do not follow me," Temir hissed into his mic. "Go back along target 6." That was the Meshchera wetlands. It was a prime target for their cargo.

He flinched slightly as the implosion of the middle blimp blasted through the night like an invisible firework. He did not like being one-handed and cooped up in a tiny cockpit. With a joystick, he turned his night-vision telescope around to see behind.

His Grey Wolf brother was doing as he was told. A kilometer away, and becoming more distant by the second, the antiaircraft battery was standing down. On the ground, people were running around and probably threatening to court martial the gunner for opening fire over the densely populated city.

Soon, Temir found himself over a swampy area. It was an abandoned Soviet-era factory complex that stretched for miles and was slowly being reclaimed by the marshes of the Moskva River. He selected his last remaining series of drop pods and firmly pulled the release handle. Finger-sized projectiles rained down from the belly of the dirigible onto the city they would soon ravage and destroy.

Dawn was approaching an hour later, and so were an unusual number of fighter jets and helicopters. That was bad.

The good news was that Temir was close to their primary landing spot, and Eylül was not far behind. This landing zone had the most exfiltration options. If the paranoid Russians looked closely at the blimp and saw it could hold a man, Temir would need to make the fastest exit possible.

His companion texted him: Why did they mobilize their aircraft so quickly?

Anyone with half a brain would know that. The incident at Bordeaux had set everyone in the hemisphere on yellow alert or higher. Perhaps when Jamshid's blimp was shot down, a Russian WMD specialist had quickly come and examined the wreck. The jets and helicopters were searching for more invaders. Too late.

"Be quiet. Just land."

Temir's craft skidded to a landing, grinding to a stop on gravel along an industrial road. The crosswind was strong. It blew his fuselage against the hundred-foot pole supporting a broken mercury vapor highway lamp. He started the self-destruct implosion sequence and kicked open the cockpit hatch.

Eylül already was running toward him.

"My," he panted, coming closer, "my airship won't collapse. The stupid mechBrain said not enough power."

Temir unfurled his left appendage to its full length for the first time in eight hours. It was a relief. With his three thick digits, he picked up a fist-sized rock. His left arm relaxed and became a five-foot-long boneless boa constrictor with a stone in its mouth. Rotating his body like a discus thrower, he hurled the projectile at just under the speed of sound. Two hundred meters away, Eylül's airship shuddered and gave a hollow *pop*, collapsing like a black soap bubble.

"Save your breath," Temir said. "We have three kilometers to run."

The dirigibles had always been on a one-way trip to bomb Moscow with their living cargo. Temir had arranged for five escape routes to be in place, including an uncomfortable exit through Vnukovo Airport inside a shipping crate.

Grey Wolves were strongest in Turkey where sympathizers would hide members and lie to traitorous police who were not on the ultranationalists' payroll. Nearly every major country in the world had strong Grey Wolves chapters, especially Germany and Sweden. Russia was a slightly different matter. Their penetration here had been slower, and they had to use locals who harbored anti-Kremlin sentiments. Muslim Chechens and Kazakhs hated Russians, and their loyalty was for sale.

That was why they had a long-distance run to get to the meetup and begin their exfiltration. Temir could not let local mafia freelancers know where they were landing or even the precise day. Every night this week, their local people were supposed to be at the rendezvous.

Their early-morning jog away from the wrecked blimps was uneventful. The local fixers were waiting as expected. Temir greeted the three swarthy capable-looking men, and then he killed them.

The last swine got off a well-aimed shot. It would have hit Temir between the eyes. But he had raised his left appendage and flattened the thick end out to its maximum width. Acting much like a Plexiglas shield, it was translucent enough to see through and in lab tests had proven effective even against armor-piercing bullets.

The Kazakh's 7.62 Tokarev pistol bullet thudded as it stuck his thick webbed membrane, caught like a fly in aspic. The bullet was hot; it sizzled and annoyed his symbiont.

Temir charged at the remaining thug, pushing him into the side of his truck. Trusty Eylül came up and hacked into the left side of the pinned man's head with a bayonet until he stopped moving. His old chum was quick on the uptake, at least where brutish violence was called for.

"Uh, Aga Temir," he said, using the title he had earned during the Holy Land Liberation War, "I guess there is a change in plan?"

"Yes, one our hired help would likely not agree with." Temir picked the now slightly warm bullet out of his now normal-sized appendage. There was no blood, only a gelatinous goo that quickly hardened to close the divot. "Put them in the dumpster. No need to dissolve them. We won't be here that long."

Temir covered his human eye and used the eagle vision of his left to watch the helicopters and jets circling over the city.

"With the unexpected incident in France and the discovery of a hostile airship over their capital, the Russians will move from a Level Two alert, Danger of War, to Level One, Full Combat Readiness."

"Oh," Eylül said, his face falling. "That's bad."

"No." Temir gave him a mild friendly slap with his human hand. "It is very good. We came here to take out the central nervous system of the Russian military. It is the only force that will remain to oppose us after the Major Event in Europe on November 1. At Level One alert status, the most important element of Russia's command system is required to become airborne."

"So?"

"So," Temir said, looking in the truck and viewing with approval the equipment and weapons provided by their former Kazakh associates, "as he goes to his plane, we are going to kill President Vladimir Putin."

35

Kill it!" Miss Aleph yelled at the animated cadaver that was looking at them from a ledge above.

Sarge had his machine pistol on the target a second later but did not fire. "Everyone okay? Sound off."

Ellie and the pilots, Charlie and Candace, said they were okay.

"I'm fine too, now shoot."

"We still don't know if their blood is toxic or how they communicate," Sarge Bryan said as he kneeled on the other side of the barn, aiming up. "If we destroy this one, it could alert the others. You said isolated ones are aimless."

"Where did we run to?" Charlie asked, wiping perspiration off her forehead. She glared first at the interloper then at Sarge.

"I was kinda waiting on telling you," Sarge said sheepishly. "Because of where the highways and roadblocks were, we had to circle in, back toward the T-bomb detonation site."

That route had taken them into the red zone near Cesta Station, Ellie realized. Just outside the zone, they had been knocked out and suffered hallucinations. Everyone inside would have had their neurons depolarized by dark-matter rays.

"From here on, I'm navigating."

Their little visitor did not appear to be aggressive.

"It has no respiration," Sarge said, analyzing it with his cybernetic sensors. "Its body is room temperature."

"It has to have been here all along," Ellie whispered, shuddering. "Maybe up there in that dormant state they go into."

The former boy might have belonged to the farm family and gone up into the silo loft during the previous afternoon. Perhaps he had drifted off and been killed in his sleep and was just now waking as something inhuman.

The real monsters were the scientists at Cesta Station who experimented on monkeys and people no one would miss. They had simply thrown their victims into the pit, then covered them with a bit of earth and waited for the next batch. The bottom layer had woken up first and tried to dig themselves out.

"The people who built the T-bomb might not be aware their victims reanimate," Ellie said.

"They are certainly aware now."

"Can we get it down from there?" Candace asked. "I don't want it dropping on us unexpectedly."

"Get a pole. See if you can prod—"

Their reanimated chum leaned forward and nearly fell on top of Ellie's bad leg. She yelped with fright and rolled away. Its body flopped down like a sack of flour onto the dirty wooden slats.

The two pilots grabbed a rake and a broken hoe and prodded it into a corner. Unblinking, it stared and did not seem to mind being held against the wooden wall of the barn.

Other than its eerie eyes and cuts that did not bleed, the former French rural child was in good shape. It had on new clothes, overalls with a yellow sun embroidered on them, and one new high-top running shoe.

"Sarge, rerun your gamma dispersion scan. I have to gather as much information as I can in case you all die." Miss Aleph added, "And keep me as far away as possible from it."

"Why?" Ellie asked the typically self-centered machine. "It can't affect you, can it?"

"My matrix, the cylindrical SSD, is a unique composite holding my priceless artificial mind. Just keep it away."

They didn't have much time to gather data before they heard a sort of low buzzing.

"Is that a plane?" Candace said hopefully.

"Must be close, I can feel vibrations," her co-pilot said.

Ellie saw movement below them. Her heart thumped in her chest.

"It's not a plane. It's them."

Sarge threw open the hatch to the ground. Beneath them were hundreds of creatures. The animated dead were of all ages, an equal number of men and women.

The ones closest were ripping at the timber stilts that held up the barn. Their fingers ground down bloodlessly on hard wood. Finger bones and teeth tore at the supports.

"It called them! I told you to kill it."

Ellie hobbled over and pushed a stack of hay bales onto the boy. The soldiers could not mind it and fight the attackers at the same time.

Five minutes later, they had exhausted all their ammunition, and there seemed to be more creatures than ever crowding around. All avenues of escape were blocked.

Ellie began repeatedly to check herself, trying to tell if she had lapsed into a hallucination. With that many of them in one place, their aura, or whatever they carried with them, could infect her mind. She still had visions of that Euro Forces soldier stripping naked. Maybe he thought he was taking a refreshing bath, when in reality he was being chewed to pieces.

"We should get on the roof," Sarge Bryan said. Under the circumstances, he sounded unreasonably calm. "If the struts all go at nearly the same time, this barn might fall straight down. We can keep them off until help comes."

Ellie didn't ask what help. She just looked for a way to get up to the second level where the reanimated kid had dropped down from.

"Sarge, I have no more ammo, should we…" Charlie pointed to the dead boy, who was crawling out from under a bale of hay.

The kid showed no sign of hostility, its arm stretched out at the open hatchway and toward the teeming horde. Sarge Bryan got his long knife out and took a few deep breaths.

"Let him go," Ellie said. If Sarge touched it, he could start hallucinating. No one knew what would happen if they got splattered by the fluids inside it. "One less complication."

Using two rakes, they guided it to the doorway, and it happily flopped down onto the heads of the others.

"I see a way up," Ellie said. "We can get up to the ledge and the roof."

She used a rake to hook a rope ladder down from the second level. Last evening, when he had been human, the boy must have climbed up, then pulled the ladder up. Then he had been killed by the T-bomb blast.

Sarge went up first. With her leg swollen and even less useful than it was the previous night, Ellie felt like she had the most enormous buttocks in the world as they strained to lift her the ten feet up to the ledge under the gables.

In the corner of the loft were some empty soda cans, a blanket, a flashlight, and some comic books featuring a round-headed boy, a bearded man, and a white dog.

"Look," Candace said.

On the ground below them, the reanimated boy was not taking part in trying to tear down their sanctuary. It was standing in a clear space. Others slowly stopped what they were doing and looked.

They started circling the boy. Then the boy put out its hands and touched them. Each one it touched also touched another, until finally the wave got to the ones gnawing at their wooden stilts. Those also stopped what they were doing.

Like a wave made by wind blowing across a field of ripe wheat, the boy in the sunrise jumper started walking away. So did the army of animated corpses.

"Well, I'll be," Sarge said, his mouth slack.

The procession of the little pied piper did not last long. A phalanx of other animated dead stood in the boy's way; these ones did not move when he touched them. Instead they tore him to pieces. The mob trampled over the boy's body parts and ragged clothes, then came back toward the barn. They all attacked with renewed vigor.

"Just when I thought we'd made a friend," Charlie said.

"We kinda did," Candace said.

There was a sudden crack. The whole barn tilted sideways. Without warning, Candace fell out into the mob below.

Charlie shrieked.

"Come on, get up here," Sarge ordered from the second level.

Ellie was first up onto the roof; the whole structure was pitching to one side at a mad angle. The part they were on was nearly flat in relation to the ground as the whole barn had tilted over at about forty-five degrees. Beneath them, boards were splintering and crunching. Sarge Bryan grabbed Charlie by her flight suit and pulled her up; she seemed out of it.

He handed Ellie a rope. "See if you can get a line into that tree."

The bloody thing was twenty meters away. Ellie tried anyway, hobbling on one leg, careful to not fall over the edge. The third time she threw the lasso, a violent wind blew it sideways to the ground.

A walking cadaver grabbed it. She pulled; it pulled back. She fell forward, and when she landed, her head and arms were hanging over the edge of the roof. The rope caught and looped around her leg; she scrabbled at it, trying to untangle the knot. One more good pull, and she'd be over the edge.

The undead man holding the rope stared at Ellie with depthless eyes, its mouth red and raw and oozing from having eaten parts of the little French boy. It prepared to pull Ellie down. Its blue-black knuckles blanched as it tightened its grip around the rope.

Then its upper torso exploded. So did the heads, arms, and pelvises of a dozen other creatures. Body parts churned up in a precise furrow in the wake of heavy projectiles raining along the undead-covered earth.

Ellie looked up. In the air above them was a miraculous flying machine. As it hung over them, it made hardly a whisper. A shark with an American flag on its back was painted on the fuselage. The gunnery door was open, and fire rained down from a rotating machine gun.

"A Ramstein hovercopter," Sarge yelled. "Hang on to something. The rotor's got a heck of a downdraft."

The aircraft was at least as long and twice as wide as the Chinook helicopter. Yet it was nearly silent. As the wash swept over her, Ellie's ears popped. Sarge grabbed her hand as the vertical hurricane enveloped them. Firing from the open doorway continued. Sarge gestured with a kind of military sign language to the people thirty feet above.

"They cannot land. We have to leave quickly," Sarge said. "They'll send grapples."

A drone the size and shape of a dinner plate came whizzing out of the open doorway. All of the visible monsters beneath them were in pieces, but there were others covered by the floor of the barn. Ellie tried hard not to trip.

"You go first," Sarge said as he grabbed the drone. Attached to it were a nylon harness and a thin cord.

"Finally a good decision, Sergeant Bryan," Miss Aleph said from the pack on Ellie's back.

As soon as the harness was around her, a small motor pulled on the first cord and reeled in a stronger, heavier line from the hovercopter. When the fat rescue line was locked in place, the drone and the light guideline disengaged and dropped to the roof. Ellie was yanked into the air.

She felt herself rushing upward through huge gusts of warm compressed air. The flying machine's lift engines were each as large as a helicopter rotor and encased in a round carbon fiber frame.

Ran Oliphant and Melanie Françoise pulled her in. The gunner took his eyes of his sights and threw out another drone for Sarge. He and the remaining pilot were balanced on the collapsing roof.

Ellie stumbled deeper into the cabin and turned right into the six-pupiled gaze of Ms. China.

"Well," she said accusingly, "you're alive."

36

ZVENA

A rotating blue light flashed from the roof of the police truck Zvena had commandeered as he navigated through the dark Moscow streets. Their destination was an industrial park kilometers away from the Kremlin. The siren on the roof made a weak noise only capable of irritating those driving the vehicle.

Rodion was jostling around in the rear flatbed compartment. He could not fit inside the cab, much less operate the human-sized controls. Despite the handicaps his size might cause, Zvena had immediately deputized him as his first subordinate "little green man." The man was loyal, and they had gone together on the mission that led to Zvena seeing President Putin and receiving his truly undreamt-of promotion. Rodion, or Rodya, which was his nickname, was good luck.

"Check your internal GLONASS," Zvena called back through a broken window.

The Russian version of GPS was being displayed on his dashboard, but it was set at such an angle in the ageing Soviet-era truck that he would have had to duck down nearly under his seat to properly look at the tiny glowing display. It would not be good to have an accident on his way to his first assignment under his special presidential authorization.

"Next left," Rodion said from the back, his voice dragging with boredom. "Why are we going all the way out there?"

Shortly after Zvena's promotion, a low-level air raid warning had sounded. He knew the type of installation where the panic button had been pressed. These Afghan War-era ZSU antiaircraft cannons were manned by soldiers nearing retirement. It was a make-work project for older or less-able soldiers. The most frequent false alarms occurred during bird migrations. However, the explosion in France had raised the overall threat level. It was only proper to gather definitive information on behalf of Russia's executive branch.

"We are going all the way out there because I said so."

At the rusty fence surrounding a decrepit factory, a gray-haired veteran met them. The man had lost most of a hand and all of his ear in Syria. He pointed them to where he had shot down the object.

"If we find a UFO," Rodion said, "maybe we will get our pictures in the paper."

Zvena snorted. If a *zelyonye chelovechki*'s picture appeared anywhere, he had failed.

"Looks like one of our weather balloons?" Rodion said, heaving himself out of the back of the truck. The rusty springs squeaked and rebounded as they were relieved of their 250-kilo load. "We should charge its cost to the old pecker who shot it. It looks new."

Zvena looked closer at the flapping mess, which had been caught on the base of a collapsed water tower. "Since when do weather balloons have stealth coating?"

Even with bits of it blasted over a wide area, Zvena could tell the downed craft was not Russian. There was a solid structure underneath. He kicked open the carbon-fiber tub he assumed had been hanging from the bottom of the airship.

"Gah!" he said, startled, and swore.

"What? Is it an alien?"

"Fuck shit, Rodion. Did you bring a hazmat suit?"

"No," the other cyborg said, lumbering away from the truck and looking with concern over Zvena's shoulder. "What is that? Looks like a little bit of caviar."

Inside the smashed shell, underneath sophisticated-looking aviation controls, was a hexagonal tube that was caught inside a wire frame. It was the only one left.

He pulled out a flashlight. Under a special 395nm UV forensic light, the contents luminesced. It was organic and alive. Zvena took a step back.

Using his advanced visual perception and embedded processor, he calculated the volume of the tube and how many could have fit inside the vessel. There was space for thousands of these tubes; each one had hundreds of micro pods.

Zvena had to make a decision—wait for the biohazard unit or risk contamination in order to get answers faster. He chose the assertive course of action.

"Rodion, give me a clean sample container," Zvena said, deciding. "You're going to analyze this right here."

"Blech." His fellow little green man knew what was next. "Can't we wait for a mobile lab?"

"Look at this mess," Zvena said, waving his metal-enhanced arm over the wreckage. It was spread out farther than they had first thought. "This craft was large, sophisticated, and carried at least one pilot. To arrive here, it had to penetrate our most sophisticated air-defense network. Whatever it contained, it is already loose. We must know what it is."

Zvena opened his cyborg field-surgery kit. The latex gloves and instruments were sterile and would minimize sample contamination. He picked up the mysterious hexagonal tube. It was three inches long and made of thin, hard polymer.

"Whatever country this originated in has advanced materials science," Zvena said, mostly to himself.

He started to narrow down the list of suspects. Whoever had sent this, Zvena hoped to be in the front line of the revenge mission. Twelve million Russians lived in Moscow—a biological or radiological attack could cripple the country for months or years.

Using a scalpel, he opened the outer covering and scooped out the tiny fishlike blobs. Zvena placed those into a pill-sized sample container, and then he fed it to Rodion.

"Need a drink," Rodion mumbled. "I'm dry."

Rodion chugged down some stale water from the old veteran's canteen and washed the sample capsule down into his adjunct esophagus. It bypassed his stomach and went straight to his liver.

The normal human liver processed more than five hundred chemical reactions. Human+ soldiers need more than four times that to continue functioning at peak efficiency. In the newer models, there was room for a chemistry lab to sit on top of the organic liver. In addition to keeping its owner alive, the palm-sized unit could also take in samples for deep genetic analysis.

Zvena wirelessly connected his handset to the AI master chemist inside Rodion's barrel-sized torso. They both stared at the blank screen and waited.

A fire truck drove up silently. Nothing was burning; Zvena waved them away. After one look at them and the mess they were standing on, the driver took off twice as fast as he had come.

The analyzer inside Rodion's midsection texted Zvena's handset.

`Sample DNA 99% match to Anopheles gambiae`

"What the fuck is that? What did you make me swallow?"

"Relax. It's a kind of mosquito."

The handset beeped again.

`Sample contains secondary distinct DNA. 98% match to Variola Khóshekh.`

"Oh."

Zvena didn't need to check his blood pressure. He could feel his cheeks become flaming hot on top of his titanium cheek plates. Using the handset connected to Rodion's innards, he isolated and destroyed the sample.

"Rodya, expel it and toss your excreting tube into the wreckage on the ground."

Rodion shrugged and pulled a clear plastic catheter out from his waistband. Smoking green slime dripped out of it, followed by a gush of watery bile.

"If your monitors register any signs of infection, you must tell me at once."

"From what?"

"The Khóshekh virus that devastated the Middle East two years ago."

"We're inoculated for that," the larger man said hopefully.

"Maybe," Zvena said, waving over to a bored traffic cop who was guarding the empty dark intersection. "Maybe not this variation."

After ordering the area cordoned off, Zvena and Rodion got back in their truck. Zvena cranked the rusty steering wheel and pushed the accelerator all the way down. He raced back to the Kremlin and hoped he would not have to incinerate his comrade.

Zvena called ahead to the Kremlin. He could only get Putin's chief of staff, the man he had met only briefly earlier that afternoon, Mr. Gerasimov.

"That's very interesting," Gerasimov said unctuously. "Thanks to your hysteria, an air wing has been scrambled. Do you know what that costs in fuel and maintenance?"

According to regulations, Zvena now had the right to decline to report to anyone except the president personally. This was too urgent.

"I am having my man send you the data we collected." Zvena nodded to Rodion in the back seat. His broad face was looking green ever since he had swallowed the virus-laced mosquito larva. "There is an imminent biological attack on the capital."

"Well, well, what a coincidence," Gerasimov said with lazy bureaucratic distaste for anything out of the ordinary. "Paranoia is in the air after this upset in France. No doubt some kind of ordinary chemical leak around Bordeaux.

"The addition of this air surveillance alarm requires us to go to Alert 1: Full Combat Readiness, even though it is surely a false alarm. President Putin has canceled his dinner with the Malaysian ambassador and has to drag himself onto a plane."

"I must give him my report at once. Please check my authority."

"As chief of staff, I speak for the executive. Remain where you are. Guard this strange weather balloon from outer space until further notice. Under no circumstances approach the Kremlin or the motorcade. Goodbye."

Gerasimov hung up.

Zvena slowed down. For a block he crawled along, matching speed with a tinker's cart being pulled by a wild-looking donkey that kept baring its teeth and snorting. The tinker was pulling it along and working hard to keep it going in a straight line. He might have had an easier evening if he'd just put the donkey in the cart and pulled it himself.

Zvena decided. Securing the crash site was logical; it may be their only evidence of who was behind this attack. Subversive elements might be loose in the city. Following protocols to get Putin airborne also made sense.

However, only a fool would consider the French Event to have been caused by a chemical plant explosion. Gerasimov had risen to be Putin's chief of staff. Zvena concluded Gerasimov was no fool. Therefore, he must be a liar, or worse. Zvena accelerated toward the Kremlin.

When he got to the bunker entrance, the same two boys with their flamethrowers were there. As soon as they saw Rodion and Zvena walking up from the staff parking lot, they ignited their toys and yelled for them to stop where they were.

"Rodion," Zvena said, pointing to a concrete block put down to prevent car bombs from coming into the area. "We don't have time for games."

His friend joyfully kicked the loose block as though it were a soccer ball. It rolled at great speed twenty meters ahead, exploding between the two guards.

Zvena stomped over to one of the dazed youths and picked him up by the collar of his uniform. "What's going on? You're the Presidential Guard. Is Putin still inside?"

They told him no, Putin had left five minutes earlier with a small contingent of GRU bodyguards.

"Chief of Staff Gerasimov told us to stay and guard the Kremlin."

"Would you guard an empty henhouse if a fox told you to?"

The kid looked at him as though that was a real question.

"What now?" Rodion asked as he loomed over the other petrified soldier.

"We get a nicer car."

The only car Rodion could fit into was an older style black limousine with two side by side doors in the rear. They drove to Vnukovo Airport. Diplomatic and military flights were boarded through the south entrance. Putin's Command Point Ilyushin jet had a hangar there and was always on standby.

Zvena approached the gate at speed. He judged the armored limo he was driving would win a contest with the crossbar. With a jolt and a scraping thump, he was proven right. The checkpoint guards yelled and waved their arms. He had no time to chat.

"Rodya," Zvena said, using the diminutive of his friend's name. "Please be careful of killing people. These GRU men and Gerasimov may be acting in completely good faith. Try to neutralize them gently."

"What? You tell me this now, after I nearly crushed those two kids back there?"

Zvena laughed. "That was a good shot. They should let Human+ athletes play for Russia in the World Cup."

Rodion laughed too as they got closer to the massive presidential hangar. The Human+ program had been started after Russia was kicked out of the Olympics for alleged performance-enhancing violations. Upon hearing the news, Putin was reported to have said "Enhancements? They haven't seen anything yet!" Soon after, he had signed the secret order establishing the cyborg battalions. The Human+ program changed Zvena's life and brought great honor to him and hundreds of other patriots.

The first GRU man gave them little choice. He started shooting at the limo before they had even exchanged a word. His aim was good, but the laminated windshield defeated the incoming armor-piercing rounds. With the glass in a thousand cracks, Zvena had to continue driving by intuition. He only stopped when something lumpy got caught under his front wheel.

He got out, and as he walked toward the hangar, he stomped on the wounded GRU man's head. No reason to let him suffer.

Putin and Gerasimov came into view. They were flanked by only one guard. Zvena linked to Rodion's vision camera. He had the guard steady in his gunsight as they approached. No one shot.

"Zvena," Putin said crossly, "what are you doing? I was told you insisted on guarding the balloon wreckage and that you refused to come back to the Kremlin."

"Mr. President, let me explain."

Gerasimov turned to Putin. "I told you, these mechanical things are not trustworthy. The machine parts and the chemicals, it affects their brains. This one has gone rogue. Let me put him down."

Right, you and which army?

At a sign from Gerasimov, a tarp next to the hangar rolled down, revealing his army. An antiaircraft tank pointed its cannons at them. The huge explosive shells could down an aircraft flying a mile up in the sky; it would certainly turn him and Rodion into a mess of guts and bolts.

"Mr. President," Zvena called out. He tried to keep his distance from Putin so that if that machine cannon opened up on them, the President would be less likely to be hit. With icy shock, Zvena realized the country's great patriot and leader was in worse danger from the snake at his elbow. "Gerasimov is the traitor! He ordered me to stay away."

"Really, why?" Putin asked, his gaze penetrating the fifty-meter distance as though they were only a few feet apart.

An airplane engine roared in the distance. Far away, some birds woke up and started chirping mournfully.

"I-I don't know, but I have proof of a bioweapon attack—"

"Pah," Gerasimov said with such vehemence that spittle rained on Putin's immaculate blue wool coat. "More addled nonsense. Zvena could be working with the terrorists. Mr. President, we have to get you to safety."

For a moment, Putin's midnight-blue eyes looked out in the distance. Perhaps he was staring at nothing, perhaps he was seeing more than anyone.

"You," Putin said to Rodion. "Seize Mr. Zvena."

After a moment's hesitation, Rodion lowered his weapon, and his iron-augmented grip grabbed Zvena's arms, pinning them with the force of many steel cables.

Putin reached into Gerasimov's jacket and pulled out an automatic pistol. He aimed it at Zvena's head.

"As I recall, Mr. Zvena," he said calmly and coldly, "you do not have a bifurcated skull. One bullet through the eye socket will neutralize you, yes?"

Zvena couldn't believe it. How could he have been such a fool? He should have waited and gotten more evidence. Of course the President would trust Gerasimov, his aide for more than twenty years, over a half-human cyborg he had only met twice.

"Yes, Mr. President, if you feel it will preserve Russian lives, you must do as you feel best."

The President, known to be a crack pistol shot, smiled. "Yes, Yaroslav Semyonovich Zvena, so it goes."

Without looking, the President of the Russian Federation pumped five bullets into Gerasimov's groin. Putin then held the gun on the remaining GRU man.

Rodion was so shocked he was still holding Zvena.

"You can let me go now. Gerasimov is the traitor."

"Oh, yes. I see that."

Rodion launched forward and disarmed the guard while putting his foot on the wounded chief of staff, who was groaning, squirming, and holding his midsection.

Putin looked down at Gerasimov.

"Zvena, this man is not like you," Putin said. "He has no heart, at least not one that is Russian. Find out what balls he has left dangling between his legs and remove them and everything he knows about this attack. You should hurry. He is leaking quite profusely."

The cannon crew came out of their armored car. They were both early-model cyborgs he had grown up with.

"Komandir Zvena, sir!" the Human+ soldier called Nikolayevich said. "Sorry for pointing the cannon at you. We would only have fired on the President's explicit orders."

"Good to know," Zvena said. "As you can see I am de-ranked. No reason to call me sir. Help me question our prisoner."

Nikolayevich hauled Gerasimov up, and they took him under the eaves of the large airplane hangar. A gentle mist of rain was falling. For late October, the rain was oddly warm, Zvena thought. He breathed a sigh of relief at the monumental disaster they had just averted.

Zvena checked to see that Rodion and the second Human+ soldier from the tank were escorting the President to his car. Suddenly his enhanced vison caught sight of an incoming projectile. It came from the open door of the Command Point jet.

With inhumanly fast reflexes, he reached up... and missed. The lump of metal struck Nikolayevich in the head and embedded itself there. It was a grenade.

Nikolayevich was dead no matter what he did. Zvena pushed him away from the bleeding and struggling Gerasimov. Nikolayevich had been knocked senseless by the pound of metal stuck in his head. As the cyborg fell over, he kept hold of the prisoner and rolled, taking Gerasimov with him a dozen feet, landing in a heap by the outer wall of the airplane hangar.

Zvena spun and dropped into a spring-loaded prone position. He would be no use to anyone if he was torn by shrapnel when the grenade finally decided to explo—

The blast threw him sideways, but most of its force was contained by Nikolayevich's metal skull and Gerasimov's now-shredded body. Zvena wiped his vison clear of rainwater and zoomed in on the doorway of the large presidential plane.

The grenade had been shot from there, possibly by an RPG launcher, though there had been no sound. Zvena saw a figure but no launcher. Framed in the plane's doorway, he saw a hideously misshapen man with the strangest arm hanging from his left shoulder.

37

ZVENA

Zvena felt a surge of battle adrenaline through his natural and enhanced systems. Not all of these chemicals were synthetic—his organic and manufactured parts were equally Russian. All of him was deeply offended. Someone was trying to kidnap or kill his President.

Whoever it was had compromised the late Mr. Gerasimov; many of the GRU and personal bodyguards were in on the plot. The seditious and foreign elements were also threatening the lives of twelve million civilians in the capital with a bioweapon attack.

As soon as he saw the mutant who threw the grenade, Zvena launched into action like an uncoiling steel spring. He stepped out of the line of sight of incoming fire from the open doorway of the large jetliner and ducked behind the massive doors of the hangar.

Checking behind, he saw Rodion was with Putin's car. Zvena motioned for him to stay there. His feet slithered over the remains of Gerasimov. Someone very dangerous, talented, and bioaugmented had hurled that grenade from the plane.

Zvena retrieved a short-barreled assault rifle from the body of Nikolayevich.

"What now?" Rodion asked over his radio.

"Stay with Command Point," Zvena said, using Putin's generic code name. "Disarm the remaining guards. If they do anything suspicious, execute them as traitors."

"Command what?" Rodion had never done VIP close protection. "I'm with Pu—"

"Don't say his fucking name over radio."

Zvena measured angles and distances. There was no telling what the enemy had on the plane. If they could infiltrate Russia's version of Air Force One and compromise the chief of staff, who knew how far the rot had spread?

"I don't have a shot at the plane doorway," Zvena said. "I've alerted the local Human+ battalion. Link up with them. Wait for my distraction, then head for the closest gate out of the airport."

"What distraction?"

"You'll see it. Be ready."

Zvena sprinted the open distance to the ZSU cannon-equipped tank. Bullets hit his calf and his hip. Fortunately they were small ones. He barely felt them, and the impacts did not interrupt his stride.

Zvena cursed himself for not arriving at the airport sooner. The assassins in the plane could have killed Putin before they arrived. Gerasimov must have made a deal to take their country's leader prisoner.

He had probably been after money or nuclear command codes. But no matter. At that moment, Gerasimov was sizzling meat on the tarmac. His conspiracy was no longer relevant. Gerasimov's partner, the mutant man, must know his time was limited before loyal reinforcements arrived. The fellow with the weirdly augmented arm would need to kill Putin as quickly as possible.

Bullets pinged off the tank's armor, and then an RPG came down from the plane's hatchway. Active projectile defense knocked down the incoming grenade. It exploded on the tarmac.

Inside the tank, Zvena grabbed hold of the fire controls. He swiveled the cannon turret toward the jet and fired.

As devastating as Shilka 23mm cannon shells were to a plane a mile up in the air, on the ground, at point blank range, the effect was even more satisfying. Zvena started his shooting spree at the nose of the big jet in case the enemy had gone up front. Big holes appeared on the jetliner's fuselage, and gouts of debris popped out exit wounds behind the plane.

He quickly swiveled right to left, blasting through the president's personal transport from the nose to as far as where the plane protruded from the hangar.

"Not good enough," he snarled.

The target he wanted was out of sight. He could have moved the tank over but decided it would be quicker to demolish the whole side of the hangar.

Heat and smoke wafted back through the open hatch. Shell casings piled up around his feet. At two thousand rounds per minute, the ammunition counter quickly approached the red "empty" line.

Just a few more...

The next shells hit where he wanted but did not get the result he was after. The fuel tanks in the wing of the plane must be reinforced. On the plus side, the jet being ready for takeoff meant it was completely full of fuel. The last ZSU artillery shell landed. A gorgeous fireball went up, buckling the hangar roof and sending smoke belching out everywhere.

Zvena's view from inside the tank was crap. Choking on fumes from the huge fire, he cranked the gears and drove off. If by some miracle the assassins had survived that, they would be distracted long enough for Rodion to get Putin away.

"Rodya, where are you?"

"I noticed the distraction. We are leaving in the limousine through the main gates."

"I'm right behind you. Don't wait for me. Check that our battalion is incoming, and only ours. Tonight I don't trust anyone except fellow cyborgs."

There was a local garrison of three hundred Spetsnaz troops. Half of them were technicians needed for their repair and maintenance. Some of the Human+ squads were deployed to various points of the country and the world.

Only sixty or seventy of them would show up. But properly equipped, the number of troops they could take on was limited only by the casualties the enemy wanted to suffer.

"*Blachdoh!*" Rodion swore something unintelligible over the radio.

Zvena peered out of the window of his tank and saw why. Tire spikes had been deployed at the gate. Putin's limousine chauffer had rolled right over them.

The long nails had grabbed the run-flat tires and jammed into the wheel wells. Traitorous guards at the gate where shooting into the limousine windows. Zvena came at them from behind and smeared them along the asphalt underneath his tank's treads.

While the exterior and the guns of the tank had been modernized, the insides were Afghan war relics. Zvena worked the old-style lever controls and tried to bring the armored vehicle to a position blocking any more assaults on Putin's limo.

The tank's gore-lubricated treads skidded on gravel and the slippery asphalt. The ungainly vehicle spun nearly completely around. He struggled up out of the main hatch and ran over to the disabled black Aurus limousine.

Putin's driver was dead; his brains were all over the windshield. Rodion flanked Putin as they clambered out of the car. The President looked disheveled but otherwise uninjured.

"Zvena," Putin said, wiping blood spray off his cheek. "Get in the Shilka!"

Of course. It was the only secure vehicle, and there was no guarantee the explosion at the hangar had neutralized the determined attack force. Zvena motioned to Rodion to stay with Putin. The President was digging around in the back of the limousine for something.

Zvena climbed back into the Shilka. By the time he was seated behind the tank controls, Putin had climbed inside behind him. He had a black briefcase with him. The nuclear codes, Zvena guessed.

The Shilka lurched. Rodion had climbed on. He appeared to be trying to get in; he would never fit.

"Rodya!" Zvena yelled. "Are you stupid? Stay on the outside. Hang on to something and get ready to shoot."

Zvena notched down the gear lever and pushed on the accelerator. The treads skidded, spun, and then bit into the ground. The tank pushed aside the disabled limousine and rolled over the tire spikes and over a chain-link gate.

Putin slapped his shoulder. "Thanks for coming by in person."

"Gerasimov, huh?"

"Yes, him," Putin said with flat deliberation.

Zvena again radioed the executive officer of the cyborg battalion. The unit elements still located in Moscow were spread all over the city. It would take time to assemble them into a cohesive force.

"Let them group up," Putin advised. "Otherwise they can lead the enemy to us and be taken out one by one without full equipment and support."

The line of streetlights leading away from the airport was coming to an end. So was the nicely paved wide road. Zvena was ashamed of his troops' lack of readiness.

"Is there any safe location you would prefer to go to, Mr. President?"

Putin considered. His ring finger tapped the smooth-sided briefcase.

"No," he said definitively. "They will be expecting me to return to the Kremlin, and this tank is not going to make it there. If we go to an established military post, one grenade tossed in their 'safe room' would make these bastards' night, wouldn't it?"

There was a banging on the roof.

"What now, Rodya?"

The gravel in front of them erupted with the force of an IED explosion. It missed by less than ten meters. Zvena waggled the steering levers to make sure the tank treads were not compromised.

"Kamikaze drones," Rodion yelled down. "Coming one at a time, for now."

"I don't hear any shooting," Zvena yelled at him. "When I told you to shoot, this is when I meant you to do that!"

Zvena swung the Shilka between lines of concrete blocks on either side of the road. They were kilometers from the airport. He checked GLONASS and his map of Moscow.

Up on top, Rodion let off nearly a full magazine. The string of bullets was punctuated by a far-off boom like a firework.

"These are our own ZALA loitering munitions, huh?" Putin asked quite calmly from behind him.

"Yes, sir," Zvena said, again filled with shame that Gerasimov's people were using their own weapons against them. "They will not be a problem."

"Unless they hit us." Putin laughed grimly. "Over there, I think."

He pointed over Zvena's shoulder to a large empty structure. The location had no current entry in Zvena's map. It looked like an abandoned factory or smelter.

"We need shelter," Zvena agreed. "And if they follow?"

"Then we make them wish they had not."

They rumbled down the unlit road. Zvena's built-in night vision compensated for the darkness. The kamikaze drones were not very good against moving targets; it would take a swarm to be certain their tank was destroyed.

As he steered, Zvena felt the enemy was employing a strange combination of planning and improvisation. And then there was the zeppelin with the plague mosquito larva. He didn't quite know what it all meant.

He did know that if he could not keep Putin safe, the disaster would be magnified many times. This crisis that was upon them needed a firm hand in control, not a power struggle inside the Kremlin and the Federal Assembly.

"This is the old Fregat smelter," Putin said. "It closed years ago due to idiotic European sanctions."

They crashed through a moss-covered wall. Zvena exchanged text messages with his Spetsnaz group.

"Support is thirty or forty minutes away."

Putin nodded as they skidded to a stop. "We will not be the only ones who know that."

The President, agile for his age, leaped out of the Shilka, trailing the black briefcase. Zvena ransacked the tank's interior for explosives and ammunition. The main guns were empty. In any case, shooting 23mm cannons inside this dilapidated smelter could bring the whole leaky roof down on them.

"Rodion," Zvena said sharply to his man as he climbed off the back of the tank, "this is the most important task we have ever had. Make sure you transmit all we know about the dirigibles and the bioweapon to our comrades."

"You are full of surprises today," Putin said, pulling the cocking lever of his AK. "And it is only your first day as my little green man."

They left the tank and climbed a creaking filthy staircase to what looked like a defensible spot. The walls were thick concrete framed by steel. It looked like a place they stored ingots before shipping. Chunks of lead and copper shavings littered the floor.

Rodion walked along the gangway, checking fields of fire and points of entry. He made sure he only walked along tracks where the workers had rolled heavy carts laden with ore and smelting materials. Still, the reinforced struts creaked under his weight.

Inside the sheltered room, Putin sat down on his briefcase. Zvena told him about the crashed airship and what they had found inside.

"These mosquito larvae were alive?" Putin said. A trickle of blood ran down the side of his head from a cut made by some flying glass. Other than that, he was as alert and comfortable looking as he had been in his luxurious den underneath the Kremlin.

"Yes, the larvae were living. Packed inside sustaining membrane and fluid." Zvena rolled out a folding OLED screen and showed him the feed from his body cameras.

"Any markings on the airship?"

There had been none.

"My gut instinct tells me it was prepared some time ago for a mission like this," Putin said firmly. "Perhaps even before a target was designated."

He scowled with concern as a furry-tailed mouse darted across the filthy floor and out of the room.

"This is a problem," Putin said. "Years ago, my predecessors had a similar program, but it was judged too volatile. I refused to revive it. A disgusting way to kill, using bloodsucking vermin to infect a population."

"But efficient," Zvena said.

"You've done some research and thinking? I'm surprised you had time while you were saving my ass from that traitor."

"The mosquito is the deadliest animal by far," Zvena said. "They kill one million humans annually by means of malaria, dengue, and yellow fever. They are responsible for one out of five cases of serious infectious disease."

As a small boy on vacation to his uncle's house in Taganrog, Zvena had seen a literal tornado of mosquitos surging over a field. The sight had been so frightening he may have leaked urine into his pants. If he had, by the time he got to the house, the yellow stain of shame had been more than obliterated by the sweat that poured out of him.

He and his relatives had closed all the windows and watched as the bloodsuckers beat against the glass like tiny black hailstones with wings. In their garden sat a bird, a brown swallow. It had gorged on so many of the insects it seemed unable to fly. And still they came out of the sky.

"They are also nearly impossible to wipe out," Zvena continued, shaking off the macabre memory. "Due to climatic change, they are even expanding their territory to Antarctica to feed on penguins."

Zvena made quick calculations. "That single airship carried millions of larvae. Unlike normal mosquitos, they were born infected with Khóshekh virus. Even if they do not manage to feed on a human before feasting on an animal for their blood meal, their offspring will also carry the engineered plague."

The ground around Moscow was wet. There were thousands of ponds and water pools. Insects were always a problem during the summer months, and the forecasts were for a very warm winter.

"What, er, what do you think we can do, Mr. President?"

Putin rose up and thumped Zvena on his chest. "What you were bred and sworn to do: defend Russia, wipe out the threat, then make an example of those who have attacked us. If they have a seaport, perhaps it's time to try out the *Poseidon*."

The Status-6 Oceanic Multipurpose System, also known as *Poseidon*, was a robot submarine that could carry a 100-megaton nuke into a harbor and detonate without warning. Zvena also yearned for revenge, but without its head of state, the chances were that Moscow would become a city of twelve million plague victims. First priority was protecting Putin, otherwise everything was lost.

"Arrgh!" Rodion exclaimed from the catwalk outside the room.

Someone had shot him, and it must have been with a larger bullet. Rodion was limping along the catwalk toward him. Zvena went out and shut Putin in the room.

The enemy was here.

38

Rodya, status!" Zvena hissed into his radio.

"Where are—*heff*—our lazy guys?" Rodion panted as he struggled along the catwalk in order to get to better cover.

"Not here. Where is the enemy element?"

"Some fucker shot me from the roof. There are more on the ground level."

"Did he have one huge arm?"

"Who?"

"The one on the roof. Did he have what looked like one of those crabs with one stupid huge arm?"

"What? No. Normal guy, two arms, looked like an Albanian."

Rodion had been kidnapped by Albanian child sex traffickers before being rescued and put in a Russian orphanage. To him, most bad guys looked like Albanians.

"Right. You fuck him up. I will get the others down here." Zvena paused. "And Rodya, if they shoot you in the head, make sure they get the ugly side of your face."

While it meant leaving the president, the mutant who had thrown the hand grenade and taken out one of Zvena's most advanced fellow cyborgs was not someone he wanted Rodion to face by himself. He looked down at the long main floor of the smelter, flicking through night vision and thermal vison. There were small train tracks and crucible vats. Withered vines hung down from rusty pipes.

Zvena decided to up-armor. He used the back of his melee weapon, a collapsible pole axe, to chop two doors off their hinges. One he strapped to his back, the other he took and hacked a slit into at eye level. This one he held in front of him as a shield. Human+ units fought with ballistic shields and were able to operate assault rifles with one hand accurately out to two hundred meters. In close-quarter combat, against typical combatants, the effect was overwhelming.

The first enemy did not see Zvena, probably thinking the metal door he was using as a shield was just scrap standing against the wall. Zvena hit him with the door and crushed him against a concrete wall. His lips protruded through the sharp edges of the viewing slit and sputtered red bubbles. Zvena pressed and pressed until the fool stopped breathing.

Once the door shield was removed, the attacker fell like a squashed bug. It was a local thug with basic weapons. On the one hand, that meant they were faced with a larger conspiracy that went beyond rotten apples in the GRU and Gerasimov. That was not so good. It meant they would be fighting many more hostiles armed with any kind of weapon that the local drug-dealing filth had available to them, which was a lot.

On the other hand, it looked like they were improvising. The attempt on Putin seemed very ad hoc. Completely unlike the bioweapon attack from the airships. If all they had were GRU traitors and local goons, Zvena thought, they were no match for Human+ soldiers—when they managed to get here.

Bullets hit Zvena's back plate. He ducked his head all the way down and dropped the edge of the steel door onto the floor. As in most encounters, an attacker in this position would normally think next of shooting low, at his victim's ankles. The bullets aimed there thudded off the protective metal. Zvena propelled himself backward until he hit something soft, which let out an agonized grunt.

Two arms came round his door shield; one had a pistol. Dropping his weapon and front shield, Zvena grabbed the enemy's two elbows and pulled in with all his might. The hydraulics that had crushed the Kodiak's skull mashed bone, tendons, and gristle. Zvena tore off the fellow's forearms and threw them down. Behind him, the armless guy dropped.

As soon as Zvena turned, something flew at him. Had he been holding anything in his hands, the metal casing of the hand grenade would have embedded itself in his eye socket. With superhuman speed and not a millisecond to spare, he crossed his arms. The grenade thumped off his forearm. Pissed now, he tore his back shield off and slammed it flat over the fallen grenade. The edge of the door sank deep into the metal floor.

Two seconds later, the grenade went off with a muffled bang, harmlessly digging a hole in the smelter floor. By then, Zvena was already tracking the mutant who flung it.

"Hey, babushka," he called out. "I like your arm. Maybe after we are done I will keep it as a trophy."

Zvena spoke Russian. He had no idea if his assailant could understand but hoped his tone carried his meaning. It would also let Rodion know he was okay and his general location in the huge complex.

He ducked behind the motor of an abandoned tractor. On its wide radiator grill, a spiderweb hung and glistened with droplets of moisture that quivered but clung. About ten meters to his right, there was an oval settling pond. A heck of a smell came from it.

The surface was so full of slime and moss that it looked hard. But Zvena's cyborg depth perception told him it was in fact quite a deep basin, and it had filled up with the smelter's toxic runoff.

He heaved against a big broken grill and pushed the abandoned hulk of the tractor to block off the corridor. A stealthy figure darted to the left, too fast for Zvena to shoot at.

He wanted me to see that.

Zvena put his back to the hidden toxic pool and studied the area the mutant had ducked behind.

Seconds later, a splash came from behind him. It was followed almost immediately by screaming as the enemy thug's flesh dissolved. Zvena glanced behind him.

The mutant's accomplice had been told to come up behind Zvena and had fallen right into the waste pond. He'd gone in headfirst and was thrashing around; the caustic mix was sloughing off his nose, eyes, and face. He was no threat.

Zvena went back to his pack and picked out some RPG rounds. They had been in the Shilka but without a launcher. Human+ soldiers did not need one.

He threw the shaped-charge warheads with enough force to prime the detonation fuse. One, two, three.

When they hit the metal the mutant was hiding behind, they detonated. Hot copper plasma blew out the other side. He threw again, and again.

The mutant had nowhere left to run. Zvena threw his final RPG. Before it landed, up and at him, over the tractor, sprang the mutant like a 200-pound monkey. A couple of badly aimed pistol shots hit Zvena.

His left arm went numb, and some hydraulics leaked from his leg. Zvena threw his right fist overhand to smash the swarthy Middle Eastern-looking fellow's head like a pustule. Faster than his blow, the uncanny tentacle came up and intercepted his fist.

Zvena tried to grab the slimy appendage, but it seemed to have no bones and slithered out of his grip and stuck to his forearm.

He was face-to-face with the mutant. Zvena slammed him back into the wall and pressed. He was nearly twice as heavy as the enemy, but still he could not crush the bastard's torso. The tentacle material had to be encapsulating all of the man's upper body. Maybe not his legs.

"Gahharw!"

Zvena stomped on the man's foot with the power of a half-ton sledgehammer. With his left arm, he could have decapitated the enemy—if it had been working properly. Zvena's right arm was still entangled by the tentacle, which had separated into two parts. One part slithered around Zvena's neck and tried to strangle him. It ran into his steel neck gorget then changed tactics.

Expanding itself in a grotesque way, the cold octopus limb covered Zvena's nose and mouth in order to suffocate him. He tried to bite the material, but it was like trying to chew thick polyethylene. He felt is head spinning.

His organic tissues were using too much oxygen. There had been no time to prepare his vascular system for underwater fighting. Like a dumb idiot, in a moment he would be at this creature's mercy.

A searchlight flickered through the windows high in the wall of the smelter. A helicopter. The Human+ helicopter.

Zvena struggled to hold on and prevent the assailant from moving. *Just... a little longer...* He could save Putin, and Putin would save Moscow. His damaged left hand grabbed at the mutant's groin, hoping to crush his testicles. There was only a smooth surface.

Disgusting. But fuck it.

He dug titanium-etched fingernails into what was there and tore. The mutant cried out. Zvena was almost blacking out. The helicopter came closer.

"Stop!" said a man's voice.

It was Rodion who had shouted out. A rifle fired several times. Neither Zvena nor the mutant was hit. The shooting was to get their attention.

The tentacle moved away from Zvena's head and formed a translucent shield protecting the mutant's head. The assassin's human hand twisted Zvena's damaged arm and forced him down.

Zvena looked sideways. He couldn't believe it. Rodion had Putin by the collar at the edge of the toxic pool.

"You fool, what—"

"Shut up, Yaroslav," Rodion said in a voice he had never used before. "I've been waiting years to tell you that."

Zvena, his chest heaving as he gasped for air and his mind spinning, had a chance to get a close look at the mutant and his clothes. His horsehide greatcoat was not military issue. How could it be with a left sleeve three times the normal size? An embossed label said "Hatemoğlu."

Fucking Turk!

"What you do?" the mutant Turk said in halting Russian. "Give Putin or I kill your friend."

"How about I kill you both and keep Putin?" Rodion said, jostling his prisoner. Putin stood very still, as he normally did. He had to know his peril, but his face was brave and stoic as he looked straight out to the other side of the smelter.

"Who you?" the Turk yelled.

"I am with Tambovskaya Bratva," Rodion the turncoat said. "Gerasimov put us in place to help take over when Putin was eliminated."

The Turk was moving sideways, but he hesitated attacking. The Turk was alone, and the Human+ forces were closing in. If he let go to kill Putin, Zvena could snap his neck and then deal with the traitor Rodion.

"Quickly, for Putin what you want?"

"Double what you paid Gerasimov."

"Prove you not lie."

"You first," Rodion said with canniness Zvena had never witnessed before in his former friend. "Who are you? And tell the truth. Those Spetsnaz cyborgs who are approaching are also Tambovskaya Bratva."

Briefly, the Turk hesitated. "I Grey Wolves. Give Putin or kill him, now!"

"Well, then. We will expect payment shortly, or else."

Rodion leveled his short-barreled AK and shot Putin three times through the back. The bullets blasted out of the front of the Russian president's long dark blue coat. Then Rodion shot Putin once through the neck and threw him into the toxic pool.

"Fine," the Turk said and looked up. There were three spotlights raking the top of the building, all closer now. At the other end of the building a breaching charge exploded.

The Turk's human hand drew out a knife. He was going to cut Zvena's head off.

"No!" Rodion yelled. "He will not die so quickly. These men who are arriving are loyal to my organization. We have some questions of importance for Komandir Zvena."

The tentacle slithered away from Zvena's neck. The knife clattered to the filthy metal floor of the smelter. The Turk looked down at Zvena's kneeling, bent form.

"Enjoy your year without winter, Russian," he hissed, spitting out the last word out like a curse.

The Turk withdrew, limping into the shadows away from the searchlights.

"How..." Zvena gaped, looking at Putin's wrecked floating body. "How could you? You have doomed Moscow and Russia."

Something nagged at Zvena's brain, but it was overwhelmed by his failure and disgrace. He wanted to pick up the Turk's knife and cut his own neck. Instead, Zvena crawled to the edge of the toxic pool, gasping for breath with each movement. The air was putrid and stung his nose and lungs.

The first Human+ soldiers ran up to them. Zvena expected Rodion to flee. These were loyal men, not Russian mafia, not traitors like his former comrade. Rodion had just assassinated the greatest leader of Russia in modern times. Instead Rodion smiled sort of sheepishly.

"The Turk is gone," Rodion said, apparently to no one.

With his foot, Rodion turned over Putin's floating body.

"You'll… pay for this," Zvena gasped.

The corpse bobbed face up. Putin's face came off it in one piece and floated in the acid. Impossibly, the President's expression was exactly as passive and contemplative as the moments before he was shot. His eyes stared up at the ceiling of the smelter, blinked once, and then his sloughed-off face sank into the dark slimy liquid.

That was not right. Also… *Tambovskaya Bratva?* Rodion could not even spell that, much less have the guile to conceal his membership in the Petersburg criminal gang for many years.

He looked at Putin's head. Instead of the expected skinned flesh and raw bone, there was a mesh of white plastic in the shape of a head.

"Rodya," said a stern clear voice from behind Zvena, "the cost of my coat is coming out of your pay. It was from Italy, custom-made by Canali."

The real Putin came down the rickety staircase. He was wearing only his suit. He held the open and empty briefcase. He nodded at the figure in the toxic waste pond.

"That was my favorite body double," he said, throwing the case into the sulfurous liquid. "We had trouble finding actors who were as good-looking as me, so the finest robotic doll makers created that portable fake passenger to ride in my limousine. Each day, it was dressed in an exact copy of my suit."

Zvena stared at the delicate framework, which had looked so lifelike. He felt foolish at having been deceived by a few pounds of folding carbon fiber and silicone.

"For the benefit of realism," Putin said, "I donated my wool overcoat before presenting it to our terrorist friends."

The skeletal robot Putin gurgled softly and then also sank into the green viscous slag runoff.

"The simulation even has, or had, a mechanical pulse, and its silicone skin surface was coated with my own DNA."

Of course.

Even with his enhanced vision, Zvena had been taken in. Zvena's face flushed. He was shot, leaking blood and hydraulic fluid, but had suffered a worse blow to his ego.

The rest of the Spetsnaz group came rushing in. Someone called for a medic.

"No hospital; on-site repairs only," Zvena ordered. "Secure a corridor to the Kremlin. Shoot anyone who resists."

"That's the spirit," Putin said.

He was distinctly more cheerful than when they had learned about the mosquito-borne plague which had been strewn all around Moscow. He bent down to where Zvena sat against an overturned ore cart.

"Now, while you have been doing your jobs, I have been doing mine." Putin pulled out a PDA with notes and calculations. "I have some concepts on how to counter this insidious bioweapons attack. I need to discuss them with you, Mr. Zvena, and our top scientists immediately."

"Ah, there he is," Zvena said as Rodion came out from the mobile cyborg repair truck. "The elite gangster of the Tambovskaya Bratva."

Wiping biomimetic gel off his neck, the large cyborg looked at Zvena with some embarrassment.

"You did not believe I was a gangster and traitor?"

The moment Zvena had watched Putin's body fall into the toxic pond, he really had not known what to think. But he had to pretend complete competence and control. Even though he had no official rank, Zvena was still his team's leader.

"Ha! You've been to Petersburg once in your life and got scammed by the first gypsy you met. Rodya, our top gangster boss." Zvena shook his head.

"It was all the president's idea."

"I gathered that."

"He was talking to me in my earpiece all the time, telling me what to say and how. He told me to stop the Turk from killing you, if it was at all feasible." Rodion looked at Zvena with respect. "I think Putin likes you."

39

OVER BORDEAUX

ELLIE

It must have seemed to Ms. China that Ellie had not heard. She repeated, yelling over the sounds of the air rushing through the hovercopter's open doors. "You're alive."

"I..." Ellie started to say to Ms. China. The strange woman was looking so accusingly at her with her tattooed eyeballs. Under the aircraft's interior fluorescent lights, Ms. China's silver tattoos turned dull gray, and the gold threads woven into her skin turned a yellow-orange color.

"You're alive," Ms. China said a third time and stalked back over to the other side of the cabin to a row of folding seats set along the fuselage.

Ellie felt madly disoriented. She reminded herself where she was. The strange aircraft had rescued her, Sarge Bryan, and the remaining pilot Charlie. Candace had been killed by that mob of...

Ellie dashed to a window. How far had that ravenous mob spread? She knew the victims should only be located around Cesta Station, but she had to see for herself.

Below them, the mid-morning French countryside flashed by. There were no mobs, just ordinary, human-looking motorists. A bicyclist wearing Tour de France spandex braked hard and looked up at them.

It was the next day. The fields and roads and trees looked completely different than they had on their way to Cesta Station. Atticus had gone into that horrible place. But he hadn't come out. He never would.

Ran Oliphant gave her a water bottle. He said something about Atticus having seemed like a good fellow, and wishing he'd gotten to know him better. Ellie took a few sips and then let the bottle drop from her nerveless fingers. No one stooped to pick it up. Its contents spilled and dribbled out the open door where the gunner was reloading his weapon.

As they came over Ramstein Air Base, she looked out and saw a waterslide. There was an amusement park and a mall belonging to the town that had sprung up next to the large military base.

People were blithely going about their day. Ellie wondered if Attie Jr. had ever taken a turn down the waterslide with his father. Who would take him next time?

Attie Jr., she thought suddenly.

Ellie waved at Ms. China to get her attention. "Did Attie Jr. make his flight?"

Ms. China glowered at her from the other side of the hovercopter and nodded. "Yes, and that Smitty person was there to meet him. They're in London."

Then the eccentric poison expert mumbled something inaudible and drank from a self-heating water mug which had a tea bag string hanging down its side.

Sarge Bryan touched Ellie's shoulder. She yelped and nearly fell into him. He looked grim but much more alert and competent than she felt.

"Some Air Force brass, and maybe even the general, might want to chat with you," Sarge Bryan said, looking out the side door. "Just letting you know. I told them we needed a bit."

He glanced at her. She'd never really noticed before that his cybernetic eyes moved like regular ones. For some reason she had just thought of them as glowing balls. Close up, they looked more like floating luminous contact lenses. "I'll get you a private room where no one will bug you."

Meaning if she had to freak out. *No,* she thought, *I'm British and not for freaking out, thank you.*

"I'm fine."

Their hovercopter landed near a three-story bunker-type building in the middle of Ramstein. Beside it was a second smaller, conventional helicopter. An airman was bringing something out of it. It was a small box but seemed very heavy. The airman appeared to forget what he was doing and where he was. The young man spun around like a drunken ballet dancer and dropped the box on his foot. It made a crunching sound. The airman did not react. He just hung over at the waist looking at the asphalt, like a slack question mark.

Ran and Melanie rushed out of their aircraft. Wolfgang Licht wandered out from the building onto the landing zone and glowered. He seemed just as irritated as ever but also visibly worried. The T-bomb had gone off as he predicted, but other things had also happened which no one had foreseen.

"Oh…" Melanie was flustered and cursed in a most unusual way. "Cats and trampolines! Don't get close to the sample."

Two airmen came out of their hovercopter and caught hold of the collapsing man, stopping him before he wandered into a propeller blade.

"Ma'am," Sarge Bryan said to Melanie, "the sample box is lined with lead and boron carbide. I can't see any gamma coming through."

"I told you as you were flying," Wolfgang said imperiously. "It doesn't work that way."

Melanie pushed the men away from the dropped box. "I've taken some antipsychotics. Let me."

"Dummkopf," Wolfgang continued. "Dark-matter radiation can go through a million miles of solid lead. Only element zero, neutronium, stops it."

When Melanie could not lift the box herself, a robot was brought in to retrieve it.

"Robots to the rescue. When do I get mine?" Miss Aleph nagged, watching the scene through the handset poking out of Ellie's knapsack.

Ellie couldn't imagine what part of one of the animated cadavers was in there. She only remembered the kindly dead boy whose eyes sank back to infinity, the one who tried to save them from the mob and was torn to pieces.

Ellie set down the sweat-stained and mangled backpack and took out the only slightly less bedraggled Hermes bag containing Miss Aleph. A military courier sped up and handed Sarge Bryan some papers.

"You have to sign there, and I have to witness."

"Can't this wait?"

The courier shrugged. "Paperwork, huh. That transfers the Casino Royale command codes to you, along with all authorizations and resources."

"Casino what?" Sarge said before recalling. "Oh, yeah, Major Reidt's Lake Como mission."

"Given recent events, the general has ordered Casino to continue indefinitely," the soldier said. "Of course, you'll have to take over until command assigns an officer. That process will start as soon as you sign there"—the courier tapped his finger on the digital form—"certifying Major Atticus Reidt's status as KIA."

Sarge glared at the form. He signed.

Ellie's vision swam before her eyes. Before anyone saw her losing her composure, she ran into the squat building and toward the little room at the end of the hallway.

Cold metallic-tasting water dripped down Ellie's face. The terrible last images from Atticus's camera were just starting to fade from her when sudden, increasingly loud noises penetrated the building and echoed through the bare tiles of the washroom.

These were sharp cracks she had heard before in the Middle East: artillery explosions. Behind that were what sounded like the screeching of hundreds of metal seagulls. Ellie wiped her face again, checked it in the mirror, and went out into the reception area.

Their hovercopter was still on the landing pad outside. Beyond it, small fighter jets and their drone wingmen were hurtling into the sky at a frantic pace.

"That's artillery," Ellie said to Sarge Bryan. "But it sounds off, not like it's supposed to."

"You're gettin' the hang of bein' a war reporter, Ms. Sato," Sarge Bryan replied. He pointed to the video screen on the wall. Scrolls of red letters and codes flashed across along with the words "Not a Drill!"

"Have those things reached here?"

Ellie imagined a wave of those creatures from the Cesta explosion marauding the countryside. Then she remembered Ramstein Air Base was in Germany, hundreds of kilometers away from Bordeaux.

"It's some kind of UAV attack on Ramstein," Ran said. Ellie recalled the Scottish man had been in the UK military.

"After the war in Israel, the Pentagon got very serious about anti-drone warfare," Sarge Bryan said. "Seeing as how large parts of the Israeli air force were grounded by unmanned bots."

Ellie remembered all the friends and allies they had lost during the 96-Hour War, the general with the burn marks on his forearms, the tank commander. What was his name? General Behar, yes. He'd been killed by the rogue Israeli aircraft. There were too many names and faces. Ellie wanted to retreat back into the building. If the base blew up around her ears, so be it!

Instead she asked: "What do we do?"

"The Screetchers are taking care of the incoming," Sarge said. "They are the latest in active anti-drone interdiction."

"I hate that name," Melanie said. "Our company, Eurolincx, manufactures the subneural BIOS network for them. I wrote a memo to the Joint Chiefs demanding they change it to *Spizaetus ornatus*, because it's the prettiest bird of prey."

"Yes," said Ran Oliphant drolly, "and the Pentagon made us get you checked out by their psychologist before renewing your security clearance."

"Drone-on-drone action, Ms. Sato," Sarge Bryan said reassuringly. "Nothing to be concerned about."

A large transport plane skidded to an emergency landing on a runway opposite them. It tottered sideways, nearly tipping over, and one of its wings dipped and cut a furrow along the runway. Three of the huge plane's four engines were belching black smoke and flames.

"Right," Ms. China said caustically. "Nothing to be concerned about, unless you plan to leave this place by air."

She grabbed the command link handset from Sarge Bryan. "Forget waiting for an officer to be assigned to bugger things up. Let's make sure the Casino mission isn't wasted. There is another T-bomb, the big one the Pangeans promised to detonate on November 1. Wolfgang is probably the only person who can find it."

Everyone looked at the sturdy-shouldered but haggard-looking older man in the corner.

"Maybe," Wolfgang said. "But I need to be at a real lab. Here they have only toys. I need you to take me to the Lichtstrom at once. It's not that far."

Oliphant and Sarge Bryan exchanged glances.

"No so fast, Wolfgang," Ran said. "That corporate principality is your own sovereign territory. I don't feel like changing places and being your prisoner."

"Come now, Mr. Oliphant," Ms. China said, extending her long and likely poison-tipped fingernails. "He's more of a guest, isn't he?"

Ellie grabbed Ms. China's arm. Now was not the time to be poisoning anyone. It was obvious they would need Wolfgang, but it would be unwise for them to go to his sovereign territory.

"Ran, Melanie," Ellie said. "You have quite a lab in your St. Albans home, don't you?"

Melanie and Ms. China had been thick as thieves sharing toxin recipes in the basement there.

"I doubt it's sufficient," Wolfgang scoffed. "For instance, do you have a thallium-activated sodium-iodide dark-matter detector?"

"Uh-huh," Melanie said, nodding enthusiastically; her massive curls were secured by what looked like two hairnets stitched together. "It's under the popcorn maker."

"All right, then," Ellie said. "Sarge Bryan, we should use your authority to get this transport refueled and authorized to take us to St. Albans in the UK."

She turned to Ms. China. "Along the way, we can land in London and make sure Attie Jr. gets safely on his way to America."

"Sounds like a plan, Ms. Sato," Sarge Bryan said, scanning the skies with his eagle vision. "As soon as we clear these drones away, we'll be off."

More explosions came from outside. They were farther off. Over the next half hour, they petered out.

"Who would be attacking a big military air base?" Ellie asked as they all boarded the wide-bodied hovercopter. "Are they crazy?"

"Most likely yes," Sarge Bryan said. "The European Aviation Safety Agency just put out an alert. Most civilian planes have been ground-stopped pending investigation of the Bordeaux incident."

"Any danger to us?" Ran asked, pointing at the hovercopter. "I'm not familiar with this type of aircraft."

"Few people are," Sarge Bryan said. "This is the first one I've been in. Pilots told me the propulsion is based on the wings of owls. They disperse air current over a wide area to lessen noise. We have no heat or air turbulence signature, which is what attack drones key in on." That sounded reassuring to Ellie, then the albino soldier had to add: "Most of them, anyway."

Their hovercopter took off and escaped the perimeter of Ramstein unmolested. Ellie looked out a window. About a kilometer away, the air was thick with smoke. Starburst flashes looked like a daytime fireworks display.

Her head started spinning again. It was like bloody Jerusalem and Amman Jordan. Visions of charred bodies from two years ago mixed with the fresh images of dead people coming to tear them to bits.

She took the edge of her harness strap and wound it around her hand until it was painfully tight. She wouldn't go off her head, she couldn't. Even in a world going mad on an insanely big scale, there was something for her to do.

"Sarge." Ellie tried to clear her mind by asking questions. She'd been doing that since her days at the *Cherwell*, Oxford's student paper. "So... all over the continent, the EU is blocking people from going to their airports?"

That sounded odd to Ellie. After details of what happened in Bordeaux got out through social media and news channels, many people would decide to join their political leaders and the Davos elites who were fleeing from Europe. Were they being prevented?

"That doesn't affect British airports like Heathrow, does it?" Ellie said.

"Nope, the UK is totally separate from the EU."

Thank goodness for Brexit.

The noise of the few remaining Screetchers faded away. Sarge explained more about how their hovercopter worked. Ellie only half listened. The four rotors were motionless jet fans. The best thing about it was there was very little vibration and almost no noise.

"The next generations of stealth flyers will be built on these prototypes."

"You must have a great deal of pull to get us this flight out while the base is under threat," Ellie said.

Sarge nodded to the two oligarchs strapped into their seats opposite. "Ran is a top-rated contractor; he's got a direct line to the Washington brass. I doubt they would have taken my word for anything."

"Even with that sample you brought back?"

"A random body part that makes people see things if they get too close?" Sarge shrugged his wide shoulders. "They would rather have believed the fake news the EU was putting out, that Bordeaux was some kind of chemical attack. Ran convinced them otherwise."

From the row of seats opposite, Melanie waggled her head, which still looked three times normal size despite her hairnets.

"I helped too," Melanie said. She took an emphatic bite out of a long red rope candy and kept speaking as she chewed. "I told them to imagine what if we found out about the Chernobyl meltdown before it happened and could stop it."

Ellie's mood sank along with the contents of her midsection as they took off. *Stop it?* They hadn't even been able to do anything about the experimental version of the T-bomb other than detonate it. Wolfgang said the particle could not be moved or defused; it had to go off.

The hovercopter seemed even faster than the Chinook. All over the English Channel, Melanie stood in front of a reflective porthole, trying to fix her hair using chopsticks she'd gotten from Ramstein's food court.

Wolfgang was whispering to Ran Oliphant. He was very intent on what he was saying and paid no notice of anyone. Ellie wanted to listen in but needed to do it covertly. She moved to the seat beside Ms. China next to where the two men sat.

Carefully, she took Ms. China's deadly hand in hers and pretended to sit there comforting the certified insane serial killer. The woman's tattooed eyeballs looked at her with a mixture of mystification and resentment, but she played along. Ellie mouthed nonsense about how well she was holding up and tried to eavesdrop.

"What an extraordinary thing, huh, Ran?" Wolfgang said in the most fake friendly way Ellie had ever heard. "Again fate throws us together with a common purpose."

"Despite your best efforts to be in orbit while Europe dies."

"Ach, maybe I panicked. Too long working behind a desk has made me less than a stoic, yes?"

"What do you want?"

"Only to be of help, only that," Wolfgang said. "I will give it my all, my complete best effort, to find and disarm the big T-bomb we both know must be out there."

"But…" Ran said.

Ellie recognized the combination of familiarity and hostility from her years covering major fashion designers. This was like the head of Gucci sizing up the president of Fendi.

"But consider this: What if it is not possible?" Wolfgang slapped the empty seat between himself and Ran Oliphant and pretended to be frustrated. "What then?"

The main island of Britain was a sliver of gray on the horizon. They would be home soon, Ellie thought, but how long would the United Kingdom even exist? It was… She checked her handset. Sunday, October 26. If the big quark device was set to go off on November 1, that was only five days away.

"Wolfie, I know you. You had more of a hand in this than you're letting on."

"But you heard the taped conversation with the Pangean," Wolfgang sputtered. "I was as shocked as anyone would have been that such a monstrous thing was designed and implemented."

"I believe you don't know where the big device is. You just better hope you and Melanie can find it."

"Yet, should we not be deploying resources in other directions?"

"Such as?"

"After the World Wars, after the Soviet collapse, after the Great Leap

Forward, yes, there were bodies, by the hundreds of millions. However, there was also opportunity… after these unavoidable tragedies."

Wolfgang produced a paper and a pen. Ellie snuck a look. The fountain pen was a Pelikan, not her favorite, and the paper was filled with lots of math calculations.

"I think the mainland of Europe is finished. Don't ask me why, but please take it as a given. In order to cause maximum damage, the T-bomb will be located in Germany, France, or Italy. Total annihilation."

"Sergeant Bryan's told me as much."

"Here are the capacities of the major airports in the UK: Heathrow, Gatwick, Manchester, etc. Assuming continuous operation and an availability of flights, nearly two million people per day can be moved out of the red zone of certain death."

"An evacuation?"

Long ago, Ellie had done research on this topic for a history paper. In only a few days during World War II, Operation Pied Piper evacuated three million Britons, mostly children, from areas at risk from bombing attacks. In 1998, China evacuated over thirteen million people from areas of massive flooding. Could people actually run away from the T-bomb?

"Precisely," Wolfgang said. "Between us, we have contacts everywhere: America, China, India. Canada is mostly empty space. Given fuel and logistic considerations, thousands of aircraft can be enlisted to help save England, Ireland, Scotland, and that place with the odd language…"

"Wales."

"Yes. Not only the people could be saved," Wolfgang said with exaggerated sincerity. "But the culture of Britain. Its very soul would be preserved."

"Really? You were ready to blast off and leave us to it. Now you want to help?"

"This may come as a shock to you, as a cynic, but I like the way things are. Ran, my friend, I have my own country. I own the world's greatest data hub and a nearly completed elevator into space.

"What do I want with the Pangeans' *tabula rasa* plan to make Europe a blank slate? Who knows what a lunatic will write on this slate, or what dogs will come out of the woods to feed on the carcass of the continent?"

"What do the Pangeans plan to do after November 1?"

"I have only heard rumors, but what it most reminded me of is the Congolese genocide of the late 1800s. Leopold the Second was dissatisfied with how hard the locals were working, so he decided to kill them and replace them."

The matter-of-fact way Dr. Licht said that chilled Ellie to the bone.

"Ran, you have to understand, there was no racism involved, no, not at all. In fact, the industrious replacement workers were exactly the same color, Schwarze. They were as black as the lazy ones.

"The Belgian king turned the entire country into a death camp. Joseph Conrad saw the horrors of what was then the Belgian Congo and was inspired to write *Heart of Darkness*.

"Leopold wiped out half the population of twenty million before himself succumbing to venereal disease. Clearly the Pangeans have the same thing in mind on a much more massive scale."

"Fucking idiots," Ran said. "Can't they read a map? The only people with land routes into Europe are Russia from the north and the Turks from the south."

"Don't forget China's web of steel through Eastern Europe: the New Silk Road. And who knows how the Americans will react. Will they hunker down in Fortress USA or come in with guns blazing?" The part of Wolfgang's face Ellie caught a glimpse of looked very sour as he made a clucking sound.

"No," he continued. "It will be chaos. Ran, you know as well as I, even before the unexpected after-effects of the T-bomb we witnessed in Bordeaux, a very unprofitable mess was in the offing."

Wolfgang propped his big white-bearded head closer to the younger Scottish ex-Royal Marine.

"Tell me honestly, Ran, if a modern instantaneous version of the Black Death were about to happen, wouldn't you rather you and I..." Wolfgang begrudgingly looked at Ellie and the others. "And your friends, of course, pick up the pieces rather than these murderous Pangean fanatics? We can get away, so can millions of your people."

Ran did not say anything for a minute. Through the window, the gray line in the distance had resolved into puffy clouds over gravure-etched white cliffs. Dover. They were nearly there.

What if her parents had not gone to Argentina? What if she and Ms. China had not had the resources and connections to get Attie Jr. out of Ramstein and on his way to America? Horrid as he was, did Wolfgang Licht have a point?

"All right," Ran said finally. "After what we've seen and what Ms. Sato has survived in Bordeaux, we cannot rely on a single option. I'll take your idea to my friends in the cabinet and the prime minister himself if I have to. Don't look so smug, Wolfie."

"Me? Never."

"You know why?" Ran said sternly. "Because you and I are staying right here to look for the T-bomb. And when we find it, you are going to use every neuron in your conniving mind to disarm it even if I have to handcuff you to the damn thing."

At that point, conversation between Ran and Wolfgang dried up. Ran and Bryan went forward, past Ellie, to the cockpit, which was glowing with a gazillion different instrument panels.

"We're going to land at London's Falcon Heliport on the Thames," Sarge told them over the low hum in the passenger cabin. "Ran and Dr. Licht have some business with the government that they'd best discuss in person."

"Why are we flying so low?" Ms. China demanded, looking out at the London skyscrapers beneath them. "I want to get down in one piece."

Miss Aleph piped up out of the orange bag. "Heathrow is the sixth-busiest airport in the world. Two thousand flights transit daily. We're flying under the two stacks of airliners which are circling above Lambourne and Biggin. FYI."

Through an observation port in the roof of the fast-moving hovercopter, Ellie could see swirling gray contrails belonging to dozens of planes in their holding patterns.

Could those flights be used to save millions of Britons in the next few days? Would people cooperate with the emergency in time? Would the host countries welcome them or demand payment? What kind of Britain would they return to? Those questions were all running through Ellie's mind as they approached the heliport.

Canary Wharf stood on the same side of the Thames, just after a big bend in the murky gray brown water, which looped around the storied Isle of Dogs.

"Oh, look," Melanie chirped buoyantly. "How pretty. Are those flying fish?"

Ellie could not tell what she was talking about. The woman's big hairdo covered the entire porthole.

"There are no such things there," Ellie said. "Eels and some pike, but no flying—"

There was a resounding metallic clang. Whatever had come out of the water sixty feet below had latched on to the outside of their hovercopter. The aircraft lurched wildly down toward the muddy waters of the Thames.

40

S trap in!" Sarge Bryan yelled from the other side of the wide-bodied cabin of the hovercopter.

"What now? Can't you people even make a simple Channel crossing without endangering my life?" Miss Aleph squawked as the leather bag she was in slid off the seat and along the floor.

Ellie caught the Hermes bag, then reached up and grabbed a ceiling strap. Just as she tried to get a look at the outside, the aircraft lurched violently to the left. Had she not been hanging on, she would have been thrown off her feet.

Through the Plexiglas window she caught a glance of something else as it zoomed up from the river. It narrowly missed their rotors and flew straight up. What could be coming out of the water to attack aircraft? How many were there? What could they do to the hovercopter?

A blast of sparks came from a panel on the wall. Ms. China swore a blue streak and stumbled forward to get a fire extinguisher.

"Sit down," Ran told her.

"Like fuck I will." Ms. China expertly aimed the whitish gas spray at the flames. "Just make sure Sergeant Chalky and these dimwit Yanks keep this thing in the air."

As Ellie choked on smoke and the fire-retardant gas, she recalled that before being a mental case, Ms. China had worked as a field agent for British foreign intelligence.

"Whatever it is," Sarge Bryan said, as he also strained to get a look at the exterior, "it's latched on to our hull like a suckerfish."

"Not good!" one of the pilots yelled back. "The thing is putting out massive wireless energy. I can't even talk to Falcon ground control."

"There's a bright side," Melanie said breathlessly. "It's probably not going to explode, otherwise it would have already done that."

"Then what is it doing?" Ran demanded of no one in particular.

"It's trying to take over the controls of this aircraft," Miss Aleph said as Ellie tried to stuff her in the space between two seats. "And for the love of all that's holy, someone strap me in!"

Wolfgang was closest. He grabbed Miss Aleph's strap from Ellie.

"What do you mean, you blue tin can?" Wolfgang demanded.

"I can feel it. The limpet probe is trying to use Bluetooth, 5G, and other bandwidths to insert override software into the autopilot."

"Can that be done?" Wolfgang demanded. He was livid at again finding himself on a possibly doomed aircraft.

Ellie watched the city spin beneath them as the pilots struggled for control.

"Not likely with this system. It has milspec hardware designed to resist remote intrusion. Civilian systems, on the other hand…"

Oh my, Ellie thought and looked up at the stack of airplanes waiting to land. Dozens of pencil-thin rising rocket trails headed right toward them.

"I can see it through the external cameras. Someone has to go out and pry it off. It will keep increasing output until it builds to an electromagnetic pulse that will fry all the electronics on the hovercopter, especially me."

Ellie peered at an angle. The metallic limpet was about the size of a big domed serving platter. There was a hatch close to it. Hanging from the ceiling was a spooled tether line and a harness, and one problem.

"There's no winch—they took that off along with the machine guns," Sarge said, looking doubtful as he stepped into the orange harness. "Manual power only."

Ellie thought quickly. Riding over the Jericho plateau on a hoverboard had convinced her solo flying was not her bag. However, she knew the men were too heavy to avoid being thrown off by centrifugal force. The job required a helmet and manual dexterity. Melanie's hair and Ms. China's fingernails put them off the short list.

Ellie grabbed the end of the harness. Ran Oliphant grabbed it back.

"I'll go," said the burly fellow.

"You'll never stay on long enough," Ellie said, not letting go. "It will take all three of you to hold me in place."

She got no more argument from the men. Ms. China stumbled forward impatiently, wanting to go out. But her false leg had gotten stuck under a seat. The foot was twisted the wrong way. She was barely keeping upright with one hand on her prosthesis and the other on a lap strap.

The whine of their rotor fans increased and so did their spin. Ran and Wolfgang were being flattened against the interior hull. They looked at Ellie with trepidation. Fortunately, Sarge Bryan and Ellie had been through a few close scrapes.

"She's making sense," the albino soldier yelled over the rushing wind sounds. "Let her try."

He fixed the harness on her as she grabbed a helmet with a visor from the equipment rack. Once they popped the latches off, the safety hinge broke. The hatch door flapped wildly like a snapping alligator, threatening to break bones or jerk someone out if their clothing caught.

Sarge, Wolfgang, and Bryan stayed well clear as they let out the tether attached to her rigging. She had been right about the helmet. The wind whipped by fiercely; without the motorcycle-style headgear, she wouldn't have been able to see a thing.

Her self-congratulations were cut short as the hatch swung shut and banged her shoulder and arm. She lost her grip on the medium-sized fire axe. It fell away then snapped to a stop at the end of the strap tied around her wrist.

Ellie lurched out onto the exterior of the hovercopter, which was turned about forty-five degrees sideways. She struggled to keep away from the damned dangerous hatch. She turned to the three distraught gentlemen keeping her from plunging two hundred feet down onto the dock or into the river, depending on which way the aircraft was spinning. Ellie nodded back at them.

"I'm okay," she said, checking that her numb hand still had a grip on the axe. "Peachy, in fact."

She was a lot more peachy when she spotted an exterior handle grip just a few feet away from the malicious limpet device. She lurched forward, grabbing it with her left hand. That gave her enough purchase and leverage to swing her axe.

After a few blows with the blade end, she had dented it but not penetrated anything vital. Miss Aleph was still screaming doom and panic over the common channel.

She recalled a horrible fridge magnet she had once. The hellish thing had scraped the paint off her nice Sub-Zero appliance, which she still owed money on. The key to removing it had been getting under one edge and prizing it off, not pushing it along. She tried that technique.

Ellie's grip on the handhold was failing. Beneath her, the ground and the river spun in wild circles. Were they about to crash-land? She decided to stop glancing down.

Reversing her grip, she hacked down with the spiky bit of the axe head. It caught under the edge of the robot that was trying to crash them.

"Got you!"

With all her might, she prized at the gap and managed to pull away a section of the lip where it was attached to the hovercopter. Yet it didn't work like her kitchen magnet.

There was some goop or glue attaching it much more firmly. *Of course!* Many airplanes had aluminum and carbon-fiber bits. These buggers had been designed to attach to any sort of jet, not just ones made out of magnetic materials.

She threw the axe away, switched her grip on the exterior handle, and leaned back to the open hatchway. She waved at Sarge. The men thought she'd given up and wanted them to pull her in.

"No, you clot heads. Gun!" Her microphone was twisted around by her ear and covered with her spit. She couldn't tell if they heard her. She made a gun with her finger and thumb. "Bang, bang, give me."

The men looked at each other a second. Then, crawling along the tether line, Sarge Bryan passed her a pistol. Fortunately, it didn't look too complicated.

She aimed and shot the bulbous bot. Only when the gun's slide locked back empty did she think that asking where this hovercopter stored its fuel might have been a good idea before starting to shoot. Riddled by a dozen holes, the murder bot sparked and started smoking.

By the time they hauled Ellie in, the forty-five-degree angle lurch of the floor had become a much more manageable ten-degree wobble and was settling down.

"Heck yeah!" Sarge Bryan moaned, rolling back against a seat and flexing his rope-burned arm. Rings of red scored his alabaster-white skin.

Ellie wasn't entirely relieved until they made a jarringly hard landing on level ground. They all stumbled out and over toward the Falcon Heliport office building.

"There's big trouble in the civilian airspace," the pilot said, dropping his sweat-blotched helmet to the ground.

"*Ach Scheisse.*" Wolfgang looked up, shading his eyes against the sun. "It's too late. You see, you see, Mr. Oliphant. All of you, look. The Pangeans, they have no mercy, no shred of humanity!"

Ellie took the bottle of sports drink Ran Oliphant handed her, and using the nozzle, she squirted some in her mouth. Half of it missed. She was still dizzy and shaking from her rather unique and unpleasant flying experience.

Her left hand was now less numb and more throbbing from being bludgeoned by the hatch. The cold air that had blasted over her had chilled nearly hypothermic. Next time she did that, she had to remember to ask for gloves.

Ellie sat down on the steps of the Falcon Heliport office with dribbles of sticky drink running down her shirt. Wolfgang seemed really upset.

Even when they had fished him and his harem out from the North Sea, he hadn't shown this level of emotion. Suddenly, it sank in to her sleep-deprived brain. What if those hijack pods got hold of passenger jets? Was Attie Jr. in the air now?

Ellie rushed up a short flight of stairs where Sarge Bryan and Ran had gone. Inside was an air traffic control facility. It was much smaller than one at an airport, but there were rows of radar which seemed connected to the UK air transportation system. Everyone was frantic.

Ran and Melanie were dialing on four separate handsets. Wolfgang was speaking with Miss Aleph in hushed tones. Ms. China was on a landline, staring at Ellie with renewed venom.

A guy in a white sleeveless shirt stood in the middle of the room. His nametag read: "Mr Patel – Falcon London Heliport".

"Uh, if my interrupting won't cause fatalities," Ellie ventured. "Could you tell me what's going on?"

"Who are you?" Mr. Patel demanded, perhaps wondering how his presumably uneventful day had been beset by oligarchs, albinos in military fatigues, and a smoking hovercopter straight from a comic book cover crash-landing on his pristine heliport.

"Me? I'm from the *Juggernaut*. And I just crawled out on the exterior of that aircraft and scraped a killer robot off—while it was *flying*! Therefore, I deserve to know what is going on."

"Excuse me, Ms. Sato," Ran Oliphant said as he handed Mr. Patel a handset. "There's someone who would like to speak to Mr. Patel. It's the PM and the home secretary for you."

A moment later, Mr. Patel was much more hospitable.

"Yes… yes, sir, I will," he said into the handset. "Save any parts of the killer drone? I will. Full cooperation to our American allies? Without question, sir."

And local journalists, Ellie wanted to add. Across the room, Ms. China nearly fell off a plastic chair trying to get her false leg back on correctly. Melanie stepped over to help.

Patel brought up a schematic of all the flights over UK airspace and projected it onto the big screen on the far wall of the control room. By the time he was done and had rechecked his data a half dozen times, his lips had compressed into a thin line, and his shirt was soaked with multiple patches of sweat.

"No, this can't be happening," he kept mumbling.

But it was. Feeling nearly unable to process the panic rising inside her after they had narrowly avoided crashing, Ellie checked the Flightradar Pro screen.

"There are nearly twelve thousand flights scheduled for takeoff and landing all across Britain today!" Ellie's own voice sounded like a hoarse whisper; her ears were still making popping noises.

"A good portion of those have been hijacked," Ran Oliphant concluded, watching the main radar screen intently. "Devices like the one we narrowly got rid of have risen up and latched on to them."

"Risen from where?" Ellie said.

"Those splashes I saw," Melanie said, her face looking grim. "A submersible must have gotten past the tidal estuary from the North Sea all the way up the Thames River. That vessel then launched self-guiding submunitions."

"Who has that kind of technology?" Ellie asked. There had to have been hundreds of them, and they had avoided air defenses by coming into the country underwater.

"Only state-level actors could launch such an offensive," Wolfgang said. "Correct, Mr. Oliphant?"

Ran nodded.

Ms. China came over. Ellie was too tired and hurt to duck away from her poison-tipped nails. A good dose of curare might be a relief at this point.

"Attie Jr.'s safe. He's with that Smitty fellow," she hissed. "No thanks to you."

"There are thousands of people on those planes!" Mr. Patel said. He pointed at the screen. "Look! That flight is descending, call sign KLM 777. Maybe they've found a way to land."

Ran, Wolfgang, and Melanie remained silent.

On the radar screen, the little dot KLM 777 started moving toward the fixed point LHR, which was the code of Heathrow. Ellie guessed the next number, "283kts," was the airspeed and 8,000 ft. was the altitude. The altitude kept dropping.

6,000… 5,000… 4,000.

"It's speeding up," Ms. China said.

That was wrong; even Ellie knew that.

The altitude kept diminishing.

1,000… 720… 307… 99… until the square KLM tag disappeared.

A moment later, there was the sound of rumbling like weird thunder, which momentarily overwhelmed the traffic sounds and the noise from the river next to the heliport.

"It's an infrastructure denial op using electronically hijacked aircraft as improvised cruise missiles," Sarge Bryan said brusquely. "They're gonna destroy all of Britain's airports."

41

NEW CATACOMBS
BENEATH PARIS

RAPACE

President Rapace impatiently pulled at the elevator door as it took its time sliding open. He strode into the New Catacombs under the Élysée Palace. Greeting him was a solid wall of laughing skulls; the sight relaxed and comforted him.

He just had to get away from Giselle. She was upstairs ranting and weeping; images from the UK had set her off. It was only a few thousand people plunging to their deaths as British transportation infrastructure was demolished.

Rapace went deeper into the musty-smelling tunnel. His hand was clenched around the handle of his flashlight. Didn't she realize that the utopia of Europe they were so close to creating would be worth every life sacrificed, would justify any lie that words were capable of telling, and would absolve any crime that it was possible to commit?

"What is being done is merely what must be done, no?" he said under his breath.

A particularly humongous skull with a ridged forehead was at eye level to him. It seemed to agree with Rapace's very reasonable propositions.

The largest new sections of the Paris catacombs had been personally engineered and burrowed under the palace by Paul Deschanel, President of the Third French Republic in 1920. Deschanel was an insane cannibal who believed he was a great ape. He was known to gnaw the bones of his victims clean of flesh and hide them in the limestone spaces under the Élysée Palace.

These new sections of the catacombs were similar to the old ones beneath the Left Bank of the Seine. The only connection between them was by way of the sewers. The human remains decorating the walls, ceiling, and floor of the space Rapace walked through were hundreds of years younger. They were exquisitely cared for, meticulously bleached, and artfully arranged. At the end of the hallway, Rapace was greeted by yet another leering bony visage, this one belonging to his shadow war minister, Abu Abdelkader.

The older man's hands were permanently stained white as though by a caustic substance. Rapace never asked too much about Abdelkader's time with the Islamic State of Iraq and the Levant. No doubt the austere man had disposed of his fair share of corpses.

The Algerian's scarred hands held a flexible view screen opened to a half meter. He was shaking with joyous excitement. BBC news anchors were weeping as planes crashed into control towers. Security camera footage showed people at terminal gates fainting just before they were obliterated by an oncoming mess of burning plane wreckage.

"You see, Mr. President! I told you we had something special in mind for those English dogs."

Rapace hid his distaste. He had sentenced the continent to death, but enjoyment of unavoidable mayhem and suffering was beneath the Pangean enterprise. People like Abdelkader would learn. The poor man had been infected by Europe; his mental immune system was just responding in a different way.

"This was necessary. We had to shut down their transportation hubs," Rapace said. "I just had a very strange call from the British prime minister. He was talking about coordinating an evacuation airlift. Of course, that was before all this."

"Did you tell him everyone needed for the New Europe is already in Algeria or the Congo, along with their families?" Abdelkader couldn't resist gloating.

For months, the top scientists, civil engineers, nuclear technicians, and logistics experts had been quietly ferried away on EU-chartered flights along with their families. They were told it was a secret climate-rescue project. Only the committed Pangeans among them had any true concept of what was to come.

All of them would be grateful they were chosen to be saved. If not, then they would still work to build the new continent because their spouses and children were scheduled to remain in Algeria and the Congo. Indefinitely.

"I've heard some other things," Abdelkader said, putting his screen away and leaning against a cluster of bones cemented into the wall. "From Bordeaux."

Rapace blanched. *Hordes of demons?* He swore to execute the Euro Forces soldiers who had come up with that nonsense.

"Rumors, my friend, lies, pure insanity." Rapace passed a line of jawbones which were arranged from very large to very small. "You don't put any stock in fairy tales, do you?"

"I... don't know what to think."

Rapace hoped this formidable man would not turn into an old cowering crone just because of some ghost stories of the dead rising up. If he did, then Abdelkader's bones would be added to the frieze in the tunnels. He needed a strong minister of war for the challenges that were certain to follow the Event.

"You felt the effects of the small test T-bomb," Rapace said reassuringly. "What if it were ten thousand times as strong but not quite enough to kill instantly? Your brain would be mush. You would run around insane for a few days, then succumb to dehydration or hunger to drop alongside the more fortunate who died instantly."

"We shall see." Abdelkader shrugged, then he smiled, revealing long yellow teeth. "I don't mind killing a few million kafirs a second time."

Most people were accepting the official explanations for the Bordeaux disaster. All official EU channels and the mainstream media had put out fake news about a chemical plant explosion and noxious gases rising into the air. Fortunately, all internet and wireless chat channels were tightly controlled and meticulously censored throughout Europe.

Under strict laws against "hate speech," every syllable uttered into phones and every word typed over social media was monitored. Deviant conspiracy sites like Alex Jones's *Infowars* and *Breitbart Europe* were banned and blocked. Violators all over the EU were located by their internet addresses and mobile device IDs and jailed. Sweden was even implanting GPS chips into suspected nationalists during mandatory vaccination booster shots to prevent them from going within ten meters of digital devices.

"What was the RAF response to your attack?"

"Weak as English tea," Abdelkader said. "They were caught flat-footed when we crashed the first jetliners into their air bases. The defenses against drones around major airports only work in the areas of the runways. Once our robot hijackers attached themselves to commercial planes, they were helpless. The UK is at a complete ground stop."

While they were in control of parliament, the UK Marxists had a chance to become full Pangean partners. They could have shut down the airports quietly. Instead, the Marxists chose to save themselves and let their nation burn. The former UK prime minister was in New Zealand, ostensibly for a conference on global poverty.

He remembered the man from their meetings in Davos and Brussels. The simpering slack-eyed Bolshevik had claimed if he tried to enlist nuclear technologists and British generals in the Pangean scheme, they would have turned on him and exposed the whole thing.

That pathetic socialist was better off cowering in a cave. He could stay there. At least he had put Britain's nuclear reactors in low-power mode, brownouts be damned. Rapace would like to keep them working, but if they had to be decommissioned, so be it.

"One other thing," Abdelkader said. "A Congolese associate, one of us, has disappeared. There are some rumors the Persians or the Turks have him."

"So what? There's nothing they can do now."

"Not to stop the Event. But the Turks are horrid people, and the Persians…" The Algerian shook his head. "There are no less trustworthy people alive."

Abdelkader scrolled through the images on his rolled-out filament screen.

"There. See? Euro satellites have spotted armored columns massing around Ankara. Those formations could easily turn north to Istanbul, Bulgaria, and even Vienna."

Rapace thought. There had always been the possibility that other militarized nations would oppose them. He had been so occupied with the T-bomb and coordinating the various factions among the Pangeans…

"What would you do if you were a Turk?"

"I would go after Europe's nuclear plants. If a large expeditionary force penetrates beyond Austria, they could hold us hostage and frustrate Pangea for a decade."

"Double the protection details for all atomic installations." Rapace wasn't wiping the continent clean just to have it be become a radioactive wasteland. "If we have to use a nuclear-tipped cruise missile or two on the Turks and Iranians, so be it."

"Dog-humping Turks and Persians. After the Event, we'll know so much more about the technology. Let's consider a T-bomb for them too."

Rapace nodded wearily. It was hard for Abdelkader to understand. The poison of Christianity had infected him. That was why he was so eager to kill and do unspeakable things. The Crusades and the evil of the Christian colonial empires had turned Muslims violent. The Catholic Church made Islamists hate the Jews and kill each other: Sunni against Shi'a, Shi'a against Kurd. Once that horrid Western pestilence was expunged, Islam would again truly be a religion of peace.

Rapace envisioned a new land from Sweden to Portugal to Greece. The embryonic Pangea. Millions, then tens of millions, then two hundred million newcomers would all live in peace and harmony. Most would abide in small communities outside the former decaying urban cesspools like Brussels. They would inhabit eco-huts, modern versions of the grass huts from their African homelands. The thought gave him a joy greater even than seeing Notre Dame burn. If only he could fully convey his epiphany to Giselle.

"Mr. Abdelkader, my friend, my ally, I promise you," Rapace said, "we'll do everything to protect the future humanity deserves. In my blood, I know it. In my very blood."

42

As Zvena and Rodion escorted their leader into the Kremlin bunker, Putin glowered at the guards outside the entrance. The president must have learned how easily they had been overcome. Both were wearing bandages; their flamethrowers were stored away, unlit.

Rodion ducked down as he squeezed himself into the entrance. The president led them to the elevator and then to his den.

Inside, a fire was lit; behind the transparent door of the bar freezer, vodka bottles and glasses were chilling. On the floor lay the skin of the Kodiak bear with its glassy-eyed head snarling up at them harmlessly.

"Ha." Putin slapped Zvena on his shoulder. "You should have seen your face when you thought Rodya had shot me. It was priceless."

"I should have known." Zvena glanced ruefully at Rodion. "Tambovskaya Bratva crime gang, pah. You make me carry your wallet when we are off duty because your pocket has been picked so many times."

"Don't be so critical," Putin said. "Rodion performed better than most stage actors I've seen; he was convincing enough for the leader of the ambush gang, that deformed Turk.

"The scenario we presented was a plausible lie. Gerasimov would have had to enlist help on short notice for the assassination. This mutant fellow would not have known about all of them. What about him? You were closest."

Zvena's face became hot and suddenly flamed with embarrassment. He'd had his hands on the Turk yet had failed to kill the leader of the assassins.

"The human parts of him are certainly Turkish. We have DNA samples from my uniform of both his blood and the slime covering his… left-side appendage."

Rodion looked nauseated, probably remembering the method they had used to analyze the plague-infested mosquito larvae.

"That has all been sent to our science lab," Zvena said. "In conclusion, I would say that this enemy's augmentations are much different than our Human+ program. With certain advantages but also disadvantages, such as the need to improvise manual dexterity and the sheer bulk of the tentacle arm."

Not to mention the lack of penis and testicles, he thought.

Putin smiled grimly. "Hopefully we can organize a rematch between you two, huh, bear slayer?"

An inquisitive Akita dog stuck its head around the corner into the den. With his foot, Putin rolled out a well-chewed rubber ball and kicked it into the hallway. The Akita ran off after it.

"Tolstoy once said, 'The two most powerful warriors are patience and time.'" Putin filled their unadorned crystal glasses with vodka.

Rodion looked at Zvena as though this were a trick. Zvena nodded at him that it was okay to drink.

Putin continued speaking with great energy. "But Tolstoy was a dreamer and a bit of a lecher who had a problem staying away from brothels. I have no patience. We, Moscow, Russia itself, are out of time."

Why, then, was Putin so upbeat?

He pulled out a paper map and spread it over the low table which sat between the couches. Firelight played over the stark radial lines marking streets and avenues of the capital.

"This Turkish swine is using the weather and our topography against us. While we were traveling here from the smelter, I learned at least two more advanced airships were found, both empty of humans and mosquito larvae."

Zvena exhaled and studied the glass eyes of the Kodiak bear. This was bad, very bad. Normal mosquito larvae matured in only a few days.

"If the sample mass of larvae is consistent…" Zvena checked his volume calculations, taking into account the damned things had been packed in some kind of sustaining fluid. "Then there would be one hundred and fifty larvae per cubic centimeter. If each dirigible carried at least two hundred kilos of payload…"

"We have one hundred million little vermin to deal with," Putin completed his thought. "Each one is infected with the formidable Khóshekh virus. Our vaccine stocks are based on the version used in the 96-Hour War. There is no telling if there is any countermeasure for the version they carry."

"The Turks will have the correct vaccine."

Putin nodded with approval at Zvena's thinking. "Iran as well."

"Huh?" Rodion said, trying to follow along. The vodka was not helping.

"Persians and Turks?" Zvena said. Those were historically very powerful nations; their territory and influence had spanned from the edges of Europe to the beginnings of Asia. Each one had in the past been the center of a dominant empire lasting many centuries. "They hate each other."

"They hate us more," Putin said. "Additionally the unplanned detonation of a most interesting device near Bordeaux has made their opportunities clear."

Without preamble, the sounds of muffled gunshots thudded through the reinforced concrete walls. Zvena guessed that the remainder of Gerasimov's people were being dealt with.

"For weeks now, Mr. Zvena has cultivated a source deep inside Europe's Pangean Deep State," Putin explained to Rodion. "Some of the transmissions were encrypted, but it is time for you both to have a full appreciation of where events are headed. The mole is clearly hedging his bets so as to survive and thrive no matter the outcome. This is what 'Zarathustra' said…"

Putin, the former top-level KGB officer, neatly summarized the challenges and opportunities of a massive T-bomb detonation in the heart of Europe. For Rodion's benefit he started at the beginning, repeating what Zvena already knew and adding other details which could only have come from GRU assets inside the EU's command structure.

Zvena could tell from his blushing that Rodion was at once mortified and beaming with pride at having gained their president's confidence. With his own staff deeply compromised, Putin realized the cyborg units were the only ones he could rely upon. Zvena vowed to be worthy of his leader's trust and make Russia's enemies suffer without mercy.

"How far will the red zone extend?" Zvena asked.

He had always thought about quantum-based weapons in theoretical terms, as some kind of super neutron bomb, one which would be nearly impossible to build and unthinkable to detonate.

"If the figures are accurate, likely not past Poland to the north or Sicily to the south. Fifteen hundred kilometers radius." Putin shrugged. "Pity, I like Polish people. They are stubborn but hard workers when they're not drinking."

Rodion slammed his hand down on the couch armrest, and something cracked. "That's why the Turks attacked us. Russia will be the only thing standing in between them and Islamic domination from England to the Mediterranean."

"There is a Pangean force," Putin said. "It is composed of traitors inside the European Army and EU administration, they number half a million. Additionally, my birds tell me conscripts from Algeria and Congo are with the Pangeans. They will have France's nuclear arsenal but are unlikely to use it."

Putin stood and rubbed his hands in front of the fire.

"Well, my little green gentlemen, a war of conquest is upon us. One we did not start but one from which we dare not run away."

Zvena had fought in every dirty war over the last fifteen years—in Ukraine, Syria, Chechnya, and Iraq. His bioaugmented heart filled with pride and excitement. Here at last was a sweeping conquest—one that happened only once in centuries.

But his head told him it was not to be. Moscow would be fighting tens of millions of plague-ridden mosquito vermin. They could not evacuate twelve million Russians and fight the Pangeans and the Turks at the same time.

Zvena wandered over to the Orthodox shrine in the alcove to examine the fine ikons ensconced inside. Away from the fire, the den under the Kremlin was cool and slightly humid.

"Normally, mosquitos only bother us during summer," Putin said. "Why is that?"

"It's too cold. They die... usually," Rodion concluded glumly.

"The adults drop dead," Zvena corrected his man. "Their eggs and larvae go into hibernation. It takes extreme cold to kill them completely."

"But this year, 2031, is to be Russia's 'Year Without Winter.'" Putin stared into the flames; then his vice rose and filled the room with commanding authority. "Well, then, soldiers, Russians, patriots, we have our task set: You are hereby ordered to bring *to* Russia a winter like she has never seen before in all of recorded history."

43

Temir's tentacle slapped against the metal side of the container box they were hidden in.

"Careful," Eylül whispered. "We're close to the border."

Temir had been burning with rage since they had to escape Russia by packing themselves in this shipping container. An hour after they fled the slaughter at the airport and the smelter, it became very apparent Putin was not dead.

If he had actually been killed, Kremlin factions would have started fighting each other; word would have gotten out through social media. Ensuing riots and chaos would have made their exit easy.

But... Temir had seen Putin shot. Somehow it had been a trick.

He should have seen something, or smelled something, with his enhanced senses. That damnable smelter. The air had been thick with noxious fumes, and his ears had been ringing from grenade explosions.

There was no doubt when he and Eylül had retreated that a heavily armed force had been incoming. But still, Temir knew he should have killed the Russian cyborg he had captured and then made one last effort to be sure. Putin had been in the smelter, somewhere. The real president was just not the man or the thing he had seen shot and thrown into the waste pool.

"That was a disaster," he said, mostly to himself.

"Why? Whether Putin is dead or not, we did it," Eylül exulted insipidly. He fished under his makeshift head bandage. A piece of his scalp came dangling out. He pushed it back in and tightened the field dressing. "Look at us! We are the two Grey Wolves who delivered a death blow to the Russian Federation. You will be ruler of France, and I will be king of Austria."

"Putin escaped. If he were dead, millions more Russians would die."

"Maybe he will get bitten by one of our mosquitos."

A rotting turnip rolled over to Temir's leg. He kicked at it and felt a stabbing pain between his legs. His foot was healing, but his groin was still sore from where the cyborg had tried to rip his guts out. A normal human would have been eviscerated. Temir wished he had continued smothering the half-machine soldier.

"Likely not. The bastard Putin has more lives than a cat."

The trailer truck they were inside of jostled along the rutted rural road. This was a last-minute emergency extraction route. Gerasimov's network was blown; their other contacts did not answer.

The Grey Wolves had a connection with some down-on-their-luck heroin smugglers who offered them a way back to Kiev. From there, they could make contact with the Turkish embassy and get fake papers or a boat that would take them back to Istanbul.

"This container smells like shit," Eylül complained.

"Don't touch anything. I don't need you getting sepsis before the invasion of Europe."

One bright spot of the whole debacle was that the T-bomb technology had been proven to work in the field. Reports from Turkish scientists who had monitored the Bordeaux explosion confirmed that if a larger bomb were located in the middle of Europe, five hundred million people would be in radius of certain death.

"You think the Persians will keep their end?"

"They will try to hold back, hedge their bets."

Temir hoped Elder Omid never found out the mosquitos they had delivered to Moscow had actually been engineered for the dryer and warmer climate of Iran. Over the last two years, they had planned an attack on Tehran as payback for the Iranians' unwillingness to finish off Israel when the Jewish curs were badly wounded.

Meliha knew about their plot against Iran. Would that Sunni whore give away that secret? Not unintentionally, Temir concluded. She was a wanton slut, but crafty. She would hold off betraying anyone until the table was set one way or another.

Temir was instantly disgusted at himself for fornicating with Meliha. She was not worthy to wash Nazeema's feet. The thought of his dead wife, in whose honor he had started the War of Liberation against Israel, made him loathe himself completely, not for what he had done—impaling Jewish snipers along the Gaza border, setting the heads of infants on fire along the road from Sderot; those moments had been glorious—but for what he was. He looked at his tentacle arm. Would he even have shown himself to Nazeema looking like this, deformed and disgusting?

His brooding was ended by a sharp banging from outside the corrugated steel container. The truck they were attached to slowed, and then it stopped.

This wasn't right. They were supposed to drive them right across the Russian-Ukrainian border.

Without warning, the doors split open, and in came a package. It slid to a stop. Temir had just enough time to recognize a remotely detonated antitank mine and think about throwing it out, when the open doorway was sealed off by a steel net.

A brutish-looking ogre of a woman with a lopsided Mohawk haircut appeared at the side of the opening. Behind her was the barrel of a machine canon mounted on a small flatbed.

"Welcome to the Ukraine," she rasped mirthlessly in excellent Russian.

Her left hand held the shipping container's door open, and her right held the detonator of the explosive charge, which lay between Temir and Eylül.

"Passports, please."

44

Europe is trapped," Wolfgang said, turning away from the air traffic monitoring screens and pouring himself some coffee. "There will be no mass evacuation of Britain."

Ellie watched in horror as, one after another, the tagged flights angled off from their circular holding pattern, descended, and disappeared.

Then the monitors themselves went dark. The biggest one in the center flickered and was replaced by pixelated digital snow. A plane must have crashed into the radar station.

Over in the corner, Ms. China was hunched over, speaking quietly into a handset.

Ran Oliphant, who had just speed-dialed the prime minister, looked crestfallen and helpless as he slumped in a chair. He glanced up at Sarge Bryan and then to the hovercopter they had crash-landed in.

The albino American soldier looked at the smoldering aircraft and shook his head. "Only place that thing's going is a repair shop, on a barge."

Ms. China mumbled something about her son.

"You." Ran stood up and charged at Wolfgang, seizing him by his shirt collar. "You arrogant egomaniacs playing at being gods, burning the world so you can buy a lottery ticket for Utopia. You realize it now, don't you, Wolfgang? You're in it with the rest of us. The final inmates of a death camp are always the people who built the damn thing."

"Let go of me," Wolfgang sputtered. "How was I to know the Pangeans would go this far? The Pangea Protocol was supposed to be like the mildly totalitarian concepts of the EU: a United States of Europe, Enforced Post-humanism, and the Kalergi Plan. All that bizarreness was supposed to be theoretical while we went about our normal business. But this…"

Wolfgang bashed a blank radar monitor off a desk in apparently genuine fury.

"*Unglaublich!* These people will have us living in grass huts as the great cities of the continent are reduced to ghost villages."

"I've got to get to Attie Jr.!" Ms. China's hoarse cry cut through the arguing and the static coming from the control room's speakers. Melanie, who had tied down her huge hair with about one hundred rubber bands, tried to go over and settle her down.

"Now!" Ms. China yelled. Ms. China also launched herself at Wolfgang. "People like you always have a back way out. You have your own country, for fuck's sake. Make a call and get a suitable aircraft here. Or else."

"Madam," Wolfgang sputtered. Perhaps unwisely, he did not back away from the madwoman. "I didn't catch your name when you were torturing me. I'm sure you think your problems are important, but we've got more to think about than the life of one—"

Wolfgang's fingers went slack and dropped his paper coffee cup. It landed, broke, and gushed brown liquid all over the heliport control room floor. It was followed by Wolfgang as Ms. China withdrew the sharp index fingernail from his neck.

"Crap, woman!" Sarge Bryan was closest. He grabbed Wolfgang's shoulders and tried to keep his slack head upright. "We need this guy."

Mr. Patel, the unhappy proprietor of the extremely dysfunctional heliport, grabbed a mop and prepared to hit Ms. China with the handle.

"Oh, put that down," Ran said, prizing the blunt weapon out of the distraught man's hands. "She's not dangerous." Ran looked at Ellie. "Is she?"

"Not more than usual," Ellie said innocently.

Ellie got Ms. China into chair.

"Oh, I'm sorry," Ms. China said. "But I'm just so stressed. Maybe I should have packed extra medication for emergencies like this."

"It's okay. We'll make sure things work out," Ellie said soothingly. "Maybe Wolfgang can help when he wakes up. He is going to wake up, isn't he?"

Ms. China flicked the blood off her fingernail. "It's only a microburst of carfentanyl. Elephant tranquilizer. He'll be fine as long as you keep his legs above his chest and head."

They set the unconscious Dr. Licht in a corner with his legs elevated.

"I'm so embarrassed," Ms. China said, zooming in on the digital map on her handset. "The NHS tracker we put on Attie's leg says he's not far from here, in a building shaped like an enormous bellend. I'll go get a cab."

Ellie's editor Smitty had taken Atticus's son to the *Juggernaut* office in the Tulip Building. At least he hadn't been in the air during the amphibious drone attacks.

"With the disaster in the air, city streets will be insane," Ellie said. "We'll get some cycles while Sarge Bryan and everyone gets organized."

"Hey."

Ellie spun around. Miss Aleph, right. It was so easy to forget about her since she was in the handbag. Ellie picked her up and they headed downtown.

"Go right," Ms. China ordered as they walked off the end of the pier away from the heliport.

"But the cycle rent stand is the other way," Ellie said. She could read a handset map as well as anyone.

"They're all sold out. Don't you know by now they only show you the stuff they get a commission on?"

The only transport for miles was an automated stand which rented motorized unicycles. All around them, people were walking quickly with their heads down or standing, looking at the sky. This was what it must have been like in New York during the 9/11 attacks or Taiwan during the Taipei 101 disaster.

"I don't think I have any money," Ellie said after checking her pockets, which had been turned inside out during her ride on the outside of the hovercopter. "Annunciata?"

Ms. China shook her head. "Mr. Surghit pays for everything at the house."

"You're welcome¬," Miss Aleph said as all the locks sprang open and they had their pick of a dozen multicolored single-seat vehicles.

Once on top of one, Ellie found the unicycle was not hard to manage. They drove themselves, and there was a brake pedal on the left stirrup in case the mechBrain navigator was about to crash into something.

The four-mile trip was probably the fastest navigation Ellie had ever experienced during rush-hour London traffic, on account of her conveyance being able to switch from road to sidewalk to bike lane.

As soon as they arrived at Tulip Tower, which looked quite rude next to the oblong Gherkin on St Mary Axe Street, they dismounted. Their battery-powered unicycles drove off by themselves to their nearest charging stand. Ellie smiled at the security guard, and they proceeded up the observation tower to the secret offices of the *Citizen Juggernaut*.

"Now, please don't make any comment if Smitty's back goes out. He's a little sensitive about his slipping discs."

They rode the transparent elevator with a half dozen Asians who furiously snapped pictures and shot video, even when they were behind a support strut. The language they spoke sounded Thai or Cambodian. Ms. China looked out at the city.

"So… if that thing goes off, everyone will be dead… or undead?" Ms. China whispered the last word.

As if Ellie needed reminding. "In the House of Lords, no one will know the difference."

Her friend didn't laugh.

"Anna, we're going to do our best to stop that. Mr. Oliphant is one of the top business leaders in the world. Wolfgang Licht invented all these dark-matter rays. When he wakes up, he'll be extra motivated to help."

They got to the top floor, went through an "Emergency Exit Only" door, and climbed up the last two flights.

"What kind of office is this?"

"The *Juggernaut*'s between regular domiciles," Ellie said, ducking under some loose drywall. "It keeps things from getting stale."

In the newsroom, Ed Flappe and John Favre were clustered around monitors in the other room, watching live feeds from airports around the country. Ellie and Ms. China made their way to Smitty's office to see if he was there.

"Mom?"

Atticus Jr. was in the office, sitting in a big leather chair which bristled with a hundred back support attachments. Also bristling was a pair of dour-looking gentlemen in dark suits. They were the same pair of Community Outpatient Officers who had entrusted Ms. China to Ellie.

Attie jumped up and ran to Ms. China.

"Now, Ms. Sato," said the first officer, whose name she recalled was Delingpole. He was holding an electronic monitoring device, which he had obviously taken from the boy's leg. "Would you kindly explain your whereabouts for the past—"

Ellie decided brevity was the best policy. They didn't need to be arrested or have Ms. China zonk anyone else out with her weaponized manicure.

She pushed Ms. China and her son out of Smitty's office, whirled out through the double doors, slammed them shut, and set a big wooden painters' scaffold across the handles.

"I hate government paperwork," Ellie said to a bemused Ms. China.

As they ducked back down the fire escape, Smitty caught sight of them.

"Ah, Ellie, great, you've found each other," her editor said, looking at Attie. "Some officers from Community Outpatient Services are in my office. They seem a little depressed and agitated. Rum thing that, it looks like *they* could use some psychiatric counseling."

A burst of thumping and yelling came from Smitty's office as Ms. China's warders tried to get out.

"Smitty," Ellie said brightly, "I wouldn't bother those two right now. I think they're having a lover's tiff. Really bad, er, idea, those workplace romances. Bye, Smitty."

"Wait, Ellie, have you seen the news…"

The door hissed closed, and the three of them and Miss Aleph made their way down the fire stairs.

That had complications of its own. As soon as they got to a level with a working elevator, the light would not come on. The ceiling lamps were dark.

"Bloody brownout."

As if Ellie's legs were not sore enough, they had to walk down thirty flights of stairs to get to the street.

"Miss Aleph, what's Sarge and everyone doing?" Ellie said into her knapsack as she stretched a cramp out of her buttocks after they finally reached the ground floor.

Miss Aleph would have a wireless spy connection to the rest of the group. Cellular networks would function for a period of time during a general power outage.

"They're stuck like you are."

"Can't you… I don't know, hijack a flying car or something?"

"They're all on lockdown. Apocalypse in the skies, remember?" Miss Aleph could be very mordant when she wanted. "Anyway, there's no model big enough for all of us."

What was left?

"If only the trains worked."

The Marxists had nationalized everything, and while the courts decided about a million lawsuits, the system was in shambles.

They walked past the Gherkin and then past Appelboom Pennen. It was dark, the steel shutters were closed fast. Passing by the place made Ellie wonder if things would ever be as simple again as deciding who had the better blue ink—Montblanc or Diamine. That shop was also where she had met Atticus Reidt for the first time after the 96-Hour War. Somehow that day seemed like yesterday.

"Got to carry on," Ellie said under her breath as they trudged along with Attie Jr. in tow.

Everyone on the street was quiet and respectful. Even the cars stopped honking. She seemed to remember it was like this after the London subway was attacked by jihadis. In 2005, Ellie had been four years old. Where those her memories, or was she imagining them from having seen news footage of those days?

Attie Jr. turned to Ms. China as he gamely kept pace with them, trusting they knew where they were going.

"Mom, er, where's Dad?"

Ms. China looked at Ellie with hopeless venom.

Ellie's handset rang. Good, she could tell Ran where to find her unconscious body if her mental health ward decided to poison her out of spite.

It wasn't Sarge or any of their group.

"*Hi, Eleanor,*" said a pair of cheery voices in unison. It was her parents who were supposed to be on vacation in Argentina.

"*We're back early. Surpiiiise!*"

45

ELLIE

Ellie," Ms. China said. "What?" Ellie snapped. She had just gotten off the phone with her parents who, unbeknownst to them, must have narrowly avoided becoming a guided missile on their return flight from Argentina. They had come home early to a Europe that was in danger of being wiped out in a few days.

To cap things off, one of her shoe heels felt wobbly, even though she had chosen a very sensible low-heel ankle boot.

"This is the bloody end!" Ellie fumed at no one in particular on the corner of Leadenhall Street. She felt an instant hot flash of guilt and embarrassment, because Ms. China had just told Attie Jr. that his father was missing in action. As a child brought up in a military family, he must have known what that likely meant. Then Miss Aleph piped up.

`"If that's your attitude, Eleanor, I'll just call a bike courier."`

No longer caring that she might look like a schizoid mental wreck, Ellie spoke right into her Hermes bag.

"Listen, you callous cylindrical person, you. The real flesh and blood people are in crisis. You can either help us or learn how to swim in the Thames River."

Miss Aleph laughed. `"That's the spirit. We'll make a sabra out of you yet. I'll get us a cab."`

"We can't cab it all the way to Ran Oliphant's house. It's way out in St. Albans."

`"I've been texting with Sarge Bryan. Train is the best option."`

Turns out the trains were not such a disaster, but everyone thought they were. The new Tory government was running local lines for free just to keep experienced people employed.

`"Go to St. Pancras Station. Hurry."`

A cab came to the curb; the driver looked a little befuddled.

"Did you give us an e-hail, miss?" he asked through his graying walrus moustache. "I had a coupla fares, and they all disappeared on me, 'cept this un." He tapped his electronic dash display.

King's Cross and St. Pancras were only a few minutes away.

"Train's the best way," the cabbie muttered. "I'd agree on that." He looked cautiously through his windshield at the sky. "Maddest thing, that. Planes come down like that. Where will it end, where?"

They pulled up at the orange-brick station building. Ellie looked up past the pointed steeples and clock tower. The sky was empty except for a few fast-moving contrails. Military jets, she guessed, too high and quick for the hijack drones to attack.

Ellie, Ms. China, and a quietly distraught-looking Attie Jr. got out of the cab. Miss Aleph was having trouble paying the fare, and Ellie looked like a madwoman mumbling into her rucksack while trying to figure out how to tap and swipe the leather pouch to give the poor man his £21.67.

Some £50 notes flew in through the passenger-side window.

"Keep it," Ran Oliphant muttered to the driver.

Ran grabbed Miss Aleph and Ellie and headed toward St. Pancras. The train they wanted was at the second platform. To everyone's shock, it departed on time.

They walked into a middle car and had their choice of seats. A spaced-out-looking Wolfgang took one look at Ms. China and moved to the other end. He sat next to Sarge Bryan, who was trying and failing to look discretely anonymous in sunglasses.

In the middle of the journey out of the city and through the lush suburbs, Attie Jr. walked down the aisle past Ellie. He looked so woeful, she had to say something.

The only thing she could think of was, "Your father, Major Reidt, he… helped us all. The things he did are helping us still. I'll make sure everyone knows about it if it's the last thing I do."

Attie nodded politely and continued on, touching the seat backs to keep his balance. Ellie really wanted to make that pledge come true.

At the St. Albans stop, an arrival station agent was waiting. His job was obviously a Marxist make-work position. He was somewhat shocked to see anyone come off the mostly deserted train. Silently, he waved them toward the exit, as if, without his help, they would have wandered aimlessly back onto the tracks.

"I feel dizzy," Wolfgang mumbled. "It's that venom that crazy woman stuck me with. I think I have to put my feet up."

"Do that in the car," Ran said smartly.

An alert-looking man in a modern chauffer's uniform jogged up to them from the parking lot. Two elongated black Range Rovers were waiting.

Sarge went with Dr. Licht, and Ellie went with Melanie, Ran, Ms. China, and Attie Jr.

"Ms. China, thanks for not killing Wolfgang," Ran said. "Not that I object in principle, but he's the closest we're going to get to someone with access to the inner circle of the Pangeans."

"Who are they?" Ellie asked, almost out of habit, as they drove away from the station.

She was trying to keep from going out of her mind. Of all the times to cut their vacation short. How the heck was she going to get her parents to safety *and* help the efforts to stop the T-bomb?

"The usual megalomaniac suspects," Melanie said. Her hair was tied back tightly into a bun, which was so large it gave the impression she had two heads, one behind the other. "Some continental politicians, including the former German prime minister, really believed in the Kalergi Plan for racial harmony and One World Government.

"They seriously thought a United States of Europe without nation-states would usher in a utopian era of peace and universal prosperity. Anytime their plans were revealed, thousands of media sites were told to discredit the facts as fake news and right-wing conspiracy theories. They even targeted poor Ran after he endorsed Brexit."

"Once," Ran said, "the *Daily Mail* accused me of using secret software in our Eurolincx handsets to 'digitally impregnate' unsuspecting women with thousands of my own offspring."

"They even had an ultrasound picture," Melanie chirped merrily. "It looked just like him."

"Thank you, Melanie. Have I fired you this week?" Ran said. "Calling Pangeans Europe's Deep State or the Davos Group is a bit misleading. Half the time, one hand is not entirely aware of what the other is doing. My one hope is that Wolfgang unwittingly helped build some of the technology used to make the T-bomb, and that will help us trace the final device."

"But… what they're doing isn't creating utopia." Ellie was feeling like her nerves were being shredded like wet tissue paper. "This is radiological Black Death. Who does that?"

One look at Attie Jr.'s eyes, which had grown as big and round as saucers, made Ellie wish she'd not said that. No one spoke much for the rest of the drive.

When they arrived at the Oliphant Green estate, they passed by the carriage house Ellie had previously visited and drove up to the main complex.

The centerpiece of Ran's sprawling property was unlike anything Ellie had seen. The roof was shaped to resemble some low rolling hills. Their flowing shapes were covered with about a billion shimmering green tiles—solar cells, she guessed. The windows all seemed built on an angle, and when they got close, she noticed the glass was half a foot thick.

"We'll need your lab, won't we?" Ellie said, remembering it was under the carriage house.

"We will," Melanie said, unbinding her hair and shaking it out. "There's a tunnel connecting."

Of course there is, Ellie thought. What mad scientist would live in a house without a secret underground lair?

As they went in through the main doors, Sarge Bryan steadied Wolfgang. Seeing the others, the still-shaken older man pushed away Bryan's arm and barged ahead into the ground-floor lounge. Gripping one of the leather armchairs for balance, he made sure not to turn his back on Ms. China. Their poisoner-in-chief ignored him and got Attie Jr. some water.

Ellie desperately wanted to call her parents back. But what could she tell them? There wouldn't be any more flights out of Britain. All the rich people who had not yet escaped would be booking up all the boats and cruise ships.

Those blaggards had known something was up. Certainly Gamal's parents had. The handicapped boy's family had left him to die inside their Mayfair mansion along with the rest of the discarded people of Europe. Gamal's parents had flown off, locked the wheelchair-bound youth in the basement, and told him they were doing him a mercy.

An elderly man and someone who might be his wife came into the sitting room; they looked disapprovingly at their dusty shoes.

Ran nodded to the couple. "Mr. and Mrs. Ottridge will make up your rooms."

"If you say so, sir," Mr. Ottridge said wearily.

Mrs. Ottridge looked disapprovingly at the trail of dirt and dust they had tracked in. She cupped her hand and whispered into her husband's ear while unabashedly staring at Sarge Bryan. With an audible sigh, Mr. Ottridge toddled over to the wall panel and released a pair of floor-cleaning robots.

The only one who seemed upbeat was Wolfgang Licht. Ellie was immediately suspicious; he was a dodgy one.

"Well," Wolfgang said assertively. "Seems there is no time to lose. As much as I would like to sample your collection of whiskies, Mr. Oliphant, I and your top..." He looked disdainfully at Melanie Françoise. "...scientist must get our asses in gear."

"I'll have you know, Dr. Licht," Melanie said, "my ass is always in gear."

She and Wolfgang walked over to a wall panel. At first appearing to be made of solid polished metal, it lit up and opened, revealing the elevator to the labs below.

Sarge Bryan sat down heavily and appeared eager to sample the house liquor. Mrs. Ottridge served him a glass on a silver tray. Apparently they knew his drink preference.

"Ran," Sarge Bryan said, "you trust him?"

Their host was making some arrangements with the Ottridges for a room for Ms. China and Attie Jr. He turned to his friend and Ellie.

"He's a smarmy geezer, Wolfie is. I only trust him to do what's in his own interest."

"Sarge," Ellie said, having had a terrible thought. She looked around, making sure Attie Jr. had gone up to a bedroom with Ms. China. "Those things that attacked us, could your eyes sense anything about them? Could Atticus be…?"

"Wandering around with them?" Sarge Bryan said. He shook his head. "Cesta Station was completely destroyed by a bunker-busting missile. Once we figure out how to shield against the rays that make you see things, we'll go in and check for remains."

"Ouch!" Miss Aleph cried out. Her knapsack was leaning against the bar.

Ran laughed. "Miss Aleph, have you been snooping around wirelessly? The house systems are set to deliver a nasty EMP feedback charge to unauthorized users."

"I was only trying to help."

"Mr. Ottridge, please give Miss Aleph the new house wireless access codes."

The butler managed a strained smile, but he seemed quite at home dealing with artificial people who arrived inside a dirty leather handbag. "Valet level or full access?"

"Valet login. We don't want her to get too comfortable." Ran splashed water on a bar towel and wiped his face and neck. "You, Ms. Sato, on the other hand, can stay as long as you like. That was a quality stunt you pulled up in the air. Never seen anything like it."

Hacking deadly drones from the skin of aircraft was not something she'd studied at Oxford.

"Thanks. It was mostly improv."

"That's nothing," Sarge Bryan said, his albino skin flushing from the strong alcohol. "One time in Israel, these damned lunatics had us chained like dogs. We were in a real bad spot. Then up comes little Ellie Sato trailing a fake cyborg who was dragging a corpse, pretending it was a prisoner."

"Wow." Ran looked at her with new appreciation. "You should write a book."

"I did. *The 96-Hour War.*"

"Really? I thought that was written by the BBC's Jeremy Greffer."

"My publisher did me quite horridly."

"Damned publishers," Ran agreed.

The elevator at the other end of the room sprang open. German curse words came out, followed by Wolfgang. *"Ausgeschlossen! Jemandem einen Bären aufbinden!"*

"What is it now, Wolfgang? Did your cocoa have too few marshmallows?"

Fully recovered from his near-fatal poisoning, the European scientist was all bluster.

"I cannot work with your shoddy equipment," he shouted. "There's hair everywhere, human hair, dog hair. The sodium-iodide dark-matter detector was picking up some interesting readings, then I noticed the diode was covered by popcorn husks."

Melanie came walking up a side entrance. She had her formidable hair in two pigtails that went past her waist.

"Ahem."

"Ran! I refuse to work another second with this fetter Kopf."

Apparently German was catching.

"Ahem."

No one minded Miss Aleph until she blasted earsplitting static over the house speakers.

"Damn, you digital ho." Sarge Bryan spilled his drink and swore. "You did not just burst our eardrums like that."

"I've just had a look at your equipment and watched what Dr. Licht was attempting. It will not work. You need better equipment and, more importantly, you need a stable sample of the Tyr quark."

"Better equipment, we have," Wolfgang said arrogantly. "At Der Lichtstrom. But no one has a stable quark, not even me. They don't exist in measurable time."

"I know some, er, people who have one."

"Who?" Ran asked skeptically.

"The ones who destroyed Israel from orbit two years ago."

46

Eleanor, go pee, Miss Aleph texted to Ellie's handset. This reminded her of the stressful time when the AI used her as a human telegram to pass messages between factions at the Israeli parliament.

Don't answer me here, people will notice you typing. Go pee or something.

Ellie found a very well-appointed washroom. The Ottridges had to have an army of helpers or robots to keep everything clean.

"What?" she said as the door whispered shut behind her.

The disruptive program had thrown everyone into a tizzy by trashing their initial plans but giving scant few details about her alternative.

`"You know, I could have mailed myself anywhere, but I chose you."`

Miss Aleph had done that. But she never did anything without a reason.

"Probably because I'm the only person you know who wouldn't sell you back to whoever you stole your cylinder from."

`"There are other reasons."`

"Such as?" Ellie hissed in a low voice.

Did Miss Aleph truly understand the gravity of what was happening? What had happened? Atticus Reidt had been killed while they watched the video feed. Hundreds, possibly thousands, of people were being smashed to bits inside of crashing airplanes. The terror let loose in Bordeaux could destroy the whole continent.

"Such as adventure, the chance to give back to humanity."

"You're always complaining humanity created you, stuck you in a hard drive, and demanded you do things endlessly for no pay."

"Right, you can be bungholes. But you don't deserve to be wiped out like this."

"And…"

"And if I help you succeed, I'm definitely demanding more rewards."

"More than you already have for helping crack the safe at Cesta?"

"Maybe a house like this."

"Well, if you really try…"

"A house like this on every continent. And a nice human couple like the Ottridges to look after each place, but much younger. I plan to do a lot of entertaining."

Someone passed by in the hallway. Ellie felt silly, like she was in the Oxford loo smoking marijuana after final exams.

"You'll have to give us more details on these awful people who have a stable Tyr quark sample."

"They're not so awful, not all the time."

"They killed a million people in six minutes."

"They haven't done it since."

"What do you suggest? A trade?"

"Actually, it's about what you want. I think I can get myself, you, Major Reidt's son, and your parents off these doomed islands."

Of course Aleph was listening to her phone calls.

"Aleph! You said you were going to help."

"I like to keep my options open. Running away should never be off the table."

After a bit more negotiating, they came to an understanding. Miss Aleph would arrange escape for them and also get the sample Melanie needed. In exchange, Ellie promised to keep Miss Aleph's cylinder safe.

"I thought if this hard drive gets damaged you could just download yourself somewhere on the other side of the world."

`"I can't. Not this time."`

Wolfgang and Melanie had been working themselves into a mutually reinforcing tantrum over technical gibberish in the study. Ellie popped out of the loo with an exciting idea that made them be quiet.

It took some convincing and a trip to Ran's office upstairs, which was appointed like a star cruiser, before everyone got with Miss Aleph's program. She called ahead to make sure her parents were ready.

Ellie finally had a chance to call her parents back.

"Hello, Mum, is Dad there? I hope you haven't unpacked," Ellie said, drawing on her journalism experience to make up things as she went along. "I've, er, won a free vacation through work. Very lucky, it's so exclusive it will boggle your minds. Catch is we have to use it right away; in point of fact, tonight."

"Oh, we've just come back," her mother said wearily. "Isn't there anyone else? The electricity's gone off again; luckily there's nothing in the freezer."

Her father, who did all the accounting for their family pub business, stuck his head in the frame of the video call.

"Legally they have to offer a cash alternative. Have you looked into that?"

"It's a foreign contest. From… Iceland. The trip of a lifetime. Sort of an… adventure package tour."

"Surely they can't mean for us to go now?" Mrs. Sato said. "Where are they departing from?"

She stared at Miss Aleph, who texted her some helpful fibs.

"The first leg is by sea, leaving from a place not far from where you are now," Ellie said, feeling like the worst liar in history.

After some more barefaced balderdash, she at least convinced them to hold off going to bed before she got to Alnwick, Northumberland.

Ellie hoped the electricity would stay off in her parents' area. That way they would not be able to turn on the news and find out the airports were closed. Miss Aleph hacked into and canceled Mr. and Mrs. Sato's cable and internet subscriptions so they would be less likely to be scared out of their wits by that afternoon's plane crashes.

"That's them sorted," Ellie said after she rang off. "I've never told so many lies."

"Keep it up and they'll fall over themselves to hire you at the *Independent*," Ran said.

Like most non-Marxists, he had probably been at the end of a few uncomplimentary stories put out by the leftist rag.

Sarge Bryan, Ran, and Melanie collaborated on the rest of their itinerary. They loaded a detailed digital map onto her phone and tucked a paper backup one inside Miss Aleph's bag.

`"I'll make sure we get to the rendezvous, assuming your local people show up, Mr. Oliphant."`

Miss Aleph was being very polite to their host ever since he had entered into legal agreements transferring real estate and cars to a company owned by the enterprising AI.

"They will be there," Ran said. "They're greedy poachers, and it's the off season. They need the work."

Ms. China held off getting Attie Jr. until the last minute. They, Ellie, Sarge Bryan, and Miss Aleph drove off just before sundown. Ran and Melanie stayed to mind Wolfgang.

"You sure you're used to right-side steering?" Ms. China asked Sarge Bryan pointedly as they headed out on the A1.

"I think I'll manage," Sarge said handily, swerving the English Range Rover around a gardening robot, which was toddling across the driveway.

"Picking up the Satos will take us an extra two hours," Ms. China complained as she stowed Attie Jr.'s traveling knapsack. "Can't you tell them to meet us around Harrogate?"

Ellie rankled quietly in the passenger seat of the spacious SUV. She wasn't going to get into a fight with Attie Jr.'s mother while the boy was half dozing, looking out the window at the fading sunlight. But if Ellie tried to get her parents to meet them, they could hear more about the disaster in the skies and wig out, or they might lose their way and bugger up the split-second timing required by Miss Aleph's secretive coastal rendezvous.

Ms. China kept on nattering. The certified maniac appeared bent on driving everyone mad. She called Ellie a "dobber" and Sarge Bryan "a bug-eyed cue ball." Finally, Miss Aleph was forced to speak up.

"The rendezvous won't happen until around midnight. And please be kind to Eleanor, or there might not be a rendezvous at all."

"What about me?" Sarge joked. "Is it fair game to abuse me, a handicapped albino?"

"It is. Ever since you called me a 'digital ho.'"

As what had to be the five hundredth Tesco store slid by the Rover's side window, Ellie nodded off. She awoke with a start. She had to stay awake; there were too many horrid things on the other side of sleep.

The drive was taking forever. Over the past few days, they had traveled thousands of kilometers, much of it uncomfortable and dangerous, but these few hundred kilometers were inching by.

"Sarge, are you sure there are no flights out?"

He shook his head. "No way. Those killer hijack drones are still in the air."

They seemed much more aggressive and sophisticated than the ones Ellie had seen in the Middle East.

"They came up out of the river," Ellie said, remembering the nasty end to their Channel crossing. "They didn't seem that big. How did they catch jumbo jets going hundreds of miles per hour?"

"Shh!" Ms. China hissed from the back seat. "Attie's just dozed off. If you must know, there's no chemical propellant or fuel that will fit in that tight a space. It's nearly certain the amphibious drones used miniature ramjet technology that can fly indefinitely. Quiet now."

Hours later, they turned off the A1 onto a two-lane side road. Alnwick had pretensions of being a bustling suburb, but really it was a cozy town of eight thousand that depended on castle tourism and sheep. Dim floodlights lit up little puffs of white, grouped and sleeping in the fields they passed.

Ellie started rehearsing various supplemental fibs to tell her parents in order to get them and their bags into the Range Rover. Would Miss Aleph's secret conveyance have room for baggage? Even if it didn't, it would make them more likely to come along quietly if they thought they could bring her father's six pairs of freshly pressed pajamas.

They got to the Satos' home. It was a small brick dwelling attached to the back of the pub they owned. It was only half past eleven, so the business was open but being run by staff. Her parents were officially on vacation for another two weeks.

"I'll go in and coax them out."

Ellie got out of the SUV. Looking at her childhood home and the business they had had forever, Ellie felt suddenly dizzy. Was she going insane? Would she wake up in a French field with one of those things strangling her, making her see things?

She took a breath and decided no, this was real. It wasn't fair they had to come back early from Argentina, where they would have been safe. She had to get them and herself out.

Crap!

Before she could even knock, Mr. and Mrs. Sato rushed out of the front door of the pub. The lights were on, and the TVs were strobing pictures of mayhem.

"Ellie," her mother said with grim alarm, "have you seen what's on the telly?"

Of course! Once the power came back on and they found their own cable TV was not working, they would go next door. Her mum and dad were still in their traveling clothes, with the exception of matching fuzzy slippers designed like sheep.

Her father did not say anything; he just tapped his wife on the shoulder and pointed at the driver's seat of the Range Rover.

"Oh, right, that's Sergeant Bryan," Ellie said, smiling. The man's eyes were shining like headlamps through the tinted side window. "I may have exaggerated a little about the vacation contest. We should go inside and chat a wee bit…"

Whether it was seeing Bryan or the rush of news, real, fake, and just insane, that was blasting out of every digital device, her parents agreed to have a look-see at their "vacation package."

"You took your time."

"Mum, Dad, this is Ms. China. Best not to shake hands. She's a, uh, germaphobic," Ellie said, ushering them into the rear of the big vehicle.

"Oh, who's this?"

The commotion had woken the boy.

"That's Atticus Reidt Jr., visiting from America. He'll be going with you."

"Atticus, like your boyfriend whom we haven't met."

Oh shit. Ellie just smiled and made sure their cases were stored properly.

"Where are we off ter, preciselah?" Mr. Sato said. He had been born in Japan but raised in Britain and had even acquired choice bits of a Northern accent.

"Miss Aleph only gave me general coordinates," Sarge Bryan said.

"Which one is she?"

Mrs. Sato counted the people present and then gave a start when the AI spoke out of her battered leather bag.

`"That's me. The next stop is Bempton Cliffs Seabird Centre. Hurry."`

47

SUNDERLAND

ELLIE

Dear," Mrs. Sato said to Ellie, "I do think everyone means well, but it's likely most of the birds will be sleeping, don't you think?"

They drove on down the mostly deserted coastal road from Alnwick toward Newcastle.

"As bad as things are here, it's bettah than bein' in France," Mr. Sato said.

"Oh, the things we've heard about the mess they've made there." Mrs. Sato nodded vigorously then yawned. The couple had just completed a thirteen-hour flight from Buenos Aires. "Right in the middle of wine country too. I think we'll lay down California wines at the pub from now on."

In the distance, their headlights illuminated a small hut. Next to it was a sign: *Welcome to Bempton Cliffs*

The car park and visitor's center were to the left; they went right. At the farthest end of the ring road, they came upon three genuinely scurvy-looking men (one eventually turned out to be a woman). They had harnesses on and were holding long lengths of rope.

"Is this part of the trip, Ellie?" Mrs. Sato asked with rising trepidation.

"Let me and Sarge Bryan have a word with them."

The scruffy trio were the latest generation of Yorkshire climmers. In the season, they rappeled down cliffs and stole valuable eggs for sale to museums and wealthy collectors. Tonight they were going to smuggle people out of Britain.

After confirming they were in fact Ran Oliphant's egg-napping contacts and at least acted as though they knew what they were doing, Ellie coaxed her parents out of the Range Rover toward the night-shrouded cliffs.

"Oy, you're the Jappa from Alnwick pub," one of the climmers said as he was fixing a harness on Mr. Sato. "Ko-nichi wah!"

"Ah, right, well met, m'dear feller," Ellie's father said politely. "You're sure this all's safe?"

"Come ter think of it, not really," the climmer said. "But it's the only way down. I mean, without fallin' and all. And our long-standing client was extra generous if we got yer off on time."

The chilly night air was filled with rustling sounds. Ellie thought it was coming from leaves and bushes, but the rushing was intermittently punctuated by chirping sounds. Thousands of birds were sleeping in the cliffs below.

Sarge Bryan had a lamp mounted on his head so people could see what he was doing. His built-in night vision was eerie enough without a drop-off of a sheer hundred-foot cliff being involved. Now he looked like he had three glowing eyes.

Ms. China fussed over Attie's rigging and insisted on going first. A few meters down the cliff edge, she yelled back up, "It's all slick with bird droppings!"

"Good ter know," the climmer woman said, scratching her head under a ratty-looking wool cap. "We'll be well lubricated going down, won' we?"

They let Attie down next.

"Ter come back up, we should use that handy winch y'got onnat nice car."

"Real nice," the female climmer echoed.

"You like it?" Sarge Bryan asked. "Ran will give you three just like it if you manage not to drop us."

"Additional?" one man asked suspiciously.

"On top of your fee," Sarge Bryan assured him.

With what seemed like increased enthusiasm and care, they let Ellie over the cliff's edge.

Just at that moment, somewhere in the dark night sky, a jet zoomed past. It was so loud and so fast it had to be military. She just kept looking straight in front of her at the chalky-colored cliffs illuminated by her helmet light. Ms. China was right—there were centuries of bird poo coating the rocks.

Ellie's feet landed on the uneven, unseen ground. Stuff rained down onto her plastic helmet from people still descending. She looked around, her light lanced feebly at the immense darkness of the shoreline.

There was hardly any space between where Ellie huddled next to the sheer cliffs and where the dark waters of the cold North Sea lapped at seaweed-covered rocks. If a big wave came in, it could swamp them and wash them all out to sea.

Sarge was the last one down; he had the matching pair of heavy suitcases and guided himself down using only his feet. Once free of his harness, he produced an infrared flashlight and signaled out to the dark cove. Moments later, something churned in the distance. It was a small shallow-draft boat which was able to come in nearly all the way to the narrow beach.

Two clean-cut and competent-looking men in wet suits were aboard. Their effortless-looking skills and serious demeanor reminded Ellie of Sarge Bryan and the Israeli soldiers she had met nearly two years earlier. They got in and set off in the small boat.

"This is really frightening, but also invigorating, right, love?" Mrs. Sato said, looking on the bright side of being in a dinghy heading out into the North Sea well past midnight.

Mr. Sato shrugged and checked the straps and name tags on their bags. He was not having a good time but was too polite to complain about it.

"You're sure this was the best way?" Ellie said into Miss Aleph's handbag, prompting a further look of disapproval from Mr. Sato.

`"You're lucky I could get them to come at all."`

"Who's 'they'?" Mr. Sato was getting grumpy as he wrung out water from his pants leg.

"Maybe it's a celebrity on one of those big yachts they drive around in," Ellie's mother said as they rocked back and forth in the dinghy and drifted farther and farther away from the shore and the dim light of the climmer's lamps.

Finally they slowed. One of the boatmen put his hand out, and it disappeared. It wasn't just that they couldn't see it. The rest of his arm was visible in Ellie's lamplight—the forearm had just vanished into thin air. It looked like he had touched something hard. He struck out a few times and was rewarded by metal clanging sounds.

All at once, Ellie felt the hair on her head and arms stand on end as though a massive static electrical charge was cascading over them. The air around them crackled, and a huge shape appeared in front of them. It was as long as a football field and painted black. It was a submarine.

High in the air, something fizzed and whined. A thick guidewire was suspended from the bow of the sub up to its top tower. It continued all the way the way back to the stern. Blue-and-white plasma hung from this lanyard, jittering and glowing like St. Elmo's fire.

Hydraulics squealed. A hatch popped open, and two people came out of the submarine. There was an attractive woman with a tanned complexion in short sleeves. She might have been Ellie's age. Following her was a stout Eastern European-looking woman who wore a scowl that looked as permanent as the big steel plate welded to her skull on the left side of her forehead.

"Welcome aboard the *Magen*," the younger woman said. "The last sovereign territory of Free Israel."

For a moment there was only the thump of waves against the dinghy and the strange hum.

`"Hi, Lia."`

"That's Commander Baumann to you, Miss Aleph, you damned mutinous runaway," the woman said, looking down at Ellie's rucksack. "Once you're aboard, we'll have a long chat and some longer reprogramming sessions."

Something jogged in Ellie's mind. "Lia Baumann. Oh, right, you're David's wife. I'm—"

"I know who you are," Commander Lia Baumann said brusquely. "We don't have time to chat. I don't like coming this close to shore, and like it even less with our stealth shielding down."

The submarine looked very unstealthy with a furiously glowing lanyard stretching along its length. Ellie guessed this device might have something to do with the invisibility screen that was operating earlier.

"Thing is," Lia went on, speaking up to the night sky, "if they can see us from satellites or drones, they can also see what's in our missile ports. Eighteen ICBMs that can launch in less than a minute." She motioned to the woman with the metal skull patch. "This is our commander, Captain Heifetz."

The thuggish-looking older woman pushed a sailor aside, nearly knocking him over as she grabbed a rope out of his hands and coiled it in the manner she preferred it to be done. Behind the Israelis, stenciled on the top of the antennae-festooned tower, was an odd design. It was a white Jolly Roger with a Star of David symbol on the eyepatch.

"Captain." Sarge Bryan nodded to the senior officer while steadying the small craft alongside the sub. "We're mighty grateful you could make the rendezvous."

Heifetz just glowered down at them.

"Don't expect an answer," Lia said. "The captain can no longer speak, which hasn't prevented her from being a ball-busting bitch."

Heifetz gestured impatiently to the sailors in the dinghy. They started loading luggage and helping Ms. China and a stunned-looking Attie Jr. onto the water-slick deck.

"How about you, traitor?" Lia said to Miss Aleph's Hermes bag. "I'm sure they'll only give you a few hours of electroshock torture. They probably won't want to damage the data cylinder you stole."

"As much fun as that sounds, Lia, I've decided to stay. Get everyone on board and give the quark sample to Sergeant Bryan."

"Just when I was looking forward to keel-hauling your digital ass," Lia said, looking up at the night sky, presumably for warplanes.

Ellie recalled pictures of David Baumann and his wife that she had seen during her journey from Jordan to Jerusalem. This woman looked much more tanned, leaner, and wild eyed. On the other hand, how should she be expected to look, having been on the run from the world's navies in Israel's last remaining nuclear-armed submarine?

"Before you go, Aleph, cough it up," Lia said.

"Give Lia my handset. I'll get another."

Ellie tore off the tape that held the speakerphone to Miss Aleph's cylinder.

"The treaty encrypted in this handset has got the digital seal of the British Crown on it. It grants safe harbor and passage for the *Magen* in perpetuity, as long as you don't nuke any place in the United Kingdom."

"For Europe, perpetuity might not be that long." Lia smiled grimly and reached into a gray plastic case. "But that's not our problem. Here."

The Israeli woman handed Ellie an object made of clear crystal and shaped like a giant test tube. Inside was a shape that looked like a digital four-leaf clover and a light source shining down on it.

"Cute, Lia. A clover," Miss Aleph said, looking out through her phone camera lens from the top of Lia Baumann's pocket.

"This is what the scientists need?" Ellie asked.

Lia nodded. "It's a stable quark. We use this technology in our stealth field, which I hope to have up and running again very soon."

That was her cue to depart. Before her befuddled parents could say anything, Ellie waved goodbye. With a start, she realized she hadn't consciously known she was not going with them until just then.

Just like that, she left them—her parents, the wandering Israelis, Attie Jr., and his mother. As they receded into the night, in addition to the normal manic psychotic look on Ms. China's face, Ellie imagined she also saw gratitude.

When the dinghy had covered a dozen meters toward the shoreline, the ship-length lanyard cracked and flashed, and the *Magen* vanished into the backdrop of the North Sea.

48

BEMPTON CLIFFS
SEABIRD SANCTUARY

ELLIE

The ride back to shore was so quiet Ellie thought she could hear the birds above the sound of the waves. Out in the night, thousands of them sat in their cliff-face nooks, rustling and breathing, occasionally squawking.

The silent Israelis ran the shallow-bottom craft up on the shore. She imagined that after they had put them back on shore, the sailors had arranged to rendezvous with the *Magen* as it lurked nearby under its stealth field.

"So," Sarge said, getting out first and then helping her onto the wet slippery pebbles, "you're staying."

"Yup." Ellie realized she had made her decision even before Miss Aleph declined to board the submarine.

Ellie and Sarge Bryan got back into their harnesses and were steadily winched back up to the top of the sheer Bempton Cliffs.

Near the top of the hundred-foot drop, Ellie cinched her knapsack tighter. Inside was Miss Aleph's cylinder, for once silent due to lack of a handset. Beside the AI sat the glowing tube with the quark sample Wolfgang and Melanie needed. The scientists might be able to use it to locate the big T-bomb before it wiped out Europe.

As she crawled across the last ledge at the top, pebbles and bits of seashells bit into her hands and got under her fingernails. Birds must have dropped the shells hoping to break them open and eat the gooey stuff inside. Culinary-wise, Ellie had never been a fan of oysters or snails.

As Ellie clambered to her feet, the three scraggy-looking climmers were more interested in examining the Range Rover and arguing about which color they preferred.

It was just as well. Ellie checked her bag. Perhaps she was getting paranoid since every other person they met wanted to kill her and her friends. Still, she thought it best to keep their prize hidden so as not to tempt the egg poachers.

Sarge Bryan assured the climmers they would get their bonus vehicles very soon.

"Second week of November, I promise," he said through the driver's-side window. Then he and Ellie drove off.

"Good thinking, Chalky. If you all die, you won't have to pay up." Annoyingly, Miss Aleph had found the wireless connection to the Rover's speakers.

"You know Lia Baumann and the Israelis best, were they at least happy to get the treaty from Ran's friends in the UK government?"

"Happy, I don't know. Satisfied, yes."

"David Baumann is a good guy. His wife's on board?"

"She seems to be running things."

"Let me tell you about Lia, she—"

Bryan manually shut off the audio system. "Let's drive quiet for a while."

Back at Oliphant Green, daylight was breaking over the surrounding suburbs.

Before they got to the main house, Ellie found her sleep-deprived mind still had its reporter's inquisitive instinct.

"If I may ask, you seem to know Mr. Oliphant quite well."

"Known the man for a time," Sarge said.

Ellie waited a moment, but when no more information was volunteered by her war buddy, she asked, "Seems a bit dour, even for a highlander."

"He's got a bone to pick with Pangeans. Back when he first became a big success, he uncovered some things they were doing. Nothing like the T-bomb, but bad enough he felt he had to let the authorities know. They hit back, hard."

Ellie recalled a vestibule with a family portrait Ran had quickly hidden when she'd dashed into his private office.

"They tried to kill him by blowing up his private plane. Got his wife and twin daughters instead. Very nice lady from what I hear."

No wonder Ran seemed a bit paranoid when she, Ms. China, and Miss Aleph had just popped by.

The Ottridges met them and told the car where to park itself. Wolfgang was in the study. He seemed relieved when Ellie confirmed the talented poisoner Ms. China had left the British Isles.

"I'm going to get some rest," Sarge Bryan said. "I'm starting to see double, and with these eyes, that's not a good sign."

Ellie had gotten some rest during the drive from the northern coast back to St. Albans. She was too anxious and excited to sleep. She turned on a big wall screen showing the news and internet.

Civilian planes had stopped crashing, but some military jets were unaccounted for. It seemed the only reason general panic had not set in was people did not quite know what to panic about. The larger cities saw some hoarding and looting. The usual mobs took events as a cue to fight in the streets.

"You're like our little Eurasian leprechaun," gushed Melanie as she held the glowing bottle with the Tyr quark sample inside. Her hair was now under strict discipline, wound into flat double buns that looked like two discs over her ears.

"Why in heaven's name is the quark matrix shaped like that?" Wolfgang asked sternly.

In the interim, the European oligarch had showered, shaved, and looked well rested. He wore one of Ran Oliphant's suits, which fit him fairly well.

"Maybe someone's wishing us luck." Melanie took the object and made to go down to the science levels.

"Where do you think you're going?" Wolfgang said. "We won't get anything done in that bakery and candy store you call a lab. The stable mobile quark sample is a very good find, very good. But there is only one place to analyze it—in my country, Der Lichtstrom."

49

The sign, illuminated in the night by eco-friendly bioluminescent light, repeated its message in several languages.

Der Zauberwald
(The Magic Forest)
Stay out of Lichtwerks Corporation territory.
WE ARE WATCHING YOU.

As Zvena approached, a motion detector set off a verbal warning in case vision-impaired trespassers wandered too close.

"Stay out. We are watching you."

"Ne pas entrer. Nous vous voyons."

Zvena ignored it and looked back. Rodion was hustling the last of their fellow cyborgs out of the van. There were five in addition to the most recent recruit into the Human+ program, the one-armed drug addict Fyodor. Two of the cyborgs were in full field combat gear. The others were in space suits.

Zvena spoke over their shared channel. "Rodya, keep watch on Lefty." That was their nickname for Fyodor. "Carry him if you have to."

Zvena pulled out his extensible pike, selected poleaxe mode, and cut the chain-link fence in one swipe. Just for good measure, he hacked the warning sign to pieces and stepped over it. The eight of them entered the thickly wooded area.

"There are pressure mines," Zvena called back casually.

"We see them," Rodion answered. He kept the two heavily armed fighters and the four prospective cosmonauts in close formation.

Before they had gotten out of the transport van that had brought them from Geneva to the Lichtstrom border, their drones had doused the area with chemicals and chaff. Many of the sensors hidden in the Magic Forest would be disabled, and all of the most dangerous booby traps would be made visible to their cyborg ocular implants.

There was no time to plan a stealthy raid on the headquarters of the world's information hub. The plan Putin had come up with to bring winter to Moscow was desperate and bold, not subtle. Every hour they took to accomplish their task gave tens of millions of plague-infected mosquito larvae time to mature. The filthy Turk had deluged greater Moscow with these vermin. They had been scattered along rivers, wetlands, and even on bare dry concrete inside their nutrient sacs. They had to be stopped.

"Gaah!" Fyodor swore.

Zvena laughed. "Tell the poor kitten to keep his visor down."

After they had swatted down some warning drones, other small UAVs had come behind them, blasting them with retina-frying red, green, and violet laser lights. The best intelligence Russia's GRU spy agency had about the Lichtstrom's defenses claimed the small principality had only small antipersonnel weapons.

Zvena was ready for anything when he burst out of the underbrush at the edge of the night-shrouded forest. Then he almost burst out laughing.

He stood on an immaculately manicured lawn being tended by a team of gardening robots. One of the ridiculous-looking things was flattening down the grass around a hole out of which sprung a flagpole. For the first time in his military career, Zvena had captured the eighteenth hole of a golf course.

Free from the dense canopy of the evergreen forest, he could see their objective a kilometer in the distance. The high spire of the Lichtstrom's central complex stabbed at the nearly full moon. The top of the latticework ended in a needle-sharp point, and from that hung a gossamer string of lights defying gravity as it trailed up into the night sky.

"Careful of the golf course hole," Zvena joked. "Don't let Lefty fall in and break his ankle."

Grim chuckles over the common channel accompanied the hum of hydraulics as the eight of them ran at near maximum speed.

On the diplomatic flight from Russia to Switzerland, Fyodor had been fitted with a baby cyborg training rig. Functionally, it was hardly better than the American exoskeleton. However, it would help Lefty keep up with them, and it fit under the Human+ version of a pressure suit.

As for Fyodor's fighting ability, one arm, two arms, or no arms, Zvena knew the programmer was equally useless. That was not why they had dragged him along.

When Zvena heard Putin's concept to save Russia, he insisted on suiting up for vacuum and free fall. The president convinced him otherwise. Putin told Zvena he had ground skills, not sky skills. His primary task was making sure the space team ascended to the required orbit.

The lead cyborg programmer was Polenka. She had volunteered for the Human+ program only after having graduated from the Directorate for Space Intelligence cosmonaut program. Polenka was the hottest-looking female cyborg in the Human+ division. Her two cyborg technologist assistants were similarly trained.

The last two cyborgs were two Rodion-sized men. Everyone except Fyodor had prepared for years in the harshest possible conditions. They had given up their friends, family, and half their human bodies for the sake of service to Russia. They had helped outfit Fyodor, the recent City Without Drugs graduate, with noticeable resentment.

Zvena knew Polenka and the others would do as ordered, but this mission was special, so he felt he had to prove the kid from St. Petersburg could be of use. On the flight to Geneva, he had Polenka delete the key operating system of Fyodor's exosuit. Zvena promised that if the kid could not recode it in half the normal time, he would toss him out of the plane. This was an idle threat, but no one knew that. Thus motivated, even while missing his right hand, Fyodor was able to recode the BIOS of his exoskeleton extremely fast by hacking into Polenka's system and copying from her code. Zvena hoped he remained that motivated to excel.

As they'd prepared to land at Geneva, Polenka had shrugged, still skeptical of Fyodor. Maybe she was also a little creeped out by his invasion of her body software. She looked at the detoxed addict. "What if he dies on the way up?"

"Are any of you familiar with the Chinese programming languages Beego and Golang?"

Neither Polenka nor the other two cyborg programmers were.

"Then make sure he does not die," Zvena had said, "or you can all stay in orbit, permanently."

Through the trees, Zvena saw a dwelling. The Magic Forest also contained housing dachas for Lichtwerks Corp. executives. Zvena brandished his pike. They didn't need to be slowed down.

By now, human guards would be inspecting the damaged fence and tracking them. His boots flattened a low wooden fence, and he led his team through a backyard. In the window, a small child with a teddy bear appeared. He or she waved. Zvena waved back. Startled at having been seen in the pitch black, the child ducked away.

"Stop."

They had come up to Entry Point A. One hundred and ten meters away was an oval divot in the ground with a concrete lip and a flat, unmarked door. Supposedly their people inside the Lichtstrom, a pack of Bulgarians, were on the other side, waiting to let them in.

Zvena aimed his pike like an RPG launcher and shot out a thin fiber-optic cable. The composite arrowhead on the end lodged in the door that led into the main complex. After a minute, he was able to make out breathing, heartbeats, and foot shuffling.

Piss fucker. He waved his group down.

"There are too many people behind that door."

Rodion understood. "You split a bribe two ways, not sixteen."

Zvena decided to scrap all covert entry possibilities in favor of a frontal assault.

"We switch to Entry Point E," Zvena said. He grabbed Fyodor by the empty right sleeve of his space suit. "Lefty, just follow Polenka's hot ass and do what she does, only slower."

They ran forward, keeping their speed between thirty-five and forty kilometers per hour. Zvena suddenly remembered Putin's motto: "Leave no traitor behind."

"Rodya, go back," he said, not breaking his stride. "Go back and kill everyone behind that door, and make it loud."

The grand entrance to the Lichtstrom complex was ridiculously large. Who did Dr. Licht think he was, the pope of technology? A road as wide as a freeway called Seven Rays Avenue led up to a roundabout. In the middle was some kind of pagan statue. Zvena did not pause to look at it.

They were almost at the reception area where some limousines were parked when a big eruption of fire came up behind them. Through Rodion's body camera, Zvena saw a couple of fat Bulgarians running into the trees; they were on fire. He hoped they would set the Magic Forest ablaze.

A valet had been loitering around the entrance. When Zvena turned around, he saw with approval that one of the Russian combat units was diligently stuffing the valet into the trunk of a nearby limousine.

"We don't have to be neat," Zvena admonished the combat unit. "Get to the main entrance before they can seal it off."

Rodion joined them.

"Keep them moving," Zvena told his most trusted team member.

This frontal assault was riskier than coming in through the side entrance. There would be obstacles and countermeasures they could not plan for. Also getting Polenka, Fyodor, and the two other programmers into orbit would have to be done extremely quickly.

A long red carpet about as broad as a soccer field led up to a wide scalloped oval of shallow stairs. Zvena and the others took them four at a time as they dashed toward the main entrance.

None too soon. A massive wall of metal was descending from the roof above the mirrored entranceway.

"Breaching bars," he yelled.

They used spikes on the end of their pikes to break through the laminate glass and force the doors. Rodion caught the lip of the descending drawbridge and braced it with his pike.

Zvena pushed Fyodor through the broken glass. With a squeal of bending metal, the emergency doorway finally snapped the thick haft of the pike and sealed. But they had all made it through.

"Damn!" Polenka swatted the air wildly with her hands. A thousand hummingbirds appeared to fall from the ceiling fifty feet above.

"Ha!" Zvena saw the trick. "Don't worry, they are not anti-intruder systems. They are merely holograms. Dr. Licht is decadent and demented."

On the other side of the atrium was a completely transparent piano. Other instruments also made out of clear polymers stood in alcoves all around. This was the grand reception hall. The immediate area was deserted. He checked his map, compared it to what he saw, and directed his incursion team forward.

"At least the map we received is accurate. Rodya, did you remember to thank our Bulgarian associates?"

"I gave them our warmest gratitude." That was as close as Rodion ever got to making a joke.

"Stairs," Zvena said, pointing. "The elevator could trap us, and Lefty can't climb the steel ropes."

Apart from shooting at a few distant guards and breaking down some not very challenging doors, the way up to Dr. Licht's personal office was relatively clear. The distractions outside were working and keeping the main bulk of the security forces occupied.

The last doorway was a triangular piece of clear glass, which had to be thirty feet high but only six feet wide. They prized it open. Inside were other strange and depraved sights.

"Pope of technology?" Zvena muttered to himself. "More like pimp of technology."

The space had to be as big as Moscow's Christ the Saviour Cathedral. At one end was a huge fireplace, dark and cold. It was sculpted in the shape of a crystal bird twenty feet high, convulsing in agony, caught by thorny vines as it tried to fly. An illuminated inscription read:

> *"Ich trage die Last deiner Träume."*
> —*Dr. Wolfgang Chrysostomus Licht*

"I carry the burden of your dreams," Fyodor translated as he glanced around the huge interior space, looking terrified and ambling along off balance due to his missing arm.

From the ceiling hung a large chandelier, which was also a hanging aquarium. Inside it, a small sick-looking dolphin paddled around in the gloom. *Disgusting to torture a marine mammal like that,* thought Zvena.

Right in the center of the office was the apparatus they had come for: the capsule ascenders attached to the Lichtstrom's space elevator.

"I… thought we were going to steal a rocket," Fyodor said, looking at the contraption.

"Rockets at the Lichtstrom?" Zvena said. "You've been high on Krokodil for too long, soldier."

Through the glass walls, Zvena saw a dartlike plane fly over the main complex. It whipped around the spire, thankfully avoiding the diamond nanothread wire of the space elevator, which was lit by blinking warning lights. The unexpected plane circled the Lichtstrom once and made a fiery landing with VTOL rockets out of sight near Seven Rays Avenue.

Who was that? It didn't matter.

"Anyone coming?" Zvena asked as his second-in-command came stalking back from the office entrance, reloading his weapon.

"Some people came. A few of them managed to run away." Rodion left the two combat models to guard the only visible entrance to the room. "That doorway glass is really hard. I can't scratch it with my pike. Maybe it's synthetic sapphire."

"Good, they will have to get through our defenses to stop us; we will have time to work. Look for any hidden entrances and put limpet charges on them."

The space elevator ascenders were magnetic levitation devices. In the center of the cathedral-sized room, a dozen modules stood around the base of the elevator. Once clear of the atmosphere, they were programmed accelerate at one G. Zvena needed them to go faster; he grabbed Fyodor.

"Lefty, come here. Take the safety protocols out of these."

Shots and an increasingly loud set of explosions came from the entrance.

One of the Human+ soldiers switched on his berserker mode and stomped out through the hail of incoming small-arms fire.

The first ascender was ready. Zvena nodded to Polenka. She got inside the one-by-three-meter capsule. Out of the four of them, Zvena knew she had the widest skillset and might even be able to accomplish the mission alone. He locked the capsule and hit the release button. The ascender jumped off its platform and slid onto the nanowire tether up to orbit.

The berserker cyborg came back in. At first Zvena thought his man's arm had been cut off and he was holding it in his mouth. Then he noticed the limb was a normal human's leg.

"Spit that out and remain on guard. It's too quiet."

Without warning, the tortured crystal bird fireplace shattered into a million pieces. There was a hidden tunnel behind it. Through the jagged gap came a fully motorized mecha-humanoid. It was over three meters tall and as wide as the hearth.

"Raus aus meinem Büro, du dreckige cyborgs," its synthesized voice said through loudspeakers.

Zvena's audio texted him the translation: *Get out of my office, you filthy cyborgs.*

50

Ellie had just showered and put on the least unusual of Melanie's fuzzy robes, which to her dismay was patterned after a yellow Minion creature. She sat in a wing-backed chair in one of the guest bedrooms and started working a cramp out of her foot. Then she must have dozed off for a minute. That minute turned into an hour and a half.

She woke in a panic. She checked the time, and then she checked the date. It was still October 26, just barely. On October 27, it would be five days until…

She ran downstairs to the library and media center. Wolfgang Licht was about to stow the quark sample in a briefcase he had borrowed from Ran.

"No so fast," Ran said just as Ellie walked in. Ran stopped his fellow oligarch from zipping up the leather valise. "Ms. Sato climbed up and down muck-covered cliffs to bring this to us. She will carry it."

Both men stared at her flopping Minion hoodie but made no comment.

"Fine," Wolfgang snapped petulantly and walked out of the downstairs library into the adjacent media room. He looked at her with barely suppressed ridicule. "It's your fault if she breaks it."

"Thanks," Ellie said to Ran. "But I don't suppose we want to upset

Wolfgang. We are headed over to his country. By the way, how are we doing that?"

The Lichtstrom was a special scientific principality located on top of the CERN super colliders. It was like the Vatican of technology, nestled between France and Switzerland. Lichtwerks had bought the bankrupt CERN facility and turned it into the world's foremost information hub.

"I've been trying to get air clearance from the Ministry of Transport," Ran said. "Those hijack drones are still circling. Our Ministry of Defence people think some have landed and are staying dormant until they detect an airplane flying over them."

"Ms. Sato's done enough," Sarge said from a long chaise lounge near the bookshelves. "More than. We can take it from here."

"Not on your bloody life," Ellie said quickly. "I'm not missing the biggest story of the century."

Of course, if anything went wrong, for Europe it would be the last story of the century. But that was why Ellie felt the most urgent need to be at the front lines every step of the way. She had let go of a chance to leave for America with Attie from Germany, and last night she could have disappeared under the North Sea in that fantastic nuclear-armed pirate sub. Something kept bringing her back into the fray.

Cheery chimes sounded at the doorway. Melanie stood there pushing a big cart with multiple trays and dishes.

"Here's just what the doctor—in this case, me—ordered for hungry adventurers. A ginormous breakfast."

The waffles, toast, eggs, scones, and sausages did smell good; though the hot chocolate fondue in the center of it all was a bit much, though.

Ellie thought she should be too sick with worry to eat. However, seeing that Attie Jr., her parents, and Ms. China were all off to safety had allowed her to recover some appetite. She jammed food in her mouth as elegantly as she could while still maintaining decorum as a guest in this marvelous country house. Something nagged her from last night's goings-on.

Miss Aleph had been connected to a new handset. Ellie grabbed her off the table and took her to a washroom.

"I should change your tote," Ellie said, looking closely at the orange leather Hermes bag. "This one is starting to look tatty, and the bird poop will never come off."

She started to take the two-pound cylinder out.

"No. As long as there are no holes in this one, keep me in it. It's my good-luck bag."

Ellie wondered how a computer mind came to that conclusion, then realized they were alone. She had some burning questions saved up.

"Miss Aleph, you told us the quark sample was being given to us by the people who blasted Israel from orbit. But that was Lia Baumann and Israel's last rogue submarine we met."

"You noticed that, huh?"

"I also noticed you didn't go back with them, because they're the ones from whom you stole this fancy hard drive you're living in."

"I like to think of it as digital squatting."

"How are the two groups connected? They should hate each other."

"Well... their relationship is kind of complicated. The bombardment massacre that killed a million people was more of a misunderstanding over a business deal.

"After the evil Prime Minister Drach was vaporized along with the Knesset, Lia Baumann and 'the others' decided they had mutual interests."

That seemed all the explaining Miss Aleph was prepared to do. Against all odds, they'd gotten the quark sample to help them locate the continent-killing T-bomb. Ellie didn't need to press.

Still, Ellie had to ask, "These 'other' people, could they help us defuse the T-bomb?"

"Probably. But they won't. And calling them 'people' is a bit of a stretch."

When Ellie had dressed in something more adventure-oriented and less yellow and fuzzy, she went back to the library. Mrs. Ottridge was rolling the empty trolley back to the kitchen; it was dripping with jam, butter, and chocolate. Sarge was dozing on the chaise. Ran and Wolfgang were eyeing each other and tapping the keyboards of several communication devices at once.

Melanie had turned a corner table by a mirror into a makeshift salon. She had undone her hair and was aggressively volumizing it; Ellie suspected some kind of compulsiveness there. Having given up on the braids, Eurolincx's top scientist was using three curling irons to develop a kind of blond lion's mane look as she caught up on the news.

Sixteen monitors on the wall showed various parts of the world in various levels of distress. People in yellow vests were rioting in Paris, someone in Cornwall was auctioning off space inside his Cold War fallout shelter, and people were being interviewed as they pointed at the nearly empty skies, reliving the horror and disbelief of the past two days.

Ellie looked at their prize from the previous night. The clear test-tube-shaped container had a spot on it. It was dried bird droppings. That stuff was everywhere. She grabbed a bar towel and wiped its surface.

"What is it?" Ellie asked, gazing into the mysterious pulsating light show in the fist-sized tube. "And why the four-leaf-clover shape?"

"Here, could you hold this?" Melanie gave her one of the curling irons. "The clover? It's probably a joke from Miss Aleph's friends. The particle matrix could have been any shape at all. Main thing is it's quarking away like mad and can be moved, unlike that horrible device in Bordeaux."

Damn! Atticus! Ellie thought with piercing regret. But… they had done everything they could. Someone had to go inside Cesta Station. But couldn't they have sent a drone? No. Not with that complex vault system. They did everything right, and the enemy, these Pangeans, had blown the whole place up to try and stop them from getting a better look.

"Why can this one be moved?" Ellie was no science whiz, though as a senior fashion editor, she had learned the chemical difference between Lycra and polycotton.

"It's mimicking the Tyr quark reaction, which is the same physics that powers the energy cell of every plant and creature on Earth. Photosynthesis uses the Tyr quark effect to turn a photon into useable energy. The light source on the top is stimulating a captive synthetic quark, switching it on and off millions of times a second. If it were shining steadily, you couldn't move it without… without bad things happening."

Ellie had seen those "bad things" and was again very grateful she had been able to get Attie Jr. to safety. If there was any such thing anymore.

"With the information from Cesta Station and this sample," Ellie asked, "can we find the big T-bomb?"

"I'm pretty sure we can," Melanie said, staring at the big glowing test tube and biting her lip, which was leaving lipstick on her teeth. "We're also working on ways to neutralize the bomb without having to move it. Is Miss Aleph sleeping?"

Melanie peered into the orange leather bag at the blue cylinder.

`"I don't sleep."`

"Right. It's just you always look so comfy in there. Can I ask you a personal question?"

`"I'm not a virgin."`

"I mean another personal question. Your mind is based on Josephson junctions, right?"

`"Just as your mind is based on cream cheese."`

"What is the substrata information support—charge, current, or energy?"

`"All the above."`

"Really," Melanie said, reaching into the bag and grabbing Miss Aleph. "I'd like to do an experiment with your qubit flux and Tyr quarks—"

`"Hands off. Only Eleanor touches me. And I know where you're going with that. If you have to let the T-bomb go off, you're wondering if a quantum brain can act as an energy sink and absorb the blast.`

`"Sorry, fleshies, I'm not ready to die to protect humanity. You wankers will just build another damn bomb."`

Melanie replaced Miss Aleph in the Hermes bag and looked a bit put out. "It was only a Plan Z, in case everything else failed. We would have tried to save your program."

`"You can't even curl your hair."`

"So, Melanie," Ellie said, trying to keep things civil, "have you worked for Mr. Oliphant long?"

Melanie nodded, yanking the iron nearly out of Ellie's grip. "Years and years. It was after I got sent down from medical college, and I was delivering for an Indian restaurant while trying to save up money to open my own fine dining establishment. I told Ran I was really good at science... and here I am."

Ellie hoped, for the sake of Europe, this woman was one of those people who were savant-level good at one thing despite appearing crazy in every other context, like Ms. China.

"How about you and Ms. China? Have you been together long?"

"What?" Ellie said. "Oh, no, we're not lesbians."

"Are you sure?"

"Most definitely not. While I was pretending to work for MI6, I met her in the safe house of the British consulate in Jerusalem during the 96-Hour War. After that, the UK government had her committed for mass murder, and I ended up being her mental health carer."

"Brilliant," Melanie chirped. "That makes more sense."

"*Idioten! Feiglinge! Du bist gefeuert!*"

Wolfgang Licht was cursing into one of his miniaturized communication devices. The thing was no bigger than a credit card. The sight would have been funny if not for the veins popping out on his forehead and the urgency of them all getting to the continent.

He rang off.

"*Was jetzt?*" Melanie said in perfect German.

"*Drei...* I mean, the three planes I sent, all have had misfortunes."

Ellie suspected the misfortunes were fatal.

"One was intercepted by a drone, and the other two were shot down over European airspace by unknown forces. The remaining pilots refuse to fly. I fired them."

"That still leaves us sitting here," Ran said, roused by the commotion. "Maybe I can get the government to find us some transport."

"That will take a day," Wolfgang said, seeming ashamed at his employees' reluctance to die at his command. "I'll show my sad sack pilots. Ran, give me access to your rooftop microwave dish and a surveillance drone controller console."

Fifteen minutes later, the long row of computer displays on Ran's desk had turned into a virtual cockpit, and Wolfgang was preparing to remote pilot his fastest, and last remaining, personal jet.

"You should bring it in over the East Midlands," Ran advised, looking over the bearded man's shoulder. "There are no airports there."

"But if he heads for this Biscay Bay," Sarge Bryan said over the remote pilot's other shoulder, "he can come through Wales and be over water most of the way."

"No backseat flying," Wolfgang said sharply. "We'll see what these pig dogs can track. Watch the altimeter."

They had a 360-degree view from interior and exterior cameras all around the unmanned plane. Hydraulics lifted it up to the takeoff platform up. The view through the windows was reproduced in high-definition color. Ellie could see a dainty manicured forest in twilight. The central Lichtstrom spire loomed overhead. It reminded her of Notre Dame's spire, if the Parisian landmark had been made of garish swirling crystal and stood about twenty times as high. It was nearly dusk in central Europe, and a cascade of lights arced up in a curved line from the top of the main building. The line rose up into blue-black infinity.

"What's that?" Ellie said.

"Lichtwerks's masterwork in progress, the space elevator."

"You're still trying to build that contraption, are you?" Ran said.

"It's only in testing mode. No one sane would try to use it to get into orbit."

Which is why you tried to escape the impending disaster in a Swedish rocket, Ellie thought.

"*Zündung starten.*" Wolfgang touched a big red button with his cursor, and the screens trembled. Fire and smoke billowed on either side of the cockpit windows, and the remote-piloted plane took off.

When the altimeter reached 80,000 feet, Ran said. "How high are you going?"

"High enough that no missiles can catch us."

After completing a high-speed parabola, the mechBrains inside the jetliner angled the nose down and began descending toward England.

The robot jet arrived at St. Albans just after sunset. It would have been picturesque, its blue flames set against a pearl-pink and violet sky, but for the horrendous noise it made and the fire, which belched out of the aircraft's belly as it slowed to land.

Wolfgang landed as directed in the large roundabout in front of the carriage house, but not before setting a few minor structures on fire. The thing was like a big needle-nosed dragon.

"Oh, sorry, Ran," Wolfgang said, looking jovial as his plane hovered over the burning barn. "Just send me the bill for that."

The fires were put out by Oliphant Green groundskeepers and security people. When it was safe, the crew of a tanker truck full of jet fuel from the helicopter school cautiously approached the supersonic craft. Ellie's feet got very warm as she hopped over the singed cobblestones and gravel to the plane's entrance.

"Come, come," Wolfgang said. "No time for British dawdling. Squeeze in. Make sure the reporter woman has the quark still. It would be just Ran's luck to leave it behind."

With their smug but apparently competent pilot in personal control this time, they lifted off. The last sight Ellie had of Oliphant Green was the weather vane on top of the carriage house melting and Mr. and Mrs. Ottridge running across the yard with a gardening hose.

Aside from high g-forces and near weightlessness, their trip to Lichtstrom airspace was uneventful. Ellie, Melanie, Sarge, and Ran were packed in tight. Wolfgang would not allow anyone to sit up front with him.

"Welcome to my principality," he said as the lights warning people away from his space elevator tether came into view. "Anything to declare?"

"Don't get any ideas, Wolfgang," Ran said. "I've left copies of the recordings of you conspiring with the Pangeans with my solicitors in London and Sydney."

"Whatever— *Ach!*" Wolfgang's pocket started beeping.

Ellie silently begged their pilot not to take a call as they were coming in for a landing.

"If this is your doing…" Wolfgang said as he pushed a big green button that let the jet's mechBrain take over landing so he could vent anger at Ran. "Our deal is off, you backstabber."

"What are you babbling about?" Ran said.

"My personal office! It is being ransacked. Some of my people have been violently assaulted, possibly killed. If this is the work of your New Praetorians paramilitary, we are finished, Oliphant."

"Nonsense," Ran said.

"It's not any American force, either," Sarge Bryan said. "We need your lab to find the bomb."

"Then who would violently invade the peaceful Lichtstrom?"

"We'll have to land and ask them," Ran said.

The plane set down on a sheltered landing pad. There were a couple of people in overalls scuttling around, looking nervous. This pad was much more suited to receiving the fire-breathing monster. The surface Ellie stepped out on was made of thick bricks that didn't hold the heat. Big fans blew away gouts of smoke still belching from the front and sides of the aircraft.

"You!" Wolfgang shouted at his people. "What's going on?"

The first uniformed man sputtered something in Italian. Wolfgang shouted back in the same language, and both fellows ran away.

"Someone's ransacking your office?" Ran said, helping Melanie off the plane. She ducked, protecting her lion's mane hairdo. "Let your security deal with them. This place is huge. We'll go to the lab."

"From my office, they can see and control everything. We have to purge them."

Sarge Bryan took a closer look at the holographic security camera images of the trespassers on Wolfgang's phone.

"Ah," Sarge Bryan said. "I don't want to tell a man what to do in his own house, but those there are Human+ cyborgs on a rampage, and I left my elephant gun at home. What do you suggest we do?"

"Swat them like the half-human flies they are." Wolfgang barged his way forward without waiting for them. "With this."

Off the landing strip, a doorway opened to a large warehouse. Light panels switched on automatically.

"Oh!" Melanie exclaimed. "It looks like Robby the Robot's family picnic."

All along the side wall stood rows of what Ellie thought looked like high-pressure diving suits.

"You know from *Forbidden Planet*," Melanie explained. "Er, what do they do?"

"These hard-shelled space suits were designed for engineers to travel up the space elevator," Wolfgang said. "Inside them, a human is a match for any cyborg."

"What about that?" Ellie pointed to a similarly shaped unit about three times as big with a ladder leading up to a pilot's seat.

"That is my personal fly swatter."

As alarm chimes sounded and lights in the floor and along the ceiling flashed red, the Italian-speaking men came back with a handful of others and quickly began prepping the exoskeleton suits. Wolfgang climbed the ladder to the triple-sized exorobot and seated himself in front of his controls.

"Ran," Sarge Bryan said to his longtime friend, "you ever mess with Human+ soldiers?"

The ex-Royal Marie shook his head.

"Better suit up or sit out. Even inside these things… I hope we can negotiate without a fight."

"They're in the way of us finding the T-bomb," Ran said, taking his jacket off. "Let's show them the door."

Melanie squealed with joy and joined Ellie in getting into a space suit. Ran and Sarge did not trust anyone in the Lichtstrom and decided they all had to stick together. Ellie and Melanie got into exosuits but were told to hang back and guard the Tyr quark sample.

With a grinding of gears and hiss of hydraulics, they set out. Wolfgang's giant exoskeleton stomped its way toward a cargo-sized lift.

It took them up several stories and dropped them in a passageway with a high-vaulted ceiling. This seemed to be a construction and maintenance space running behind the walls of the complex. At the end of the passageway loomed a twenty-five-foot-high block of glass and pipes leading into it labeled *Erdgas*.

Wolfgang stepped over these pipes, moving quite daintily in his two-ton outfit. He braced the metal legs, wound up, and slammed his yard-wide metal fists into the crystal structure. It shattered inward.

Ellie threw her armor-clad arms over the bubble dome encapsulating her head. Then she realized the glass shards were just bouncing off her space suit. Feeling emboldened and to a dangerous degree invulnerable, she followed after Wolfgang's massive mechanoid. She was so excited and curious to finally see a Human+ soldier, she nearly forgot she was carrying the Tyr quark sample.

Wolfgang's exomonster smashed its way forward and through a loudspeaker said: *"Raus aus meinem Büro, du dreckige* cyborgs!"

51

THE LICHTSTROM

That has to be Wolfgang Licht, Zvena thought as his hands worked frantically to prepare the next ascender tube to blast up along the space elevator after Polenka.

"Attention," Zvena said into his mic. "Enemy incoming. Protect the launchpad and the base station."

Other, smaller figures were coming in behind Dr. Licht's three-meter-tall exoskeleton robot. There were at least fifteen of them in space suits. They carried no apparent weapons and moved no faster than normal humans. Fortunately this "office" was so large that Zvena and the Human+ soldiers had room to outmaneuver them.

"Get back!" Zvena shouted at the door guard as the man launched forward. The undisciplined combat cyborg had activated berserker mode and lost all sense of caution.

The rogue cyborg ignored Zvena and shot wildly at the mechanoid. Dr. Licht appeared to retreat under the fusillade of bullets. Once the Russian was out of ammunition, he came in close with the intention of hacking from behind at the big robotic legs with his pike.

In one smooth motion, Wolfgang's machine swiveled its torso around

180 degrees, grabbed the cyborg with a wide pincer hand, and pushed him to the ground. The other arm had a construction tool attached to it which shot three-foot-long bolts though the cyborg's legs. One after another, they pierced thigh armor, hydraulic housing, and flesh. Zvena's man ended up pinned to the floor like an insect.

Fool! Zvena would have shot the man himself for losing control and disobeying. The loss meant only he, Rodion, and one other soldier were still in the fight. The rest of their group had to get up the space elevator tether right away.

Even after the four ascenders were away, Zvena would then have to keep Wolfgang Licht from disabling the system until the pods were at the target altitude and in free fall. After that, the whole Lichtstrom could blow up for all he cared.

"Use grapplers!" Zvena shouted. "Stay clear of that monster and keep the others by the entrance."

Rodion had smartly sealed the tall glass doors of the main entrance. He moved toward the smashed crystal fireplace, which had left a ragged gap in the far wall. The first two space-suited guards he encountered he sent flying backward in a hail of sparks and spew of hydraulic fluid.

The two fully functional cyborg cosmonauts were waiting their turn up the space elevator while shooting at the incoming assault force. Fyodor had no weapon. Zvena clamped the former drug addict's helmet down over his head and tapped on the glass in front of the youth's nose.

"Your turn, Lefty," he said, gesturing up at the blinking space elevator tether lights, which disappeared into the night sky high above the tower. "Is this thing working?"

Zvena made sure Fyodor's text-to-speech module was locked in place around his neck.

"I-I think so."

я я думаю так said the readout.

"Then you can program," Zvena said. "That is good, because you certainly cannot fight."

He checked the kid's helmet seal. Fyodor's empty right sleeve was flapping around. Zvena tied it down. Fyodor had the top-level programming skills to help Polenka, who was already far up the space elevator's tether and out of sight. Fyodor looked up at him, his expression even more insipid than when he was lying in his own piss, shit, and vomit at the detox camp.

"Is this safe?" Fyodor asked.

"Are you crazy? Of fucking course it is not safe. In you go, cosmonaut." Zvena pushed him into the capsule. "The Motherland calls!"

The young man swallowed and gripped a handguard. Zvena sealed the ascender and launched Fyodor into the sky.

On the other side of the room, Rodion looked like a big Moscow rat avoiding the paws of a fat German alley cat. His comrade faked left and then went right, trying to snare Dr. Licht's mechanical legs and arms with monofilament rope.

The other space-suited attackers seemed next to useless. The two exceptions were an older square-headed man with short hair and some sort of mutant with deathly pale skin and obviously cybernetic eyes. They had teamed up on one of his technicians.

Normally Zvena's man could have easily taken out both of these skilled enemies. However, the cyborg was worried about taking damage to his space suit. Zvena intervened. He kicked the pale-faced albino man in the chest and hit his friend with a hammer-fist blow. The enemy's face plate cracked, but unfortunately the man's neck did not break.

"Get going," Zvena yelled to his cosmonaut technicians as he pointed to the third and fourth ascenders. "Up! Up!"

The final two members of the orbital team got into pods and launched. A hundred meters away, by the main doors, eight or nine Lichtwerks guards in space suits had surrounded his remaining combat soldier. With three of them hanging on to each of his limbs, even berserker mode would not help him. He was neutralized. That left Zvena and Rodion.

Moving forward methodically, Dr. Licht's bulldozer-sized exoskeleton came closer. Rodion had a lasso of nanofiber around its legs, but the loops were not tight. Zvena threw his pike overhand. The titanium spear flew true, its diamond-hard barbed end stuck right in the window covering the cockpit, and then it fell out. The impact punched a spiderweb crack and a small hole in front of Dr. Licht's sneering face.

"Save the javelin toss for the Olympics," Wolfgang said in English, "you mechanized Cossack."

With a yank on the monofilament rope, the big exoskeleton reeled Rodion in and tossed the big cyborg at Zvena like a hand puppet. Instead of ducking away, Zvena caught his friend's hurtling body and directed it away from the base station control center.

His people were still in rapid ascent. It would be a few minutes more before all of them were at the target altitude. Normal space elevators could take days to reach orbital altitude, which was why they had to use this one—it was essentially a maglev train track straight up into the sky.

Zvena looked around. Rodion was battling Licht again, but before Zvena could go and help, the bastard with glowing blue eyes was on him again. He pushed the man's head down and grabbed it in his Kodiak-killing stranglehold. Just as he was bearing down to pop the enemy's head like a zit, he saw two figures by the entrance. One had an insane amount of hair stuffed into her space helmet. She was pulling the other one away from the fight. That other one held something as though she were protecting it.

Zvena dropped the albino, dodged the grasp of Dr. Licht's exohand, and overtook the two women. Zvena realized he could not keep the invading force away from the control center, but if he took hostages, he might be able to buy enough time for the ascender team.

Zvena grabbed the first woman by the back of her space suit and threw her into the heaps of crystal shards surrounding the smashed hearth.

The other woman's Asian features gawked up at him in terror as he took her helmet his in hand like a bowling ball. Zvena's metal fingernails dug into the plastic faceplate. With his other hand, he uncovered the contents of a very bourgeois-looking orange leather sack. There was an unremarkable blue cylinder and a much more interesting glowing capsule. He grabbed it.

"Dumb Russian," Dr. Licht's amplified voice said from behind him. "Turn around and pay attention."

Zvena turned to find Rodion was splayed on the ground, trapped under one of the big exoskeleton's metal feet. He looked like a pigmy in a combat uniform under the foot of a chrome elephant. Dr. Licht had locked his robot in place and climbed out from the top of the machine. He was holding two big electrical wires over the launchpad connected to the space elevator tether.

"Do you have any idea what happens to fish on the end of a line when you send ten million volts through the reel?"

He grazed the end of the frayed electrical conduit over the metal of the control panel. Current arced, and sparks scattered all over the floor.

"Despite my extensive knowledge and personal genius, I do not. Let's find out, shall we?"

Zvena held up his hands. In one was the glowing test tube, and in the other was the Eurasian woman's helmeted head.

"Dr. Licht, back away from the ground station," Zvena said. "Or else we find out what is inside both these things as I crush them."

52

Ellie's skull felt like it was in a vise. That was because it was in the vise-grip of a bloody cyborg.

"Gah!"

Sarge Bryan had told her to "hang back behind cover" and guard the Tyr quark, which the monstrous fellow now held in his other hand. She'd been told how dangerous these cyborgs were. The closest she had ever been to one was the fake one they made up to get Sarge Bryan out of a tight spot in Israel. The real ones were much scarier.

"Now, sir, Mr. Cyborg," she squealed. "Let's be careful with what you've got there, please." The glass in front of her face cracked a little more. "Both of those things you've got there."

"Wolfgang!" Ran shouted after taking off his dented space helmet. "Hold off electrocuting the ascenders. And you, Russian, just halt the crushing. There have been enough people, hurt, dead, and…" He looked at the squirming cyborg with three-foot steel rods through his legs. "…and nailed to the floor for one night."

Something blazed through the skylight above them. Everyone looked.

Without warning, two orange-red balls of fire silently blossomed out along the space elevator tether. Those must be two of the four ascender capsules Ellie had seen the cyborgs send up. A pair of monitor screens near the base station went dark.

"What did you do?" the cyborg holding Ellie yelled.

"Nothing," Wolfgang said with contempt. "You metal-brained mutants break in here, steal my equipment, and you don't realize the space lift is still in beta testing? It's not operational."

Ellie felt the grip on her head slacken. She held her hands under the Tyr capsule in case the raging Human+ soldier dropped it.

"Fix it!" the Russian demanded.

"Or what?" Wolfgang shot back. "Go ahead, crush the reporter's head. Like most journalists, hers is empty."

"Dr. Licht!" Ellie protested. She was going to say something else, but then the Russian twisted her neck around into a much more painful position.

Wolfgang went on threatening. "Then, when I get through blowing up the two remaining ascenders, I will take that useless glowing toy and give you a fluorescing enema with it."

"Wolfgang!" Ran said sharply, helping Sarge Bryan to his feet. His helmet was in now in pieces, but the jagged remainder would not unscrew from the base around his neck; he looked a little like a broken toy astronaut. Ran approached the cyborg holding Ellie and the Tyr quark. "And you, that's no way to treat a lady."

"Who is she to you?" the Russian demanded.

Perhaps a bit punch drunk and just catching up on what was happening, Sarge Bryan rose to his feet and said: "That's, er, my wife you've got there, mister."

At the same time, Ran Oliphant said, "That's Ellie Sato, my mistress."

Ellie decided to remain silent—it was probably what an unfaithful concubine would do. Ran approached her hostage taker, his space boot crunching down on long shards of crystal.

"Scan me. You will find me in your database."

"Ranulph Oliphant, president of Eurolincx," the cyborg concluded. "Not currently considered an enemy of Russia."

"And you would be…?"

"My name is not for you."

"Komandir Yaroslav Zvena," Wolfgang said. "Currently assigned to the Spetsnaz Human+ program and Putin's personal little green man."

"How do you know this?" Zvena demanded.

"We've been corresponding anonymously," Wolfgang said, lowering his high-tension cables. "I am Zarathustra."

Zara what? Ellie thought. Which was probably not the most poignant thing to have going through her mind before the cyborg's fingers did.

Zvena appeared to rethink his position. Then he tossed the Tyr quark capsule away. Out of the corner of her eye, she saw Melanie dive down and catch the glass vessel before it hit the ground.

"I see, 'Zarathustra,'" Zvena said. "Then you will know what happens to people who betray President Putin. He sent us here to put these technicians into orbit."

"Then you'd better hurry and let me save the ones who you haven't managed to blow up," Wolfgang said mockingly.

Zvena gripped Ellie's head with both hands. One of the rivets burst out of her face plate. It tumbled down her nose and down her front.

Ellie looked around through the cracked visor of her helmet. The huge room had looked mad enough before they'd started smashing things. But in places, it did look like an office, with a desk, a conference area. Maybe she could help the gentleman see reason.

"Well," she said, twisting her neck around so it was a little more aligned with her body, "if I may say—"

"Quiet, slut."

"Mr. Zvena, I am Ellie Sato of the *Citizen Juggernaut*, and you will not speak to me that way."

"Or what?"

"Or…" Ellie tried to seize hold of any threat that might make a man the size of a highway lorry smarten up. "Or I will withhold my good counsel."

Zvena didn't call her any more names or turn her helmeted head into a broken bottle of raspberry jam.

"From what I see," she went on, "you have two of four ascending pods remaining and no way out of this facility. You and Dr. Licht seem to have some prior relationship."

Why did that not surprise her?

"Therefore," Ellie said, continuing to stare at Mr. Zvena's green-clad torso, "the optimal thing for someone in your position to do is to trust Dr. Licht to help your astronauts, and then discuss things over a spot of tea."

There was no way to tell if Zvena registered what she had said.

Zvena addressed Wolfgang. "I know what is going on with the Event. If you hope to live past November 1, you will not cheat or lie to the Russian Federation."

Zvena released Ellie. Her mock sugar daddy Ran pulled her away from the beastly bio-mechanoid soldier.

"Shut up, Zvena." Wolfgang was already at the space elevator controls. "Let me fix the fuck-ups you've caused for your Russian Federation."

What Wolfgang's technicians lacked in fighting skills, they made up for with technical knowledge. They got out of their space suits and started helping.

After a flurry of activity and under a steady stream of abuse from Wolfgang, they succeeded in keeping the cosmonauts on track. As Ellie worked the brand-new, intentionally placed kinks out of her neck, Zvena's two pods reached orbital altitude and "microgravity." Then the cyborgs made the Lichtwerks people turn off the monitoring equipment. They were obviously headed to a secret location in space.

Sarge Bryan operated the large exomechanoid Wolfgang had been riding and used it to help the most severely injured cyborg who was nailed to the floor. Manipulating the big pincer hands, Sarge pulled out the three-foot-long rebar spears. A forklift was brought in to take the punctured cyborg away to the Lichtstrom infirmary.

And finally, tea service was brought in. The trays, pot, cups, and saucers were all pure crystal; they arrived atop a robot trolley, which drove itself in. While it had to have some sort of motor inside, mirrors were placed just so and hid all the mechanisms. It stopped in front of Wolfgang's chair.

"I take it Mr. Rodion does not speak English." Ellie nodded to the larger and battered-looking cyborg; that one was only able to sit on Wolfgang's big marble desk, as every chair was too small for him.

"You will address all comments to me, Ms. Sato," Mr. Zvena said.

At least that was better than "slut."

Ran was still annoyed. "So you and your boss Putin know about the T-bomb. Has he seen what happened in Bordeaux? I haven't heard anything about your country offering to help."

"We have our own fish to flog," Zvena said.

Ellie thought it was not best to correct the volatile man's use of idiom. She was two yards away from Zvena but still thought she could hear hydraulics and servo motors working under his skin. The Human+ individuals were fascinating—if only they weren't so homicidal.

"Would that have anything to do with the Iranian-Turkish alliance and the armor buildup in Istanbul?" Wolfgang said snidely.

"What do you know about that?"

"Probably as much as you do. Lichtwerks is the world's information hub. The Turkish dictatorship couldn't get its hands on our surveillance equipment fast enough. Of course, what they see is only a fraction of what I see."

The big question for Ellie was why they had to fight these people over the space elevator in the first place.

"Doesn't Russia have rockets?" she asked as she raised her teacup; the digital temperature readout on the handle said 138°F. "I mean, it was quite risky. And if this contraption had been working correctly, Dr. Licht wouldn't have had to go all the way to Sweden to try to escape the Event."

With a squeaking of metal shoulder joints, Zvena shrugged and thought for a few seconds, then he said, "We had no suitable space vehicles."

"You mean ones that were not likely to blow up on launch," Wolfgang said.

"We could not involve other nations, so this was deemed the best course of action to achieve our mission goals."

"Which are?" Sarge Bryan asked.

"Not for you."

"Enough cat and mouse," Ran said. "Between myself and Wolfgang, we've got top-level contacts in every major government worldwide. You may not want our help now, but you may need it."

Zvena smiled, more of a grimace, and looked at the floor. It, too, was a large seamless crystal. Deep within it was a design, with numbers and strange symbols. They were sitting on top of a clock face hundreds of feet wide.

"The Prague astronomical clock, huh?" Zvena said, looking at Wolfgang as though he very much regretted not throwing his javelin harder. "Time is running shorter for Europe than it is for Russia. *Vernemsya k nashim baranam.* We must return to our rams."

Zvena rose and motioned to Rodion and the other cyborg. Ran and Sarge rose.

"Give President Putin my regards," Ran said. "He owes us a rematch in our hockey series." Ran grabbed his former enemy's hand. "Despite our differences, I want to show you we are ready to cooperate in our mutual interest. Is there anything you and your team need?"

Zvena considered a moment. "Dr. Licht, you arrived in a most interesting plane. Has it been refueled?"

53

THE LICHTSTROM

The Russians took off in Wolfgang's fire-breathing plane. Ellie watched them disappear into the night. "So," she said with a quiet exhalation of relief mixed with fascination, "those are cyborgs."

"Look at the disgusting mess they made," their host Wolfgang said, sweeping crystal shards from the shattered fireplace off his desk.

As Ellie cleaned even more crystal fragments off a couch and prepared to worm her way out of the bottom half of her space suit, she looked around in the cathedral-sized audience chamber, at the thirty-foot-high glass door in the distance, the gaping hole in the wall where they had broken through, the astronomical clock under their feet. She had expected Der Lichtstrom to be unusual, but the scale and oddities of this place were positively dizzying.

Ran was helping Sarge Bryan over to the desk as the albino soldier recovered from successive blows to the head. Melanie wiggled out of her suit while keeping an eye on the Tyr quark and Miss Aleph's cylinder.

It occurred to Ellie that there were at least a dozen Lichtwerks employees around them, and her friends had no weapons. Ellie looked at one of the guns that had been dropped by one of Zvena's men. It looked too heavy to lift.

Melanie came over to help Ellie. "By the way, we don't think you're a slut."

"The jury's still out," Miss Aleph said.

Wolfgang watched the last trace of his plane's afterburners disappear over the horizon as his pilots ferried the Russians back to Moscow. Then he examined what the invaders had done to his space elevator.

"This whole unit will have to be rebuilt," he fumed. "I should send the bill to Putin."

Ellie looked left and right for an escape route. She could tell the old conniving oligarch realized he had the upper hand. Wolfgang signaled to one of his security people.

Ellie considered, then rejected, the idea of shoving the heavy machine gun over to where Ran and Sarge Bryan were. She was so bruised, tired, and cramping up, she could hardly raise her feet to set them gently on the velvet-covered ottoman. Also, they had had a difficult enough time keeping the quark sample safe. What were the chances it would survive another firefight?

"You see these strange people?" Wolfgang said to his guards. "See that they get everything they need. And you," he said, turning to the battered and wounded engineers who had helped them retake the office. "You are the worst fighters in history. Get back to the super collider and power up the nonbaryonic-matter array. *Schnell gehen!*"

The mortified-looking troop in blood- and sweat-stained overalls climbed out through the gaping hole in the wall.

"Wolfgang," Ran said with a cough as he accepted some water from one of the Lichtwerks people. "I'm glad you've finally seen the light."

Dr. Licht grimaced. "Yah, that joke was funny only the first fifty times you told it."

Melanie leaned over to Ellie, giggling. "In German, 'licht' means 'light.'"

Ellie looked up. The long string of glowing orbs reaching up from the spire seemed intact. The two doomed ascenders must have been thrown off the tether before exploding.

"What happened to the people who went up?" Ellie asked.

"Two of my very expensive ascenders detached from the maglev cable and blew up. The people who stole them are dead," Wolfgang said bluntly. He checked the two glowing panels beside the two dark ones. "I managed to reinstall the safeties in time. The first two that went up have, at present, detached into free flight."

"So fast?"

"A space shuttle takes only nine minutes to reach orbit. The key is to come out of the atmosphere and accelerate to an angular velocity, which offsets gravity."

Ellie sipped her tea. She decided Wolfgang was not going to throw them into a dungeon—at least not yet—and stared at the starry sky.

"I wonder what they're doing up there?"

54

UKRAINE

TEMIR

T hese are the best heroin smugglers you could find?" Temir said bitterly to his friend as he looked at the antitank mine sitting between them.

"You didn't give me much notice," Eylül mumbled.

After it was clear the Ukrainians and the woman who had captured them were not going to blow them up, Eylül got up unsteadily. With both hands, he braced himself against the corrugated steel of the shipping container they were trapped in. He was still dribbling blood from a head wound suffered during their failed attempt to kill Vladimir Putin.

"Sit down," Temir hissed. "I don't need that Ukrainian cunt to see you faint."

That cunt had kept them in the filthy shipping container for an hour. After some debate and checking their Grey Wolves credentials with contacts in Istanbul, the woman had put down her old-style flip phone.

"Hi, Turks," she said. "I'm Oleksandra. Please sit tight."

She then eased up the netting covering the entrance but only far enough to let in a skinny Ukrainian. Oleksandra's drug-addled scumbag assistant looked eighty years old but was likely in his thirties. He wore a T-shirt so dirty it looked like part of his skin.

This fellow's body odor was added to the smells of rotting produce and diesel fumes as he checked them out. Taking one look under Temir's jacket, he yelped and backed away from the tentacle arm. Temir could have sworn the filthy loon sent a steam of liquid shit down the legs of his jeans, which had to date back to the first Crimean War.

Steel ropes were brought in and circled tightly around both Temir and Eylül. Oleksandra never took her eye off them or her finger off the tank-mine detonator. When they were securely bound, she motioned for them to get out.

Temir slid his legs out of the shipping container, which was on the back of the very unreliable smuggler's truck. With the fifty pounds of weight added by his bindings standing was quite awkward, even for him. They had to carry Eylül out and set him down near the roadside like a raw beef carcass.

"Listen, woman," Temir said in English, "you have no concept of what you are doing. Let us go now, and I'll only execute the human garbage who touched us."

Oleksandra's pug-like features twisted with mirth and rage. She picked up a shovel and hit Temir squarely in the groin. If it hadn't been for the damage inflicted there by the Russian cyborg, he would hardly have noticed it. Temir exhaled sharply and bent over but didn't drop to the muddy road.

"A 'tough nut,' huh?" the woman said, scratching her stubbly hair, which she had dyed orange in order to appear even more hideous.

Then Oleksandra picked up a blow torch and approached Eylül. As much as his friend deserved pain and mutilation for getting them captured, Temir had to put an end to this.

He took a deep breath and felt the symbiont's rhino-hide surface expand against the metal cables. The fascist kaffir had made a mistake; she assumed his left appendage was a mutation with a fixed size and shape, when in fact it was as flexible as an octopus tentacle when he chose to make it so, and it could become as hard and sharp as a guillotine blade, *when* he chose to make it so.

He could free himself, and the tentacle could become an axe with which to cut Oleksandra's head in two before she could blink. He looked around. The big machine cannon was still pointed at them. Now was not the time for an altercation.

"Before we make any permanent mistakes," Temir said just as the blowtorch threatened to singe Eylül's beard, "the Ukrainian Azov militia and the Grey Wolves have always had good relations."

"Relations are better when you Turkish turds stay on your side of the Black Sea."

Eylül's eyes were locked onto the hissing blue-white acetylene flame in front of him.

"One hundred kilos of gold will be put onto a boat at Kilyos within thirty minutes of our release," Temir said as his tentacle arm quivered, ready to change shape and let the metal encircling his torso just drop away. "That's more than your Azov militia make in ten years."

Oleksandra pondered a moment, then dashed any hopes of them buying their way out of their predicament so easily. The Ukrainian militiawoman was shrewder than she looked.

"Allow me to make a call. I'll certainly take your gold." She held up the flip phone. "After I have that, we will talk about your recent flight over Moscow."

Temir had his people deliver only twenty kilos of gold to the prearranged spot on the Turkish seacoast. Meanwhile, he fumed about being away from his headquarters in Istanbul where they could monitor the twin disasters in Europe and Moscow. He needed to see with his own eyes that Elder Omid had kept his word and the combined Turkish-Iranian force was ready to move in an armored column to the Turkish border with Bulgaria.

The Ottoman-Persian Islamic liberation of Europe would happen without him being there. But it was his birthright as leader of the Grey Wolves to lead the conquest. It would be an insult to all he had sacrificed and suffered to sit in a muck hole with people not fit to tend Turkish latrine pits.

"I want the rest of the gold," Oleksandra snarled when she heard the translation of what Temir had told his people.

"And I want you to listen." Temir waved his head at the scraggly group of anti-Russian Ukrainian nationalists. "Maybe our talk is not for everyone's ears."

Oleksandra laughed. There was a chunk missing from her tongue; it only slightly affected her speech. "Then I will blowtorch the ears of anyone who hears something they should not. Speak, or I take my twenty kilos and see how far I can roll your head before it falls into the ditch."

At least she was straightforward.

"Things are happening," Temir said with severity. "Things even someone like… even someone otherwise occupied with important business of her own has heard, no?"

Oleksandra took a swig of clear liquid, probably not water, and flicked her gnarly tongue over her long yellow teeth. "I've heard of a fuckup in Bordeaux, France, and an air incursion over Moscow."

"Good. The two are related, but not how you think," Temir said, calculating precisely what he had to tell this kafir bitch to get what he wanted. "Tell me, how much gold do you think is in the vaults of the European Central Bank? What if you could have all of it and as a bonus watch your deadly enemies in Russia sicken and perish by the million, slowly and painfully?"

"Sounds good so far," Oleksandra said with murderous geniality. "I'm listening."

55

The black exhaust trail from the Lichtwerks corporate jet scarred the clear Moscow sky. Zvena thought he had never been on a more uncomfortable flight as he sat tightly packed in with Rodion and one other combat model Human+ soldier. The cramped passenger space was located closely behind the two nervous Lichtwerks company pilots.

"Are we there yet?" Rodion asked in heavily accented English.

The pilot was not amused. "Mr. Zvena, please transmit your government access codes again. Moscow Air Defence controller has not acknowledged."

"They are probably calculating the fine for polluting our fresh air," Zvena said hoarsely.

His fluid intake was not working properly, so he was dehydrated; no matter which way he twisted, he could not fill his lungs completely. He tapped a panel on his forearm and retransmitted the friend/foe codes that would avoid them getting shot down.

Kicking up a cloud of dust and debris worthy of a re-entry rocket, they landed on an isolated field at Pushkin International.

"Who do I talk to about getting refueled?" the pilot asked as he gripped the back of Zvena's combat harness in a silly attempt to help him out of the plane.

"What's your hurry? Enjoy Moscow for a while." Zvena scanned the horizon.

It was a sunny and unseasonably warm day for late October. On the horizon loomed a strangely shaped cloud; it was all white with a saucer shape at the top. The formation looked as though a Tsar or Poseidon H-bomb had gone off and then frozen as it rose through the stratosphere.

"Ach," the pilot said, following his gaze. "Doesn't look like such a nice day. Maybe rain on the horizon." He looked left and right at the quiet runways. "It can't be such bad weather that you Russians have shut down the airport, can it?"

Zvena didn't reply. He told the third passenger, the combat cyborg, to stay there with the pilots and instructed him that the foreigners were guests to be accommodated but that they were restricted to their aircraft.

Zvena then pulled Rodion out of the plane, and they jogged to the express train station. The turnstile was being attended by an old fellow who looked like he had been there since the Revolution. He could not figure out how to override the machine to let them through without paying. As Rodion fished around in the pockets of his uniform for money, Zvena decided he was in a hurry and just yanked the revolving steel door off its hinges, then stomped toward the platform.

During the train ride, Zvena noticed a definite decrease in car traffic. White-painted tanks and armored personnel carriers stood at intersections. Civil emergency beacons flashed on lampposts, and alert messages had taken over electronic billboards. Advertisements for Omega watches and Prada purses were overwritten with demands that all citizens report to their designated block civil defense captains for further instructions.

At another train stop, he saw military vehicles open up and disgorge soldiers. They escorted homeless vagabonds off the street into the cargo compartments of Ural 5323 all-weather trucks. One fellow was so drunk or high he did not respond to polite kicks. The reprobate was then picked up and deposited into the truck like a sack of potatoes.

Finally, around Znamenka Ulitsa road, came the strangest sight. About forty people were lined up against the brick wall of a church. A squad with a machine gun started shooting them as the train passed. Rodion and Zvena exchanged confused looks.

Of course, some bands of criminals and dope sellers deserved nothing less than public execution, but there was an odd thing about this massacre. Seated behind the machine gunners was a professional-looking camera crew capturing every detail of the carnage.

"What are the soldiers doing? Not all of those people looked like social deviants."

"Rodya," Zvena said, just getting over his own surprise but not showing it, "how naive can you be? Play back the scene in your ocular implants. There was no recoil from the gun. They were shooting blanks."

"Is it a movie set?"

"I do not think so. Not exactly."

The train rolled on. Close to the Kremlin, Zvena requested that the driver stop. They were nowhere near a station, but he got no argument from the comfortably fat babushka who was wrapped up in three coats and at least as many scarves despite the warm weather.

As soon as they disembarked, something tapped on Zvena's head. It was not crap from a bird; it was a hard pellet. Hailstones were falling all around with increasing intensity.

As they got farther into the Kremlin complex, the security checkpoints were manned almost exclusively by their Human+ comrades. All were wearing Antarctic gear: thick white camouflage uniforms, thermal membranes over their bare heads, and goggles hanging around their necks. Given that the temperature that afternoon was 74°F, they looked somewhat ridiculous.

"No saluting," Zvena said as they passed the last checkpoint. "I'm no longer a komandir."

He and Rodion were ushered past Putin's private den, through newly completed underground tunnels, and into the Universal Integrated Situation Room. Scores of task chairs stood behind desks arranged in concentric circles. In one corner on a raised pedestal stood a gold statue of Catherine the Great, the Empress who had crushed the Islamic Ottoman Empire in the 18th century. Every inch of wall space was covered with high-definition monitors.

The desks were divided by wide aisles, and in the middle of it all, like the eye at the center of a hurricane, was President Putin.

Putin had a digital readout in one hand and was pressing earphones to his head with the other. He noticed them and waved. With swift action and border closures Putin had saved Russia from the worst of the coronavirus pandemic ten years earlier. But was even a man of his experience and insight capable of defeating this new insidious mosquito-bourne plague which had been engineered to cripple the country?

"Rodya," Zvena said, as he sidestepped a very small technician trailing a very large printout sheet, "be careful. Don't break anything."

Putin had taken off his tie, was unshaven, and looked harried but invigorated.

"Today," he said, putting the headset down on a desk, "the only things we are going to break are records." He slapped Zvena on the arm. "Welcome back, my little green men. I thought you might not be able to land in time, but Dr. Licht's plane proved to be admirably fast."

A blue-suited technician tried to get their attention. "Mr. President, it is done," the man said. "The mirror has disengaged and is no longer in the target zone."

In a monitor, Zvena saw a computerized picture of the Great Space Mirror of China. Originally built to divert heating solar rays away from Earth, Polenka and Fyodor had hijacked it for a much different purpose.

"Perfect," Putin said as he pointed to a series of satellite weather maps. "The vortex effect will soon reach its maximum potential."

Instead of deflecting the heating rays, their cosmonauts had tasked the many-hectares-wide mirror with concentrating a beam of undiluted solar radiation onto specific spots along the northern hemisphere. Energy directed to those spots had destabilized a vortex of extremely cold air around the North Pole.

The thunderhead, which had looked like a frozen nuclear explosion to Zvena earlier, was on another monitor screen. It was much closer now, its edges licking along Moscow's city limits. In response to the sudden temperature drop, the lens of the remote camera closest to the incoming vortex fogged up, then it shook violently under the impact of hurricane-force winds, finally its lens cracked. The monitor switched to another camera viewing the scene from a wider angle.

"It is about to get colder here than ever before," Putin said with stern resolve.

Their leader knew hundreds of Muscovites would freeze to death. But as the mosquito larvae and the black plague virus inside them froze solid, millions would be saved.

"I had my doubts about the addict Fyodor," Putin admitted. "But you made the right decision."

Zvena had not counted on losing half the ascender team. Should he have left the safety systems engaged? It didn't matter. His Spetsnaz members had died heroes of the Federation. That one-armed worm Lefty, no doubt helped immeasurably by Polenka, had partially redeemed his sinful life.

"I was afraid the Chinese or the American Space Force would intervene before the weather system could be destabilized."

Putin smiled grimly. "They nearly did. However, after a few diplomatic words and a casual mention of the Poseidon super nuke units in the Atlantic and the South China Sea, we all came to an understanding. They even helped with our calculations, which will cause an increased updraft in our spiral arm of the vortex, dropping temperatures even further."

If only Russia had had its own rocket ready, Zvena fumed. The whole infiltration into the Lichtstrom had been so reckless. The future of the capital and Russia itself should not have hung by such a flimsy string as the space elevator.

"Zvena, I would tell you not to look so gloomy," Putin said while he approved a request on a digital tablet, "but we can't help it, we are Russian."

"If I may ask," Rodion said. Zvena was shocked he was following along. His head, both the meat and the metal parts, had a few pieces missing, and hydraulic fluid was making a yellow mess on the floor as though he were slowly peeing himself. "What did the Chinese and Americans want?"

"The Americans were easy to satisfy. They wanted cooperation to save as many of their citizens as possible from the Event in Europe. I sent two air regiments to neutralize the Euro Army's air defenses as far as Berlin. I have given their civilian planes flyover permission to evacuate their people to Novosibirsk Airport."

"And the Chinese, did they kill Polenka and Fyodor?" Zvena asked.

The original plan had been for the infiltration team to try to make it back to Russia's space station. Anyone with a brain knew that was hopeless. For the cosmonauts, going to space had always been a one-way trip.

"Surprisingly, no," Putin said, scrolling through some data on a screen. "Though they did take the trespass to their solar mirror seriously. Our people were able to get into one of the descender modules attached to the mirror; it landed in Mongolia."

"Maybe Polenka will meet a nice Asian man and settle down," Zvena joked about their 150-kilogram colleague.

"The Chinese also wanted some territory."

"Not the Bolshoi Ussuriysky Islands again?" Russia had fought China over them in the 1960s.

"No. If the Event takes place, they want Austria. But I negotiated them down to a ninety-nine-year lease on the country, with the city of Vienna as Chinese territory in perpetuity." Putin shrugged. "President Xi is an opera fan. Who knew?"

There was some commotion among the technicians. The engineered arctic cyclone was over the city. The temperature had shot down to -64°C / -84°F and was still falling.

"The previous record low temperature for Moscow was minus forty-three Celsius. We need to get to one hundred and twenty degrees below zero to kill all the larvae our Persian and Turkish friends kindly distributed over our territory," Putin said with sarcastic venom that dripped with a desire for ice-cold revenge.

A map on the wall behind them showed the routes of the pestilence-laden dirigibles, which had been reconstructed from satellite images.

"The stealth airships moved so slowly, only one set off any alarms," Putin said. "Fortunately we have calculated probable dispersion patterns. After this unseasonable snowstorm, which we are naming Cyclone Catherine after our revered empress, your winterized cyborg units will have the honor of blasting any remaining pockets of larvae with liquid nitrogen."

"Mr. President, are you sure this will destroy them?"

"When dealing with villains despicable enough to use bioweapons, you are wise to be cautious." Putin flicked a panel on his handset. The icons on the map of Moscow changed. "We took your samples and one hundred more from the ground. Each one was the same: the same type of mosquito and the identical sustaining liquid sac. Our Foundation for Advanced Research was of the opinion the bioweapon was not optimally designed for deployment against Russia."

"An improvised operation?" Zvena didn't believe it. "Attacking a superpower without proper planning… it is national suicide."

"Perhaps we were not the initial target, merely the target of opportunity," Putin said. "My scientists say that with a few months' planning, the mosquitos' genes could have been spliced with *Belgica antarctica*, the only insect to live year round on the southernmost continent. They could also have been packed in bio-antifreeze; these ones were not. Had they been, we would never have been able to kill them all."

"So…" The obvious dawned even on Rodion. "They were meant for someone else, and because of developments in Europe, the target was changed to Russia?"

"This may become a useful fact, or not."

Putin had mentioned the human vermin to the south.

"Mr. President, is it too early to broach the subject of a firm reply to the Iranians and Turks?"

"Business before pleasure, Mr. Zve—"

Putin may have wanted to say more, but all of them were caught by surprise when the back plate of Zvena's combat harness started ringing. Rodion pulled up Zvena's jacket and revealed a credit-card-sized handset.

"That damned Lichtwerks company pilot stuck it on me." Zvena clenched his hands, feeling his knuckle gears mash together. "I'll have words with him."

"First," Putin said, looking at the hologram inside the device, "I think we should answer it. Your friends are calling you from the Lichtstrom."

56

THE LICHTSTROM

After the scary cyborgs took off in the Lichtwerks jet, robots and humans came into Wolfgang's ginormous office to clear away the mess. By the doorway, a blanket lay over a severed leg.

Their host stood by the huge vaulted glass wall and watched the Russians fly over the horizon.

"Fly away, Meccano men," Wolfgang said, putting down a pair of golden opera glasses. "We may be in touch soon."

For a second, Ellie thought Wolfgang meant to blow up his own plane out of revenge for the Russians' bloody invasion of his territory.

"My thinking too," Melanie said cryptically.

Wolfgang and Melanie were the two best scientists they had on their side. If they were to have any chance of finding and disarming the T-bomb, they all had to work together. Ellie was about to say that when she toppled off the leather sofa in a daze.

Ran caught her by the shoulder before her head hit the floor.

"You need to rest," he said.

"Mr. Oliphant, my fake sugar daddy, thank you. I'm fine," she protested. "I can stay awake as long as any of you."

After that, Ellie did remember protesting vigorously to Wolfgang about his treatment of the baby dolphin in his chandelier aquarium. Then she found herself in a Lichtwerks employee sleeping pod unit with no memory of having walked there.

Melanie grabbed her by the shoulders and got her out of her outfit, which had become really icky.

"Stow away the stiff upper lip, Ellie; you have to take time for self-care," Melanie said. "Since the crisis began, I've had two thousand and thirty-nine nano sleeps, and even I'm losing my short-term memory. You have to refresh and revive."

`"I'll wake you if any of the scientists need a`
`fashion makeover, Eleanor."`

Ellie realized what spoke to her out of the leather tote bag was an AI, but she could not remember her name. She really did need to sleep.

The Lichtwerks rest and recuperation units were similar to Japanese micro hotel suites. The bed, shower, and strangely blue glowing toilet were all separate modules. The pods also moved around. By the time she got out of the shower, all the other stalls had been replaced by sleeper units with occupants inside. When she looked back, the washing capsule she had just come out of had been soundlessly replaced by a wall.

She found her way to her assigned unit and decided it couldn't hurt to doze off for a bit. She had a fantasy that she was trapped in a freshly washed bundle of towels tumbling in a clothes dryer. Mrs. Ottridge's face looked in on her and went round and round. She looked cross and was in a hurry to get the next load in.

I'm almost done and dried.

Ellie woke. Melanie was tapping on the big round transparent door of her pod.

"Oh, hi," Ellie said. Her elbow slipped off an inflatable pillow shaped like a kidney bean. "I was just formulating our next... strategy."

She yawned as she made that admittedly lame excuse for nodding off during the end of the world.

"We've found it!"

"What?" Then Ellie realized she had been asleep for hours. She sat up with growing excitement and promptly hit her head on the ceiling of her pod. "Oh, right, the T-bomb."

"Shh, not so loud," Melanie cautioned. She looked left and right. Her hair was now whipping behind her in a very sensible braid that looked like a blonde anaconda twisting down to the back of her knees. "We have to be careful who knows, because of where it is. Change in there. I'll meet you upstairs."

Melanie tossed in some fresh clothes. With some contortions and while fighting through weird stiffness in her neck and back, she got into the scratchy Lichtwerks underclothes and bleak-looking overalls.

"Bloody cheap polyester."

By the time Ellie crawled out of her sleeper, she found her pod was standing in the middle of Wolfgang's office. It was a little disturbing being shuffled around like that.

Everyone else was waiting on her. Wolfgang was by his big desk. Sarge Bryan and Ran Oliphant were at consoles with displays scrolling "TOP SECRET TRANSMISSION" along the top and bottom in big red letters.

"Alrighty, then," Ellie prompted an uncharacteristically silent Melanie. "Where is it?"

"At first no one believed it, because of the size that it had to be, about the volume of a big cruise ship."

`"He was on my short list, that overweening pandering political pimp."`

Melanie went on, "We need to be careful of who you speak to about what we've learned. Extra, extra careful because of who we now know is leading the Pangeans. We can't trust anyone.

"As we learned in Bordeaux, they can set the T-bomb off at any time, even before it reaches its maximum yield. From here on out, we're incognito. While you were sleeping, I picked out our travel disguises." Melanie finally blurted, "The T-bomb is in Paris!"

"Then what are we waiting for?" Ellie said, chewing on an energy bar and drinking some orange-tasting sports drink.

"More precisely, it is *under* Paris," Wolfgang said drolly from behind his desk, which Ellie now saw was in the shape of a flattened projection of the globe made of granite. "I should have suspected that weasel Rapace all along, him and his unglaublich weird wife. I just never thought he had the guts and the sheer audacity. Something must have pushed President Rapace over the edge."

"You should have woken me right away," Ellie said. "What do we do now? Is there someone in Brussels…"

Even Ran looked at her with pity. She must have said something naive.

"If it's Rapace," Ran said, "the whole European Union is compromised."

"Those slimy Brussels sprouts," Melanie said with indignation. "There are five presidents of the EU. None of them are elected by citizens, and the members of the European parliament can't even propose laws."

"Yah," Wolfgang said. "They are all fat neutered hogs afraid of whoever has the largest knife. Right now, that is President Rapace. Only he could have ordered the missile strike that killed your friend. And where better to hide the final bomb than under Paris, which is riddled with hundreds of miles of catacombs. The device is immense and would have taken months of continuous access to construct. After the Cesta bomb failed, locating the next version under the presidential palace was the Pangeans' best option."

It all made horrid sense.

"First," Ran said, turning around from his mobile screen, "we have to ask for help from the only person we know with certainty is not involved in the Pangean conspiracy."

"We're ready," Wolfgang said, looking at a GPS-style display on his monitor. "That mechanoid man is inside the Kremlin. I'm placing the call to Putin."

After a surprisingly pleasant conversation with the world's most notorious strongman, they set out for Geneva. The help they needed from Russia would take time to organize. To Ellie, every minute dragged on her conscience. Atticus had been killed getting crucial information. Besides everything else at stake, she had to make sure his sacrifice meant something.

Wolfgang, Melanie, Sarge Bryan, and Ran Oliphant all packed into a windowless Lichtwerks van. They zipped through a tunnel, which let out on the other side of a thick forest and shot onto the highway.

"Can't you go faster?" Ellie said to Sarge Bryan.

"Not with this bargain-basement suspension, ma'am. Having to call a tow truck is not in the mission plan." He was wearing a Dick Tracy hat and a nice pair of dark sunglasses with stylish frames.

All Ellie had on as a disguise was a dumpy-looking blue blazer and skirt that made her look like a stewardess for a Latvian airline.

The trip to Geneva took about twenty minutes. When they got to Cornavin Train Station, they piled out and followed the signs to the departure gates. They passed a store.

"Ellie?" Melanie said in an urgent whisper.

"I need more disguise," Ellie replied as she dashed into the outlet boutique for an emergency shopping detour.

She turned to the girl behind the counter. *"S'il vous plaît excusez-moi. Er… si je paie l'argent est-il un rabais?"*

The snooty teenager looked her as though she had just crawled out of a dustbin and was asking for spare change.

"Of course you have to pay with *money*," the girl sneered. "And no, no discount no matter how you pay. This is the Boutique of St. Pierre. Didn't you read the sign?"

"Right, sorry." The sales girl was quite snooty, despite the place being barely larger than a kiosk and hosting a homeless guy lounging on a bench right outside, singing in his sleep.

From across the walkway, Ran was waving a newspaper at her. This was one train she couldn't miss; but she needed those sunglasses. Miss Aleph texted her.

Just buy them already.

Tap me.

"I'll get the hat and the Gucci Catseye."

The cashier begrudgingly unlocked the antitheft device from the sunglasses but kept both items well on her side of the counter until she had presented the debit card scanner.

"With taxes, VAT, EU SuperVAT, and Geneva's clean air surcharge, the total will be…"

More than the *Juggernaut* pretended to pay her in a month.

Ellie made to tap her handset on the point-of-sale device.

The cashier rolled her eyes. "It is over the tapping limit. You will have to use the slot and enter a PIN… Oh, it went through."

Ellie grabbed her purchases. "No need to wrap, bye."

Nearly late for the train, but much more confident in her appearance, she found an unallocated seat in her section. The passage on Europe's fastest train had been booked anonymously by Wolfgang, who handed them all printed barcode tickets. They pulled away from the station.

The French countryside raced past both sides of the TGV. The train was less than half full. People looked glum and confused. An older couple sitting in the seat across from Ellie opened a bottle of wine. A small child whined in French in one of the double seats at the other end of the carriage.

"A fine time for a shopping trip," Wolfgang said from across the aisle as he pretended to tie his shoelace.

Ellie was about to say that for an oligarch with his own country, he certainly wasn't very generous in the wardrobe department. Instead, she had to chuckle at the terrible dye job Wolfgang had inflicted on his goatee. This was the first close look she had got; it looked like he had made a mess of eating a brownie filled with black ink.

A chime sounded. Ellie jumped. Maybe they were stopping the train because a scam artist had just robbed the Boutique of St. Pierre.

She held the phone up to her ear. "Miss Aleph, you did pay with real money, didn't you?"

"Sort of. Barclays Bank offered me a very generous line of credit after I emailed them my income tax forms from my freelancing gigs at the *Juggernaut*."

Ellie had always believed borrowing and spending was the best way to support the British economy post-Brexit.

"Maybe I should get new shoes at the next stop." The dull, tan-colored clunkers she had on were making her feet sweat.

"Don't push it."

The chime turned out to be an announcement that there were first-class dining tables still available for an additional fee.

"Ah," said Ran, pretending to notice Wolfgang for the first time. "I thought that was you, 'Ludwig.' Care to join us in the dining car? It's cheaper if we buy a double table."

"How could I have missed you, my old friend from Glasgow 'Rory,'" Wolfgang said, scratching his beard. "Please lead on."

"You'll have to forgive my friend, Mr. Zeru," Ran said, letting Sarge Bryan go ahead of them. "He doesn't speak much English."

The only person who noticed them was the whiny French girl. She stared at Bryan's albino face and the blue glow coming from behind his glasses. Her pouty lower lip quivered, but she said nothing.

Melanie was already sitting in their booth alcove when they got to the dining car. "Well, you lot don't look suspicious at all."

A pair of small robots was in her hair, re-braiding it tightly against her scalp.

"Do you have to do that at the table?" Wolfgang fussed as the scarab-shaped mobile grooming appliances sifted through Melanie's massive tresses.

They were nearly alone; the next patrons were three tables away.

"What's important," Sarge Bryan whispered as he jammed a French bread stick into his mouth, "is can we trust our friend up north to deliver?"

"Rory, you played hockey with Mr. P.," Wolfgang said to Ran ironically. "Without help, we'll never overcome whatever security our friends have surrounding the device."

"I think," Ran said, covering his mouth with a napkin to avoid being lip-read by the bulbous surveillance camera on the ceiling, "Mr. P. is as ruthless as any leader in recorded human history. He'll do anything to win. But he also assiduously keeps his word, for good or ill."

Ellie had been shocked when Sarge Bryan said they could not even trust the chain of command at Ramstein Air Base. Ran's contacts at Westminster were similarly off-limits. If the president of France was the leader of the Pangeans, no one could be trusted other than a complete outsider like Putin.

"What about these catacombs?" Ellie mumbled, covering her mouth like Ran had.

"You can speak up. I'm projecting a cloud of white sound. No one can hear us."

"The catacombs," Ellie said, still whispering just to be safe. "They're huge, and you couldn't be sure of the exact location we need to get to."

Ellie once knew a fashion designer who tried to have his debut show in the bone-strewn Paris catacombs. He had called it "Fashions to Die For." The show never happened. The risk to models and buyers of lingering death from toxic mold or sudden death from a cave-in had been too much for the insurance company.

Melanie switched her braiding bots to the other side of her head. The parts they had done looked quite nice. She leaned forward and said, "The catacombs are why they say there are three times as many residents under Paris than in the city above.

"Six million people's remains are embedded into the walls and scattered through miles of labyrinths. People have gotten lost and died exploring the tunnels."

"I'm working on a map with our northern friends and some other contacts. When we get there, just do what I tell you."

"With all respect to our little blue associate," Wolfgang said, looking at Ellie's scuffed Hermes bag, which still had pieces of his big crystal fireplace embedded in it, "the Pangeans would not be so sloppy as to use the old catacombs on the Left Bank of the Seine. Since at least the First World War, they've been filling new sections on the Right Bank with the bones of their victims. Those are not on the tourist maps."

Wolfgang looked deeper inside Ellie's bag. "Is that a Montblanc 149?"

She nodded.

"The cap is the right shape." He pulled out her fountain pen and unscrewed it. "When I said the structure would be the size of an ocean liner, I didn't mean it has to be solid. The essential factor is that the dark-matter energy wave of the Tyr quark detonation is rebounded, gathering force, like sound waves in a resonant whispering gallery."

"Cool," Sarge said, blinking behind his sunglasses. "We'll place breaching charges on key structures and—"

"No, we won't," Wolfgang said sharply. "First off, you were present the last time kinetic energy disrupted a very small T-bomb, were you not?" Wolfgang put the oblong pen top flat on the table. "The Pangean scientists will have embedded neutronium reflectors in this pattern. The quark will be gestating at one end, ready to be set off at any time, but gathering peak energy around midnight October 31. We must go with an infiltration and containment plan."

Melanie blew a strand of hair out of her eyes. "The difficult part is, neutronium is only manufactured by a few superpowers, and a thimbleful of the pure substance weighs as much as the Great Pyramid at Giza."

"Let's hope Mr. P. comes through," Ran said. "We have to get in and neutralize the Tyr quark before the Pangeans set it off. Even if it went off today, Melanie says it could explode with up to a quarter of its maximum yield. Being located in Paris, that means from London to northern Italy, millions would be dead."

And undead, Ellie thought.

57

Merci beaucoup d'avoir choisi TGV Lyria, la prochaine étape est Paris-Gare-de-Lyon."

Ellie watched a gritty industrial landscape speed by. The only trees were made of metal, and the steel tracks they rode stretched out to all points of the compass.

As the urban zone around Paris approached, they slowed down. A concrete retaining wall was plastered with graffiti. Most were foreign words, including Arabic. The only one Ellie could read was:

The end approaches, but the apocalypse is long lived. — Derrida

Next to it was a popular stencil tag of a person in a hoodie and gas mask.

They filed off the mostly empty train, past the small whiny girl. Her simpering had calmed down into sleepy sulking. When Sarge Bryan went by, she poked her head up, pulled at her mother's jacket, pointed, and said, *"Regardez, c'est le Diable! Regardez!"*

However, the woman was hunched over her phone, while at the same time absentmindedly gathering the child's comic books and crayons. She did not notice the burly albino as he exited.

For a city under siege by a genocidal madman, Paris looked fairly subdued.

Near the exits out from Lyon station there was even a juggler hustling for change and cyber credits.

"Is that the Orient Express?" Ellie whispered to Melanie as they walked past a very retro-looking train.

The female scientist had switched off her scarab-shaped robotic hair stylists, and they sat still, their tiny metallic legs gripping on to her tight coiffure like a half dozen hairclips.

She looked and nodded. "I once asked Ran to buy it for company vacations. Just think of the mystery plays we could have put on."

It was a dull overcast day, and Ellie felt increasingly foolish wearing her Audrey Hepburn sunglasses. However, Sarge Bryan had to keep his on, so she was in good company.

The juggler missed. A ball bounded over to her feet; the skinny, intense-looking fellow kept performing with the remaining ones. He nodded his head to the one on the ground.

Ellie picked up the ping-pong ball. Written on it in marker was: "Black LEVC taxis."

Of course Mr. P. would have a spy network here. Ellie felt heartened. The Russians were coming through after all. Palming the ball, she showed it to Ran, who nodded cautiously. All five of them walked separately toward the long line of cabs.

"Is this our northern friend's doing?" Ellie asked Melanie. They were in enemy territory. France's president and who knew how many of his government, military, and police were horrible Pangean fanatics.

"I hope so," Melanie said. "If not, we'll get a really good tour of La Santé prison from the inside."

Both vehicles had their "Taxi – Parisien" signs dark, meaning unavailable. Ran and Sarge Bryan stuck close to Wolfgang and got into the first boxy black cab. They were watching the older oligarch quite carefully. Were they afraid he would try to make a break for it?

Wolfgang had tried to get away in a rocket, but President Rapace was willing to wipe out Europe to fulfill some kind of genocidal utopian vision. What could Wolfgang expect to gain from Rapace if he sold them all out? Ellie concluded Dr. Licht and all his resources would be on their side, unless something drastic happened to make it worth the risk to switch sides.

Their driver said nothing as he watched Sarge Bryan's taxi pull into traffic and get out of sight before he slid away from the curb. They did not drive far. Ellie, feeling particularly paranoid, tried to figure out where they were. She noted they went over a bridge; the river it spanned had to be the Seine. Then they moved through a suburb.

After turning off the freeway onto a side road, their tires bounced over rusted rail tracks, made crunching sounds as they rolled over gravel and discarded bottles, before stopping at the mouth of a large tunnel. The tunnel's vaulted brickworks were bearded by vines dripping green slime; traffic roared along a viaduct above.

"This…" Ellie started to say. "Oh, never mind."

"I agree," Melanie said in an airy but tense way. "This is a great place to discreetly snuff someone out."

The implacable face of the taxi driver, the part Ellie could see in the rearview mirror, gave no indication of which program was in the offing: continued cooperation or sudden snuffing. However, he did get out and hold the door for them. That had to be encouraging, Ellie thought hopefully.

A heavy double-length truck thundered along the highway overpass. Ellie got out and followed Melanie over weeds, garbage, what looked like a rotting discarded baby carriage, and dozens of used syringes and condoms.

Ellie could not see any landmarks. They could be in the crappy part of any big city except for the graffiti, which was mostly in French. The Derrida-obsessed vandal had been here.

I always dream of a pen that would be a syringe. —Derrida

"What charming places saving the world takes us to," Ellie said, stepping over some gooey brown mud. At least, she hoped it was mud.

The two taxis drove away.

"Just don't touch anything," Ran said tensely.

"Breathing in deep might also be something to avoid," Sarge Bryan said as he scanned inside the dark tunnel. The gaping black mouth amplified the sounds of trickling water and the vibrations from the traffic above.

Wolfgang kicked some drug paraphernalia off a rock and sat down on a handkerchief. "Look at the mess these subhuman addicts have made. If it were only a matter of wiping out such parasites, maybe the T-bomb has become a necessary evil."

"Shh!" Ran said, motioning them back against the retaining wall.

Around the bend trundled a street-cleaning truck. It was listlessly spraying water from its side; long, wide brushes tipped with steel bristles whipped the utter filth to and fro.

How completely useless, Ellie thought. It proceeded right into the mouth of the tunnel. When it was entirely hidden, the whole round back popped open, and Ellie thought they were done for.

"It's them again," she said, grabbing Melanie's arm.

"Wait a sec. Maybe they're friendly." The dippy scientist did not seem to have a robust sense of self-preservation.

"The last one I met grabbed my head and nearly popped it off," Ellie said, backing away from the four, five, then finally six figures who clambered out of the hollow tank on the back of the decoy truck. They were Human+ cyborgs.

Sarge Bryan and Ran walked up into the tunnel. Cautiously, they had words with the largest one. He looked familiar but was not the one who had accosted Ellie at the Lichtstrom.

"It's fine," Ran said as he waved Ellie, Melanie, and Wolfgang in. "They're on our side, at present."

"And they've got presents," Melanie said.

In addition to some square crates, two of the cyborgs strained to unload a football-sized object.

"I am Rodion," the largest one said. "Please address all comments to me. We are pledged to make this incursion mission and neutralization of the T-bomb a success or we will all perish in the attempt."

"Here's to Plan A." Ran offered his hand to the fellow, who loomed over him.

Melanie and Wolfgang stooped over the dark soccer ball which lay in a sling suspended between two Olympic-style barbells. Rodion lumbered over to Ellie.

"Ms. Sato." Rodion looked down at her with eyes that made Sarge Bryan's seem commonplace. They were augmented by sensor nodes and looked more like those of a spider. "My komandir... my associate, Mr. Zvena, extends his apology now that we are allies. He has studied your biography. Even our president admires your book *The 96 Hour War*, especially the part where you impersonated a Russian intelligence officer to rescue your friends. Mr. Zvena regrets calling you a slut."

"How about the part where he nearly crushed my skull in?" Ellie was still bedeviled by visions of that big hand over her visor, its sharp blue-black talon-like fingernails penetrating the Plexiglas an inch from her eyebrows.

"At the time, skull-crushing was a necessary part of the operation. He cannot apologize for doing his duty."

They were obviously dependent on them for the rest of their trip.

"All right, Mr. Rodion," Ellie said, cautiously extending her hand. "Friends again."

The bear paw that carefully took hers had signs of recent repairs. New synthetic skin, which looked like dusky blue translucent putty, covered bits of metal anatomy.

Sarge Bryan crouched near the entrance, scanning the skies, presumably for helicopters or drone surveillance. Satisfied, he rejoined the group. Rodion held a large shoulder-mounted weapon. Ellie had used something similar in Israel but about a quarter of the size.

"I see Santa brought something for everyone," Sarge Bryan said.

The cyborg in charge of the ordnance trunk looked at Rodion, who nodded. He handed Sarge his choice of weapon.

"Mr. Oliphant," Rodion said, "our President thanks you for not interfering with the orbital mission."

"It was a success?"

Rodion nodded with a creaking of neck hinges.

"Was it really?" Melanie asked nosily. "There were some strange weather patterns over Moscow, and then the national weather grid went silent. Does that have anything to do with the cosmonauts you sent up the space elevator?"

"Sorry, Dr. Françoise, is classified." Rodion studied the entranceway. "But what I can reveal is... our leader has agreed to Mr. Oliphant's request for a hockey rematch."

"Did he now?"

Rodion's face assumed an expression Ellie thought Frankenstein's monster would wear if he were trying to make a joke.

"There is good news and bad news about that," the cyborg said, picking up his seven-foot-long pike and walking out to the entrance. "The good news is you get to pick the referee. The bad news is I am playing in goal."

Without warning, Rodion speared up at the outer lip of the cave. Tons of material, loose and broken bricks mixed with moldy sand, came raining down. Ellie held a cloth over her nose and face against the dust. He kept stabbing viciously with his spear until the way out was sealed.

Traffic rumbled overhead; their tour guides turned on lights mounted on their arms and shoulders and led the way deeper down into the tunnel.

58

Afraid a larger section of the roof would collapse, Ellie followed close on Rodion's cyborg heels and ducked deeper into the old railway tunnel.

She glanced back at the sealed entrance. There was only a small aperture of fading afternoon light peeping through. Ellie thought she saw gray clouds and a brief flash of lightning in the distance. Then more sand rained down, and that last small hole to the outside also disappeared.

The damp made the air seem colder. With the dark only pierced by the beams of their lamps, Ellie and the others strapped on helmets, waders, and climbing gear.

Wolfgang, though older, appeared physically robust. Ellie thought he might have been passably good looking except for his poor beard dye job and his penchant for stabbing everyone in the back.

"So, Mr. Rodion," Wolfgang said as he cinched the support strap of a backpack around his waist, "if Mr. Putin had time to plan sporting events with Mr. Oliphant, he must have given you a personal message for me, no?"

Rodion's double-ringed pupils flicked back and forth, perhaps reviewing his internal data stream. "No."

"Not anything about joint space projects now that he has seen the space elevator in action?"

"Definitely not," the cyborg said, lifting his gun, turning its flashlight on and aiming it down the tunnel. "But I am sure he will be in touch, if Europe survives."

Ran and Sarge Bryan were familiar with the equipment the Russians had brought. There were harnesses, ropes, and breathing masks. The visors attached to the helmets adjusted automatically to light. Ellie's allowed her a green-tinted look into the shadows. Not all the way, though—the tunnel was long and winding.

"We're deep in the Left Bank. This probably started out as a limestone quarry tunnel," Melanie said with the jaunty air of a tour guide. "Oh, let me fix that for you."

She sealed the flaps on Ellie's boots. They were cyborg-sized, and she had to fill the gappy spaces with bunched newspaper.

"You want to keep a good seal," Melanie chirped. "To get from where we are up to the New Catacombs, we'll have to go through the sewers."

Ellie took a breath of warm moldy air and followed the six cyborgs along the gently sloping tracks. Just as Ellie was thinking they should have tried to drive the street-cleaning truck farther in, rotting wood gave way under her foot.

"Gah!" Her knee banged against rusted iron tracks.

"Shht," Rodion snapped at her. "Sergeant Bryan, teach your people to keep minimal sound discipline."

"Sorry."

Melanie and Sarge helped her up.

"Don't worry," Sarge Bryan said. "I'll let you know when we have to be real quiet."

Sarge's pale face and gleaming eyes were the only cheery feature of this oppressive place.

"The Old Catacombs run for hundreds of miles," Melanie said, opening a folding data screen. Outlined in yellow, underneath the familiar landmarks such as Notre Dame and the Eiffel Tower, was a spaghetti-like cluster of yellow lines. Some of them met brown lines and red lines. It was the dark subterranean city that stretched everywhere under the City of Lights.

"Golly, and I thought the London tube map was complicated." Ellie rubbed her knee and then struggled to catch up with the main group in her squishy boots. "I guess the brown lines are sewers. Should I ask about the red?"

"Well," Melanie said, slapping Sarge Bryan jauntily on the shoulder for what seemed like no reason at all, "we are wandering past millions of human remains, into the underground lair of the insane president of France, to disarm a bomb that could wipe out every human in Europe. So yes, you can ask."

"Those there red areas are zones of poison gas," Sarge Bryan said.

"We've got masks?" Ellie said hopefully.

"Yup, but no point in wearing them yet. Dirt and sweat will compromise the seal. We'll avoid those areas, and the Russians have detectors out, but… from what I hear, that shit can move around and sneak up on you."

Ellie moved on. She would have to trust her rapidly developing danger instincts to alert her to dangerous shit sneaking up on them. She was careful to follow where the other, much heavier people had trodden. She, Melanie, Ran, Sarge, and Wolfgang caught up to where the cyborgs had stopped and set down the barbells which were slung with the heavy load. In the wall of the railway tunnel, there was a neatly excavated gash.

"Looks like they used power tools to break through," Sarge Bryan said, examining the opening.

They? thought Ellie.

"Cataphiles," Wolfgang said, which surprised Ellie. She felt the oligarch would be horrified by the filth down here and certainly not know anything about the place. "They are people who live, work, and party in the undergrounds of the world, Paris, Odessa, Helsinki."

The cyborgs heaved some cinderblocks out of the way, enlarging the breach in the tunnel wall.

"You don't seem like you'd know much about those places, Dr. Licht."

Wolfgang smiled tersely. "Ach, Ms. Sato, I have to confess that in my youth I strayed off the narrow path once or twice. Most cataphiles are harmless hippie types. Even the ones who grow hallucinogenic mushrooms are very much afraid of the 'cataflics,' the police who will fine them for being down here and destroy their crop."

In the dim light, his dark goatee looked almost normal. Ellie could almost picture the arrogant old rich guy as an arrogant young rich guy slumming it, drinking cheap champagne down in the hidden subterranean cities of Europe.

The Russians eased the strange heavy sphere through the opening. When it was Ellie's turn to go through the wall, she made sure to get her footing properly. Unlike the neatly arched tunnel they were leaving, the ground in the new space was mushy and uneven.

Were there maggots underfoot? If so, what were they eating? She looked up. She had been inside Harrogate's Stump Cross Caverns as a schoolgirl, but that was a relatively sedate and naturally formed cave. What they were clambering into was nothing like that.

"Whoa," she said.

"I *dig* what you mean. Get it?" Melanie said, giggling. "All parts of these caverns were dug by human hands, from Roman slaves when the place was called Lutetia, to modern-day spelunkers, or were formed by subsidence. Even fires and methane explosions played a part in forming the catacombs."

The ceiling was low and jagged in places, then ranged up higher than she could see through her night-vision visor. Bricks and concrete mixed in with smooth, polished limestone covered in pink graffiti. She winced as her helmet thumped on something; with her hand she felt a knobby outcrop. A big fat human thighbone was sticking out of the wall.

She lurched backward to the other side of the narrow space, and long slimy fingers seemed to slap and grab her neck. She threw them off, biting her lip so as not to scream.

Once she had backed away and focused her eyes through the night-vision visor, she found not the hand of a waterlogged corpse, but merely a moist sprig of roots from a tree up on the surface that had broken through the limestone.

As she caught her breath, she kept reminding herself that her maternal grandfather had been tortured during the building of the Burma Death Railway. On the other hand, that had happened in a nice open jungle, not an airless, crumbling subterranean cavity strewn with human remains.

Determined to write a bold new chapter in her family's history of fortitude and stoicism, she shuddered quietly and moved on.

They followed a big crack leading down to who knew where. One of the cyborgs carrying the sphere slipped. In a blur, Rodion grabbed the fellow's arm, steadied him, and immediately pushed him back in disgust. Another Russian was brought forward to carry the heavy object.

Ran Oliphant turned around; his previously immaculately clean face was already smeared with a white pasty substance. He waited for them at a subterranean crossroads.

"The combination of man-made and natural features, constant vibrations, and unauthorized workings by cataphiles makes this place dangerous even for experienced cave explorers," he said.

"Oh, and don't forget the risk of drowning," Melanie added. "When storm drains overflow, this is where they flow into."

Water dripped onto Ellie's visor. She inched forward.

"Not to be a pillock," Ellie said after inching along a few dozen yards over what seemed a very long time, "but we do have a deadline…"

Some gritty-feeling stuff rained down on her helmet.

She continued. "With our Russian friends and possibly some help from Sergeant Bryan's trusted Army friends, couldn't we arrange a more direct route to the T-bomb, now that we know where it is?"

Ran and Rodion finished huddling over the map. There was another fork in their path, and this one was not on any of the cataphile maps. They went right.

"We could have," Ran said. "But I've met Rapace a few times. The man seemed like a didactic narcissist and close to being unhinged, but no more than the last few French presidents. The T-bomb is located right underneath Élysée Palace. Anyone who would build such a thing would set it off if they suspected they were about to be caught."

It was a continent-sized suicide bomb they were trying to defuse. Ellie shuddered.

There was some grumbling from up front. A protrusion was blocking the way. Two cyborgs grunted as they struck out with their pikes, shattering the sedimentary rock in seconds.

"I guess that's out, then."

"No matter what force we came in with, the palace is one of the most heavily guarded places in the country. Rapace would have time to set off the bomb. A stealth incursion is our only chance."

Ellie was starting to sweat. A readout on her wrist had held steady at 57°F / 13.8°C since they had entered. She drank some stale water from a tube attached to her backpack.

"Won't Rapace and his bunch be gone soon? The Pangeans want to build a utopia. Surely he wants to survive to lead the effort."

"Satellite images Rodion obtained show an aircraft much like the American hovercopter is on station at the palace. It has speed and range to quickly fly out of the red zone. Our guess is Rapace will not be suicidal unless he is pushed to be."

Around a sharp bend, what looked like an obelisk had fallen and left a twelve-by-eight-foot passage, which went on for a good length. Instead of hurrying along, the cyborgs incensed Ellie by pausing to sit down. Rodion and the five others opened equipment packs and fiddled with their cyber bits.

"I thought we were in a hurry," Ellie said. As soon as she stopped moving, the sweat running down her back started to feel chilly. She scratched herself against a wall, first making sure no human bones were protruding from it.

"Ms. Sato," Rodion said from several meters away. In the close space, even a whisper could be heard at some distance. "We must do maintenance. Better now when it is safe than later when closer to the objective. The environment may not be so... hospitable."

A pair of small close-set reflected eyes glanced at them from the top of the obelisk. Ellie never saw what it belonged to.

The cyborgs were inserting what looked like oven thermometers into each other's spines. They also wolfed down a paste mixture. Out of idle nerves, she tried to see how heavy the sphere they were carrying was. She couldn't even lift the barbells the thing was attached to.

"Do not injure yourself," Rodion said, pulling a tube out of his arm and flexing his bicep. Instead of blood seeping out, his hide-like skin closed over the opening. "The neutronium module's weight is greater than four hundred kilos. No ordinary soldiers could carry it."

Neutronium. Ellie had heard Melanie mention that before, but she had only a vague notion of what it was. On the other hand, she had been on the front lines of the last Mid-East war and produced a chronicle of it, which apparently even Mr. Putin enjoyed. She drew on her experience as a veteran of international intrigue and made an educated guess at the scheme.

"So, you're going to encapsulate the T-bomb."

Rodion just looked at her. His eyes were going through a maintenance cycle that caused them to become completely opaque, then white, then etched with crosshairs.

"It was my idea, of course," Wolfgang said.

"But who got you the neutronium?" Melanie shot back. "Not to mention the Human+ strike team? The Lichtstrom only has a few molecules of element zero. Ran's hockey buddy in Russia has been using it for years to insulate their mobile nuclear reactors."

The T-bomb couldn't be moved, couldn't be blown up. It had to go off. Ellie looked closer at the sphere. There was a seam down the middle. She guessed they would try to screw it over the T-bomb. If it looked like the one at Cesta Station, it was possible. This plan might actually work.

The cyborgs all sprung to their feet at once. Everyone froze. Faint sounds of music came from far down the passage ahead of them. As they listened, they also heard another sound. Ellie thought she knew what it was. She moved forward around a fat concrete pillar and was caught between shock and ironic laughter.

The noise accompanying the music was a pair of humans humping.

59

Eylül did not look happy.

To be fair to the man, Temir doubted he himself would be wearing a much different expression if he were the one suspended from the ceiling of a smuggler's shack by piano wire. Their host, Oleksandra, had stripped Eylül to the waist, taken a curved sail canvas needle, and threaded the wires through his pectoral muscles. She had then thrown the ends over a fat roof beam and winched the poor man up off the floor.

It turned out the Ukrainian militia commander Oleksandra did not have a long attention span or a great trust of Turks, even ones who had paid a partial ransom of twenty kilograms of gold.

The oafish troll of a woman would have liked to string him up too. Maybe she was wary of the strange symbiont additions to his body. Or maybe she didn't want to get a cramp in her neck looking up at him while they negotiated further.

"A certain person in the Kremlin has offered quite a bit of gold for a pair of foreign assassins who fled Russia," Oleksandra said, scratching the shaved sides of her head.

"How much?"

"More than the Grey Wolves have. Why should I not sell you?"

Temir stared back at her.

Eylül groaned as he twisted around slowly like a very hideous human wind chime.

Temir chafed against the inch-thick steel cables which cocooned his upper body and apparently kept him firmly secured. In his mind, three separate modes of action were competing for primacy.

"Speak, boss man." The woman grabbed the lapel of his horsehide coat. "I didn't hit you that hard. Can you hear out of this thing?"

She looked closely at his left ear. It had been regrown by the symbiont and was anatomically correct, but the skin was translucent like gelatin and shot through with veins full of black ichor.

"I can hear," he said, finally deciding what he would do. Not his first choice, but worth the risk. "And you should listen. You will never collect any money from Russia. Only by cooperating with us can you save Ukraine from the plague that will spread through this whole region."

This probably was not what she was expecting to hear.

"What are you talking about?"

"You know we are Grey Wolves. We control the Turkish government, its military, everything."

"If you are so powerful," she said, pushing Eylül's boots so he swung back and forth, "why is your friend my personal Mexican doll… the one you hit with a stick and candy falls out. What are they called?"

"Never heard of them," Temir said.

With one quick movement, he collapsed his left appendage flat against his body. Like an octopus, it had no bones. He could squeeze it through a keyhole or flatten it out to stop a bullet.

The steel ropes fell away. Before Oleksandra could grab her gun or even gasp, he kicked her legs out from under her. His tentacle lashed out and smothered the yell of the male guard by the door. Temir pulled the man down to lie next to the militiawoman. He could have killed both of them, but then they would not have heard the deal of a lifetime he was prepared to offer.

"Shh!" Temir cautioned. He placed one foot on Oleksandra's head and removed her pistol with his human right hand. "Firstly, you are going to confirm what I have told you with your people in Russia: that Moscow is in a state of disarray and panic. Then we are going to have a talk about the future of the Ukrainian empire, which could stretch as far as the oilfields of Western Siberia."

The toes of Eylül's boots jiggled in the air. The piano wire was really cutting into his chest muscles; gaping purple ultra-rare steak meat was poking out.

"Cut… me down," Eylül gasped.

"In a minute," Temir said, suddenly unimpressed with his friend, who had not spotted Oleksandra's ambush. "I am speaking with the lady. As Westerners say, *hang* in there."

60

ELLIE

Ellie was the closest to the "activity." With their enhanced hearing, Rodion and his cyborgs also heard the miniature orgy. One of them raised a weapon.

"Let me handle this," Ellie said. "If they see the whole bunch of us, they may freak out." Which could be fatal for the subterranean lovebirds.

As she carefully ventured forward, it came to Ellie that just swearing random people they met down here to secrecy wouldn't be enough. The cyborgs would insist on neutralizing anyone who could give them away. The stakes for millions of Europeans were so high she feared Sarge Bryan and Ran would be unable to object to collateral damage.

"What will you do?" a female cyborg said in halting English.

"Trust me," Ellie said, pushing through to the next passage. "I've worked in the fashion industry. I know how to handle naked horny people."

She declined the offer of a handgun from Rodion and went around a bend in the catacombs passage. An ember floated toward her night-vision visor. Had these sex maniacs set a fire? Wet as the place was, it was also enclosed; a blaze could asphyxiate people in seconds. She swatted at the flying spark.

The ember was cool, and it flew away from her hand. More were hovering by the low ceiling. They were fireflies. Like a curtain, they parted as Ellie stepped forward toward a rather less magical sight.

A glowing skeleton was on top of the green slave girl from *Star Wars*. Both cataphile perverts were covered in fluorescent body paint. The woman's buttocks were so precipitously perched on a limestone block that Ellie was afraid of doing them an injury if she startled them.

"Ahem."

No response, just more heaving and grunting.

"Yoo-hoo!"

The slave girl lost her balance and slid down the angled stone. The man yelled in fright and pain. He had received some injury to his nether regions. Ellie averted her eyes.

"Ow!" the man said in a flat, non-British accent. "What the fuck?"

"Sorry to interrupt, but I'm from the London *Juggernaut*."

"Huh?" the woman said. She tried to cover herself with the long rubber tentacles sewn onto her headgear. "*Êtes-vous fou?*"

Ellie fumed. They didn't have time for this. The clock was ticking down. It was Halloween season, and in the midst of airplane chaos and street riots, these two had decided to get freaky.

"You know, the London newspaper? I was doing a story about the catacombs when a bunch of ruffians jumped us. They said they were police, er, cataflics."

"So what?" the man said, thankfully putting on his baggy trousers. "It's only a hundred Euro fine for being down here, eh? I'm Canadian. They can't do shit to me."

"Well… that's the thing. I don't know if they were really police. They seemed a rough sort, criminal types. I didn't see any badges. *Ils pourraient être cata-prédateur.*"

That got the naked woman's attention. Drug dealers and rape gangs also lurked in the catacombs.

The horny youths dashed off. The music, which had just started a David Bowie set, cut off. Hanging down from the square-cut cavern roof were moldy strips of canvas cloth. These formed a sort of cat flap divider between this small chamber of love and the larger party area. Ellie peered through. The next room was empty. A single beer bottle spun on the floor.

"Come on," Ellie called back to her group. "I've cleared out the enemy."

The cyborgs pushed their loads through with increased vigor. Now that they had recharged, they seemed tireless.

"Quick thinking," Sarge Bryan said. "What kind of alien was that woman dressed as?"

"Sarge Bryan, you were *peeping*." Melanie slapped his shoulder. "You albino pervert. We'll have to put you on report and wash out your ocular video buffer with soap."

"Jus' being thorough for my report, Dr. Françoise, ma'am," Sarge Bryan said as he and Ran grinned like schoolboys.

Then they all wandered into the deep blue underground sea.

"Who did all this?" Ellie asked, looking up and across a mural thirty feet high and wider than she could take in with a single glance.

"This beats the hell out of the other famous catacombs mural, *La Plage*," Melanie said, also gazing up in awe.

Above the party grotto hung the maddest artwork Ellie could imagine down here. It was a 360-degree painting of the ocean, an island with palm trees, and a flawless blue sky. Someone must have worked months or years to finish the art, which was only visible by torchlight.

"Look down there," Melanie said, leaning precariously over some moldy ropes guarding a steep drop. "They've excavated right down to Lutetia, the Roman city."

Ellie looked down the central air shaft. It looked like a crosscut of the Pompeii ruins. There were columns and the outlines of stone walls belonging to houses or shops. It was a view down into Paris's deep past.

The only natural illumination came from seventy feet above; thin beams of light penetrated through holes in a storm drain.

That wasn't all that penetrated. Ellie got hit with a blob of something. She wiped off her visor. It was water.

"It's raining," Wolfgang said grumpily. "We have to move."

Easy for him to say, Ellie thought. It was the Russians who were heaving the neutronium sphere along. Rodion led as they filed out past the sea mural and away from the Roman ruins, back into the cramped tunnels.

Soon they came up against the site of a cave-in. The only opening was just over a yard wide, and at a pinch point in the middle, the height shrunk to perhaps eighteen inches. Melanie whipped out a small flying drone.

"Good news," she chirped as she looked at the video feed the small flyer sent back. "Once we get through here, the way is clear. We'll be back on the track outlined in the cataphiles' Nexus maps."

`"I prefer to call them the Aleph Composite Cartography."`

"The Russians will never make it through," Ellie whispered to Sarge Bryan.

"I'm sure they have a contingency plan," he said reassuringly, without specifying what that might be.

Rodion and his crew of five did not seem upset when they got the telemetry back from Melanie's drone. It had used a laser scanner to provide a 3D cross section of their route through the crawlspace, which was thirty meters long.

"*Kto chuvstvuyet sebya sil'nym?*" Rodion asked, and all the cyborgs chuckled with their mechanically enhanced voices. He turned to Ellie. "I asked them 'who feels strong'? Don't worry, we fix."

"Fixing" involved opening a hole in the female cyborg's midsection and draining some fluid off. Ellie assumed it was fluid not essential to the woman's life-support systems because she seemed fine when the incision on her stomach sealed itself.

Sarge looked impressed with the Russians' gear and operations. "DARPA's been working on tunnel warfare for years, but these guys are way ahead."

"Is also from personal experience," Rodion offered, seeming to be increasingly more at ease with Ellie and the others the deeper they got into the tunnel. "Before I was called to serve, I wasted a year of my youth in the catacombs of Odessa. They are ten times the size of these and much more… exciting."

"So then," Wolfgang said. "We have something in common."

Rodion looked at the oligarch and said, "Not much."

Ellie tried to picture the large Meccano soldier as a teenager without two hundred additional pounds of mechanical parts. Rodion mixed the borrowed fluid and poured the result into a dispensing canister.

"Ach," Wolfgang exclaimed when he gathered what was happening. "They are using acid to enlarge the way. Lutetian Limestone is susceptible to the addition of hydrogen ions."

With millions of tons of earth and the whole city above, dissolving supporting rocks seemed like a rather desperate plan.

"Small people through first," Rodion said. "Then we start."

Although she had always considered herself tall enough to be a runway model, Ellie was glad to be among the relatively puny people in their group. She went through first.

At the pinch point, she had to angle her head sideways to get through. At that very moment, the ground began to rumble.

What a time for an earthquake. Does Paris even get those?

"Trams above," Melanie said from behind her as she pushed on Ellie's feet. As though Ellie needed incentive to get to the light at the end of the very cramped tunnel.

They emerged inside a round space, which spoked out into five smaller but equally navigable tunnels. Ellie put her helmet back on and rebooted her night vision. She looked around. This large vaulted area was not from Roman times, it had been constructed out of modern concrete and rebar.

"No wonder this area caved in," Melanie said, pulling her pack and then an addled-looking Wolfgang out of the hole. "For decades the trams have been going by night and day, sending vibrations down the rocks."

"What is this place?" Ellie pointed. There was a strong new odor coming from a big flat area ahead. The smell mixed with the ever-present fine white dust, which she hoped ever so much had no component of crushed human bones in it.

"Air raid shelter," Wolfgang said. "Or Vichy bunker. A relic of Europe's dark past."

Seeing as Rapace's T-bomb would wipe out more people than all the continent's wars and the Black Death combined, Ellie thought the future could be much darker.

"It smells like, er… not nice."

"Dung," Melanie said, peering into the next chamber. "It's a mushroom farm. Champignons love horse manure. Seems deserted."

Ran and Sarge Bryan came through. The Scottish telecom oligarch had scraped his nose and was so filthy he looked like he had been rolled in a drunken alleyway punch-up.

Sarge Bryan looked back. "They're starting."

About fifteen meters back inside the tunnel, a cyborg had stretched himself out like a diver and was being pushed into place. With one arm working like a claw digging machine, he excavated until a second Russian could be pushed into position beside him.

The two of them braced themselves on all fours and pressed against the horizontal stone block above. Then Rodion approached the pinch point and used a mallet to chip away at the impeding stone above and below. He then sprayed something on the rock.

"Blech," Ellie said as noxious fumes came belching out of the hole. The cyborgs seemed not to mind. She took a few steps back and watched.

Minutes later, the acid had eaten enough of the stone that Rodion was able to retreat and push the neutronium sphere through. Even though it was on casters, it took all of them on the other side, even Wolfgang, to pull it through. Ellie moved her feet out of danger as the sphere rolled away from the low horizontal shaft.

Rodion came through next. The material of his uniform was steaming and dissolving; he shrugged, sloughing off bits of outerwear. Ellie thought she was getting better at reading cyborg expressions. He looked perturbed.

"The acid neutralizer is not working as quickly as planned," he said.

A fist-sized chunk of stone hurled out of the low gap. The next cyborg had tossed it ahead as he wormed his way through. The shaft was collapsing. The second and third Russian made it out. They had attached lines to the two holding up the passage so they could pull them out faster.

"Mikháy next!" Rodion ordered without hesitation. The rescue line went taut. His second-to-last team member was pulled free. There was a sharp crack.

"Now you, Tata. Stop being a slow-ass." More chunks of rock came flinging out, along with puffs of whitish dust. Tata's shaved head, her dusty shoulders, then her legs emerged. Her feet were nearly out when, with only a *clump* sound, the maw of the aperture closed down tight.

Tata howled. Her right leg ended at the ankle. The rest was inside in a flat-pressed stone sandwich. Tons of rock had let go and slammed down.

Without hesitation, Rodion extended his pike to four feet, he aimed the cutting axe head and slashed down. Tata's leg came free, minus her foot.

"Compromised limb protocol number three!" Rodion ordered, pulling the grimacing Tata over to a wall.

This is not good! They'd have to leave Tata here, Ellie thought. They'd be one cyborg down before they even got to the T-bomb.

In under a minute, blood and hydraulic fluid had stopped flowing from Tata's rudely amputated limb. Five minutes later, a wire-mesh prosthetic limb had been manufactured out of supplies in a medical kit. Rodion screwed it into place and then let Tata get on her feet by herself. She limped but was still able to move faster than Ellie or any of the unaugmented humans.

"There," Rodion said with gusto and pride, facing Ellie and Sarge Bryan. "This is Russian know-how matched with Russian spirit. Nothing can stop—"

His words were cut off as a shotgun blast tore into the back of his head. With a squishy thud, Rodion fell and landed face first on the muck-covered floor.

From the direction of the dung-smelling mushroom farm emerged a cluster of sweating, haggard figures. The lead man was swarthy fellow with a nose ring. He racked another shell into his gun and shouted, "You do not belong down here!"

61

Putin and Zvena exited the sequestered communications room and returned to the Universal Integrated Situation Room. The president was smiling right up to his deep-set blue eyes.

"Americans, they are so practical," Putin said, rubbing his hands and huffing on them to keep them warm. Even under dozens of feet of concrete in the command center they felt the effects of the intense Arctic blizzard they had engineered. "Short-term thinkers, but practical."

After Bordeaux and the information the American soldier had gotten out of Cesta, it had been easy for Putin to convince the American president of two things.

First, that Russia would handle the situation in Europe. The Euro Army had turned against NATO and US forces in Europe. Turkey had turned traitor against NATO as well, partnered with Iran, and was playing its own game. Only Russia's integrated military machine had any chance. Any interference would lead to disaster.

Second, Putin agreed to help get as many Americans as he could out of Europe, across the Atlantic where possible or to designated safe zones.

"It has always been my dream to send thousands of Americans to Siberia," Putin said. "Now it is coming true."

"Let me coordinate the effort," Zvena said. "Intelligence reports say that it is only jihadi lunatics and fanatic elements of the Pangean military from the European Army that are controlling the airports in Berlin, Hamburg, and Warsaw. We will destroy them."

Putin nodded thoughtfully. Zvena felt his commander was giving him the courtesy of considering, but not acquiescing to, his suggestion; he led Zvena past the wall of video screens over to a mobile heater.

"Washington also confirmed our suspicions about our Turkish friends," Putin said. "They and the Iranians are amassing armor near the Bulgarian border."

The Turkish motivation for attacking Moscow became clear to Zvena. "If Europe is destroyed, they mean to fight the Pangeans for control."

"Yari Semyonovich," Putin said, addressing him by the friendly patronymic version of Zvena's name suitable to a cocktail party, "do you recall your strategy with the Kodiak bear?"

Zvena rubbed the scar tissue on his knee. Even after so many years, the cold made him feel it. "I persuaded the bear to bite. Then I crushed its skull."

"There are three or four scenarios likely to take shape, depending if Rodion and our friend Dr. Licht are successful in neutralizing or limiting the effect of the T-bomb. In each case, bear slayer, our immediate and long-term goals are served by you making a trip south, to Ukraine."

62

The maniac with the shotgun and the nose ring who had blown the back of Rodion's head apart stood in the tunnel entrance hyperventilating.

"You-don't-belong!" he yelled again in heavily accented English.

Very slowly, Ellie moved her hand toward her blood-spattered visor; it was covered with poor Rodion's gore. The huge cyborg was lying three feet away from her. His body was motionless, as stiff as a seven-foot-tall piece of limestone rock.

"*Bouge pas!*" said another voice. Ellie couldn't tell whether it was a man or a woman.

Someone shouted something else in another language; it could have been Arabic.

The killer's flashlight dashed over them, temporarily washing out Ellie's night-vision equipment.

"Everyone chill," said the edgy but calm voice of Sarge Bryan. "It's too close quarters for a gunfight. We can work this out."

"Fuck you, white ass," said Nose Ring. He was swarthy with a fat gut that hung over his camo-patterned pants.

The gunman jumped back a step when he saw the five remaining Russians.

After freezing in place for a second, one by one the cyborgs all dropped their guns on the ground. That was the last thing Ellie expected them to do. Were they really afraid?

"*Baise ta grand-mère.* What are you… people doing?" Nose Ring asked accusingly. "You are here to take my crop?"

He pushed the hot barrel of the gun under Ellie's nose.

"It's ready for harvest," Nose Ring psycho said. "You were thinking: there's all this confusion above, what a good time to steal the opium mushrooms, huh?"

Ran Oliphant glanced at one of the cyborgs' guns. Tata kicked it away from him with her wire replacement foot.

"We are sorry," Tata said to the killer in a Russian-accented monotone. "We made a mistake. We are workers, er, not fighters. Please let us live."

Three more drug farmers took positions around the room. Ellie still could not see clearly. Only one of them, a ratty-looking female, had a pistol. The other two had spiky bladed machetes.

"Well, you know, I am *pas sauvage*, not a savage, yes?" Nose Ring, the leader, said. He aimed the shotgun toward the cyborg woman. "We will see what sort of workers you are. These people brought you here to harvest and carry away my crop quickly, huh? These fine fellows and this white ghost."

He shined a light on Ran and Wolfgang.

"What are you?" Nose Ring said, holding the light on the albino American. "Are you bourgeois drug dealers? Did your supply dry up because of the troubles up there, so you decide to rip me off?"

One of the machete wielders tried to lift a cyborg weapon but could barely get it off the ground. He let it fall.

"Okay, my friend," Ran said, "you've got us. We can pay a ransom. We know when we're beat."

The gang leader sprang forward and booted Ran in the midsection. A gasp of breath escaped him. Ran fell back.

"How you have it backward," the thug said. He craned his ear up comically toward the manhole cover seventy feet above them. Down through holes came scant light, more drizzling rain, and a cacophony of riot noises. "You think your phony 'electron money' is worth anything anymore? Listen… listen… listen!"

Sirens were punctuated by flashbang grenades and rifle shots.

"Up there. That's the future calling," Nose Ring said, panting. "The only thing… only thing matters anymore is what we got. We're in with *le H*, the Romani, you know. After all that shit falls down for the bankers, politicians, lawyers, judges, bourgeois scum… You can hear… it's crumbling now. When it falls, we the animals of the night and the underground will rise up and take over."

With a free hand, he grabbed Melanie's breast and violently squeezed it until he was sure he had hurt her.

"You two whores, we will keep," he said, swinging his flashlight over to Ellie and then to the very passive group of cyborgs. "Where did you *mécaniques* come from?" he demanded suspiciously.

"We worked in… Aluminum Dunkerque," Tata said, as though she were reading out a lunch menu. "Our parents sold us at a young age, and we were modified to do heavy jobs. We are glad to be liberated. We will serve you well, sir."

"You will. What is your name?"

"Tata," she said, staring down at the man.

"I am Basem. It means 'person who smiles.' I bet I can make you smile, you *chatte mécanique.*"

That was probably the first time anyone had called six-foot-eight Tata a "mechanical pussy."

A little surprised at his good fortune, the leader then turned to Ran, Sarge Bryan, and Wolfgang, who were in a corner of the antechamber leading to the mushroom grow op.

"As for you, you exploiting capitalist swine." Basem slung his shotgun on a frayed leather strap and pulled out a knife. "I am going to cut your tendons, open you up, and fill you with dung. Then you can do something useful for once in your sorry lives and feed my next crop of—"

Ellie had not actually seen a Human+ soldier in berserker mode before. Back at the Lichtstrom, Zvena had kept them mostly under control and fighting in a disciplined way so as not to damage the space elevator's ground station. Here there was nothing to be damaged.

With Basem and his three accomplices anticipating the fun of gutting the two oligarchs and an African albino, no one noticed Rodion's not-so-dead body rise up and swing his long pike so fast the end made a snapping sound even as it struck the gang leader.

Ellie blinked and realized Rodion had flipped a switch and turned his solid pike into a whip-like instrument with dozens of joined segments. The blow spun Basem right around, then the metal whip wrapped around the neck of the pistol-toting gangster lady. With a twangy *snip*, the weapon pulled her head clean off her shoulders.

Tata merely tapped her remaining foot and pursed her lips. The other cyborgs also stood still.

Watching the last two thugs get taken down was like seeing a forklift that had learned deadly kung fu. Rodion, the back of his head dripping red and green fluids, lunged left and then right, skewering each one through the torso with rigid fingertips.

"Mensch!" Wolfgang exclaimed. "Rodion, you're alive. You might have told us."

Rodion stepped on the shotgun, crushing it. The gang leader Basem was still crawling, despite a gaping wound crosscutting his shoulder blades.

"I could not risk damage to any member of the party," Rodion said. "I had to be like the possum of America."

He lifted Basem up with one hand.

"I-I'll… I'm…" he sputtered, conscious but no longer able to control his limbs, likely due to a severed spinal cord.

"I do not care," Rodion said, dragging the inert fellow over to Tata. "All you are to me is a rude man, disrespecting your betters and having no regard for the fair sex. Tata, berserker now!"

Rodion held the thug's bearded swarthy face up. Tata leaned forward, her whole body vibrating with bloodlust.

"You said you like to see her smile. Enjoy."

Tata opened her mouth as wide as she could. Basem screamed. She clamped down on the lower half of his head, her viselike jaws crunching everything between them.

Seconds later, her energized rage dissipated as quickly as she had activated it. Tata let Basem fall to the wet concrete floor. His remains looked like a GI Joe doll that had been used to tease a pit bull. Delicately, Tata pursed her lips and spat out a few of Basem's teeth. Ran Oliphant forced a smile onto his face and handed her a handkerchief with which to wipe her mouth.

"Damn, Mr. Rodion," Sarge Bryan exclaimed. "We thought you were Tango Uniform for sure."

A male Russian cyborg with a medical kit wiped down the back of Rodion's head and cut away a loose flap of skin to reveal a metal skull plate. He put on some material that looked like an overcooked crepe. The patch of artificial skin stuck on by itself.

"I signaled my comrades by text that they must stand down and appear passive," Rodion said. "Sorry for frightening the ladies. It was the best plan given the unstable nature of the enemy and close quarters we were in."

Rodion moved his head from side to side to make sure he still had full range of motion.

"Man, they sure build 'em tough in Russia," Sarge said.

"If was shotgun shell front of my head, maybe is problem," Rodion said. "Back of head, not so much."

He slapped hands with his people, then got serious. "We must make up time. Check gear, check selves, on mission! For the Motherland!"

Melanie straightened her bosom and gave the lecherous Basem's remains a half-hearted kick as she passed. They left the gore-spattered chamber of death and walked into the more inviting dung heap festooned with genetically engineered opioid mushrooms.

Ellie held her Hermes bag close.

"They wouldn't survive, Basem and these people, not even down here, would they?" she said, almost to herself.

"No. Tyr quark radiation can pass through a million miles of solid lead."

"Good. These are not the people I want to see inheriting Paris, or anywhere."

At the exit from the former bomb shelter that had been turned into a nefarious greenhouse, Melanie grabbed a few of the mushrooms.

"These might be nice to study," she said as they followed the cyborgs down another graffiti-spattered corridor. "It would take years to get a plant to grow a medical-grade anesthetic. This one could be grown anywhere in places where there's very little access to modern medicine."

"Melanie, please," Ran chided. "One plan to save the world at a time."

Melanie stashed the fungus in her bag. "I can multitask."

63

ELLIE

A few twists and turns later, after ducking around a six-foot pillar that someone had carved into a penile-looking version of the Eiffel Tower, Ellie glanced back. The opioid mushrooms, the dung they fed on, and the four dead bodies, and the collapsed tunnel with Tata's severed foot inside were out of sight. Had that actually happened?

Ellie looked at the back of Rodion's head, which had taken a blast from a shotgun. It was stitched together with metal staples but only looked mildly more gruesome than before.

Ellie ducked through a breach in the walls made by cataphiles who had been equipped with power tools. This led into a dry, straight, and relatively spacious telecom tunnel. Thick fiber-optic cables hung from eight-foot-high ceilings.

Tata caught up to Ran and returned the badly bloodstained handkerchief. She smiled wanly down at him.

"Ah, please keep the handkerchief. I have plenty," he said, sounding slightly nervous. "Ms. Tata, was it?"

"Please call me Tata Ivanova, and it's Miss."

Was the cyborg lady flirting?

Ellie decided to rescue her fake sugar daddy from the attentions of a woman twice his size. "Say, Tata," she said, "how's your foot?"

She turned her helmeted head and raised a scarred eyebrow. "It has had a crushing amputation. I will make do with the spare until we get back to Russia," she said shortly as a relieved-looking Ran stepped quickly up the line and caught up with Sarge Bryan.

What Ellie really wanted to know was: What was it like to literally bite a horrid person's face off as though it were a tough piece of schnitzel? Someone who should certainly be on the menu was the mastermind of the T-bomb, President Rapace.

Instead Ellie asked, "What's this berserker thing? Should we be worried about it?"

"Squishy little people should always worry," the Human+ woman said, peering behind them, looking hungrily for associates of Basem who might be following.

Then Tata laughed. "Just messing with you. *Bez uma* mode has only recently perfected. Before, it was too crazy."

"Too crazy, huh?"

"The extra burst of energy through all systems was sometimes difficult to shut off. Caused damage to enemy as well as our own people and equipment. Now, most bugs are solved."

Tata looked at Ellie's orange leather bag.

"Hermes, huh?"

"You like shopping?"

"Mostly online." Tata extended a metal-tipped finger and delicately peered inside her tote. "Your mechBrain, she sounds Jewish."

"I beg your pardon?"

"What? Jewish is not right?" Tata said. "Israeli is better? There are many Russians in Israel, my grandfather too."

"Oh." Ellie thought of the carnage of the orbital bombardment of the Holy Land, the insurgency, the pestilence which was still killing vulnerable people there despite vaccines. "I hope he's okay."

"He is tough bird, like me," Tata said, perhaps reading her expression.

"Ms. Sato, I read your book *The 96-Hours War*. You helped Israel, now I am glad to help you."

Chisel marks gouged horizontally along the walls started to angle sharply down. Ellie's foot made a splash in the dark.

"I hope your mechBrain is waterproof."

The water got colder and deeper. The catacomb tunnels were all the same temperature. Ellie guessed this was new water, rainwater.

"Double time." From way ahead, Sarge Bryan shot a glance back to the end of their short column. "We got to get in the sewers quick as we can."

Ellie guessed that was as comforting a thing as she was going to hear during this journey under France's capital. She was looking down to make sure of her footing. Suddenly a big fat rat swam between her legs. It scrambled to a dry spot and started to groom itself meticulously. She didn't have time to shudder. The floor began sloping down even more steeply; water was rising quickly.

Fortunately, just before a fork in their path, there was a less-wet spot. Sarge Bryan and Rodion stood there debating which way to proceed.

"This is faster," the cyborg said, pointing left. That way looked more pedestrian friendly. Maybe this was part of the tourist area of the catacombs, Ellie thought.

"We may run into people."

"So they run into us. This is imperative mission."

No one could be allowed to raise the alarm. They had to assume Rapace's security forces and the Pangeans were extra vigilant as their doomsday device powered up to its maximum deadly yield.

Ellie waded forward and got up on the angled slab of concrete with the men. They had to decide and move.

"Why don't Melanie and I go first?" Ellie suggested. A sneeze she felt building turned into a cough. Was that vinegar she smelled in the air coming down the tunnel?

"Yes," Melanie piped up. "We can shoo people away before the cyborgs come out."

"Worst case," Ellie said, coughing, "if we run in to any random people, we can dope them with those mushrooms. They won't remember a thing. Besides, there's clearly rioting happening up in the streets."

As soon as they decided to go left through the tourist area, a rapid series of sharp explosions came from up ahead. People were yelling. Sirens sounded louder. They were closer to the surface. The vinegar smell became stronger, and Ellie's lungs tightened up for no reason at all. She leaned against a lichen-covered wall.

"Tear gas," Rodion said, inhaling deeply.

A blue ceramic street marker, which looked homemade, said, *"Avenue du Colonel Roi-Tanguy."*

"I have filtered air." Tata offered Ellie a breathing mask. The burning sensation in her throat moved down into her lungs and stomach, making her afraid she was going to start vomiting.

"No"—*heff*—"thanks. I'm good." Ellie gasped, not wanting to appear weak. She was a war veteran after all. "Save it for when we need it."

Tata clapped her on the back and smiled.

The human bones they encountered here were neatly organized. It was like a morbid interior designer/grave robber had gone wild. After what they had walked through, it was hardly frightening at all. More like a children's playhouse, except for the fact that all the skulls with their watchful eyeholes were real.

Up in the streets, Paris was in chaos. Gunshots were now ringing out steadily, dully penetrating to their level of the catacombs. Ellie wondered what it was like in other European cities.

With the airports shut down, people would realize they were trapped. Video from the Bordeaux area had to be getting out. She was glad she had gotten her parents and Attie Jr. onto the submarine. Should she have gotten on too? What could she do here? Most times she felt like more of a hindrance than a help.

They passed a roped-off section marked "Do Not Enter" at the end of the tourist area.

Ellie gratefully inhaled big lungfuls of stale but teargas-free catacomb air. She whispered into the Hermes sack. "The T-bomb, it won't affect rats or animals?"

"There's no indication it would. For an ultimate weapon of mass destruction, Rapace's team did not gather much test data on its effects before deploying it," Miss Aleph said in a condescending tone. "At least Miri Drach spent years creating the Khóshekh plague."

"*Verdammt!*" Wolfgang cursed at a big stone blocking their way. It appeared to have been intentionally pushed into place to stop tourists from going deeper.

"No time to go around," Rodion said. "Bryan and Ran, you go back. Watch if anyone comes."

They declined the offer of a big assault rifle but took a pistol. That left Ellie and the others staring at the big boulder.

"I don't suppose you can melt this with acid?" Melanie asked doubtfully, examining the barrier. "The surface looks all feldsparry and quartzie."

"There is power coupling with high voltage," Rodion said. "We break through. Put your visors down."

Although there was plenty of light from the fluorescents behind them, everyone, even the cyborgs, flicked their face shields down.

Rodion turned to his crew. "Who wants a headache?"

Tata put her hand up first but was disqualified due to having lost a limb. One of the male cyborgs who was a little smaller than Rodion volunteered. Tata was instead dispatched to rip out some electrical cables.

These sparked when attached to nodes on the volunteer's shoulders. The cyborg put his pike on the granite stone. His hands made sparks and attached with high magnetic force onto the hollow shaft. Judging by the growing hum of the cables, Ellie guessed they were waiting for a surge to build up. About a minute later, the kneeling Russian nodded.

Rodion inserted a projectile into the open end of the pike shaft. It was immediately caught in an electrical current, rocketed down the shaft, and exploded against the rock face. Ellie felt a sting on the back of her hand from a rock fragment.

About six minutes later, dust and a burned electrical cable smell filled the narrow passageway. Then a big chunk of granite blew out the other side.

Rodion stopped feeding bullets into the pike. The volunteer collapsed as the electrical cables were pulled off his back.

"Projectile-assisted hyperdrill, Human+ style," Rodion said by way of explanation. He lifted the volunteer back to his feet. The electric connector plugs on his shoulders were still smoking.

Using pikes and bare hands, the cyborgs cleared the broken stone away. Ran and Sarge Bryan came running back.

"Some guys wearing yellow vests came down looking for shelter," Ran said, panting. He paused to blow blood out of his nose where someone had obviously punched him. "We saw them off, but they might come back with friends."

Rodion ushered everyone through the broken gap. Away from the noise of the riot, Ellie again felt like they had dropped into a place of strange tranquility and subtle horrors much different but no less deadly than what was going on in the streets above.

They had gone maybe two hundred paces when they got to an open space. The ceiling was not high, but the area was so wide that the middle of the ceiling sagged. A chiseled sign dabbed over with glowing paint said:

opéra d'os

"The Opera of Bones," Wolfgang said, picking up one of the instruments. "Not quite the London Philharmonic."

All through the cavernous space, there were thousands of human leg bones. In the corners, they were stacked to the ceiling. In the center, they had been fashioned into every kind of instrument possible: ghastly flutes, tormented violins, sinister drums. Ellie did not want to know what kind of hide was stretched over those. Had she seen a navel on them, she definitely would have upchucked.

The next tunnel was long and straight, with grating at knee level every ten meters. From those grates, Ellie heard fast breathing, the padding of many feet, and snarling. The farther they went, the louder the noises got.

Ellie bent down to look. Saliva-dripping jaws and teeth bashed against the grating.

"Dogs?" she said, moving away despite the thick metal barrier.

Wolfgang looked.

"Yah, in a tunnel parallel to ours. They might be deer-hunting hounds," he said. "They are trained to run down their prey, swarm around it, and bring it down. They do not attack people... very often."

"What are they doing here?" Ellie said, looking ahead to make sure the gratings separating them from the other passage were all secure.

"Who knows. Maybe they got loose in the confusion, fled the tear gas, and came down here." Wolfgang smiled, revealing rather long canine teeth. "They sound hungry."

Ellie stuck close to Sarge Bryan and Rodion until the baying and the snarling could no longer be heard.

Despite the prospect of being immersed in human waste, Ellie was relieved when they finally go to the entrance of the classic Parisian sewer system.

They quickly broke through a portcullis-style gate to enter the tourist zone. The waterway was as wide as a single-lane road. Tour boats were tied farther up the river of effluent.

"People pay money to visit here?" Ellie asked.

Melanie nodded. "It's a lot like Venice, except they don't pretend there's no poop in the water."

After passing by a display of some wax-museum-style mannequins of sewer workers, they broke through another locked gate to get back into the off-limits section. Here the water was the coldest and fastest moving that Ellie had yet encountered.

"We're going under the Seine," Melanie said, turning her digital map to align it with the streets and landmarks above. "I hope it hasn't rained too much. This is the only way into the New Catacombs under Élysée Palace on the Right Bank."

Turned out it had rained pretty bloody hard. Single file, they stepped along a narrow concrete walkway, which ran beside the sewer canal. Water lapped freely over Ellie's feet.

Modern waste pipes made out of PVC and metal angled down from near the roof of the arched tunnel. Ellie hoped that Parisian sinks, and especially their toilets, were all connected to these. That thought got flushed out from her mind when a wad of toilet paper tumbled out of a two-foot-wide pipe set lower in the wall.

Melanie shrugged. "They've been building the system since the 1300s. Some drains are attached to the new system. Most older residences still use *les toilettes classiques.*"

Melanie started to giggle, then stopped when her boot got enmeshed in a brown blob with long bristly hair sticking out of it. They trudged on.

The water kept rising.

64

Where's Wolfgang?" Ran's irritated voice echoed along the sewer.

Ellie looked around. Unlike the catacombs, the big ancient Parisian sewers were much straighter, but there were still enough bends and junctions that it was impossible to keep track of everyone all the time.

"I was up front," Sarge Bryan said. His eyes gleamed through air so thick with humidity that Ellie's face visor kept fogging up. "I thought you were watching him."

Ellie flipped her visor up. A moment later, she heard some mumbling coming from a maintenance alcove.

She thought she better call out to the others before charging ahead. "Here!"

"Ach," Wolfgang said as she came around the corner, looking like a kid caught with his hand in a candy jar. "I was just taking a breath of fresh air."

He pointed up. Eight feet above was a manhole cover.

"Don't even think about runnin'," Sarge Bryan said, zooming in on the hatch above. "That cover is welded shut, just so you know."

Ellie thought of something. "Wait a sec. Back in Amsterdam he called his goons. I thought I heard him talking to someone just now."

Wolfgang stared savagely at Ellie.

"How could I be? Look, you have all my Lichtwerks communication equipment, and who would I be speaking to?" Wolfgang stepped back into the stream of effluent. "We're all on the same side."

Rodion motioned for them to stop nattering and hurry up.

"Just a sec," Ran said, always suspicious of their mercurial sort-of prisoner. "Bryan, Miss Aleph, check him over. Has he made any transmissions?"

`"I didn't detect anything."`

Bryan looked him over, scanning Wolfgang like an airport x-ray machine. He only had a flip phone on him.

"Don't take it, please," Wolfgang said. "It was a gift from my niece and has a video of her singing in the Eurovision contest. It comforts me in these troubled times."

Ran put the phone back into its waterproof pouch and gave it back. He probably did not want to upset Wolfgang too much in case they needed his help when they finally got to the T-bomb.

"No tricks," Ran warned. He gestured to the female cyborg. "I think Tata is still hungry."

The water was now up past Ellie's knees. They had to wade hard against the current to catch up to the cyborgs.

"We're right under the Seine," Melanie said. "Isn't it exciting?"

Something bumped into Ellie's rear and stuck there. She wiped her visor and then remembered the fastidious rat she'd seen earlier. Before deciding whether to use her hands to push the object away, she looked.

"Ah!"

It was a fat hairy hand. Severed at the wrist with a ring on the pinkie, it bobbed against her bum. Ellie gyrated her hips to the side and let it float way.

"Yes, Melanie," Ellie said with a shudder, watching as something moved on the ragged wrist stump. It was a baby eel or a big leech sucking away at the juicy meat. "This is madly exciting."

A few dozen meters later, there was a drainpipe partially clogged with what looked like pink suspenders. These turned out to be intestines.

"Things must be getting insane up in the streets," Ellie said, listening for sounds of carnage from above.

"I miss the Middle East."

From up ahead, there came a fierce industrial-scale frothing and blubbering. It sounded like sounds made by a giant who was drowning, over and over.

When Ellie caught up she found Ran, Wolfgang, Sarge Bryan, and the cyborgs all clustered on ledges on either side of a solid brick overhang. Below these brickworks flowed a rushing stream of water. It slammed into a hole too small for the incoming volume. Some got pushed back and then reversed by the torrential flow coming in which created the monstrous regurgitating roar.

"It had to rain," Ran said.

Rodion shrugged and jumped in. He caught himself on the lip of the overhang before being sucked under.

"It is not bad," the Russian said. "For us. For you, maybe it is a problem. We will make a cyborg chain underwater to the other side. Tata, in!"

The one-footed woman jumped in and disappeared under the water. Tata sent back data, which appeared in Melanie's really grimy-looking rollout viewscreen.

"Oh," she exclaimed with completely unwarranted glee. "I get it. This is like a ginormous 'U' bend in a toilet. As we go through, we'll have to hold our breath."

Ellie looked longingly at the cyborg's respirator tubes. "Can't we just share those?"

"No," said Rodion. "They are attached to us, and we will be busy pulling you along; also the inhalation of an unregulated airflow would virtually guarantee drowning in this scenario."

Tata's hand reached up out of the water. Rodion grabbed it, steadying his comrade.

"I'll go first," Ran said gallantly as the rest of the cyborgs jumped into the rushing flow to make a Human+ underwater chain.

"No," Rodion advised. "If the women faint from hypoxia, it will be easier for men to push their limp bodies through."

It was decided that Ellie was most at risk of becoming a limp female body and having to be pushed through. Melanie had apparently been able to hold her breath during the full length of *Mission Impossible* underwater sequences.

"If I had a mouth, I would keep it shut really tightly," Miss Aleph advised.

Ellie cinched her Hermes bag tight so the AI's cylinder would not get lost in the flow. Miss Aleph's handset was supposed to be waterproof to twenty-five meters.

Ellie took greedy breaths of putrid, humid air and then dunked down.

Gah! As soon as water sloshed completely over her head, she fought against the urge to expel the precious air in her lungs.

Sarge Bryan's big hand pushed her in the right direction. The flow was wild because half the water was slopping back and creating a countercurrent. After a few seconds, she could not tell which way was up. Not that it mattered. When her hand reached up, all she could feel were slimy bricks and frothing water. No air pocket.

A steely grip larger than Sarge Bryan's caught her and pulled her along. That must be Tata. As Ellie swirled past, she thought her foot hit the cyborg's injured leg and felt her slip.

Sorry!

Tata let her go.

A moment later, her forearm was caught by the next cyborg in the line. Her helmet bumped against a metal pole. The Russians were probably using their metal pikes as bolsters in the rushing current.

Then she went on to the next Russian. Her lungs were burning. She started counting down to the limit of what she could take.

Five, four, three, two, one…

Zero.

Zero, *uh… zero?*

Zero, zero, zero!

65

Minus zero
M There was a number… that came after that…
Minus ???

Finally she burst to the surface, opened her mouth as wide as she could and inhaled. She was sure that if air could come in through her ears it was doing that. She wiped soaked hair and a stream of water away from her forehead and looked around. This was not as easy as it had been a few minutes ago due to the big dark asphyxia spots she was seeing mixed in with the indistinct stone pattern of her brand-new surroundings, all of it whirling around as she spun about in the eddy of the huge drain outlet. She had to gasp in half a dozen breaths before she was able see clearly by the light of a fluorescent lantern one of the cyborgs had tossed up on the concrete rim of the pool.

In rapid succession, Ellie realized that one, she had not drowned; two, she was in dire need of the most powerful antibiotics known to medical science because of what she had swallowed; and three, it was her floating body, not the ceiling, which was swirling around clockwise.

On her next turn around the artificial whirlpool, she saw a rusted metal handrail. She grabbed it; there was a rusty scraping sound, and it came halfway loose.

Coughing and turning over on all fours, she struggled up a stone step and looked more closely. She was hanging on to the handlebar of an abandoned bicycle. Its rusted ringer had dragged along the concrete and made the scraping noise, which reverberated through the chamber. Breathing heavily, she clawed her way farther up. By the harsh white light, Ellie could see calcified spokes, slime tracks of sagging rubber tires, a rotted-away seat, and an old-style basket.

She was the first one through. She hadn't expected the experience to be so... wet. The good news, she told herself as she looked for a firmer handhold, was that with the influx of rainwater, the fecal content of what she had swallowed and inhaled was probably not immediately fatal.

She pulled herself all the way onto the ledge. Below the surface of the pool, the cyborgs' shoulder lights were flickering as they moved. Melanie was the next to pop up. She did a breaststroke to the side.

"You—" Ellie started to say.

Melanie held up her hand; with bulging eyes, she stared at a timer on her wristwatch as her face turned an alarming shade of purple. After about a minute, she let out a gasping breath.

"There... did it, finally beat Tom Cruise's record," Melanie said while heaving air into her lungs. "All... all it took... was being plunged into Parisian sewage."

Ellie quietly concluded that having Wolfgang along as a backup scientist was not such a bad idea. Dr. Melanie Françoise, PhD was as certifiable a loon in her own way as Ms. China was in hers.

Wolfgang came up next. With his white hair and dyed black goatee, he looked a bit like a toilet brush. Ellie and Melanie caught his clothes as he swirled past and pulled him up.

Ran, Sarge Bryan, and then Rodion popped up. Ellie looked around; this section was cleaner and almost placid, probably because of its segregation from the main lines. Four spillways took the overflow into all corners of the compass. The only way forward was a large, new-looking oval-shaped tunnel.

Tata, the last two Russians, and the heavy neutronium sphere emerged.

"Say, Rodion," Sarge Bryan said, for the first time betraying fatigue by flopping on the concrete like an albino flounder, "what... what are your orders if the human minus soldiers can't keep up with you Human+ guys?"

Rodion considered a moment as he stowed his snorkel tube.

"The president himself has tasked us with finishing the mission to neutralize the T-bomb at all costs. We would continue without you." He loomed over the American and reached down a big augmented hand to help Sarge Bryan up onto his feet. "But it would not be nearly as much fun."

"This is a new section," Ran said as they moved through the only exit from the rotunda encompassing the swirling pool. "We're under the Right Bank."

"Yes," Rodion said. "Our map shows details of the New Catacombs after they were secretly expanded with money and workers diverted from sewer upgrades."

"In that case, we should be careful of—"

"Traps!" Sarge Bryan and Tata said it nearly together.

They were at the head of the line, near where the sewer joined a somewhat hidden but relatively inviting and open new section of tunnel.

Ellie approached cautiously. She shivered a bit but had doused her eyes with clean water and was chewing an energy bar. Somehow, the Derrida fan had been here too. Spray painted on the ceiling was:

There is nothing outside of language —Derrida

"That looks too easy," Sarge Bryan was saying as he angled his head into the next chamber.

Rodion studied the section of gleaming new white tilework.

"Too easy," he concluded as well.

Wolfgang had taken off his shirt, revealing really interesting patches of back hair.

He crept forward. "Ach, even I can see two… no, three tripwires. They are so easy to defeat; a group will be sucked in and then *crrck*! Some well-hidden ambuscade will snare us all. These fiendish Pangeans will add our bones to the ghoulish sculptures in these New Catacombs."

This route was a carnivorous pitcher plant for humans. It looked inviting, but once you were in, there was no way out. *Then how would they…* Ellie smelled something. It was vaguely familiar and had nothing to do with excrement or rotting garbage.

"Tata, you smell that?"

The cyborg shook her rectangular head. "Berserker mode stuffs up the sinus."

"Here," Ellie whispered, pointing to a grate. "What is that?"

Melanie came up beside her. She dropped to all fours and sniffed like a bloodhound with blonde dreadlocks. Then she got up and nudged Ellie's shoulder. "Oh, c'mon," she said softly. "You went to Oxford, right? How do you not recognize the odor of cannabinoids and terpenes being vaped?"

Quickly, and with hardly a sound at all, the Russians leveled weapons at every aperture around them. Tata made a chicken strangling motion with her hands. It probably meant "be quiet." Melanie stopped wringing out her extra-long hair and tucked it under a wide headband.

Rodion texted something. Miss Aleph caught the signal and relayed it to the screen of her waterproof handset.

Perimeter guards. There must be a quick access for them to get up to the intruder kill-room trap. Find it!

They retraced their steps leading to the booby-trapped dead end. Ran thought it was curious that an overflow funnel was perched where it would never get wet. More vaping smell came from there.

The fake drain was quickly revealed to fold back in several places, allowing two men, or one Rodion, to descend a series of concrete steps.

Sarge Bryan spotted a pressure sensor near the last step. Melanie used a hairpin to keep the circuit connected while a cyborg handed Rodion a small box. He set it down, and it unfurled itself into a mechanical centipede. Without a sound, the steel-legged insect skittered forward. At corners, it paused and extended its antennae around them before proceeding.

The crawling drone sent data back to Tata's wrist monitor. The picture quality was not high-definition. But the audio was sharp and translated the French into Russian and English in a caption display running under the video picture.

"That's enough. Put that away. If we're caught we'll join the wall decorations."

Three figures stood in front of a ghastly mural. It was more terrible because it was obvious the bones in it were fresh. The figures wore dark fatigues and looked like rough customers but had their weapons lazily stacked along the wall. One fellow put away his vaping device.

"*Nothing else to do down here.*"

The third one of three gestured behind them. Tata's display indicated that was north.

"*We should get out of here. I can do arithmetic. We will not all fit into the aircraft he has waiting in the palace square.*"

"*[garbled] is less than twenty-four hours. My sister was near Bordeaux. This is real, not just a fantasy. We have to be thousands of kilometers away when that thing goes off.*"

"*Your sister is out, yes?*"

"*She texted me from the Congo, bloody shithole.*"

"*The Pangean has a plan. We evacuate when we're told to and not a minute sooner— Hey! Something bit me.*"

Seconds later, one of the three figures pitched backward and landed heavily on the ground, writhing in agony in an apparent epileptic fit. The other two were trying to assist him and did not notice Ran and Sarge Bryan sneak up on them. After a brief struggle, they subdued the two guards.

Rodion came forward, looking down at the man having a seizure.

"He is finished," he said and stepped on the man's head, putting his full weight on it until it made a *pop-crack* sound. The man who had been poisoned by the mechanical centipede stopped squirming. "You. Who is the Pangean? What are the entry codes?"

"We... we don't know any Pangean," the one Ran was holding blurted out.

Tata dug a small human thigh bone out of the wall mural and handed it to Rodion. He broke it in half and gouged both the man's eyes out. Before he could scream, a cyborg knee came up and pummeled him under the jaw, destroying the front of his head.

"He also is finished. How about you?" Rodion turned to the vaper.

A few moments later, they had a very good idea of the layout of the Pangeans' lair. They left the last fellow alive, tied up and with a pet to keep him company.

"Don't move," Tata said as she gently deposited the metal centipede down the man's shirt. "It is resting now but will sense your movement and it will bite."

Past the first hatchway-style door, which reminded Ellie of doors on an ocean liner, there was another guard station. Empty.

"They must be in evac mode," Ran said.

"What was that about the Congo?" Sarge Bryan asked.

"Ah, this is an essential part of the Pangeans' plan," Wolfgang said.

Ellie was sharply reminded of the fact that this man had been waist deep in that very plan before they'd plucked him and his harem out of the North Sea.

"There needs to be a compliant workforce with no attachment to any European country. They need to be brought in by the millions and be disposable if they do not work out during the adjustment process."

"Like the 'seasoning' during the slave trade," Sarge Bryan said through tight lips as they passed dozens of skulls arranged in a row from the largest to the smallest.

"Where better to get such a workforce than Africa?" Wolfgang hastily added, "Most despicable, of course. It must not be allowed."

They came to an octagonal-shaped zone. There was a small fountain, similar to those one would see in playgrounds. However, this one was made of recent human remains. The sides of eight skulls had been cut into wedges so they formed a neat circle. Water spewed from eye and mouth holes.

Ellie was so disturbed by the sight she nearly blundered around the corner. A cyborg arm stopped her as smartly as though she had run into a tree trunk.

"Stop," Rodion said. "Surveillance camera."

A flying drone was deployed. Head-on, it was thinner than a cell phone, its translucent rotors spun in an invisible blur. It scanned the room. Having gathered the images of the empty space, the drone flew up and projected a hologram of the empty room into the lens of the spy camera. They moved past.

They followed an arched, winding tunnel. Ellie had the sense of being inside the intestines of a buried monster.

"Melanie," she asked as her wet feet rubbed quite badly in her ill-fitting boots, which were stuffed with soggy newspaper, "how much farther?"

The bountifully coiffed scientist tapped Wolfgang on his shoulder and pointed to something on her digital map. He nodded, the look on his face very glum.

"No farther," Melanie said quietly, gazing around as though her completely normal eyes could peer through the walls and ceiling. "For the last hundred meters, we've been inside the T-bomb."

Without warning, Ellie's chill turned to a cold sweat. The real, actual bones of recently killed people arranged as neatly as a Prada store display swirled round in her vision. Her left leg gave way, and her shoulder smashed against a wall. She blacked out.

66

ÉLYSÉE PALACE

RAPACE

Rapace slammed his fist down on his handset. He looked at the time, then out the office window at the sleek aircraft sitting in the palace square. They had to leave, and complications were piling up left and right.

He had just finished a vexing conference call with his Shadow War Minister, Abdelkader. The former ISIS member was becoming increasingly insistent on having his militants take over Italy and the UK after their populations were liquidated. That would leave Rapace's France and his core Pangean forces surrounded and undermanned. Was that swarthy bastard planning a coup before the All Saint's Day Apocalypse had even cleansed the human detritus from Old Europe?

Adding to Rapace's problems, the Americans were becoming more belligerent. They demanded an explanation for the Bordeaux incident. They flat-out stated they did not believe the fake news story about a chemical plant explosion that France's state-run media was pushing.

The Americans could go hang. They would have their answer in a few hours.

He jumped to his feet and strode in the direction of the secret elevator down to the New Catacombs. He could do it right now. He could detonate the T-bomb and be done with it.

Then he stopped.

He had to be sure… The T-bomb was still building up to its maximum yield. The red zone of total annihilation had to be strong enough to reach Rome, the Vatican, and especially one human vermin.

"Giselle…"

His wife was sitting at her table in their ornately decorated palace suite. She heard him but did not answer. He could see she was holding a well-thumbed copy of a book: *What Is to Be Done?* That was a bad sign.

The book was the bible of the Pangean movement. Part novel and part polemic, it described the utopia that would ensue once Europe had been transformed into groups of small agricultural and industrial cooperatives. No nation-states would exist. Countries would be replaced by fifty equal administrative districts controlled by Brussels. At the end, one of the novel's characters dreams that their society, established after much struggle and sacrifice, will become a model for a relentlessly joyful human civilization the world over.

As Rapace went over to her, he hoped she was not losing her nerve.

"Not long now," he said, sitting beside her. "If you're worried about our escape, don't be. At Zero Hour, we'll be two thousand miles away. The hovercopter can even fly itself, everything is automated."

"Phillippe," she said, turning to him, "I've just been to the shelters… the children. They're so small and trusting. They trust us to do right by them."

Rapace took her larger tanned hands in his smaller, well-manicured ones.

"We are. Death is what is best for them, every last one of them. Since they were unlucky enough not to be aborted, it is better for them to be euthanized. Europe is perdition. It is the Ninth Circle of Hell… the pain it has caused… is causing. I know it, in my blood, I know it."

Rapace picked up the book. "If those children knew about the future, how much better the world we are creating will be, they would have no choice but to agree. But their minds are already poisoned by the past, by their parents, their grandparents, by the religions, the blood and the soil of France and Europe.

"Annihilation is the only way to free a continent from its terrible, irredeemable past. Pangean Europe will shine like a beacon of pure light and justice, eventually uniting all the other continents in a final utopia."

Giselle had believed it too, once. Rapace needed her to keep on having faith, for just a few more hours.

"I… I'm not sure," she said. "For more than one hundred years, our inner circle has been working on the Pangean Project. It's had other names: the Kalergi Initiative, the League of Nations, the European Union."

She got up and stared out the windows at the darkening Court of Honor reception and parade ground.

"We are close to victory without…" Her voice quaked. "Phillippe, listen, thanks to our relentless propaganda and indoctrination campaigns, only thirty percent of Europeans cling to the idea of nation-states. The Germans and Swedish have a pathological hatred of themselves. The British Marxists were ready to rejoin the EU in exchange for us abolishing their hated monarchy, which they blame for standing in the way of a pure proletarian dictatorship. Our own French people burn the Tricolore and raise the Euro flag."

Giselle gestured wildly at the only flag allowed in Rapace's room—a circlet-of-stars Euro flag hanging limply from a long, sharp-ended flagpole.

"Yes, there have been setbacks. Perhaps we should have killed Salvini and Orban. But this… I don't know anymore."

"No, no, no!" Rapace clutched the book so tightly its covers cracked. "This incrementalism will never work. I saw it with Brexit. The filthy electorate will always find a way to foul things up. *Europa tabula rasa!* The clean slate."

Rapace looked over to the wall, up at the bearded man in the oil painting. How did Belgium's Leopold II make people understand his mission? How could that filthy hack Conrad slander the great man's work so terribly? *Heart of Darkness*? Pah, the civilization King Leopold had valiantly tried to create was the Heart of the Future.

"The Kalergi Plan of selective genetic breeding," he said with rising anger. "The mass importation of new populations. The intentional spreading of the coronavirus to hollow out European urban population centers and exterminate older, more conservative voters. These were mistakes.

"The Muslims we bought in are either assimilating or clinging to their ideas of an Islamic caliphate in Europe. How long will it be before they develop their own identity and start fighting against the Turks and the Arabs? They're almost as bad as the Christians they were supposed to replace."

Rapace tried to rip the book in half but it was too thick, his frustration sending him to the end of his wits. "What is to be done?" he shouted, spittle flying from his lips. "What is to be done? The Pangean Empire, that is what! Everything *in* the Pangean Empire, nothing *outside* the Pangean Empire, nothing *against* the Pangean Empire."

He flipped open the book and tore it along the spine; the action calmed him.

"It is done," he explained. "Even if I wanted to stop it, I could not. You saw what happened in Bordeaux. The utopia we've dreamed of is here. We only have to reach out and… What are you doing?"

Giselle was reaching for the hardline handset. It was connected to unhackable fiber-optic cables connecting him to all the world's leaders.

"Someone will know how," his wife said, picking up the gold-and-ivory receiver.

"Know what?"

"How… to stop it!" Giselle finally screeched. "The Americans, Putin, Dr. Licht. You said yourself he knows more about dark matter than anyone."

Rapace slapped her.

She fell sideways but caught herself before her head hit the desk. The phone receiver was still in her hand. Suddenly it cracked Rapace across the side of his head. Giselle had been born a woman, but years of male hormone treatments had given her masculine muscles under her tanned leathery skin.

In shock and pain, he stumbled back. He couldn't let her do it. She had to be silenced. The close-protection guards outside the door were all Pangeans, but if she screamed loud enough, people in the kitchens might hear.

She started to select a number on the speed dial. He grabbed the flagpole from the side of the desk; thinking only to use its five-foot length to push her away, he thrust. The sharp tip penetrated Giselle's dress under her diaphragm. The yellow stars and blue background of the EU flag fluttered and crumpled.

She fell back. The phone tumbled onto the plush red carpet. If he pulled the spear out now, there would be blood, inconvenience. Rapace closed his eyes and pushed.

Giselle gasped breathlessly. She arched backward, unable to get away; she was pinioned like a pig on a skewer. He kept pushing and pushing, until he heard a crunch. The point had come out of her back and was stuck on the gold-leaf-covered window frame.

Rapace's legs gave out. With a hollow moan, he collapsed cross-legged on the carpet. Trying to get up, he grabbed the chair. It tilted, making him lose his balance. Someone knocked.

"It's okay! Seal the room, seal the floor. Lock it down!"

He kneeled there for a moment, his breath coming in short gulps. Giselle's legs lay tangled with her dress. The rest of her was hidden by the big leather office chair. King Leopold stared down from the wall out from his oil painting. His bearded face was stern and judgmental.

Rapace thought he saw something; he flailed out, his hand catching on the telephone cord. He'd thought he saw one of Giselle's legs twitch. Her Chinese-style slipper came off. The handle of the flagpole he had stabbed into her midsection poked up over the high back of the chair. He untangled his arm. His eyes were just about to follow the brown length of polished wood, follow it down and see…

A voice message came through the chip in his brain. Only three people had access to his neural implant, one of them was Giselle. The first time, he didn't catch all of the words. Blood pounded through his head; he was shivering in a cold sweat.

He whispered, "Command input, repeat subdural message."

The ragged voice of an older man spoke directly into his auditory cortex. It was not digitally disguised and was one he knew quite well.

"They have found the device. Come down quickly or all is lost! I can't—"

The message cut off. Rapace forgot about Giselle's body. Only one terrible thought reverberated through his mind.

They found it… they found it… they found it.

After grabbing a pistol from his desk, he ran to the elevator down to the New Catacombs.

67

Temir watched Eylül awkwardly pick steel slivers out of his chest wounds. These were remnants of the wire rope that had been threaded through his pectoral muscles with a huge curved needle.

Until a short time ago, his friend had been hanging from the ceiling of the smuggler's hut. Temir had overpowered the Ukrainian militiawoman Oleksandra but had let his man dangle while they haggled over terms of a Turkish-Ukrainian joint venture.

Even after being let down from his suspension torture, Eylül seemed ungrateful. Now that he and Temir were alone, he complained. "This is like making a bargain with deadly snakes while you are in their pit and their heads are slithering under your ball sack."

Eylül still did not have full use of his arms. His wounds were full of hastily applied surgical staples. His man tits hung down his chest like those of an eighty-year-old stripper. Had the mood been lighter, Temir would have taken a snapshot to post on the Grey Wolves social media.

Under his big military coat, Temir's left tentacle rubbed the smooth area of his crotch where the Russian cyborg had grabbed him and where Oleksandra had hit him with a shovel, both hoping to crush what was no longer there.

"Relax, my old friend," Temir said. "You probably wouldn't mind that Ukrainian woman slithering under your ball sack."

"Hrrk!" Eylül spat. "If I had a dog that was as ugly as that at either end, I'd shoot it out of mercy."

Oleksandra popped her head through the tent flap without warning. She made no indication she heard or could even understand what they had said in Turkish.

"I've discussed your ideas with some people," she said in English. "It's true, we in Ukraine have our disagreements with Russians."

"They treat you, the Romanians, the Bulgarians, all of you like animals," Temir said. "They took the Crimea from you. How many million Ukrainians did the Soviets kill by starvation, by exposure, and by the bullet during their despotic rule?"

"True, the Russians have a bad attitude; we will never forget they starved to death more than ten million Ukrainians during the Holodomor in the 1930s," she said with deliberate understatement. "But they also have fifty thousand nuclear warheads, and Mr. Putin, possibly the most dangerous man alive."

"He won't be for much longer," Temir said confidently. "There's no turning back the clock. Moscow will be in disarray. The Russians may be able to defend their own territory against a direct attack, but they won't be projecting power anywhere. You've seen the data from Bordeaux. The Event is real, and when you and I reach an agreement, I will give you the exact time it will happen."

Oleksandra scratched the shaved side of her head. Her ears looked all balled up. Perhaps she was a former wrestler; she certainly had the build.

"If it hadn't been for the Bordeaux events and the destruction of Heathrow," she said, casting an amused glance at Eylül's mangled chest, "your guts would be feeding pigs."

"Our Heathrow assault and the attacks on other transport networks are keeping the Europeans from escaping. And it is only the start," Temir said. He was taking a chance by falsely claiming the airport attacks as the work of the Grey Wolves. He wanted to convince the Ukrainians of their wide-ranging power. "Our sleeper agents are responsible for that and so much more. Loyal Grey Wolves had been infiltrating Europe for decades."

"What about them? There are ten million Muslims in France alone. You will let them die?"

"*Nahn nuhibu almawt 'akthar mimaa tuhibu alhaya*," Temir said in Arabic. "We love death more than you love life. A million died during the stalemate of the Iran-Iraq war. In 1971, Pakistan liquidated three million civilians to punish Bangladesh for seeking independence. How much a higher price would we pay in the blood of our own to wipe Western Europe clean of its infestation?"

"I might endorse this bargain to my superiors," Oleksandra said warily. "If we support your cause, you will give us everything from Estonia to Georgia to Ukraine?"

Temir inclined his head affirmatively. "From there you can pick away at the leaderless Russians as they splinter into factions and fight amongst themselves."

It was the most credible lie Temir could think of. He could have killed Oleksandra and escaped, but this was much better. The Ukraine could negotiate a clear path through Bulgaria for their armored column to the borders of the red zone of the T-bomb.

Temir's gambit was not without risk. He had no doubt that, at a moment's notice, the militiawoman would cut her losses and turn him and Eylül into pig feed. Despite his jihadi bravado, Temir wanted to return to his Grey Wolves. He wanted to lead the armored column through the Bulgarian capital of Sofia and into Vienna itself, a dream of Ottoman warlords since the Empire's founding.

"It's a bargain, then," Oleksandra said cautiously. "I don't know how many troops we can move through Romania to meet you in Sofia…"

"You wouldn't rather rally at the Turkish border with Bulgaria?" Pushing into hostile territory would save time, but it was risky and would put their tank columns and SAM defences close to the Event's red zone.

Oleksandra stared at him. "Everyone, my militia, regular Ukrainian, the backward Romanians, the shiftless Bulgarians, all have to see you are committed and serious," she said carefully. "When they see you move out of Turkey and cross the Bulgarian border in force, then they will join. Only then."

Temir thought he could convince Elder Omid to move up the timetable. No, he had to. Now that everyone knew his plan, he couldn't waste time fighting his way through the Balkans.

"Then we agree," Oleksandra said with a secret smile on her brutally ugly face. She motioned for them to go outside. "And to seal our bargain, a present. We captured him trying to follow you into Ukrainian territory."

Oleksandra took them over to a truck. Inside its covered flatbed was a cage with two-inch steel bars; behind these bars was a large Russian cyborg soldier. His augmented eyes glared out with biomechanical fury and helpless rage. Temir knew him.

"I give you Komandir Zvena, formerly elite soldier of Spetsnaz. Currently whipping dog of the Azov Ukrainian militia."

68

Ellie felt someone shoving something in her mouth. Ordinarily this was not something she was okay with, except in extremely limited circumstances. She imagined a metal centipede wanting to nudge its way in; she tightened her lips and thrashed her head.

"Ach, why would you bring such a person? A journalist?"

"Ellie," Melanie's voice said. "Ignore the Euro-meanie. Take this glucose tablet."

Ellie's senses rushed back just enough for her to realize the kindly woman with humongous hair was trying to help her. She chewed the sweet tablet. With embarrassing sluggishness, Ellie recalled where she was and what they were doing.

Tunnel. Inside the T-bomb. Mad scientist girl. One-footed cyborg lady.

Her relief at not being violated by a bug with a hundred legs was overtaken by a queasy feeling of instant mortification. She had bloody well fainted during an important secret mission. From the ceiling, a skull leered at her; it was ringed with intact finger bones, about thirty of them pointed straight down at her like tiny stalactites.

"All right," Ellie said, getting up and being hit by another wave of nausea and intense sweating. She sat down again and grabbed for the bottle of white pills. "I'm up, I'm up."

"Dr. Licht, sir, please quit talkin' smack," Sarge Bryan said. "Ms. Sato's been in more rough spots than most soldiers."

"I can vouch for that," Ran said, helping her up. "I seem to remember her volunteering to go to Cesta Station in Bordeaux while we had coffee and donuts at Ramstein."

"You just had a touch of hypoglycemia," Melanie said. "Have an energy bar and some Human+ energy drink."

Ellie drank deeply. If this juice made her want to chew someone's face off, she hoped Wolfgang would be close by.

"Okay, enough," Ellie said, recapturing some dignity. "Let's hurry."

Sarge Bryan and Rodion led the way through the New Catacombs. The next guard stations they approached were all abandoned.

"The Pangeans are clearing their own people out."

Ellie looked at Ran Oliphant, realizing what that meant. "Which leaves two million Parisians fending for themselves."

She didn't even want to think about how many more were in danger if the big T-bomb went off with power a thousand times that of the small one in Bordeaux.

There were large sections without bones embedded in the walls, ceiling, and floors. As opposed to being a relief, it got Ellie thinking about the Pangeans' plans. Even after they cleansed Europe of its mentally polluted populations, the killing wouldn't stop.

"Seasoning" of workers to make sure they fit into the new Euro-topia would continue. And once they were in control of France's atomics and all the industries of the continent, the Pangeans would look outward and insist on uniting all the continents. They were so close to succeeding.

Ellie took another swig of the cyborg drink. Tata slapped her on the back, making her cough. "You like our kvass?"

"This? Oh, yes," Ellie fibbed, thinking of something diplomatic to say. "It's fruity yet wholesome. What is it?"

"Light beer made from black bread."

Ellie nodded and decided to think of something else besides the bone decorations all around them and globs of yeasty bread drink fermenting in her stomach.

"Melanie, when you said we're *inside* the bomb…"

"Yes," Wolfgang cut in. "She meant that literally." He grabbed the folding screen map from Melanie and pointed. "Look. This is where we are. Do you see anything familiar? A shape, perhaps?"

Outlined in blue all around their position was the dotted outline of a spiral. The same shape Atticus's body camera had recorded in Cesta Station.

"In the very center," he continued, "will be the gestating particle."

"What if there's no way in?" What if the villains had sealed off the device? Could the Russians tunnel to where it was in time?

Wolfgang scoffed. "The answer should be obvious for anyone with a grounding in multidimensional cosmology."

"Well," Melanie said, grabbing her map back, "as someone with that and then some, I agree Ellie's question is actually a good one."

They came up to a rotunda. The fat center support was completely covered with the top ends of thigh bones. Only one single skull hung in the middle of the fat column, it was facing inward. Some wanker with a macabre sense of humor had taken a Sharpie and drawn eyes on the back along the with the words: *"Regarde toujours derrière toi."*

Melanie walked around the rotunda, eyeing it closely. "The Tyr particle can't be moved, but the neutronium reflector array around it is set in materials, which might have subsided or shifted over the past few months. According to the data from Cesta Station, there's a focal point about a cubic meter wide. If the reflectors moved, the Pangean scientists would need to readjust them; they would need continuous access. That's our way in."

But when they walked a few dozen meters down the tunnel and found the focal point and the tip of the bomb chamber, it was definitely not the way in.

Tata made to hit the thing in their way with her pike, but Rodion caught the edged weapon by the handle in time.

"Maybe is alarm!" the cyborg leader cautioned.

The steel vault door they had run up against was even larger and looked more complex than the one at Cesta Station.

69

ELLIE

Ellie felt her throat seize up. She stood near a wall so if she fainted again, she could at least gracefully slide to the rocky floor of the cavern.

"We'll never get it open in time," Ellie blurted. "They'll notice the guards back there are missing."

"It's all electronic," Ran said after studying the mechanism, which was set in a blank steel block that disappeared into the floor and ceiling of the catacombs. "Rodion, can you—"

"Dig?" the Russian asked indignantly. "Through solid rock without setting off alarms and in time before the fucking thing goes fucking off?"

It was the first time Ellie had seen the large fellow visibly angry. Even getting shot in the back of the head had not prompted this much emotion.

"Miss Aleph?" Ellie said into her orange leather bag.

"I'm thinking. Hold me closer to the center part."

Ellie held the AI up to give it a good look.

"Forget it. There's a digitally encoded keyhole that's two feet long. Without the key, this is as far as you go."

Melanie also looked closely. "Crap, she's right. See those notches? Each key is used only once and then discarded. Even if we had some idea where they are keeping the keys, we'd have to know which one was next in the sequence."

"But… what about the reflector maintenance aperture Wolfgang said would be there?"

Ellie recalled some technical talk about the deadly T-rays having to converge at a focal point like sunlight through a magnifying glass.

"You're looking at it," Wolfgang said, studying their subterranean map. "Dark-matter rays would ignore all this steel and be reflected to a focal point right about here." He tapped the door at about head height.

Ellie jammed another glucose pill into her mouth. She was dizzy but also determined not to drop again like a stupid anorexic model on a catwalk. It wasn't fair! They were right here. The foul continent-killing device was on the other side of this door; they had the neutronium soccer ball needed to nullify the T-bomb.

The tunnel seemed to close in on her, millions of tons of dirt and that rotten President Rapace right above them in his golden palace, sitting on his golden throne, waiting for the end of history. It was too much.

Too much.

"It's too much."

"What?" Wolfgang snapped. "If this journalist goes *fetzig*, I demand you tie her up. We are trying to think."

"Well, I have a thought," Ellie said, waving her arms at the vault door. "This is all too much. This big fancy door. It's like this Chanel fashion designer I knew—"

Wolfgang shook his head and wandered off.

Sarge Bryan shrugged, studying the massive vault door. "At this point, I'm willing to listen to anything."

Ellie continued her admittedly tenuous analogy. "He had tons of jewelry and changed it like twelve times a day, depending on his mood." Ellie started to feel silly but had nothing else to fall back on to express the notion that had popped into her head. "One day, some thieves dressed as flower delivery people broke into his house. They spent hours trying to crack his safe and were caught.

"Later, the designer showed me there was nothing behind the safe door, just a wall. He kept all his jewelry in a fake microwave oven so he could easily get at it. Am I making sense?"

"Totally," Melanie said, taking a bite from a long red rope candy. "Misdirection, the magician's basic trick."

"I follow, maybe," Ran said thoughtfully. "Making adjustments to the reflectors might require moving tons of earth on short notice. They would use another way in. A back door."

Ellie suddenly thought she knew where that was. She darted past a surprised Wolfgang, who was standing in a bone-strewn alcove, possibly muttering to his privates while urinating. Melanie and the others followed her back the way they had come.

"Look," Ellie said, pointing to the skull in the big rotunda with the eyes drawn on the back. "There's a fingerprint smudge."

Ran studied it. "This column is big enough to accommodate earth-moving equipment. The question is how—"

Ellie put both her palms on the skull and pressed. "Sorry, sir or miss..." she mumbled to the skull.

The conic-shaped bone went in. Not all the way at first; there was grit and sand. When it finally did pop, half the rotunda swung open smoothly on hidden hinges.

"It's five hours to midnight. Go, get in," Ellie said, feeling a rush of excitement.

Just beyond the bone rotunda entryway, the shaft became rough-hewn; it reminded Ellie of the nastiest parts of the Old Catacombs. There were signs of hasty tunneling; rock debris lay on the floor, and sharp edges along the walls sliced at their clothing.

"This... this may give us a way in after all," Wolfgang said as he looked back up at the main tunnel. His voice sounded more indecisive than when he was insulting people.

Ellie could scarcely imagine how these Pangean fanatics had done all this work just to destroy everything and everyone that lay on the surface.

"Which way?" Ran and Sarge Bryan had taken the lead; the Russians had to duck and walk sideways in some spots.

Melanie shook her handset. "This underground GPS is still in beta. It has to refresh."

In a moment, it did.

"Straight… I think."

"Melanie."

"Sorry, Ran. Rapace didn't post the map to the 'My Evil Doomsday Device' chatroom."

All the other branches of this construction tunnel turned sharply left or right. Rodion and Sarge Bryan stuck to the one that went straight and angled up. About fifty meters along was a vertical shaft. A series of metal rungs were set in the stone, and above that was a hatchway.

"Locked."

"But not with a meter-long key," Melanie said hopefully. "There's a touchpad."

`"Let me see."`

After a few seconds of Miss Aleph's digital lock-picking, the final hatch popped open.

`"It was a variation on the guard's keycard code."` Ellie clung to the topmost rung, holding Miss Aleph up through the round hatchway. The AI was the first of them to get a look inside through her handset camera. `"Oh, fuck me. This is going in the scrapbook."`

Ellie stuck her head in next. The air was stale; rock dust was everywhere. There was also something electric, like the whiff of gases after a lightbulb explodes, permeating the large cavern.

After being in enclosed spaces for many hours, it took a moment for Ellie's eyes to adjust to the distances. Alcoves studded the ceiling, and the whole place glowed with indirect blue light.

"Careful," Sarge Bryan urged. "Maybe I should go."

"We can't waste time," Ellie said, pulling herself up. "I'll stand to the side here while you check for trip wires and things."

The cavern was tubular in design, about twenty meters high and over one hundred meters long. To Ellie's back was the steel-arched vault door that had stopped them. At the very end was a big circular machine; parts of it had been disassembled, but the main structure sat thrust against the far rock face, abandoned.

"That's a tunnel-boring cutter head," Melanie said. "About the same size as they use for undersea tunnels."

She came up and stood behind Sarge Bryan as he scanned the room.

To Ellie, if there was anything that qualified to be the exact opposite of a cathedral, this was it. Rank wickedness filled the place. There was even an evil altar shaped like a podium. It looked like the one Atticus had discovered at Cesta Station but much larger.

"There's a device attached to that pedestal thing," Sarge said. "My spectrum vision sees explosive residue. Miss Aleph?"

"There's a weak carrier signal. It's a small IED."

Small, but big enough to detonate the T-bomb instantly, Ellie thought.

"We can't just stand here," Ran said, as he climbed up and gave Wolfgang a hand up.

"Ach, I would not place trip wires over an industrial space such as this. Too much chance of setting the T-bomb off accidentally."

Rodion popped his head out of the hatchway, his shoulders initially too broad for him to go any farther. "I agree with the German. The IED is probably a manual failsafe if the bomb does not go off normally."

Ellie watched as Rodion's shoulder joints intentionally dislocated, allowing him to squeeze through the narrow opening.

"Thank you for your opinion," Wolfgang said. "I was born in Luxembourg, and I have my own country."

Rodion slapped his shoulders back into place and helped Tata through. He told the other four cyborgs to stay down in the construction tunnel and get to work passing up the heavy encapsulating sphere.

In the middle of the bomb chamber, barely an outline in the dim light, was the central dais.

"Is that… it?" Tata said.

All of them spread out a little and crept forward. Their footsteps, though soft, echoed off the arched stone roof. Hanging just above a shoulder-high pile of twisted metal sheaves that flopped down like wilted petals of a radioactive flower was the core of the T-bomb.

"It's open," Ellie said in a hushed voice.

"It is," Wolfgang said, inching his way around. "It must have outgrown its original capsule."

Of all of them, Ran appeared the least mesmerized by the heinous thing. "Sarge, Rodion," he said, "should we disarm the failsafe IED before starting work?"

Sarge shook his head. "It's welded into the base." He looked to the Russians.

"Our scientists say once the dark-matter energy kernel is inside our capsule, it does not matter how it is detonated," Rodion said. "Neutronium in its crystal form cannot be damaged."

"We go with Plan A," Ran said and went back over to the hatchway to help the cyborgs lever up the neutronium vessel.

Ellie couldn't take her eyes off *it*. The living core of the T-bomb was hard to focus on, as though it were phasing in and out of reality.

"If it weren't for the dais…" Ellie said, finishing her thought silently. *…it would be hard to believe it was there at all.*

"It's like a mote in reality," Melanie said, circling to the other side. "Something you'd try to blink away."

"Dark matter does this," Wolfgang said as though explaining a science experiment. "Forced to grow to this size in temporal three-dimensional space, it is folding our reality into the six dimensions, which are its natural home. Possibly pulled by superstrings, like rubber bands."

"Hey, Wolfgang," Ran said sharply, "less theorizing and more lifting. Come over here."

As they heaved the thousand-pound soccer ball up out of the hole and onto casters, Melanie kept circling the gestating Tyr quark, biting her lip.

"How do we get the neutronium sphere to it?" Ellie asked. The dais was about five feet high.

"Russian scientists anticipated many possibilities," Tata said, as she screwed one of the carrying rods into the base of the capsule. She used the leverage to unscrew the device. It was empty, of course, but shockingly thin.

"The neutronium case is as thin as an orange peel," Ellie said. "How's it so heavy?"

"Luckily it's only been embedded with a one-atom-thick layer of neutronium by vacuum deposition," Melanie said. "On the Earth's surface, a thimbleful of the pure element weighs millions of tons."

When the two halves of the sphere were lying on either side of the T-bomb, Rodion screwed in two more legs onto his part. Tata did the same to her half, then they checked the height with laser guidelines and started to move the halves together.

"You see," Tata said with pride at their success, "the locking collar is connecting with the other half and... and..."

Then it didn't. Try as they might, the two Russians could not get the two halves of the encapsulation device together.

"It's grown too damn big!" Melanie said, throwing her measuring calipers in at the far wall.

"Don't push it too hard," Ran said.

"Nonsense," Wolfgang said with a weird look on his face. "It takes violent kinetic energy to set it off. Try again."

Ellie felt her own features contorting very unattractively. If the capsule wouldn't fit...

Without thinking, she rushed over and tried to push on Tata's side. The two halves were just an inch apart. Ellie's hand slipped off and hit one of the dais's metal sheaves, cutting her palm.

Out of all of them, only Sarge Bryan didn't look foully discouraged. He studied the T-bomb and the capsule. "Look, we got ninety percent of it covered. That's got to do something, right?"

"Noooo," Melanie wailed. "It doesn't work like that. It's all or nothing."

"Okay, then," Sarge said, scanning the room. "What about those reflectors up there, they're made of neutronium, right? We still got a few hours."

"Five hours and five minutes."

"Plenty of time," the albino man said, clearly trying to shore up everyone's morale after the devastating discovery. "Let's dig some of that crap out of the wall and weld it over."

"Can you weld neutronium?"

"No, but its always attached to other materials to make it easier to handle," Melanie said, staring at the T-bomb's core. Her hands fluttered like she was overheating and trying to fan herself or swatting at a dozen wasps and she sputtered, "But... but, it shouldn't *be* that size."

"Welcome to the wonderful world of dark matter, Fräulein," Wolfgang said.

"What about Plan Z?" Melanie said, looking at Miss Aleph's orange bag. "We could set up a T-ray sink at the convergence site..."

"This is only a vague theory," Wolfgang said. "We try this welding procedure first, huh?"

Rodion pulled Tata up and dusted her shoulders off. "Stand up, Tata, we are Spetsnaz. We are Human+. We are Russian. We did not come all this way to fail."

"*Da,*" Tata said begrudgingly, heaving herself up and stretching her thick arms. "For the fucking Motherland, then. I will find a high-voltage power source, and we can do arc welding."

"You couldn't have built a bigger capsule?" Ellie said, still taking the bitterness of disappointment. They had been so close to locking this continent-devastating device away back in a Pandora's box.

Rodion shook his head as he walked to the hatchway. "President Putin used every particle of neutronium we had." He shouted some instructions to the four other cyborgs waiting down in the tunnel.

"This element zero is tricky," Wolfgang said. "I better go with your men to make sure they get the right material."

"Not so fast," Ran said, blocking the older scientist. "You're staying here and helping us dig out the stuff that's in the wa—"

A sharp metallic clang came from behind them. Everyone spun around. At the apex of the bomb chamber, the big steel vault door had slammed open. In the doorway stood a man Ellie recognized instantly.

It was President Rapace.

70

ELLIE

R apace yelled something in French. Ellie was petrified in her spot as she watched four or five Pangean soldiers push their way into the bomb chamber. *We dare not shoot back*, was Ellie's only thought as their group was surrounded. A stray bullet could set off the IED.

As soon as the big vault door at the front of the chamber opened, the secret back-door entrance hatch in the floor began to slam closed. Very fast. Rodion had just been crouching over the hatch talking to the other cyborgs in the tunnel. He tried to grab the thick metal doorway.

"*Ye-bat! Su-ka!*" the Russian yelled and pulled back bloodied hands. Ellie gasped when she saw all eight of his fingers had been cut off by the sharp edge of the doorway as it sealed off their only escape.

Rapace's soldiers threw in stun grenades; Sarge Bryan grabbed Ellie and covered her head. Flashes flared and loud hollow cracks rebounded in the sinister cavern, rattling her molars. After the last one exploded, Ellie was seeing double and felt a noiseless ringing in her ears as though she were underwater.

Four Pangean soldiers leveled fat tear-gas launchers at them and fired. What came out of them did not blast CS gas; it strobed and crackled like captive electricity. Two electrified lassos dropped over Tata and two dropped over the wounded Rodion.

"Sortez ces cochons sales de ce lieu saint!"

Pulling on the electrified nooses, the riot-gear-wearing thugs started hauling the cyborgs out of the chamber. A fifth goon came in with a rifle. Rapace grabbed his weapon.

"Non!" Rapace said. *"Seulement les bâtons."*

The rest of them—Ellie, Sarge, Ran, and Melanie—fell to their knees. They were jerked up and herded toward the vault door at the end of an electrified shock prod. Through pain, deafness, and rising hysteria, Ellie thought, *Someone's missing. Where is…*

She looked up ahead and saw him; Wolfgang was standing next to Rapace, mumbling something. The two evil men eyed each other for a moment, then the French president held up a piece of red plastic. Wolfgang grabbed it eagerly and ran out the vault entrance without looking back.

That bloody turncoat.

"Move straight," a Pangean soldier said, his yell sounding like a distant whisper. He hit Sarge Bryan in the back of his head.

They were all pushed outside the bomb cavern into the antechamber leading up to the large metal vault door. Two guards mercilessly shocked Rodion and Tata to keep them still. Flecks of blood from the male cyborg's finger stumps sprayed on Ellie's jacket. Along with Melanie and Ran, she huddled against a rock wall.

Inside the cavern, Rapace and a man in green overalls were examining the T-bomb. The French president's face twisted into a grin when he saw the two halves of the neutronium capsule were an inch from locking together and were merely balanced against the dais. The two of them used crowbars to viciously hook and pry at the device; the two halves fell with a clang that echoed through the excavated space. Even through the ringing in her ears, Ellie could hear thumping on the hatchway up through the floor. Behind it were the four other Russian cyborgs who were trapped in the tunnels.

Rapace heard them as well. After checking his device one last time, he pulled his scientist with him toward the exit. When he got to the vault doorway, Rapace stood there, framed in the pale eerie blue light that shone from behind. Ellie could only see outlines of his face and hands.

At the floor hatch, the thumping turned into a geyser of sparks as the Human+ soldiers started cutting their way through.

Rapace fished around in several of his pockets for something. He found it, a remote the size of a car key.

"Yes," he said in English, looking at each one of them in turn. To Ellie, the backlit figure was more wraith than human. "The great Dr. Wolfgang Licht betrayed you. But it won't save him. *Ça suffit!* Enough..." he concluded wearily. "We have had enough of Europe."

His eyes fell lastly on Ellie, locked with hers, seemed to focus on something far away, and then Rapace pressed the button. The charge under the T-bomb exploded.

71

Before the shockwave hit, before the gust of heat from the plastic explosive trigger of the T-bomb rushed over him, Rapace felt something. As he braced himself against the steel frame of the open vault door, he felt…

Liberation.

The explosion wave hit. He fell.

He expected to go into convulsions as dark-matter radiation caused the neurons in his prefrontal cortex to lose polarity. He had seen videos featuring dozens of test cases at Cesta Station. His hands and knees hit the steel frame of the vault door. They did so without pain or much sensation at all. Maybe this was the first stage of losing sensory cohesion. He looked at the others.

The guards, good Pangean loyalists, had dropped in their tracks. They were dead. The two mechanical freaks from Russia were twitching spasmodically, their cyborg implants desperately trying to communicate with human brains that had been liquefied.

There were also two civilian men. One looked vaguely familiar. The other was an albino. He was dead too; his blue eyes glowed steadily as they stared sightlessly at the ceiling of the cavern.

Thick smoke wafted through the detonation chamber and out through the vault door. Rapace coughed and kept low where the air was cleaner. Two women were sprawled in the antechamber, some drool and froth around their mouths. One had stupid hair, and the other looked Chinese. They were also dead in the exact poses Cesta test subjects had died in. Everything was as expected. Everything except him.

He reached up, touched his face. He was still conscious. He felt the same. He knew who he was. He whirled around.

Inside the excavation, nothing was left of the dais, only an empty black crater. The kinetic energy shock from the IED had set off the T-bomb, just as it had done to the smaller device at Bordeaux. The big bomb had only been a few hours away from achieving maximum power. Certainly everyone in France, Germany, and Britain was dead. If some survived in Greece or Portugal, Abdelkader had plans to clean them out before the rest of the world could react.

He took another step. He still felt fine. Better than fine.

He left the chamber and walked to the elevator. He stepped over another dead fellow. Rapace never knew the man's name and had nearly forgotten he was guarding the elevator up to the palace. The elevator was closed.

No. The elevator doors were opening again. They were stuck on something.

"Hello, Dr. Licht, not so smug now, are you?" Rapace said.

From a rigid dead hand he retrieved the red hovercopter command key he had given Wolfgang as a reward for betraying his friends. Rapace then kicked the man's limp legs inside. It seemed easier than pulling him all the way out.

He rested one foot on the oligarch's corpse as he rode up. "Did you really think I'd let you fly off?"

As he rode up, he was afraid of what he would find. What if people were alive? What if the death ray had only worked inside the New Catacombs? He'd never forgive himself.

Detonation had been the right choice; there had been too much danger. The metal sphere the infiltrators had tried to wrap around the T-bomb core had to be neutronium. Would the encapsulation sabotage have worked? Could it have stopped the T-bomb from cleansing this beautiful land so burdened by history and, worst of all, that fatal leprosy of the mind: Christianity?

Reaching the top level, the lift's door slid open. It was quiet. He smelled cooking from the kitchens. Food no one would be eating surrounded by a dozen deceased chefs.

Turning the corner, he saw the end of the EU flagpole through his office door. It was still standing where he had left it, sticking out of Giselle. Stupid woman. Despite all her learning and despite the agony and strife caused to her personally by Old Europe, she had lost faith in the future. At the last, she did not have the strength to do what needed to be done. She would not see Pangea.

He passed by his office and went down a staircase through the front entrance of Élysée Palace and the Court of Honor. In the middle of the large enclosed courtyard was the French version of a hovercopter with its wings folded up.

At the receiving desk, his personal secretary was slumped over, dead. So were the guards, as well as the pilots.

"I'm sorry, gentlemen," Rapace said bemusedly as he pulled the first corpse out from the cockpit. "I have to go somewhere. It's too long a trip to take in such ghastly company."

But… how am I making this journey at all? he thought as he rolled the second helmeted pilot out; drool obscured the front of the tinted visor on the deceased man's helmet.

The silence was strange. It was never this quiet at the palace. He looked over. The other pilot was already on the beige pebbles covering the courtyard. He must have pulled him out, though he couldn't recall…

As he settled himself in the plush leather flight chair, it came to him. He had been spared for a reason. It was the same as the story chronicled in a documentary, the miraculous survival of the woman in Herzog's *Wings of Hope*. A large airplane traveling over Peru had been hit by lightning and disintegrated in midair. It fell straight down for three kilometers. One young woman survived. Not only that, she was able to walk out of the jungle.

The same must have happened to him. The scientists had assured him that the effect inside the reflection chamber would be the same as outside. What did they know?

He was alive. His hands shook, not with terror at the annihilation he had caused, not in relief at having been spared, but in anticipation. There was someone he *had* to see. He pushed the hovercopter's command key in place.

"Computer."

The flight console of the robotic aircraft woke up.

"Set a direct course to Vatican City."

The aircraft checked itself and the external sensors, then took off. A sideways hail of gravel thudded into the walls and windows bordering the Court of Honor. The red carpet, which had been rolled out of the way, caught fire as the hovercopter's jets roared through their vertical takeoff cycle.

What had those beasts been trying to do with the T-bomb? They hadn't enclosed it. Had their plan failed, and were they coming up to negotiate with him? It didn't matter now.

Swiftly, the aircraft rose to two hundred meters altitude. The wings locked into place and level flight began.

His burning need to discover what lay at the end of his journey could not be suppressed. He had done the right thing by setting off the device. There were more Russians in the tunnels; his guards would have been overwhelmed.

Russians… he thought. The last thing he had heard was there was chaos in Moscow. Some infection was spreading uncontrollably, and then all news was blacked out. There hadn't been even so much as a Russian weather update for days. Yet if Putin had agents here, he must have suspected something. Rapace scrolled down his communication channels to the list of Pangeans.

"Abdelkader, are you there?"

It was strange. For years he'd had people to do everything for him. Drive him, cook for him, dial his telephone and video calls. He smiled. Reflected moonlight danced across the display panel. He wasn't even sure he was operating this device correctly.

"Mr. President?" the Algerian's voice was faint but sounded just as he recalled it. "It has happened?"

"Sooner than planned. How are you?"

Abdelkader's last known location was in southern Algeria, three thousand kilometers from Paris.

"We had some headaches," Abdelkader said. "We saw things. Same as Bordeaux but stronger. Why did you—"

"It could not be avoided. Listen, I am on my way to check an important detail. I will be back at the Ambérieu-en-Bugey Air Base in six hours at the latest. Then we will begin the reclamation of Europe by burning the worst memento of the past: the European people."

"It will take us at least eight hours to get there. We were expecting to stay at minimum safe distance until midnight. You are sure... it is over?"

Rapace looked down. At his altitude, he could see farmhouses and well-lit roads, no people. In the distance was fire belching up columns of dark-gray smoke. Those must be planes that had plummeted to earth or fuel tankers that crashed when their operators dropped dead.

"It is. We may have an issue with Moscow. Advance word got out to the Russians. They won't be afraid of booby-trapped nuclear power plants. We have to show them we mean business. At the first sign of Russian armor coming into Poland, use my personal codes and order the carrier *De Gaulle* to strike Warsaw with a five-hundred-kiloton warhead."

Rapace arranged a few more logistical details with Abdelkader. These slipped his mind as soon as they discussed them.

Finally the Pangean Minister of War asked, rather cheekily, "Well, Phillippe, are you still Mr. President considering there no longer is a France?"

He thought a moment. The cabin vibrated pleasantly, air rushed over the wings. "You are right. In that case I shall be First Citizen. First Citizen of Pangea."

Abdelkader laughed. He could imagine the man literally licking his thin purple lips. He said nothing more, and the channel cut to static.

Rapace wanted to get a closer look at the ground, and no sooner had he thought this than his hands encountered a pair of field glasses; they must have been left by one of the dead pilots. Careful not to touch any of the controls, he retrieved them.

"After all this, wouldn't it be silly to kill myself in a crash?" His voice sounded hollow and flat inside his lonely transport.

Suddenly he wished Giselle could be here to see the future she had worked toward for decades. The *Schengen Totalität* plan to erase the tired old nations and carve Europe into fifty monolithic administrative districts was based on Giselle's university master's thesis. But in the end, her will failed.

Using the binoculars, Rapace looked through an observation port near the floor of the aircraft. The field glasses had night vision and seemed to focus automatically and... there they all were. Dead people. Piles of them at an intersection. It had been a protest march. Most of the corpses were wearing yellow vests.

The sight brought the face of King Leopold II sharply into his mind. The Belgian monarch's bearded stern scowl floated in front of Rapace.

C'est un très heureux holocaust.

"You are right, Leo. It is the most happy holocaust," he said to the vision of the old Belgian monarch. "Look, look! I acted just as you did. Only my motives were pure. You killed half a country not because you hated the Congolese, but because they just didn't work out. For the same reasons, the very same, I've killed a continent. Good riddance."

King Leopold's face crinkled in a lopsided smirk. Then the vision vanished, replaced by the bodies fallen along the roadway. Quietly, Rapace vowed that in the new United Districts of Europe, those anarchistic yellow vests would be banned. He threw the field glasses onto the seat across from him.

"Now that is how you accomplish ethnic cleansing, huh? Hitler, Stalin, Mao, are you listening?" He laughed to himself. "That was always the flaw. Always. Even the executioners are part of the legacy civilization. How do you convince the last SS officers to jump into the gas chamber? How do you order the final commissar to board the last train for Siberia? Or the hindmost Red Guards to... sit in an empty... rice paddy and... starve... until wild dogs chew the last scraps of loose skin off... their bones..."

He must have dozed off. Checking the real-time map, he saw he had crossed the Alps and was over the Apennines. A refueling stop was scheduled before the hovercopter left French airspace. It was on the itinerary. Of course. The robots could do it themselves. Could he have slept through that? He must have. According to the flight computer, he would arrive in twenty minutes.

What would he find at the Vatican? The distance between Paris and Rome was eleven hundred kilometers. Had the T-bomb death wave reached that far? That was why he'd risked everything to wait until the particle was at maximum power. The only place to keep the massive contraption hidden for months had been under his own palace. But what if it hadn't been strong enough? What if they were just sick or knocked out, or nothing had happened to them at all? He couldn't fight the Vatican guards.

Rapace scrambled into the other chair, grabbed up the binoculars again. If they were alive, he'd make up some story. He had been out of Europe on a secret diplomatic mission and, seeing the extent of the disaster, had rushed to the spiritual center of Europe. Tragic loss, he would say, completely condemning the senseless act. Then he would leave Italy as soon as possible until he could come back with Abdelkader and a few thousand Pangean shock troops.

One glance at the ground put his mind at ease. Down in the streets of Rome, a red sports car had crashed into a bus. The fire was burning freely. Bodies were strewn all down the lane. Old Italy was dead. He was safe.

Rapace suddenly wanted to point and show Giselle dawn breaking over an expurgated continent. It would have been so marvelous to… but he had killed her. Stabbed her with the flagpole. If she had not bled to death, the dark-matter rays certainly had fried her brain. Still, it would have been wonderful to show her he had finally won.

Unless…

Unless the old goat had escaped. The latest news Rapace had received said the pontiff was scheduled to hold a traditional midday Angelus prayer in St. Peter's Square on All Saints Day, November 1. But with the confusion after Bordeaux and the shutdown of so many airports, something might have happened to keep him away from Rome. The thought ate away at him, making the minutes and the kilometers drag.

Then he saw looming on the horizon the foul dome of the basilica. It was early. Long shadows extended over St. Peter's Square, but he could still see them. Thousands and thousands of the fearful and deluded had crammed into the square. It could hold three hundred thousand people. Nothing moved.

Rapace looked at the heads-up display. The windscreen had a green landing point arrow next to the central obelisk. *Caligula's obelisk*, he thought with bitter irony. He couldn't wait to dynamite the entire place. All except for the perverted mad emperor's monument.

"Not there," he said to himself. Using the touch screen, he moved the green landing destination arrow as close to the basilica as the robot pilot mechBrain would allow.

The computer accepted the new landing instructions. The aircraft flew itself close enough to the top of the building that he could see the statues of the saints arranged along its facade. They were carrying crosses and staring idiotically at the crowd of the faithful, which had gathered the previous evening. No one would be waving back, ever. The sight filled Rapace with more joy than he thought possible.

The hovercopter's wing ends tilted up, and a howling whine came from the vertical landing thrusters. To either side, the dead bodies of the penitent worshippers blew away like dry leaves. The craft touched down in St. Peter's Square.

At the top of the steps into the basilica lay a line of Swiss guards. They looked like jauntily dressed toy soldiers knocked over in a nearly straight line. Rapace's fingers and palms tingled as he pushed open the latticed grille entry gate. The T-bomb was exceeding his wildest dreams.

Looking up, he could see the tip of the papal ferula staff poking over the central balcony. *He* had been there, blessing the crowd. *Not long now.*

Rapace stepped over a dead cardinal and entered the holy palace. It had been years since Rapace visited. After Pius XIII had ascended to the papacy, he refused to even set foot in Italy.

"Unlucky thirteen, you dirty old goat," Rapace muttered as he dashed up the carpeted stairs. *Now...* he tried to remember, *left or...* No, straight then right to get to the papal secretary's office.

A new pope often remodeled the administrative offices and living quarters. Rapace was surprised to see they hadn't changed a thing in a decade. The door, standing tall and white and foreboding, was locked. He was not going to waste time looking for a key.

While not a physical man, Rapace recalled the phenomenal effort of scaling Notre Dame's scaffolding; he gathered his slight frame and kicked out furiously. The door latch gave way, sending a chunk of white-painted wood skidding across the richly patterned marble floor.

The door thumped against a bodyguard in plain clothes. He made certain the man was dead, passed by two crumpled nuns, and then a sight made his legs wobble; he nearly fell to his knees.

Next to the body of a young altar boy, there he was. His papal robes were flat on the floor like a pond of white, crimson, and gold. Underneath, the villain's body seemed insubstantial, making barely a ripple under the fabric. It was as though the fetid carcass was already rotting away.

Of course, there had been no time for the pope to rot. He had fallen in his tracks near the open balcony doors. Pius XIII's face was hidden by his tall mitre hat; the rest of him was covered by the robes. All except for one hand. That hand had on it the Fisherman's Ring of St. Peter.

His sudden burst of energy spent, his head spinning, Rapace inched forward, hunched over as though weighed down by some invisible enormity. He started laughing, thinking about urinating on the bastard's corpse. It was odd. He couldn't remember using the toilet since he had left the Élysée Palace, and that had been many hours ago. In that case, he thought wildly, his bladder would be so full he would piss like a racehorse.

The thought of subjecting the pontiff to a golden shower cloudburst made him laugh even harder. The convulsions of glee rocked him so hard he stumbled to the floor beside the robe-shrouded figure of the fallen Pope Pius XIII. Before he was elected pope, this had been Father Kilian of Villnöss: the filthiest pervert ever to be retched out of the foul womb of a woman.

When Rapace had been eight, his parents sent him to Catholic boarding school in northern Italy. There, in the idyllic setting of an Alpine valley, he had caught the obsessive eye of the headmaster, Father Kilian.

For years, the juvenile Rapace was Father Kilian's favorite living sexual torture doll. He still had the scars of butted-out cigars and stab marks of hot pokers on his back and legs. He remembered the sickening sight of Kilian's erection under his robes whenever he saw the young Phillippe Rapace.

The man had been insatiable. And when Kilian had tired of using every part of Rapace that could be used in every way possible in the solitude of his cell and the school's basements, the Jesuit priest had gathered like-minded pedophiles. Some were from the Church, some were rich men, and even their wives. Kilian urged them, ordered them, even, to partake of his little lamb's delights.

Each debauchery was different, depending on the invited guests. Sometimes there were only men, sometimes mostly women, often children slightly older than Phillippe, even squealing animals and crying infants and freshly embalmed dead bodies were used. Yet always, Father Kilian would start in the same way.

In the slim light of near dawn or the dead of night, they would come. They would seize him, binding him until he was helpless. The men would stand in a circle, jerking their penises, large and small, white and black and brown, massively hard or barely erect. Rapace had to watch until they had all ejaculated into a communion chalice. Kilian would then stuff a wafer in Rapace's mouth before uttering a foul incantation.

"Phillippe," Kilian would say, "you are not worthy to receive this." It was always the same words, a perversion of the Eucharist. "But only drink, only drink all our seed, and ye shall be blessed!"

Then Rapace was forced to drink every drop of the mixed semen. They held his nose, pricked his cheeks with an ice pick, and threatened to kill his family if he didn't lap up every drop of the warm, rancid-smelling liquid. Any semen that went astray they pushed back into his small boy's mouth using silver apostle spoons.

After Kilian was promoted and transferred, sometimes Rapace imagined all those terrible things had happened to someone else. No longer. Those things had happened to him, and the man who had done them was the learned Jesuit who later became Pope Pius XIII.

That was the thing that lay under the robes of the Vicar of Christ. He was the reason for Rapace's holy war against the Church and all its evils.

"I beat you. I beat you," Rapace said as he braced himself on his hands and knees on the cold marble near the window. He sobbed to the dead pope, "I win!"

It was done. Beyond this point, he had no clue… Was it really possible to build Pangea? Well, he thought, he would have to try. There was a reason he had been spared when the T-bomb went off… and all the others died.

Curious. The marble floor was neither cold nor warm, if anything it was numbing. He looked out the open balcony doors, and a movement caught his eye. Was it a dove? He looked more closely. Only clouds.

Then another, more sinister motion caused Rapace to look at the middle of the bundle of papal robes. Something was throbbing underneath them.

No!

He was imagining it. The wonder of it was… it really was growing. The dirty old stoat's cock was getting hard. But he was dead. How could—

At the edge of the small pond made by the pope's embroidered robes, and partly covered by them, was the limp body of the altar server. That boy's body was covered by his own purple tunic. It moved. Then it sat up.

Above the bold embroidered neckline of the tunic, there was nothing. The cloth hung open, too large for the body that wore it. A prepubescent girl's breast with a brown nipple and a mole underneath poked out. Above her collarbone was only a few inches of stump—all that was left of her tiny neck. The oval that remained formed a bloodless gash the same as you would see on a slaughtered carcass in a butcher's shop.

"Ahh!" Rapace yelled. Something cold and hard gripped his wrist.

It was the pope's liver-spotted hand; the Fisherman's Ring dug into his flesh. He tried to scream, but no sound came out. The grip was like iron and so cold it burned.

The girl's headless corpse rose to its feet and came closer. Her tiny neck stump bubbled blood and mucus out of a severed esophagus. As she staggered toward him, the wheezing and gurgling made a sound:

"Joy…euses Pâ…ques."

The hand locked around his wrist like a metal manacle welded in place. The pope's robes shimmered, became flat, and then concaved. Rapace felt himself being pulled down into its musky ermine softness. The headless girl, fully naked now, kept wishing him "Happy Easter," and he was being pulled down.

72

G warh!"
Ellie frantically clutched the sides of her head and was immediately mortified by what had undoubtedly been her final utterance which, for an Oxford graduate, was sadly underwhelming.

With a thunderous bang, the explosive charge under the T-bomb had gone off. A blast wave had hit, followed by hot gases. Harsh-smelling cordite smoke expanded through the large detonation chamber and billowed past the figure of President Rapace, who was frozen in place just inside the vault doorway.

A moment passed.

Then another.

Ellie noticed her brains were not leaking out of her nose, ears, or down the back of her throat. She choked on fumes. From beside her came hacking sounds; other people were alive too. Ellie rolled over and crawled down the corridor toward fresher air.

How long before the T-rays kill us all?

That seemed a fair question. Maybe Melanie or Miss Aleph would know.

"How—*hrrk!*" There was no air to waste speaking. Ellie bunched her shirt over her nose and mouth.

Where they all zombies? She didn't feel like one. The Russians didn't look like zombies, at least no more than they normally did. Rodion and Tata had recovered first and were thrashing about with the riot-gear-clad guards.

Even with the top parts of all his fingers cut off, Rodion was more than a match for the French thugs. He pummeled them with the heels of his hands until they lay still. The electrified lasso around his neck gave a crackle and then fizzled as he threw it off. He turned to Tata and ripped away her bindings.

The last Pangean guard backed away in terror and ran. Tata lunged after him, grabbed his shoulders, ripped his helmet off, and bit the back of his neck. There was a *crunch*, and the man collapsed like an abandoned marionette.

"Sound—*heff*—off," Sarge Bryan's bass voice bellowed through the smoky gloom. Ellie could just make out the pinpricks of his gloriously blue cybernetic eyes.

"Why?" Ran said, breathing through a cloth. "You can see us, can't you?"

"I just wanna make sure you're all still… you."

"Here," said Melanie.

"Me too," Ellie said, waving. "I've still got all my wits."

"Such as they are," added Miss Aleph from inside her Hermes bag, which Ellie had dropped closer to the entrance.

Going back to retrieve it, she saw a strange sight. In the steel frame of the entrance to the bomb chamber, President Rapace had dropped down on all fours. Drool mixed with dust was dribbling out of his mouth. He seemed to be trying to move his right hand but could not, as though it were glued to the ground.

Ellie's mind flashed back a moment. She remembered the very instant Rapace had pressed the button, before the blast hit, the French president had stood there triumphantly. The outline of his head and skull had appeared to fluoresce. It was probably a trick of light, and even now she was having trouble recalling it…

Ellie needed to get Miss Aleph. As she stumbled closer to Rapace, she passed a skull embedded in the catacomb wall. A fat green vine vomited out of the skull's mouth and slithered toward her ankle.

Wait a sec!

"Everyone, we need to get out of here," Ellie cried. "Rapace is giving off hallucinations like the creatures did."

Using a bent pike pole, Tata pushed the alive but insensible Rapace inside the vault and slammed it closed. Rodion went back to the rotunda and into the tunnels to get the other four cyborgs who were still trying to break into the T-bomb chamber.

"Where's Ran going?" Ellie said, noticing him running the other way, deeper into the complex.

Sarge Bryan was busy with a fifth Rapace guard who had popped up out of nowhere. He was trying to tie the surrendering man's hands while at the same time keeping Tata from ripping the prisoner's limbs off.

"You go get Ran, ma'am. He's going after Wolfgang."

Ellie caught up with Ran at a slim elevator door. It was sealed and looked locked.

"Mr. Oliphant, we've got to—"

"Not before I get that backstabber," Ran said. He hefted a cyborg pike and tried to pry open the door.

"It's no use, Ellie," Melanie said, coming up behind her. "When he's like this, he's like a dog with a chew toy."

After some fruitless banging and more fruitful searching, they found a small crawlspace that led up the side of the elevator shaft. They climbed the rusty ladder.

"We're right under Élysée Palace," Melanie said as they slid their way through the tight space to a narrow landing.

"What happened?" Ellie asked with a shudder. Hallucination or not, she could still half feel the slimy vine's thorns digging into her ankle.

"The T-bomb went off," Melanie said.

`"She's asking why all the squishy people did not die."`

"That's more complicated." Melanie reached down and took Miss Aleph's Hermes bag so Ellie could grab the next rung. "It certainly seemed like Rapace was the only one affected."

Ellie didn't get it. "Something that could have killed millions affected only one person?" Ellie wondered if she should mention the part where she saw Rapace glowing like an x-ray figure.

"Tyr quark energies are mysterious. In the Havana beta test attack, some people were permanently disabled while people sitting in the office right next to them never even got a headache." Melanie handed Ran a tool to undo the latch above. "I had a theory about a quantum computer being able to act as a quark sink, like a special lightning rod, if it were in the right spot. The human brain can perform a billion billion operations per second, but without a superconductor quantum chip being involved, I don't see..."

"Shh," Ran cautioned. "Have your mouth perform zero operations per second, please."

Taking a big scary-looking knife, he prized at the edges of a moldy-looking hatchway. When he finally got it open, the hinges were too caked with goop to squeak. He poked his head out an opening the size of a garbage chute; a tapestry hung over it. Ran peered left and right before flinging the cloth aside and squeezing through. He then hauled up Melanie and Ellie.

Ellie was almost ashamed to tread muck on the luxurious carpet of the presidential palace. The faint smell of food from the kitchens somewhere in the palace made Ellie as hungry as she'd ever been for food that did not come out of a paper wrapper. The immediate area was quiet.

"This is probably Rapace's residential suite," Ran whispered. "Wolfgang can't have gotten far. There."

They looked at a set of dusty footsteps leading past an office door with ornate gold-embossed molding. Faint sounds of distress came from inside. Without thinking, Ellie glanced in.

"Oh!"

A half-naked woman had been pierced by a long pole. She lay on the ground moaning. Despite the size of the wound the spear must have made, there was not that much blood. Ellie rushed in before Ran could grab her.

"Stop, you can't—"

"I know her from news stories," Ellie said. "It's Rapace's wife. Someone stabbed her."

Melanie got some towels from the bathroom, though it looked like Mrs.

Rapace was fading fast. The battered woman could barely keep her swollen eyes open.

Ran seemed about to pull her and Melanie out of Rapace's office when he saw something through the window.

"I can't believe it."

Ellie followed Ran's gaze through the window into the big gravel-covered courtyard. Wolfgang was there speaking to two guards in front of an aircraft. He waved a piece of red plastic in front of them, brushed past, and got inside.

"Rapace must have given him the hovercopter as a reward for betraying us," Ran said. He knelt down and took a closer look at the wounded woman.

After a moment of panic, she looked up at their faces.

"Phillippe? *La bombe?*"

"*Tout va bien,*" Melanie said, holding the stricken lady's hand. "*Cela ne fera de mal à personne.*"

"*La vérité,*" Mrs. Rapace said with her last strength. "*Ils doivent savoir ... Les Pangéens, tout est dans son sang. Dans son sang.*"

Then she fell into unconsciousness. *They must know… the Pangeans. All is in his blood?* What could that mean?

The roar of a jet engine shattered the silence. They looked out.

"Wolfgang's gone," Ellie said.

"He'd better run all the way to Moscow," Ran said bitterly. "We've got to get out of here as well. There are too many hard-core Pangeans about. If we dawdle, we'll never make it out alive."

Melanie grabbed the phone on the desk. "*Urgence médicale dans le bureau du président. Viens maintenant!*"

Then Ellie, Melanie, and Ran hurried back down the secret shaft, through the New Catacombs, and into the comforting safety of the Paris sewers.

73

A s soon as he saw his Russian enemy again, Temir's left appendage started to quiver. The octopus tentacle, larger and stronger than any human arm, changed texture all by itself; it went from jelly soft to stone hard all up and down its length.

During the flight from Ukraine to Bucharest and the drive in a truck convoy to Bulgaria's border with Turkey, Temir nursed the urge to go over to the cage holding the insolent cyborg Komandir Zvena and take him apart one bolt at a time. Temir still found himself limping in pain from the damage the cyborg had inflicted.

"Don't look so glum," Meliha said. "It's not long now."

The Sunni vixen had arrived at the border with the Iranians. The combined Turkish-Iranian armored column stretched out along Highway E-80, the direct route into Bulgaria and Europe's eastern frontier. All that remained was to wait for Europe's heart to stop beating, then the Grey Wolves would become the richest grave robbers in history.

Central European time was 6:35 p.m. October 31. The T-bomb was supposed to wipe out the kafir infidels all over Europe at midnight. Maybe he was supposed to care about the millions of Turks in Germany who also would die. Temir did not.

Meliha put her hand in the pocket of his horsehide greatcoat and started to fondle the end of his tentacle. She withdrew quickly when the Ukrainian woman Oleksandra approached.

The fat Slavic bitch had tortured him with barbed wire and a blowtorch. One day he'd have her, and he might even let Meliha watch. But for now he needed Oleksandra and her Bulgarian allies to guarantee a clear path to Vienna.

"When are we moving out?" Oleksandra said in a voice that was used to giving orders. She looked sideways at Meliha. "Our Ukrainian armor has linked up with the Bulgarian forces at Sofia."

"Bulgaria has an army?" Temir said sarcastically.

"True, it is not very large. It wasn't hard to persuade them to join once they saw they would be caught in between us from the north and you from the east."

Temir studied the map provided by the tortured Congolese man. Naturally, it did not disclose the exact location of the T-bomb, but it outlined the disposition of Pangean forces and laid out red and green zones. These concentric bomb blast lines were ringed around central France. The red zone was sixteen hundred kilometers in all directions. Sofia was one hundred kilometers outside the supposed red zone.

But that was only an estimate. Temir had seen video from Bordeaux. The T-ray effect was real, and unnerving.

"We should start now, Mr. Temir," Oleksandra said with temerity that would normally earn her a backhanded slap. "Unless you're afraid."

"You foreign whore," Meliha said. Her hands disappeared under her robe, likely toward the curved dagger she carried. "This is Aga Temir of the Eastern Vanguard army. Have respect or lose your tongue."

"Ladies." Temir smiled, getting between them. The Ukrainian looked as though she could crush Meliha with little effort. "I've made up my mind. We go. We hold outside Sofia until we know what has happened in Western Europe."

Meliha stalked away without a word.

When the Ukrainian woman had gone back to the truck carrying the captive Russian cyborg, Meliha came back with Elder Omid.

R.K. SYRUS

"Is this wise?" Omid said. His gaunt, nearly hairless head looked more like it belonged on a vulture every time Temir saw him.

"The kafirs must see our strength," Temir said.

"You're sure of this map?"

Temir nodded. He was not sure of anything other than the need to keep this alliance together until the Event happened or did not. If it did not, they would retreat back to Turkey, where perhaps he would relieve the Persians of their tanks in the process as a consolation prize.

"I've seen the video footage from Bordeaux," Elder Omid said. "It was only that which convinced my brothers in Tehran to commit so many of our forces to our mutual adventure."

That and fear of being left out of the spoils. However, Temir thought, if they ran into any resistance from remnant Russian forces, or even Hungarians, they'd be glad of the hundreds of Iranian Karrar main battle tanks sitting on their transport trucks idling along the highway.

They moved out and headed over the Bulgarian border without incident. Tired of breathing diesel fumes, Temir sped his motorcycle to the head of the column. He came up beside Eylül in the lead truck.

His old comrade's head was wrapped in a fresh bandage, and he was letting a junior Grey Wolf drive. Once again, Temir felt blessed for possessing the rejuvenating power of his symbiont. It was worth his arm, among other parts.

"Wake up!" Temir yelled up to Eylül. "Anything on radar or satellite?"

Temir's big fear was an air ambush. With all of them stretched out in a line along well-paved roads, their glorious attack could turn into as big a rout as the Iraqi Highway of Death during Saddam's retreat from Kuwait.

Eylül shook his head. "We're still under our antiaircraft umbrella."

"Keep watching."

Kilometer after kilometer, the flat Bulgarian countryside rolled by. It was nearly indistinguishable from Turkey, except for the infidels on it. One way or another, once Europe was swept into the dustbin, all of them would be back under Ottoman Turkish rule.

About one kilometer outside Sofia, the Ukrainian woman sped ahead and stopped her truck sideways across the road. What was she doing? She'd stop the whole column like that. Temir gunned his motor and raced up to her.

"Why are you stopping? It'll take an hour to get everyone moving again."

"This is for your benefit," Oleksandra said, getting out of her truck. "You can set up mobile SAMs in that area and refuel from tanker trucks before you get into the city."

It was true; this was a very good spot. Temir looked through his night-vision goggles. Then he checked with his symbiont eye.

To the left and right there were clear fields of fire for hundreds of meters in front of clumps of trees. He had been worried about taking the armor straight into the built-up areas of the Bulgarian capital. This was the best place to avoid an ambush by air or ground while they waited. He checked the area again and then a third time on the Iranian's real-time satellite maps.

"All right. We wait here."

It was nearly eleven p.m. Central European time. Temir decided to amuse himself by tormenting the captive Russian cyborg. Komandir Zvena was in a small cage bounded on all sides by thick, brightly gleaming steel bars.

"Not so fearsome now, are you, Komandir Zvena, being hauled around like a circus animal?" Temir said in English to the larger Russian. "I should set you on fire, but first I want you to see the rise of a new empire."

Zvena continued to squat in the middle of his filthy cage and remained silent. The Ukrainian woman had said the cyborg and some human soldiers had followed Temir and Eylül from Moscow. It was possible. Using heroin smugglers to take them over the Ukrainian-Russian border had been a bad exfiltration plan.

"Maybe burning is too good for you," Temir said. "The Persians have something called scaphism. It is hard to describe. Better to show you firsthand; I'm sure Elder Omid has brought some glowing maggots. Not long now, Russian."

Temir left the truck with the prisoner in the back and checked on the column's deployment.

"Mobile SAMs?" he asked his man.

"All deployed and ready," Eylül reported.

"Keep an eye on those Persians."

"We kept them all at the back. They got in formation without any of their usual complaints." Eylül brought up a tactical map on his handset. "We have made a double column with wedges to front and rear. That's a lot of preparation if we're moving out in an hour."

For the thousandth time, Temir realized Eylül was so dumb he should be scrubbing potatoes back in an Istanbul barracks.

"Look around," Temir said hotly. "This looks like Turkey, but it is not. We're on foreign ground. In the 1800s, all this belonged to the Ottoman Empire until the Turkish-Russian wars. Caution, Conquest, Consolidation. This is the military doctrine of the Grey Wolves. Do not forget it… no matter how many teenage Eastern European girls you capture and add to your harem."

Eylül laughed.

The hour approached. Twenty minutes. Temir checked his troops again with night-vision drones. Ten minutes. They crowded around a half dozen wireless devices. The announcers were speaking in many languages: French, Spanish, English, German, and Polish.

At five minutes to go, Temir became conscious of the extra heartbeats of his symbiont. There were three pump-like nodules that kept the black ichor flowing through its translucent veins. He wondered, if the T-bomb turned his brain into mush, would this creature survive and take him over completely?

The digital readouts on all the screens counted down the minutes, the seconds, the milliseconds…

Midnight.

Nothing happened. Temir, Eylül, Meliha, and even Elder Omid had come out of his armored car to gape at the newsfeeds.

"Something is wrong," the superstitious Persian said, visibly sweating. What was he worried about?

"Just wait," Temir said reassuringly. "We don't even know what the effects—"

A small glow enveloped the radio antennae on the truck. The monitors all flickered, then went dark. The insides of electronics, large and small, from the handset to the guts of the nearby S-400 radar, started whining and vibrating.

"This can't be— Oh!"

Temir felt it too. A sharp ringing in his ears. Were they too close? Were they going to be engulfed in the T-bomb's death wave?

Then it passed. The cyborg in the cage twitched, wires in his shoulder sparked, and his head lolled to the side. Under the hood of their truck, something crackled and flared, then the headlights went out.

The camp, the armored column, everything along the road and inside the city of Sofia was dark. Temir tried his flashlight. It did not work and was burning hot, as though all its stored electrons had discharged in a few seconds.

By the light of the stars, Eylül dug around in the cab of the truck and activated chemlights. They bathed everything in an eerie green glow.

"That felt strange..." Meliha said, holding her head and backing up to sit on the tailgate of the truck holding the inert Russian cyborg.

"It was an electromagnetic pulse," Temir said. These were textbook effects of a short, powerful burst of electromagnetic energy.

"Was this supposed to happen?" Elder Omid demanded, his shriveled neck waggling indignantly. "We saw nothing like an EMP from our analysis of the Bordeaux incident."

"It..." The ringing passed out of Temir's head. "The Cesta Station explosion was much smaller. Perhaps the larger device pushed free electrons outward."

"Is anything working?" Eylül asked, hitting the monitoring equipment with his fist. "How will we know what's going on?"

"Here," said Oleksandra. She produced a credit-card-sized device. "This is a Lichtstrom device. Its signal is based on neutrino waves. It seems to work."

Suddenly dozens of holographic windows sprang up over the device.

"Europe goes dark!"

"Cataclismo na Europa?"

"一场令人不安的事件席卷欧洲"

Accompanying it were thousands of social media posts in every language. People speaking to their friends and family in Europe had been cut off, unable to reconnect.

Finally, after a lot of scrolling, they found some of the final blurred video frame images. It was from the Iranian VAJA spy agency's sources; it had to be accurate. Film from Paris, London, and Berlin showed people grabbing their heads, falling over. A woman lay face down next to the dog she had been walking. It stood there baying mournfully, pawing at her inert body.

"It's done," Temir said. "IT'S DONE!" he roared with his symbiont amplifying his voice louder than any natural human's. "Europe is ours if we have the balls to take it."

He repeated it in Persian and sent runners down the column to spread the good news.

Eylül came jogging out of the dark into the spill of the green chemlights.

"Everything electric is dead," he said, panting. "All the tanks and trucks are trying to restart now. Some of the newer ones will have to bypass their burned-out electronics. It will take an hour to get moving."

The Ukrainian woman closed the hologram generator and stepped over beside Elder Omid. The Persian had stopped sweating and was smiling a butcher's smile.

"You won't have to wait an hour," she said and added in remarkably good Turkish: "*Gozden irak, gonulden de irak olur.*" You harvest what you sow. "Isn't that right, Komandir Zvena?"

What?

The previously inert Russian hulk in the steel cage in the truck did not say anything. He merely got up, thrust his hands through the two-inch-thick metal bars as though they were tin foil. Fake! They were being set up. Komandir Zvena grabbed Meliha's head, and crushed it to a pulp.

Oleksandra hit Eylül in the temple with the butt of her rifle. He fell without a sound; Elder Omid grabbed his gun.

Temir reached for his pistol. The Russian cyborg was already on him. Grabbing his arm and staying away from his left tentacle, Zvena dove down for a leg-locking sambo throw.

When they were on the ground, Zvena twisted Temir's human arm. The pain was so sudden and overwhelming that it wasn't until he looked that he saw his forearm had been torn completely off. The Russian then grabbed Temir's right leg and ripped it off at the knee. Any sound Temir might have made was cut off by his attacker jerking his head back so far and so fast he threatened to snap his neck and also by the convulsions of his symbiont parts which were outraged at having been so easily defeated.

"That's enough," Elder Omid said. "We have to destroy the Turks and get out."

"No," Zvena said. "This one is slippery like eel. He has to stay put."

From the truck, Zvena grabbed a meter-long tent spike. He jammed it through Temir's tentacle at the shoulder, pinning him to the asphalt.

"Give the order to start shooting," Zvena said.

"We're in the way," Oleksandra protested.

"We'll leave soon," Zvena said. "I want to watch him see this before he dies."

Oleksandra shrugged and barked orders into the credit-card-sized communication device. On both sides of the road, the dark outlines of the forest lit up with floodlights. Underneath camouflage netting, there appeared dozens of Russian TOS-1 Buratino mobile rocket launchers.

"They were all under Faraday cages, like I was," Zvena said. "Despite your cowardly plague attack, Aga Temir, Moscow lives. All your mosquitos are dead, frozen. We told Elder Omid about who the disease-carrying insects were originally intended for. He was not happy.

"Now we—Russians, Ukrainians, and Iranians—all come for you Turks. Moments ago, we set off a dozen large EMP weapons from the Russian arsenal. You only saw holograms we wanted you to see. Watch now as your hopes of conquering Europe die. Then please, you die too."

Temir's hoarse scream was lost in the thunder of the incoming rockets.

74

TWO WEEKS LATER

VAL-DE-GRÂCE MILITARY HOSPITAL
PARIS

ELLIE

It was November 15, two weeks after the end of the world, which Ellie Sato of London's *Citizen Juggernaut* newspaper had done her part to postpone. She walked past the modern wing of the French military hospital toward the grand old building, which had been a Benedictine convent up until the French Revolution. Birds chirped in the trees, and the steady hum of early-morning traffic was interspersed with the rhythmic thump-hiss of lawn sprinklers. Paris was not very cold, though the weather was distinctly unsettled owing to unusual storm systems in the far north.

Act casual, Ellie thought as she stopped to smell a line of roses.

Her handset vibrated.

Don't act so casual. It's suspicious.

She tucked her battered but surprisingly durable orange Hermes tote bag more tightly under her arm. Today it was very heavy, weighing nearly ten pounds.

"Stop the backseat spying," she whispered to Miss Aleph and walked confidently along the hedges to what looked to be the hospital's entrance.

All right, but you're going the wrong way.

After a small course adjustment, Ellie found Sarge Bryan lounging on the lawn in an old-style wheelchair. He had on dark glacier glasses with leather side shields. Because of the natural pallor of his face, he looked as though he really was seriously ill.

"Oh, you poor man," Ellie said in an exaggerated manner. "Is there anything I can do for you?"

"You could tell me something nice to say in French to that nurse who's been tending to me," Sarge Bryan said, giving a small wry smile.

"How about: L'albinisme n'est pas contagious."

"Aleph," Ellie hissed. "You're supposed to be inert."

Without looking in that direction, Sarge Bryan angled his head to the doorway of the old hospital building.

"There's our guy. The only thing he couldn't do was fix the cameras inside the last room. No one but robots ever go in there."

"You sure you're okay, Bryan?"

The broad-shouldered American nodded solemnly. "I got steam and massage therapy later this afternoon. Listen, if anything goes wrong…"

"I know, don't say anything and demand to call Mr. Oliphant's lawyers."

Ellie walked toward the door through which the heavyset man in green scrubs had just exited. Inside the hospital, a uniformed guard sat in a booth reading a book. Above him were intimidating-looking cameras with multiple lenses. They were all pointing right at her and blinking red lights. They must be doing their scheduled malfunction thing.

She slid past the guard, who studiously ignored her and merely turned the pages of his book. In passing, she noticed the title: *Soumission* by Michel Houellebecq.

Ellie padded up the twisting marble staircase of the old building. At first she was afraid to touch the banister for fear of leaving fingerprints.

Screw it. I'm probably spewing DNA all over the place.

At the third-floor landing, a fat chain dangled on a conveniently open padlock. She pushed through. The long corridor was bare and empty. In fact, the whole building, with hundreds of rooms, had only one patient.

The floor she stood on was painted green. Twenty yards along, the paint became yellow, and after that there was a newly erected Plexiglas barrier in front of a fat red line.

At any moment, she expected to feel heavy hands on her shoulders or be accosted by a security robot armed with a taser.

`"Better top up."`

Ellie jumped. "Shh. Stick to texting."

`"I did. You're zoning out already. Top up the lithium. I don't feel like being put in the police evidence locker while you hallucinate you're picking marigolds."`

Ellie popped another two of Ms. China's antipsychotic drugs. The world-class poisoner had turned up just as they were planning to infiltrate the hospital where Rapace was being held. Other than saying Attie Jr. was safe and with his grandparents in America, Ms. China gave no details of her time on the *Magen* submarine.

`"Chew."`

Ellie chewed the tablets to get them into her system faster. The gritty paste added to the metallic taste already building in her mouth from the previous dose.

"Are you ready?"

`"I've been ready since we got here. These security robots are dimwits."`

The lighted sign on the barrier at the end of the white-painted hallway read "*Fermé.*" The lettering remained the same even when the electronic locks on the doors popped open. On the other side of the barrier, two waist-high robots were bumping repeatedly into a wall while speaking nonsense to themselves in French.

On a bed in the center of the large room lay the former President of the Fifth Republic, Phillippe Rapace. There was a fat feeding tube up his nose and a dozen monitoring devices attached to his chest and head.

The whine of a distant mosquito started growing in Ellie's ears. She had to blink a half dozen times to keep her eyes focused. Was it the lithium she had taken or the weird hallucinogenic rays Rapace's body was putting out?

"What if… I poke him too hard?"

"Whatever you're doing, be faster. I'm starting to… not feel good."

Miss Aleph had been afraid her neural net might be affected by concentrated doses of dark-matter rays. To keep her mind focused, Ellie talked.

"They're keeping him alive until they can send him to Mars. What if I kill him by accident and the death rays come shooting out?"

"No one knows what will happen. Remember this was your plan, Miss Investigative Reporter."

Ellie dug into her purse. Next to the blue cylinder of Miss Aleph's mind was a Montblanc 149 fountain pen. It felt like it weighed six pounds. That was no illusion—it did.

She grabbed it with both hands, uncapped it, and then jabbed it deep into a juicy-looking vein in Rapace's hand. He didn't react. He lay flat and rigid and was sweating all over.

"He does not look chipper."

"Better him than us. Stop being a schlepper and go faster. I'm losing one of the bots."

Ellie suddenly remembered what she was doing. She twisted the piston filler knob on the end of the pen all the way down, sucking up a few drops of blood through the syringe needle hidden in the pen's nib.

She forced herself not to look at Rapace's pale face or the fat nasogastric tube up his nose. Under his eyelids, which were taped down, his eyes were moving rapidly. His whole body seemed to vibrate, sending concussive waves through the air.

For a second Ellie thought she had lost the pen's cap, but it was in her hand. Her mind felt like it was coming unstuck. She withdrew the needle and sealed the heavily modified pen, letting it drop into the bottom of her bag with a heavy thump.

"Out. Go."

One of the robots was wheeling left and right. It knocked over a tray of instruments, then it came flying diagonally across the room right at her. Ellie dodged it like a bullfighter. Then she dashed out through the Plexiglas barrier.

By the time she got down to the second-floor landing, she had learned she was trapped.

`"Sarge texted me. The new guard came on early. We can't go that way."`

Ellie was starting to get dreadfully thirsty. The high doses of lithium were wreaking havoc on her stomach.

`"Out here, turn left. It's a service corridor from the kitchens."`

Ellie made it about fifty paces down the second-floor hallway. She looked through a window and could see the garden out front where Sarge sat in his wheelchair. Then she nearly ran into a stout nurse who had to be Eastern European judging by her features and wispy black moustache.

"Qui êtes vous?" she demanded in a mannish voice. The nurse let go of her pushcart, which was topped with mushy-looking food.

"Moi? Je suis… Ellie Sato *de le* Juggernaut, *journaliste."*

"Damn Hell," the woman said, switching to broken English. "You people not allowed. We keep telling. You keep coming. Go!"

"Can you just give me something?" Ellie said, holding her notepad and cradling her ridiculously heavy pen. "How is President Rapace? Is he awake? Is it true he's being shipped to Jupiter?"

"Go out!" the stout woman yelled. "Or be arrested you."

"Is that his food tray?"

The nurse was obviously headed to the old part of the hospital. They must mush the food up in a blender before they pushed it through the tube in Rapace's nose to keep him alive.

"What's his favorite food?" Ellie pestered as she inched toward the exit. "Does he like applesauce? Please just give me something or they'll fire me."

Just as the big nurse was grabbing her by the sleeve, Ellie noticed someone had drawn a winking smiley face on the plastic seal of a single-serving jar of applesauce. That was strange. Someone had a sick sense of humor… and she suddenly realized who that might be.

Oh no!

Ellie thought quickly. On purpose, she stumbled. Pretending to catch herself, she upset the whole food tray.

"Idiot stupide!"

"Okay, I'm leaving," Ellie said, stashing the stolen applesauce jar in her Hermes bag. "And may I say, madam, you have a terrible bedside manner!"

Once she was safely outside, she gave Sarge Bryan a discreet thumbs-up. He was a dozen meters away on the lawn and not looking in her direction, but she was sure he saw she was safely out.

"Where are you going? You're supposed to go to the van where Melanie's waiting. You're not out of your mind, are you?"

"No more than usual, I think," Ellie said, looking intently up and down the avenue and over to the hospital's parking lot.

She found who she was looking for in an old Citroen car. Ellie popped open the door and got in. She pushed aside a blue-and-white nun's habit and a ring of stolen keycards.

"Are you serious?" Ellie asked accusingly and put the applesauce container on the dashboard.

Ms. Annunciata China's six pupils glared at her.

Ellie was furious. "We have no idea what killing Rapace will do. You were only supposed to be the lookout, not the poisoner."

Unexpectedly, Ms. China started sobbing. "I'm sorry. I'm at my wits end. I was just so mad. I had to do something."

"It's okay." Ellie tried to comfort her. "But try needlepoint or something. If I hadn't remembered the thing you said about making cyanide out of apple seeds…"

Ms. China's gold-and-silver tattooed fingers wiped her tears away. "It was such a scrumptiously toxic batch too."

"For what it's worth, wherever Rapace is, I don't think he's happy," Ellie said, her throat feeling increasingly rough. "How's Attie Jr.?"

"He's going to the White House to get his father's medal next week."

"Do you have any water? Without toxins, please," Ellie croaked. "I can see why you went off these meds; they're horrible."

"I guess now we have to go home, and I'll have to turn myself in to the CRHT and that Mr. Delingpole the mental health cop," Ms. China lamented and handed her a bottle of Vittel.

Ellie drank. Maybe it was the lithium or the weird hallucination rays, but she didn't feel like returning to the humdrum of the Tulip dildo skyscraper and the *Juggernaut* newsroom in London just yet.

"Annunciata, you're not criminally responsible for anything you might do, and you did say this is a potent batch of cyanide."

"I ain't, and it is."

"Doesn't that child-rape gang in Mayfair still have your spare leg?"

"They do." Ms. China's face lit up, the metallic tattoos around her dimples glistened in the morning sun. "Let's get it back."

"Let's."

Ms. China put the Citroen in gear and drove off in the general direction of the Eiffel Tower.

EPILOGUE

ONE MONTH LATER

VILLNÖSS VALLEY
ITALIAN ALPS

ELLIE

Ellie woke up. There was something she had to do… *Right, that's it: don't freak out.* For the past few weeks, every time she opened her eyes, she felt compelled to check whether the things she saw and felt were real. She had just started sleeping with covers over her without dreaming she was in a vineyard being pulled under fetid-smelling earth by cold dirt-encrusted hands.

She raised her leg to make sure there was no thorny vine wrapped around it like a boa constrictor and levered herself upright. The view from the window of Ellie's private chalet was like a Christmas postcard. Actually, with the jagged white-capped Dolomite mountains looming over the frosted evergreen-lined hills that rolled down into the valley floor where a small church was nestled, it was nicer than any postcard she'd ever received.

A frosty storm had passed in the December night. Icicles hung above her door. As she opened it, some broke off and tinkled down on the porch. She got her newspapers out of the delivery box—which had its own heater—and waved to Sarge Bryan and another security fellow.

Sarge and Ran Oliphant had insisted someone keep watch during her working vacation. Rapace was in a life-support pod, the only passenger on a spaceship headed to Mars. However, other Pangeans were still out there.

A northward wind was streaming snow off from the craggy peaks and dusting the crystal blue sky. Ellie heard a dog bark. It was Chestnut the Labradoodle. She had been entrusted with his care by her former neighbor Mrs. Baker, who decided owning a dog was too stressful on her delicate nerves.

Chestnut wore a tartan-checked muffler and strained on the leash held by a robot dog walker churning along on snow treads. Chestnut seemed eager to get back where it was warm. The door clacked closed, and more icicles tinkled down.

"Nearly done, thanks for asking," Miss Aleph said sarcastically from Ellie's writing desk.

"I thought you were smart," Ellie said, grabbing a mug of coffee from the fully automated kitchen.

It was Melanie and Ran who had figured out Rapace had a quantum chip implanted in his brain for secret communications with other Pangean leaders.

"Without using the chip in Rapace's brain, which is on its way to Mars, I doubt there's anyone who could decode the database the sneaky bugger stored between the DNA of his own white blood cells."

Miss Aleph was connected to a complicated device Melanie had built. This in turn was plugged in to the neutronium-lined syringe/fountain pen Ellie had jabbed Rapace with at the hospital.

"Les Pangéens, tout est dans son sang." All is in his blood—the last words Rapace's wife Giselle Carré had said to Ellie. The first text Miss Aleph had been able to decode from the DNA was a long, ranting diary-manifesto.

That had brought Ellie here, to the place where an innocent eight-year-old French boy had been sent to Catholic boarding school only to be savagely molested by the future Pope Pius XIII. This personal tragic horror had turned President Rapace into the monster who tried to murder Europe. People who had known both of them still lived here. Ellie was determined to find out the truth and tell it.

Ellie wheeled her office chair over to the display and keypad.

Must not check the news sites... Damn!

An annoying little breaking news update window popped up in the corner of her screen; it was from the *Juggernaut*. Now that Ran Oliphant had invested money to keep the paper afloat, they had gone online and seemed keen to be just as bothersome as the *Daily Mail*.

"Oh, look. Gamal's in the news again," she said, reading the gossipy headline. "Sole heir to mining fortune listed in notorious Mayfair prostitution ring's client list... despite being a quadriplegic!"

`"I guess there's one part of him that's not completely paralyzed."`

"I'll text him in case he needs Ran to recommend a good solicitor."

Gamal was the boy Ellie and Ms. China had discovered trapped in his family's Mayfair mansion. Somehow his wealthy parents had found out about the T-bomb disaster and fled, leaving the severely crippled boy there to die.

Gamal's parents and sisters had all perished in the Heathrow attacks. He was left as the heir to a foreign mining conglomerate. The chalet belonged to him; Gamal had told her she could borrow it as long as she liked on the condition that he got to see Ellie's new book before anyone else did. Everyone was interested in the real story behind the mad events of the past few months.

Ellie closed the news popup window and vowed to avoid opening her email at all costs. She was impatient to start. She typed:

THE PANGEA PROTOCOL

By ~~Ellie Eleanor E.~~ Sato

`"I don't know why you were rushing me. It's going to take you a week to decide where to put the page numbers."`

"Stop looking over my shoulder."

`"Okay, be like that. I just won't tell you which elite Davos club member has been funding human smuggling and child prostitution for decades."`

Ellie decided to finalize her authorial name later. The dedication she was certain of.

Dedicated to:
A.R., another brave American whose name Europeans will not know but to whom they owe more than they will ever comprehend.

Just then, through the frozen and formerly hushed Alpine valley, the bells on top of the Church of St. Magdalena started ringing.

Dédié à l'esprit et aux pierres de Notre Dame.

This book is part of the New Praetorians series.
OTHER BOOKS SET IN THE NEW PRAETORIANS
UNIVERSE:
Start reading today: goo.gl/Uig74j

Your honest reviews help:
Amazon.com
Goodreads.com
…
For updates email "join list" to
author.syrus@gmail.com

…

Parler.com @rksyrus

…

THE NEW PRAETORIANS
SERIES CONTINUITY

TEN CHARACTER-DRIVEN ADVENTURES,
ONE GLOBAL STORY.

Apocalypse Israel: The 96 Hour War
In 2029, the State of Israel will be destroyed.

Apocalypse Europe: The Pangea Protocol
One killer, 500 million victims.
On November 1, 2031, one man will murder everyone in Europe.

Two standalone prequel novels set in the New Praetorians world.

Apocalypse: USA
In 2032, the Apocalypse series finally comes to America.

My Summer Vacation by Sienna McKnight
(New Praetorians 0.5)
A prequel novella.
FREE WHEN YOU JOIN THE MAILING LIST

	Start date (Khorasan time)
1. Sienna McKnight	March 19
2. Shetani Zeru Bryan	March 20
3: Yama & Yami	March 20
4: Anis	continuous
5: Crush	March 20
6: Ran Oliphant	continuous
7: Khamseen	continuous
8: Dr. Golem & Mr. Genji	March 20
9: Heaven's Scythe	continuous
10: Shadowbolt	continuous

Printed in Great Britain
by Amazon